Flashman and the Knight of the Sky

1

ISBN-13: 978-1499777024

www.paulfmoore.com

This is a work of fiction.
Whilst many of the characters existed, the story
is entirely from the imagination of the author.

In Memoriam

Private Sidney George David Moore
2/22nd (County of London) Battalion,
The London Regiment (The Queen's)
Killed 19th July 1916 near Arras
Age 19

Back Cover Image

Men of the 2/22nd Bn, London Regiment.
Second from right (sitting) Pte SGD Moore

Chapter 1

I could not believe the amount of bloody clobber. Just to have a ride in one of these new aeroplanes. It was only a wager for Christ's sake. I should have known better of course but I was young, in my twenties and now I was about to be launched into the air strapped to a tea chest held together with string and dope. I couldn't help but reflect on the fact that boredom, the root cause of my original gamble, was an altogether most satisfying occupation.

My guts began to churn faster and for once when near paralysed with fear my face turned white.

"Ma God Flash," said O'Connell, "ya look like ye're abite to have a baby."

"I think I am," I stuttered.

"Ye're worryin' abite nuthin," the great mick said in his now very disturbing Irish brogue. Not only was I about to take to the air, I was going to do it with a bogtrotter. "Can't back ite nye," he whistled cheerily as he began to pull at bits of his aeroplane. How they never came off in his great fists I'll never know. However, after what seemed like an age, he left off attacking the craft and motioned at me to…. well, what I wasn't sure. It wasn't like boarding a horse or a woman. Apparently, I wasn't particularly good at it judging by the comments aimed at my rear and

4

the great paws guiding my feet to avoid treading on anything flimsy! Quite how one distinguished between what was flimsy and what wasn't was beyond me. At last, I was seated. In a bucket. A very uncomfortable bucket at that. The point of wearing goggles was now obvious. I couldn't see a thing, which struck me as positive. The leather helmet also prevented me hearing much as well. It was therefore something of a surprise when the engine suddenly burst into life. By what means this had happened I was totally unaware. What I was aware of was the extremely cold draft that was now washing over me like the Niagara.

O'Connell started waving his arms around frantically. I wasn't sure that I could take much more of this. The Almighty knew what emergency we were having now. What was beginning to concern me was the possibility of my having an emergency. Something hit me an almighty crack up the behind and suddenly I realised the ground was disappearing below me.

"Jesus Christ," I yelled at the top of my voice. It was futile I know but seemed somehow appropriate. Then I started to hear a strange whine. I strained every nerve in my body to hear it clearly and decide what it was. Surely it couldn't be the…. no, it was the bloody mick singing! Singing would you believe. As if he was the Angel Gabriel. God knows what it was. Mind you, it could have been anything from the National Anthem to the Death March for all I cared at that moment.

I suddenly noticed he was pointing over the side. I looked over expecting to see something terrible and could not have been more wrong. What I saw was captivating. It was like looking at the world in miniature. I could see the field we had just left with the tents and kit all over the place. I could even see other people moving around like ants. It left me quite speechless. It was beautiful.

Now he was waving his arms about again and mouthing something.

"Me," I shouted disbelieving. "How on earth would I know what to do?"

"Just put your hands on de stick and follow me troo," he cried.

I didn't dare, at least for a few minutes. Then I thought well what the hell. I can't be worse than him. I got hold of the stick and hung on for grim death.

"Not loike dat," he yelled, "she's not a bloody harse."

"Obviously," I replied. "There's nowhere for it to sh…"

The rest was lost in the slipstream as we suddenly headed for the ground at high speed. Instinctively I shied away and at the same time, I pulled the stick back. My view was filled with clouds and I had a sudden feeling that I didn't know where the ground was. I pushed again but not quite so hard and the horizon reappeared. It was quite clever really.

"Let's troy turning," my mentor yelled. "Pull it roight and back a touch to keep de horizon in view, den use your roight foot on de rudder bar. Not too much dough or you will have us over."

I did as he said, comfortable in the knowledge that he was watching over me. I heard him start to sing again as we traced a circle in the sky.

"Troy with less rudder and den with more rudder and ye will see what de difference is."

I did this and discovered.

"Hey Flash," he cried, "let me have her for a tick. See yon natives doine dere."

He pointed downwards and at the same time, I suddenly recalled that until he took her back he had been sitting with his arms folded behind his head. A sudden chill came over me, worsened by the fact that we were now heading for the ground again. I looked out, my gaze frozen on the two horsemen who were now filling my view. We whistled past them at great speed and I had a glimpse of one of them shaking his fist and the other taking a tumble from the saddle, from which I deduced that he was angry. We flew along close to the ground and it was exhilarating. It beat the feeling of horseback into a cocked hat. We suddenly pulled up and away from the ground, flew in a gentle arc, and floated down to the field where we had started.

"Well dere you go Flash. How d'ye loike dat." This in an unnaturally loud voice.

"Bloody marvellous. Bloody marvellous." It was all I could say. I am not by nature an easy man to impress being a dyed in the wool cynic, but that was something else.

"And you're a natural."

"A natural what?"

"A natural aviator. Ye've definitely got de touch. Well ye did once ye stopped trying to trottle it."

"You must be joking," I said laughing.

"No Flash, Oi have never been more serious. Ye should dump dat nonsense Cavalry outfit, get your ticket and come and join us."

Thus, my fate was sealed.

Chapter 2

It was summer 1906. A momentous time, at least it was for me. I was shortly to leave the School and I suppose I was getting careless. What with warm days, cricket on the fields, the fags at one's beck and call and even the odd tumble in the hay, the world seemed to be entirely in order, with me at its centre. My Father was the only fly in the ointment, as he seemed to think I should be thinking about what I was going to do with my life. I had already made up my mind but I think our views were a little at variance. He, being Lord God Almighty, the Bishop Flashman of Knowall, thought I was off to the Varsity before I became something useful. I, on the other hand, had decided that the Varsity was a total waste of time and would teach me nothing I didn't know already. Nothing of use anyhow. Latin and Greek and all that bosh had no particular value in my plans. No, I had much better ideas than working for my living. We might not be the most sought after family in society but we were at least halfway there. No thanks to my Father though. We were still living on my Grandfather's reputation and had been for at least half a century, but it was still bright enough to guarantee my place with the other well-heeled loafers who generally made life interesting and meant I could avoid the thorough bore of having to work.

It was these and other charming thoughts that were passing through my head as I tooled round to the chapel. It was nearly the end of the year.

Examinations were over and it was speech day with a vengeance. All my mentors (or tormentors!) were there, presumably to make sure that I left, and they had even wheeled in Flash Harry, my namesake and Old Rugbeian, Brigadier General Sir Harry Flashman VC etc to tell us all about Courage apparently. I'd heard it all before of course, but this would be the last time, at least at the school anyway.

Thoroughly pleased with myself I planted myself down well out of sight of the bench with my unsuspecting 'chum' Burberry, and waited. Eventually, the beaks and so forth shuffled in and we all stood up and sang a hymn. The speeches started, my Grandfather delivered his customary half serious lecture which always baffled most people, especially those who had all the supposed virtues contained therein, and finally we stood up to sing God Save the King.

The timing was perfect although I say it myself. Just at the crescendo, you know the place, where we are about to send him victorious through crowds of cheering peasants, there was what can only be described as an enormous explosion. The organist, being a deaf old bastard simply carried on, which only added to the confusion. He obviously thought that it was a perfectly normal occurrence. Half the school carried on singing, while the other half smirked or cursed, depending on their point of view. The Headmaster[1] simply went purple.

---

[1] The Headmaster at this time was Henry Armitage James, also known as 'Bodger'. He was Head between 1895 and

When the dust had cleared a little, and the organist had finally realised that something was up, a deathly silence descended, broken eventually by the Head's voice saying quietly, "General Flashman, you may wish to resume your place." This was because he was currently hiding behind a curtain, much to the boys' general amusement. However, he now looked down on all of us in much the same way as a cobra regards its lunch. He didn't say another word for two full minutes.

"Whoever was responsible for that may wish to meet me in my study in exactly five minutes from now. If not, you will all remain here until I decide your fate. Gentlemen, we shall retire."

I didn't know where to put myself, but Burberry was positively terrified. You will have guessed of course who was behind the explosion. I had set Burberry up by suggesting that we cause a little disturbance and he fell for it like the mug he was. He thought we were going to make a little bang later on and cause some minor embarrassment, but I had better ideas. I had needed his chemistry, which he excelled at to pull it off though. It had only required a promise that I wouldn't use all the explosives he made and that I wouldn't kill anyone and he was mine. Well, he knew what my promises were worth now. It only took a quick glance through the doors to see the results and very gratifying they were too. The wrecked statue of some Greek hero on the lawn outside the chapel was there for all to see.

1910.

However, it was now that my chickens began their quick march home to roost. Burberry, appalled by his complicity no doubt and shaken by the Headmaster's threat, suddenly leapt up and ran outside. This commotion attracted far too much attention for my liking and I near as a toucher joined him. He hadn't given the game away yet although legging it from the hall was bound to attract comment. I was fairly sure he wouldn't confess as in spite of his association with me, he was still infected with that true puritan spirit, but if he did, I could lay the blame squarely at his feet, as the rest of the unused chemicals were in his desk. I had of course placed them there at a suitable opportunity as insurance before we went in. No doubt that would be the first place the peelers would look.

I should have known better of course. Five minutes he held out before spluttering to a now livid Housemaster that it was all Flashman's fault and he had been bullied into it. Now you saw the fine spectacle of my quaking carcass being hauled from the hall to see the Headmaster. Five minutes. Well, he would pay for that if I had anything to do with it.

I was taken to the waiting room and left by myself for a little while, no doubt to contemplate the error of my ways. But here was a fine mess. I could deny it for all I was worth but my word would be worthless compared to the sneak Burberry. So I had to scheme my way out of it. Ten minutes and I had it all pat. Wasted time though in the end.

It was about half an hour later having left me to stew for long enough, that the Grim Reaper arrived in the form of my Housemaster. Hauling me along by the ears, I arrived in double quick time at the Headmaster's study. As I went in, I realised that my audience consisted of both the Head and my Grandfather. Very strange I thought. Suddenly my story seemed very thin, especially with the General there. He was the only one in the family who always knew when I was not quite telling the truth. (Mainly of course because he was just the same although I was as yet unaware of this side of his nature.) The Head dusted some plaster from his cape and simply said, "Well?"

I looked at my feet for inspiration and finding none I looked up again but before I could begin my tale the General shouted "You stupid little bastard, you could have killed us all, what the hell were you thinking of? Eh? Eh?"

"Well, Grandpa, I thought…."

"No you didn't! You didn't think at all!"

The Head was turning redder by the second at all this blasphemy. Personally, I couldn't understand what Grandpa was in a lather about as it didn't matter one jot to him and he was still in one piece.

"I think, General Flashman that perhaps I should have a word with the boy and then he can accompany you away from the school. Come with me."

At this, he turned and stalked into his private room and I meekly followed.

"Flashman, we have recovered the substances so neatly stowed, by you I take it, in Master Burberry's desk. I assume you meant to allow him to take the entire blame for this appalling spectacle? Am I correct?"

"No sir," I stammered. "I wouldn't drop the lit… my honourable friend into this mess and then allow him to reap the consequences alone."

"I assume that is why you were in such a hurry to join your honourable friend in my study? Flashman, I will not tolerate this kind of rebellion.[2] I do not want to hear your lies, excuses or apologies. I have heard all possible combinations before. Fortunately for you, no one was hurt. Also fortunately for you, your Grandfather is a man of influence. That means that although you will be expelled, it also means that to avoid the charge of malicious damage, which the School would undoubtedly bring against you, you must comply with your Grandfather's wishes to the letter. If you choose not to then I will have no hesitation in calling the Constable. The choice is yours, Flashman. Choose wisely as you will not be allowed to change your mind once you leave this room." With that, he left.

---

[2] This could be a reference to the 1797 rebellion, when some of the boys had obtained gunpowder and were shooting cork bullets. After a shopkeeper denied selling them the powder, they were accused of lying and flogged. A door was blown in with a petard (small explosive charge), a bonfire was made of the Headmaster's books and, the riot act having been read, eventually a recruiting party of soldiers was used to quell the disturbance.

Well here was a fine kettle of fish. Burberry seemed to be entirely forgotten and I was to get the blame. Not only that but I would have to submit to my Grandfather's scheme, whatever that was. Oh yes, I had no illusions about that. I had no choice. If the coppers arrived, it would be down to the clink for a short chat and then ignominy and disgrace, at least for a little while, whereas at least my own Grandfather wouldn't disgrace me. At least I hoped he wouldn't.

A sharp rap on the door brought me back to reality. I felt like telling the owner to make himself scarce when the door opened unbidden and there was my Grandfather. Not much time to make up my mind I thought but didn't say. I had hardly opened my mouth before he said "Expelled then? In disgrace are we?" I nearly denied it but it would have been pointless.

"Yes," I replied.

"What was it? A wager, drink or women? And don't you tell me it was none of those because it always is."

I looked at the floor and said, "It was all a misunderstanding. Burberry, he, well, he…." I tailed off.

He snorted in what I imagined was anger but was in fact a great hoot of laughter.

"Caught smashing up the statues, you bloody scoundrel. Ha! And I thought you didn't have it in you! You know what I was expelled for don't you?" I didn't and I had no idea. I had always thought he was your true blue hero. "Getting beastly drunk. Ha! Up before the beak before you

15

could vomit and sent packing. The Old Man was pleased as I am sure yours will be." My beloved Father I took this to mean. "No doubt he'll lecture you on the ungodliness of it all and send prayers for strength on your behalf, and bore us all into an early grave with the shame of it if I'm not mistaken. Well, we'll see soon enough. In the meantime, James thinks I should decide what is to be done with you. Either that or leave you to the local vultures. Well, I hadn't decided until I came in just then, but I see you are a chip of a very old block unless I am much mistaken. Therefore, I will decide your fate, not that old goat. My solution is rather sensitive though so you have to decide whether to leave it to my judgement or not. Up to you my boy.... Oh and by the way, you should always look whomever you are lying to straight in the eye. They might just believe you then." And with this baffling me, he left. I thought perhaps he was beastly drunk again but he had walked out steadily enough.

Well, what a choice. The prig James or my Grandfather who may or may not have been half cut. Of course, I knew the solution already.

******

It only took the best part of the next day to get home. I had decided wisely (?) to accept my Grandfather's judgement, as it had to be better than James'. It was suppertime before my Father appeared. Someone had intercepted him and passed on the glad news, which I suppose saved me from doing it, but didn't affect the mood he was in. Moses would have been proud. If there had been any water to part or bread to multiply or whatever else these people do it would all have happened then. From my point of view, the miracle was how well he took the news of his only begotten son's disgrace.[3]

"A criminal," he murmured as though someone had farted in church. "You, my boy, are a criminal". Quite what I was meant to make of this statement I did not know. As a crowning insult, it was hardly the most frightening thing I had heard. "You are unfit to grace my presence." Something else I could live without. "You will leave this house shortly and only return when you have redeemed yourself in the eyes of the Lord." Now that was a bit more difficult.

"But Father," I said in my best crawling tone, "Where am I to go? What am I to do?"

"That is your dilemma my boy. As ye sow, so shall ye reap.[4] You have until the end of the week

---

[3] Flashman's relatives are mentioned occasionally in the original papers, notably in Flashman and the Angel of the Lord where there is an episode involving four great grandchildren by his granddaughter Selina, herself daughter of Harry Albert Victor, Flashman's legitimate son and also in Flashman and the Tiger where Selina is mentioned again just before her marriage. She was aged 19 in 1894 and as far as it is possible to tell, there is no mention of siblings until now.

[4] Presumably a misquote of Galatians vi. 'Be not deceived; God is not mocked: for whatsoever a man soweth, that shall he also reap.

to make up your mind. Use your time wisely. My Father wishes to speak to you."

I couldn't have summed it up better myself, the blasted hypocrite. Still, I had a week to get round the old bugger and persuade him that God would damn him as well if I were forced to accept my Grandfathers scheme, whatever that was. You see, I was fairly sure when I left the school that I would get round my Father as my leaving would hurt him a lot more than it would hurt me. He would then sympathetically do the honours with his, and hey presto, we would see who was going to submit to some madcap scheme. At least that was the way I planned it but of course things never quite work the way you expect them to and this time they were all after me, especially my interfering Grandfather who had suddenly taken an unhealthy interest in my fate. It's always the way with elders and such like. They cannot keep their big noses out of other peoples business, least of all mine. And they always infuriatingly know what is best for you or me and everyone else. God it makes me angry. And what they had in store for me would have had Canterbury himself cursing like a trooper. If I had known, I would have absconded that night and saved myself a deal of unwanted trouble. But I am getting carried away, memories you see.

When I look back at it all, I can't complain too much. Nor can the army of satisfied women. I suppose those I helped into the afterlife might have a comment or two but time enough for that when I join them in the pit.

I could have cried at the time though.

It was next morning, after a restless night, that the messenger of doom appeared, larger than life, in the form of General Sir Harry Flashman VC. He looked very cheerful, and well he might. He wasn't hopelessly in the cart.

"You have spoken with the Lord then my boy?"

"Yes," I replied.

"And what did he think of his charming son's behaviour?" He didn't give me time to reply but just carried on with his discourse. "No doubt he had a jolly good laugh at the idea of you being incarcerated for criminal damage. I know I did. Lectured you on the damnation to come and then proposed a second expulsion from this house I suspect. Am I right?" he sniggered in that holier than thou way known only to parents.

"Yes," was all I could manage.

"So what do you think you are going to do now then?" he asked.

Silence was all he got from me, not through insolence you understand but bafflement, simply because I really hadn't a clue. I had thought about my fate but all my plans rested on the Bishop letting me eat humble pie and stay in the end, repaying him at some vague later date. My Grandfather gave me short shrift there.

"He won't let you stay you know. And he would be right. You should get out in the World and make something of yourself, just like I did."

I felt sure he was laughing at me and said so.

"We are brave aren't we," he said. "I can see you got your manners from the Flashman side of the family, just like me again." This was followed by another great snort of laughter, which really got on my nerves. The trouble was he was the only member of the family who could really give me the willies. I dreaded to think where all this was leading. Perhaps he was just venting his amusement at my predicament.

"I have thought a great deal about the, er, situation you find yourself in. It is not unlike my departure from Rugby many years ago, not that you would know anything about that of course. All very hushed up since. Couldn't have a Brigadier General with the VC and thanks of Parliament traipsing around having tea with His Majesty if it was generally known how I came to leave Rugby don't ye know. That wouldn't do at all. But, when I was removed, for being beastly drunk as that squirming bastard Brown once said, I decided to join the Army. It didn't quite turn out how I expected, but then that is the way of things my boy. Looking back, knowing much that you won't until I am dead, I can say that on the whole, it was a life well spent." His eyes glazed over as he stared into the past.

Confused? I was I can tell you. Of course I hadn't seen his memoirs, his real memoirs, and didn't for many years to come. When I did however, and discovered the true nature of my Grandfather, many things were explained. At this precise moment, all I wanted was to be left alone to scheme and curse. Something however was nagging at the back of my mind. It hit me with a flash, excuse the pun. Like an idiot, I had been only half listening to my Grandfather and his tales of woe and glory, and suddenly I could see the path he planned for me clearly. Well he could keep his bloody Army with its bullets and bayonets and death and so on. One look at his evil grinning face told me I was right.

"You will join the Army my boy. I didn't mention this to your Father last night as he wasn't in the mood for me, and I like his pious platitudes as much as you obviously do. But he will see the sense in it. If only to remove you conveniently from the scene of your disgrace."

Well, I wasn't having that and started to tell him so. I did have the presence of mind, just, not to whine though.

"It's impossible," I said. "I cannot join the Army. I have my education to finish, and I am sure my father will agree with me. Besides, how will I get to Sandhurst? And who will support me? He is not a wealthy man, despite his position."

"Oh, I wouldn't worry about the money. I can more than provide you with a decent income and maintain you in the style to which you will become accustomed." This sounded ominous. "And as for your education, you seem to be coming along nicely without that mongrel James[5] to help you. His daughter perhaps..." He tailed off. He had it all planned I could see, and it was going to take a deal of scheming to extract myself

---

[5] James was not married so did not have a daughter. Flashman may simply not have known this.

from this precarious position. "I shall go to see him directly," he said.

"No," I squealed, "surely there is some other way?"

But the glint in his eye told me that there would be no other way. He spun round at the door, and with what I can only describe as hideous pleasure, he quietly said,

"I am afraid that this time, Cinderella[6] will most definitely go to the Ball."

I nearly wept.

But the Flashman will to survive prevailed. Just. Nothing would happen straightaway. There would be some time before he managed to sweep me out of the house, and many things could happen before then, especially if I had anything to do with it. And if the worst came to the worst and I had to go, there would be ways out. There always were. Little did I know, of course, of my blasted Grandfather and his big interfering nose. The trouble was, which I found out much later, too late to do anything about of course, he was positively enjoying himself. He didn't get too many chances to hurl people into the soup, and this was one of them. From the safety of old age

---

[6] Cinderella is an old folk tale, first recorded in English in 'Tales of Mother Goose' in 1729 which was itself a translation from the French 'Contes de ma mere l'oye', a collection of oral tales compiled by Charles Perrault in 1697. It was Perrault that apparently added some of the more traditional parts of the tale such as the idea of Cinderella going to a ball, dancing with the Prince and leaving before midnight. It is possible that the story is an even more ancient story from the east.

and in my weaker moments, I actually think there was some goodwill in his concern.

Maybe not. The conniving bastard.

Chapter 3

My optimism was unjustified to say the least. I thought I would have a few days at least to collect my wits, or at least to recover slightly. I have always been at my best (and worst) when nothing appears to happen. Hope resurfaces and everything appears in a much rosier light. Threats are a dim and distant memory. But if there is one thing experience has taught me it is that when you are up to your neck in the mire, there is generally only one person to get you out. There are two reasons for this. Firstly, no one really wants to help the leper in case the infection rubs off. Secondly, those responsible take great pleasure in your predicament, especially if they are Bishops.

It was the following afternoon when my Grandfather appeared again. I was in the Library, not being allowed out of the house in case anyone should see me.

"Hollo," he said cheerfully.

I just glared at him.

"I have just come from the Horse Guards where I saw Paget. Distant relation on your Great Grandmother's side. His father used to sort out the Flashman family woes when I was your age, if only to maintain our respectable image at Court. He despises us generally and wouldn't be seen in public with us common Flashmans. Fortunately, the King believes otherwise and thinks we are rather dashing. Just the sort he needs to keep the natives in check in his Empire. Anyway, I have obtained your place. Some formalities to deal with. Start in January."

Just like that. As casual as could be. Here you are boy, kicked into touch at the first opportunity and good riddance.

"What," I shrieked. It was all I could say. He had left me virtually speechless.

"Sandhurst is near Camberley.... That's near London. In case you didn't know," he said as he headed for the door. "Cheer up. Just think of the alternatives."

I could think of several more pleasing ones.

"I will see you damned to hell for this," I shouted.

"Oh, I am going there already," he replied, "but I will keep you a prime seat as I have no doubt you will need it some day."

And with that, he left.

So there it was. The Army and Sandhurst, or.... well, what really? I had no idea. I decided to appeal to my Father's good (ha!) nature but it was just wasted time. He said I needed to win my spurs and prove my worth and be a good Christian and redeem myself and more of that sort of piffle, and if I didn't go to Sandhurst, he would cut me off without a penny. Some Christian.

Even I could see the futility of whining any more. They had decided and I would suffer. At least I wasn't dead. And as I thought about it, my spirits revived a little. My Grandfather had survived after all, and an Officers lot was still a very privileged position. A Rugby education would help. If I could survive public school, then the Army would be simple. And one day I would return and make them all pay. Thoughts of revenge were just what I needed and this set me on a different track altogether. Perhaps if I threw myself at this Army business I could make it work. Not for them though. Just for me, and in my own way. We would see who suffered.

I don't know if the weeks of waiting helped or not. I doubt it because I wasn't allowed out of the house much. I was forced to study for the exam, something I had not appreciated initially, but the consequences of failure were made painfully clear. In the end it was not the ordeal I imagined and having passed, it was not long before the day of reckoning arrived.

I had decided to ride to Sandhurst as it was warm despite being winter and my Grandfather had provided me with a decent horse. The rest of my things went by carriage. Horses were one thing I had in common with the old bastard and we had spent many days riding when he was home. He had taught me all sorts of tricks that he had picked up over the years, which would at least prove I wasn't a complete novice when I arrived at my new lodgings. He had also provided an allowance of £400 a year as well as fitting me out with all that a new officer needed, which was more than the Old Man could have done and nearly softened my feelings for him. I say nearly because with all that happened subsequently, I could have murdered him without a second thought.

I won't bore you with the details of the road. Suffice to say it was like every other road I have ever travelled and led to death and destruction, occasionally via depravity and lust, the lust on this occasion being a giggling blonde piece at a roadside inn and the depravity an education unlike anything the Masters taught at Rugby. It was quite a wrench to leave the next morning, and I was disappointed for about five seconds. I was on the last stretch now and I cantered into a deserted barracks at about eleven in the morning. As I seemed to be alone I decided to take a shift around and see what was what. It didn't take me long to find what was obviously a mess of some kind, and having done so, I made myself at home. I had just poured myself a stiff drink when in came a cheery old buffer who looked as though there wasn't enough alcohol in existence to sustain him.

"Hollo," I said, deciding in that instant that some caution was required. Much as I didn't care two hoots what anyone thought, I also had the sense to see that my usual set of nine lives was currently somewhat depleted, and returning home in disgrace for the second time most certainly would not enhance my situation.

"Hollo yourself," the cheery one replied. "Mind if I join you."

He already had as far as I could see, but of course I said, "Please do, just having a wee snifter."

"What you here for then? Sent packing myself. Regiment fed up with hearing the same old stories over and over again, shouldn't wonder."

Me too I thought, and I have only known you thirty seconds. Just like a damned yank, always dying to tell you their life history. "I am here to join the Army," I said.

There was another of those pregnant pauses with which life, mine in particular, is punctuated.

"Ah," he said after the pregnant pause had finished. Apparently, that should have been enough to explain my situation, but when I didn't vanish in a puff of smoke, he continued. "Wrong place old boy. Not to join the Army of course. Right place for that. If you want to be an officer that is. Students. Not in the mess. Still, just arrived. Can't be helped. Guardhouse useless of course. Well, toodle pip. Sure we'll cross swords again. By the way, what's your name?"

"Flashman."

"I think you'll find its Flashman Sah. Any relation to Harry Flashman are you?"

I said my Grandfather was indeed General Sir Harry Flashman. "Ah," he said again. "Mine's ah, Leonard. Sah to you of course."

The conversation closed and I was dismissed. Where to I didn't know. Or particularly care. I mention all this of course because it has some bearing on the events to follow my arrival, which, apart from going inadvertently into the mess reserved for real officers and the like, was completely uneventful.

I soon discovered the same applied to the course itself when it eventually got started. Like all military courses from the beginning of time to the present day, I learnt very little of any use, I was systematically abused by my inferiors and virtually deafened by an excessively enthusiastic RSM. I won't bore you with the details as they have little relevance to my story, except for one incident that got my career off to a flying start. Literally.

My fellow travellers were pretty dull, all in all. My Grandfather would have written them off as Addiscombe tripe,[7] all except one. A short wiry man, he was very tough and hard-bitten. We got on famously, mainly because he was a proper gentleman but not high born, just like me really, except that I wasn't a gentleman underneath but knew how to carry the role off. He also had no money whilst I had bags of it and if anything still counted in the Army, it was certainly money. Bernie resented that fact. We both rubbed along together fine though. In the summer exams, he was judged excellent, even though he was placed only 87th, and I was judged a bit of a nuisance. They couldn't sling me out though because I found I liked it. Well, up to a point. I was a good horseman, a fair sportsman and a decent linguist I discovered. Military theory escaped me entirely but then why would one need to know how the Light Brigade should have charged? Or how

---

[7] Addiscombe was the former military seminary for the East India Company and closed in 1861. Flashman's negative opinion probably reflects that of General Flashman but why is impossible to tell given that he is referring to a generation who would mostly perish on the Western Front.

Cetshwayo had managed to destroy Chelmsford's entire column at Isandlwhana? Life seemed altogether bright and it was certainly a sight less dull than school, with decent fillies to mount, both at stable and in town, good company and the prospect of easy life ahead. At least until the end of the year when the postings would be announced. That was the only fly in the ointment. But at least I thought I should be able to avoid India. That seemed to be the place to go with a commission in the Indian Army. At least the real Army types thought so and consequently the competition for places was high. One had to be placed in the top thirty or so to be guaranteed a plum job. Bernie was all for it, mainly because he wouldn't need an allowance and could live off his pay. Personally, I felt something further down the list and a nice safe billet at home in a dashing uniform would be more my style. Of course, fate was waiting in the wings to take her usual hand.

It all happened so quickly really. It started just like beating the fags at school. Bernie in particular had conceived a poisonous dislike for a cadet whose name I don't now recall, and as leader of Bloody 'B', he had resolved on a plan to rag him before guard duty or some such and spoil his mess kit, and thereby possibly his chances of bigger and better things. As a Lance Corporal, Bernie had ordered me to follow along. Not that I minded. I was all for it. He was a stuck up prig who had ignored me from the first and clearly didn't like me at all. We Flashman's were still not quite the thing amongst the real nobs, so a little revenge seemed entirely in order.

Consequently, we broke into his room, Bernie, myself and our little gang and caught him with his trousers down. In Tom Brown fashion,[8] we pinned him and set fire to his shirttails. This was where all started to go awry. The defendant shrieked as the fire took hold - pretty combustible shirts in those days - and tried to throw himself away from the flames and avoid the bayonet someone else was brandishing to prevent him escaping. The stench of burning flesh now penetrated my throat and I started to gag. I then joined in with the shrieking as I discovered that someone had also set fire to my uniform. It was then I realised that with all this racket and the smell to boot it wouldn't be long before the boys in blue appeared, followed, if I was any sort of a judge, by an ambulance made for two. I decided to decamp if it were at all possible. I shrieked again in agony, as my arse felt like a goose at Christmas and like a man possessed staggered to the door. A few dark looks followed me but at least I had an alibi for lighting out for the frontier. I clung to the doorframe for a second or two just to check the way was clear and then my legs took over. I ran along the corridor and found an

---

[8] In Nigel Hamilton's three-volume biography of Montgomery, he uses precisely this phrase, which suggests he may have been inspired by Flashman's account of this well-known incident. If so, it is odd that he does not mention Flashman's involvement, although this may well be more to do with the apparent shared dislike of the protagonists after the event.

apparently unmarked door. I just had the sense not to kick it down, but tried the handle. It opened and I slipped in. As I closed it behind me, I noticed two things. One, the closet contained a few old pots of paint and such like, two, that voices were approaching the scene of the fire at light division pace.

I sank down onto the floor amongst some dust covers and settled in for a wait. I had no illusions about the results of the previous debacle. Friend Johnny had a nicely singed arse. He was going to want to know who had fried him and return the favour with interest. I thought about running away entirely but that would only confirm my guilt. No, there was a better way, and one that would see me out with honours.

It was all round the camp in no time. The perpetrators were in the nick, all except for one H. Flashman esq who hadn't been seen for some while. This was because he had dozed off in the cupboard, natural reaction setting in after a shock. I woke up wondering where on earth I was. It all came back pretty sharp though. Fortunately, I had formulated my plan already. All I had to do was account for the time lapse in appearing. It couldn't have been that long though. Gingerly, I opened the closet door. No one around. Slipping out, I noticed it was fairly dark, so I resolved to put my plan into instant action. I found my way out of the cadet quarters and round to the Officers Mess. Dishevelled, clothes burnt here and there, and a generous helping of ash, which required a small conflagration, (I had some matches in my pocket) to smear on my hands and face. Once I was happy, I set off for the Colonel's quarters, neatly avoiding the guards.

Faced with the great man's door, it suddenly didn't seem such a good plan. What if they had given the game away already? I might find myself joining the criminal fraternity in the guardhouse. No, it couldn't be. Bernie always was an ass for taking the blame and not squealing on his weaker colleagues. I rapped on the door.

"May I ask who is...." the servant said. "My word, it is one of those golliwogs. Be off with you sir, before you soil the porch."

"Who is it at this hour," boomed a Colonel's voice from within.

"Nobody sir, at least, nobody you would wish to see." Typical bloody butler, taking on the airs and graces of the house, turning away perfectly respectable callers even if dressed like the coalman. Now was my only chance.

"Cadet Flashman to see Colonel Capper[9], sir."

"One of the cadets?" boomed the voice.

"It would appear so, sir," replied the servant. At this point, the Colonel himself appeared in the hallway.

"Good God, what the hell is going on here? First, we have cadets setting fire to each other. Now we have one who appears to have set fire to himself. What do you want boy, and make it

---

[9] Colonel W.B.Capper was Commandant at Sandhurst in 1907.

33

quick. It had better be good or the memsahib will have me crucified."

"Well sir. It's like this."

And so began my long and tortuous career in the service of the King. I told him the truth. Well, nearly anyway. Slightly embellished to make myself appear the real villain, which was not what he was expecting at all. How I was the ringleader, had dreamed up the whole plan, and then carried it out, realising that it had been a cock up and that I would have to pay for it. I offered my resignation there and then.

What, you may wonder, was I thinking of, making myself look bad. Well, it's a strange thing about lying. Try to make yourself look good and you just appear a show off. Try it t'other way and sure as eggs is eggs, no one will believe you. At best, they will think you are just covering for someone else, and therefore what a thoroughly good egg you must be.

"Well, Flashman, did you say. We will see about resignation but that is quite a story and certainly ties up with what I know already. You were not alone in confessing your guilt. You are alone in visiting me at this late hour. The other perpetrators are currently in choky and shall remain so until I see fit to decide their fate. I will decide in the morning what is to be done with you. You may wish to know that your friend refused absolutely to identify his assailants. Goodnight sir."

With this, the Colonel turned away and I took it that the interview was over. Well, at least

Bernie had kept his big mouth shut. As I left, I just caught the tail of the conversation between the Colonel and his butler.

"Daft thing to do Fellowes. Still, just the sort for the Army. Knows when he's made a balls of it. Father's the VC man. First in at The Charge and so on. Chip of the same block no doubt. Have to punish them of course. Seen to do the right thing."

"Yes sir," said Fellowes, sounding like he didn't care a fart. All sounded very promising to me though. Wonder what the punishment would be. Must have meant my Grandfather of course. With these happy thoughts, I went to bed, well pleased with my days work. Style. All that mattered.

Next morning, Nemesis appeared in the shape of the adjutant. He formally arrested me and took me to join friend Bernie in the guardhouse. I winked at him when he caught sight of me arriving. It did nothing to cheer him up though. In fact, he gave me a look that would have frozen hell. The next hours were my first, but not my last in a military prison. It wasn't long before we were summoned. I hadn't spoken a word to Bernie and nor was I allowed to now. We were marched over to the Colonel's office and stationed separately outside. Bernie was up first. He was joined by a woman I took to be his Mother. The Bishop, his Father was nowhere to be seen. I wondered if anyone would come to support my cause.

After a long wait, they appeared again. Bernie looked distrait but relieved at the same time. He was still wearing his cadet insignia, minus the lance-corporal stripe, so he must be staying. The adjutant appeared again and announced me. I entered the Colonel's lair and crashed to attention, whereupon I became aware of another clergyman in the room.

"Oh Christ, my father is here," was my first thought. My second was along the same lines but with my Grandfather substituted.

"Well Flashman," said the Colonel, "we are gathered here today to decide your fate." Fairly obvious I would have thought. "I have noted the facts of the matter, particularly that you saw fit to admit to this misdemeanour without prompting. That does not, however, mean that it will be taken lightly. I have spoken already with your Father and Grandfather. Between us we have decided upon a course of action."

Well here we go again I thought. No thought for young Flash, just here's your medicine, hope you like it, tough if you don't.

"Yes sir," I said.

"You will not leave after Christmas but remain here until the summer[10]. I am unable to demote you as you have remained as a gentleman cadet. When you do leave, you will be posted to the Indian Army. I was at first unwilling to

---

[10] Although this does not sound like a severe punishment, it was regarded as such because those whose Army careers began with being held back a term were marked men already and tended to suffer from slower promotion as well as having a lower seniority. Clearly, this was not the case with Montgomery who ascended as high as it was possible to go.

sanction this course of action as the Indian Army is regarded as the elite posting. Your Grandfather has convinced me that in this case it would be a wise decision. I am sure you appreciate why. If anything like this occurs again however, I will remove you from Sandhurst without compunction. Do I make myself clear?"

"Yes sir," I said again.

I was dismissed and left the room alone to wander back to my quarters, where a little while later my Grandfather appeared, uninvited for a change.

"Interestin' what! Chucked out of Rugby and now close to the same at Sandhurst. I can see I will need to watch you my boy." I didn't say a word. I was still thinking of the heat and filth of India, and the fact that the locals seemed a trifle unfriendly to Johnny Redcoat most of the time. "Of course it all had to be hushed up. Can't have the Bishop's son being disgraced. Lucky choice of friends. You will like India, I promise you. Oh I know what you think now. (This was because I had squawked in disbelief.) But I thought the same. It didn't do me any harm and it won't you. Just boil your water, keep yourself clean and only go to the high-class brothels. All the rest have the clap or worse. Earn your spurs lad."

This with a particularly infuriating smirk on his face. He left and I didn't see him again for some years. I am sure he had planned it all. I don't know how, but I am sure.

So that was it. A few months later, months without incident I can assure you, I left. I had toyed with the idea of getting myself slung out completely, but the result of that didn't bear thinking about. I was only twenty remember, and in spite of my worldly instructors still a griffin. At least they sent me to a cavalry regiment. I hadn't spoken a single word to Bernie since the fateful day. I knew he was joining the Warwicks and that he was bound for India as well. But I thought, in my innocence, it wouldn't matter. I had made an enemy but a poor one with no influence. No need to worry then. I should have known better of course.[11]

---

[11] This incident is well known and is described in most accounts of the career of Field Marshal Viscount Montgomery of Alamein, KG, GCB, DSO. The incident was very serious and the cadet involved was badly burned but did not name his attackers. The culture at Sandhurst at the time allowed the cadets to do as they pleased in their free time with little interference from the officers. It was assumed that as young well brought up men they would behave accordingly. Montgomery was lucky in his choice of parents as his Mother was indeed a strong and influential woman and probably saved his career, although the fact that his Father was also a Bishop and had recently been appointed Prelate of the Order of St Michael and St George probably helped as well. Flashman's involvement is not mentioned anywhere but he was also lucky, not only that a precedent was set for Montgomery, but also that his own ancestors were influential in their own right. There is no doubt the General would have pulled on the right strings if it had been necessary.

Chapter 4

I still have no idea how he did it. Perhaps he knew I was bored. What I do know is that if it was his first stab at revenge, it was a pretty good attempt at seeing me off to my maker. Just didn't work out quite like that, for either of us.

After Sandhurst I had been posted to the 1st Bengal Lancers[12], and now I had been in India for about a century it seemed. I had seen enough garrison life to last me forever. I had even written home. I told them what a bloody bore it was. I shouldn't have done that.

It was cold on the Northwest Frontier. I had been soldiering there on and off for a couple of years now and if nothing else had learnt how to stay alive in trying conditions. I suppose I had grown up. I had all the adult vices including gambling. Gambling was a way of life. We gambled on everything and continued after dinner one evening when the great mick O'Connell had sidled in. He had brought his aeroplane with him

I had seen him occasionally but not out in the wild before. Normally a relatively quiet reserved chappie until, being Irish, he was full of the waters of the Liffey, he turned into a more interesting character altogether. And so it proved. His skill at cards and games of chance was minimal when sober so it wasn't long before he was losing money at a fine old rate. I can't remember who it was but someone suggested

---

[12] The full regimental title was 1st Bengal Lancers (Skinner's Horse).

drawing for a ride in his bus as he called it. Lowest card took the honours, which gives you some idea of the life expectancy of the lucky winner. If I had thought quickly, I would have made some sharp remark and let someone else draw for the chance to kill themselves. But I was too slow and before I could say a word, the cards were on the table. We all flipped them over together. I looked at my seven thinking I was all right, until I heard the squawks of delight that Flash would show old O'Connell here how to fly. Had he ever seen him hunt? My face was ashen. No one noticed. I was too shaken even to attempt to wriggle out of this dilemma.

"See you in the mornin' Flash," O'Connell said as the party broke up.
Well, you've seen what happened and it was the beginning of a long road. In spite of my previous horror and denial of O'Connell's assertion that there was 'nuthin to it for a man of my ability,' he had set a train of thought running. I was bored with life in general and India in the extreme. Perhaps it might even get me a ticket home, so more out of general indifference than anything I applied for a transfer. The Colonel gave me a stare and said he thought he'd be damned before he got in any sort of flying contraption. Cousin tried to fly once. Mad though. Fell awf the roof of the summerhouse. This concluded our interview.

There were two conditions for joining the RFC at the time. The first was that I would have to obtain a Royal Aero Club Certificate at my own expense before I could be accepted for training although it appeared that I could do this when I got home.

The second was an interview to assess my suitability for the RFC, O'Connell's word being not quite as acceptable as he imagined. It was quite an ordeal.

I forget who it was who conducted this interrogation, but it began with the question, "Why did I want to join the RFC?"

"The excitement, Sir," I blurted out.

"Do you ride?"[13]

And that was that.

It was months before anything happened of course, India being that sort of place. Postman murdered and so on, so I had given up and resigned myself to dying on the Northwest Frontier. Then all of a sudden, I was on my way to Bombay for a ship at least part way home. Here it was that fate took another hand through the divine intervention of the blasted mick O'Connell again. I had taken one look at the garrison mess and decided I wouldn't let my Father stay there. Consequently, I decided to look for somewhere local. When I say local, I mean of course a decent house with a decent memsahib to look after my every need, not some flea-bitten pit with the natives.

---

[13] This interview has long been ridiculed for its simplicity and apparent irrelevance, but in reality, a good horseman was as good a bet as any to make a good pilot. The skills for both were similar, balance, good hands, self-confidence and acceptance of a challenge.

I made some enquiries and before long found something that appeared suitable and sent in my card. The reply was little short of astonishing. A loud voice whooped with delight from somewhere deep inside the house and was then heard to exclaim, "If it's really dat bugger Flash tell him to gae somewhere else and drink."

Slightly offended I resolved to puncture this pompous idiot's balloon and was just preparing my reply when the approaching noise of stumbling boots mixed with curses revealed one O'Connell. I stood with my mouth open.

"Catching mossies are ye Flash? Plenty of 'em ye know."

Speechless again.

"Are ye gaein tae stand iteside all the day?"

"Why no, no of course not. Where on earth…."

"Jist passin' troo. On ma way home as it happens. Waiting for the bluidy boat. Ye would nae think this was a port wouldye nye."

So he had found me again. I have no illusions that it was the other way around. I am absolutely certain he was expecting me somehow. Well of course I had no option but to stay with him and wait for the bluidy boat. It was going to be a long passage home.

The next week passed very slowly, partly in a smoke and drink fuelled haze, until at last our numbers were up. We trundled aboard with our luggage - not too much of it as I had certainly learned to travel light with just the essentials and O'Connell had lost what possessions he had at the tables and now appeared to own only the clothes he was wearing. We found what were fairly salubrious accommodations and settled in for a long haul, at least part way back home. Initially we had planned to complete our journey partly overland from Suez to Alexandria, and Suez was where our ship now headed at a snails pace. O'Connell got bored very quickly, as he didn't have anything to do and he couldn't gamble being broke. I had learnt to pass the time more easily and wasn't quite so like a coiled spring when we finally docked.

Suez, like every port I have ever been in was teeming with every colour under the sun. Chinese coolies shoved past local porters and British tars. Arabs, Jews, Africans of all sorts, contributed to the mass and consequently the appalling stench of spices, oil, smoke, sweat, oh and death. There were more than a few bodies floating in the harbour and the odd one in the street although the locals did get a little upset about this, as they didn't like to be seen to leave corpses lying around as it might affect the trade. It was at least two hours before a gangplank appeared. A snottie informed me that it wasn't called a gangplank but the real name was lost in the din behind us as we set off on the next stage of our journey. O'Connell was virtually bursting by now which fortunately meant he got used to being back on land quickly.

"Ah've got to foind a drink, Flash," he said as we stumbled around the docks.

"We will," I said, "but not just yet. We have got to find the rail office or we will never get out

43

of this rotten place." With that, I dragged him off towards what at last appeared to be a ticket office, inside which was, thank God, an Englishman.

It was not good news. The gyppys were causing trouble apparently and he advised us to stay with the ship this time. I dragged O'Connell out of the office but no further than the drinking establishment next door which looked suitably seedy but which the Englishman said was actually rather good and could be relied upon to feed you without killing you. Having taken a rather extended advantage of the facilities, we returned to the docks to board the ship. But it was not there.

I stared around for some time, cursing the damned thing, cursing O'Connell, cursing the gyppys, in fact anyone I could think of, before accepting that our ride was gone. We returned to our haunt where O'Connell got drunk. Not wishing to sample the delights of Suez for too much longer, I tried to arrange passage out. Fortunately, our Englishman from the ticket office appeared before I sank into total despair. I was on the point of taking my chance to Alexandria and had I known what lay in store, I believe I would have, but our man promised that next morning he would arrange everything. He was as good as his word.

We had to wait about two days, but not before time we were boarding a steamer, which took us not only through the canal to Port Said, but also on to Cyprus where we docked at the port of Kyrenia in the north. As a colony, the place was civilised if one could ever call the colonies civilised and we decided to stay for a few days having found a reasonable Mess inland at Nicosia.[14] It was a welcome relief, as I was heartily sick of boats. O'Connell, whilst exploring our temporary home and considering its occupants, and being well known in aviation circles, soon found one Skene, who had been doing distance trials in his Avro 504[15] along with his chum Gooding in his. They had set off from Netheravon and finished up in Cyprus. God knew how and we should have as he spent the best part of two weeks telling us every detail of his journey and how pleased his superiors would be when he got back. I didn't say but I thought they would think he had gone berserk and have him confined together with Goodboy or whatever his name was. Apparently, there was only one problem and that was that his sidekick had reported sick and was unable to fly. This left them with the dilemma of what to do about getting home, as it was quite clear that Gooding wasn't going to be flying for a while. I was beginning to get seriously bored with all this talk until O'Connell came up with the wonderful suggestion that perhaps he could fly Gooding's

[14] Cyprus was not in fact a colony in 1914. It was nominally ruled by the Turks but controlled by Great Britain, which paid an annual fee. When Turkey joined the Central Powers in 1914, Cyprus was annexed but did not become a crown colony until 1925.

[15] The Avro 504 was designed in 1913. Easy to fly it was used briefly for bombing and reconnaissance but was not suited to these roles and was relegated to a training role early on.

aeroplane home while he went overland. Skene thought this was a marvellous idea and told Gooding who was all for it. It was a good idea. It would be twice as quick as the boat or train. I had seen enough of the limited pleasures of garrison life in Cyprus and O'Connell was becoming even more of a liability than usual with his drinking, gambling, and general collection of debt. So we took up the offer, and whilst O'Connell would do the flying I signed on as gate opener, prop swinger and char wallah.

I had not been airborne since my first ride with O'Connell, which was somewhat hair-raising, but now I rediscovered the delights of aviation as we leisurely made our way through the Ottoman lands, skirting the high bits and following the coast passing Rhodes and various other islands, on into the land of the Bulgars and continuing through various Slav lands. At one point, given my family history, I asked if we were near the Crimea, which showed how much attention I had paid studying Geography and received an incredulous stare, which clearly said how on earth do you expect to fly an aeroplane around if you don't even know where the Crimea is?

Eventually we arrived in a place called Sarajevo. It was the 27th of June 1914.

Chapter 5

We put the aeroplanes to bed for the night and then looked for some transport into town, intending to paint it red. We eventually thumbed a lift on a farm wagon. None of us spoke the lingo but with a bit of arm waving and various gesticulations, the message was conveyed. Our spirits were high and were higher still once we had had a couple of sundowners. Perhaps it was the drink or maybe just the fact that after what seemed an eternity I was nearly home. Whatever it was, my guard was down somewhat. O'Connell of course, being Irish, never had a guard in the first place. It was pure chance. At least it seemed that way.

We had noisily discovered the diplomatic and foreigners quarter and between the three of us, we had loudly discussed our flying exploits and what brave and wonderful chaps we really were. Of course, we had become the centre of attention in what was after all a fairly small town, albeit the provincial Capital, with an equally small society. It wasn't until after we left a particularly friendly place, the name of which I couldn't recall then or now that we seemed to have an entourage of about fifty in tow. No one cared and the party drifted on well past midnight. Somehow, we found somewhere to stay and we woke up feeling pretty awful in a strange house. Almost as soon as I awoke, I smelt danger but then a friendly foreigner appeared and started to serve up breakfast. Kidneys, kippers, eggs, bread, you name it, it was there and just how I liked it. We didn't therefore ask too many questions and those we did were skilfully deflected for later.

Sated from overeating on a fragile constitution, someone suggested we think about getting under way. At which point, as if by magic our host appeared.

"Gentlemen, gentlemen, you cannot rush away so fast. How was your feast? Forgive me for detaining you but we have a parade and some important guests in Sarajevo today and it would be my pleasure to introduce you, albeit briefly, to some of our European royalty. Not as grand as your own Family of course, but nevertheless, of some consequence."

Here I thought he had taken leave of his senses. I had sensed immediately something not quite right but couldn't put my finger on it. Then all this talk of royalty. Who did he think we were? Not that I could actually remember what we had told anybody the night before. As for the royal family being grand, well my Grandfather said that in the Old Queen's day he used to see them wandering about like a family of tinkers looking for bellows to mend. Still the place was comfortable enough and what harm was there in sponging off them for a while. They, whoever they were, seemed harmless enough despite my gut instinct.

This appeared to be the general feeling as well.

"Marvellous," said Skene. "Could do with a break what. Nothing like a good parade for keeping the rabble in order. Show 'em who's boss what."

We all laughed, including the Colonel, despite the fact that he plainly didn't have the faintest idea what Skene was talking about. He was right though. We had been flying virtually non-stop for days now with stops only to sleep, refuel and fix the machines when they broke or went wrong.

So we settled back and looked forward to meeting royalty.

******

Our host turned out to be some sort of local nabob. His name was Dimitrijevic, Colonel Dragutin Dimitrijevic and it ought to be splashed all over the history books but isn't because what happened next we kept very quiet about and only now, from the safety of old age can I tell what happened to us that day. It all began with digging out our dress uniforms. Skene and O'Connell had what passed for RFC best bib and tucker and I had my Cavalry rig. Once we had beautified ourselves, we were collected and taken into the centre of the town.

"The parade is in the city this morning with the Archduke. I thought you might like to see how we do these things in Bosnia," the Colonel said.

None of us really cared a tinker's cuss but it would have been impolite to refuse. I thought we would have a privileged spot. This was apparently not the case as our chauffeur left us standing in a side street. The crowd was somewhat thinner.

"Ah, Gavrilo," Dimitrijevic suddenly exclaimed. A small shifty looking boy appeared from nowhere. They gabbled away in the local lingo for a few minutes, and then the shifty one nodded to me and vanished in the crowd. Quite why he chose me was odd but I just supposed I looked the part of the leader, even when I wasn't.

"Shouldn't we...." I started. My words were drowned out by an explosion. People started rushing about. Dimitrijevic and ourselves? I instinctively ducked, checked to see that the foreigners hadn't noticed the Englishman's cowardly instinct and looked to see where the others were. They were pointing excitedly down the road at a cloud of smoke that presumably indicated the source of the bang. I could see they were desperate to investigate so I diverted them by saying, "Care for some lunch? I am famished. Presumably that's the end of today's excitement."

"Not at all," replied Dimitrijevic. "This sort of thing happens all the time. There is no need for worry. I think perhaps we follow the crowd."

This was the last thing I wanted to do but there appeared to be no choice. Off we went following the chattering mob. We eventually reached the source of the crime. The local peelers were on the scene already and appeared to be giving the nearest dosser a pasting. Same the world over. Eventually they thought better of it and threw the alleged miscreant into the local equivalent of a black maria. Dimitrijevic had watched all this in silence.

"This way," he said in a rather flat monotone. We followed him further down the road. It was somewhat chaotic but whether that was normal or caused by the apparent explosion was hard to tell. Having stared wondrously at what the tourists would now call the sights, we passed through some heavy and menacing wrought iron gates into a large building. Someone told me much later it was the City Hall. From then on the entertainment turned decidedly dreary, like most meetings with royalty. The food was dreadful and the wine tasted of castor oil. Shortly after giving an angry speech vilifying the locals, we all lined up to meet the great man himself. It turned out to be none other than the Archduke Franz Ferdinand, heir to the throne of the Austro Hungarian Empire. I gave him the bow I reserved for underlings and foreigners then shook his hand like a proper Englishman. He seemed slightly surprised, particularly when my name was mentioned, but the others took the hint and did likewise. They couldn't carry it off quite the same in their RFC school uniform but it left an impression. I think. Our host was nowhere to be seen and the reception dragged on interminably. It eventually came to a head when the Duke slung his hook and the Germans and Austrians relaxed which to them meant drinking anything to hand and collapsing under the table. Worst of all they turned into bores. As if from nowhere (it was becoming a habit) our Colonel appeared. He was dressed in ordinary rig and quietly suggested we take our leave now the bigwigs had gone.

Dimitrijevic was still behaving oddly, and we followed him back to where we had started. A rumble in the distance announced the arrival of the Archduke and his parade of cars. They drove past us, the Archduke scowling at all and sundry and his wife smiling and waving. Then, for some reason, the cars stopped. There was shouting and then they were reversing towards us. Suddenly there were shots. And now there was chaos. The crowd surged and the friendly atmosphere suddenly became highly charged. We were on the edge of a riot. Dimitrijevic sensed it as well.

"Something's wrong," he said. Couldn't have put it better myself I thought. "I think it's time we went home."

There was no argument from us.

There was a somewhat excitable atmosphere about the house when we arrived. There was also no sign of the Colonel who had made himself scarce a minute or so after we got there. It made the hairs on my neck stand on end. Once we, or at least I, couldn't stand it any longer, we wandered outside the main house for a smoke. He finally appeared in a large vehicle big enough for all of our luggage and us. We set off for the field where we had left the aeroplanes.

The Colonel was strangely quiet, almost as if he was revving himself up to say something. As we approached the field, he finally plucked up the courage to ask what was on his mind.

"Gentlemen." He stopped, presumably wondering how to continue. "Gentlemen," he said again. "I have a small favour to ask of you."

We assumed the furrowed brow required when the foreigners who have let you use their house for a while send in the bill, particularly after the somewhat strange events of the day so far, of which we still knew very little.

"It is inconsequential I can assure you. Nothing more than helping a brother officer."

Ah well, that was more like it.

"How can we be of service," Skene said loudly intimating to the rest of us that all was now well and we wouldn't be required to cough up.

"Well, Sir. It is a simple matter of….. well, avoiding the, how do you English say it? The long reach of the law. Is that it?"

How we laughed at this simpletons grasp of English.

"You'll be meanin' de long airm of de law," squawked O'Connell.

"Ah yes, that is it, exactly."

"Well den, ite with it. What has your friend been up to?" There were grins all round now. No-one of course likes to get one up on the rozzers more than your average Englishman, except of course an Irishman and here we had a perfect example of that breed who was permanently one step ahead of them.

Dimitrijevic. "Well, my friend was found in a politically compromising position."

"Politics. Is that all," bellowed Skene.

"Not quite, my dear fellow. Sarajevo is the provincial Capital and my friend only just managed to get his trousers on before the Mayor came into the room to find his wife. You see the situation of course. Here there are men, even policemen, who will kill for a few krone, and the Mayor has more than a few krone. It seemed best to arrange a post outside the Province. You are travelling west and will cross the border before you land again. I think you have a spare seat?"

He left the sentence hanging for a few seconds. He didn't need to.

"Of course old boy. He can squeeze in with O'Connell here. We'll get him away from the boys in blue."

And with that, we arrived at the aeroplanes. He was there already, the absconder. He didn't speak a word of English but we slapped him on the back a few times and gave him a couple of shots of appalling brandy from our flasks. I apparently was the only one who recognised him from the brief exchange at the parade that morning but I didn't let on.

"Princip," he kept saying.[16] We thought it was the local equivalent of 'bottoms up'. We were only slightly wrong.

---

[16] Flashman's account is the only apparent reference to Princip's attempted escape. All other accounts state he was arrested at the scene of the murder. It would appear that Dimitrijevic tried to engineer his escape. Why is unclear and without further information from Flashman or other sources it is impossible to verify. See appendix.

We heaved our minimal amount of baggage aboard, said some cheery goodbyes to the Colonel who was looking more nervous by the minute and proceeded to start up the engines. Once we were both running, he whipped the makeshift chocks away, walked quickly to his vehicle and started his own engine. I was somewhat surprised to see that he didn't appear to be hanging around. We taxied to a suitable point to begin the take off run and turned into wind. Then we saw them. Tennyson's poem and my Grandfather sprung to mind as at least a Regiment of Cavalry began charging towards us. Afterwards O'Connell said he thought it wasn't any more than a Squadron, but believe me it looked like it from where I was sitting. Skene hesitated.

"For Christ's sake go," I yelled at him. "They're not here for a dance."

He took the hint and opened the throttle. O'Connell obviously had my yellow streak as he was already ahead of us bouncing over the turf and picking up speed. I saw O'Connell get airborne and I already had enough of a feel of the aeroplane to know we weren't far off and thank the Lord as the bullets were starting to fly. Cavalry being cavalry they were more likely to hit a hedgehog with a howitzer. At which point there was an appalling scream that died into a gurgle and we acquired several new holes in the floor. The scream was Skene as he had half his head blown off shortly after which the aeroplane lurched sideways and downwards as he slumped on the controls. At about two hundred feet, this was not good news. I grabbed frantically for the controls and heaved as hard as I could. It was enough to stop us crashing instantly but ahead I could see trees and somewhere behind us were some irate cavalry. I couldn't remember Skene being this heavy before but now leaning on the stick he weighed at least a ton too much to get us properly away. We were level with the treetops and just about gaining height when the engine coughed ominously. It recovered momentarily but then entered a rapid decline. Quite clearly, Skene wasn't the only one to have lost his head. I didn't have time to think. Just beyond the trees was a field. I desperately tried to point the machine at it and began praying.

It was pure luck of course. We scraped over the last branches and sank towards the ground. I had absolutely no idea what speed we were travelling at and whether it was appropriate or not, and nor did I care. I waited until I was really really scared and then just heaved the stick back as far as I could. It must have been Skene's body that stopped me stalling and nosing in. Whatever it was, the wheels touched first, always a good start, we bounced ever so slightly and touched again. This time it was more of a pronounced thump and to start with, we rolled forward over the ground. I let go of the stick and a few seconds later, I felt the tailplane start to rise behind us. This was not good. Two things passed through my mind. First, that Skene had slumped further forward on landing and given the elevator a nose down deflection. Second and most important I pleaded with the Almighty not to leave me with a broken neck. I decided to shut my eyes.

The grinding and crunching continued for an eternity before all was silent. I could feel no pain except where the straps were digging into my crotch. I just had the sense to open my eyes before I released the straps to see where I was. My face was about an inch from the ground and suspended above me I could see shattered aeroplane. It seemed a good time to depart. As I clambered out the events of the last few minutes flooded back. All became if not clear then less murky. The Colonel knew. I looked around wishing Princip was nearby so I could smash his teeth down his throat, particularly as he was only about five foot two, but instead there was a less than rewarding view to where the cavalry were now emerging from the trees we had just missed. I am never paralysed with fear and this was no exception. I turned to run and suddenly realised what all the noise behind me was. O'Connell, having presumably seen what had happened, used his bonce for once and landed to help. I ran over to his machine shouting and gesticulating. Fortunately, he had the wit to keep the engine running.

"Skene's a goner," I was shouting.

"What about the….."

"Never mind him," I continued. "This old bus won't take us all anyway." This as I reached the side and started to climb on. Princip, presumably judging the English by his own nation's standards, bless him, had worked out the likely outcome, had hopped out, and was now running like a hare. Presumably, he was hoping the Colonel would turn up to help. Personally, I thought that was unlikely.

This time we made it comfortably and my last view of Princip was as he disappeared into some trees. The cavalry were already moving to surround him. He was as good as caught.[17] They hadn't even bothered taking a shot at us.

We breathed a sigh of relief all round and it was only then that it hit us that Skene was gone. O'Connell seemed particularly upset. I just thought what a damn lucky thing he had been wedged on the stick or I might have been burning down below as well.[18]

This particular leg of the journey was very quiet. I had never seen a man killed in so violent a fashion at such close quarters. I had seen plenty of dead people as one couldn't avoid tripping over

---

[17] Gavrilo Princip, variously the architect of the assassination or the tool of the Serbian Black Hand depending on which version one reads or believes, born 1894, tried and convicted in 1914, sentenced to 20 years hard labour as he was too young to receive a death sentence, died in prison in Theresienstadt in 1918 of tuberculosis.
[18] Flashman does not quote Skene's full name, but it is just possible that this was Bob Skene, a pilot renowned as the first Englishman to perform a loop, former Company pilot for Martin-Handasyde, who was officially killed just after the outbreak of the war trying to take off in an overloaded aeroplane which crashed and was listed as the first RFC casualty of the war. It would have been easy to concoct a crash to avoid reference to the Sarajevo incident, but so far, we only have Flashman's evidence that Skene was killed this way.

them in the streets in India. But this was different. We had been chatting merrily moments before and now his brain was spread over the remains of our erstwhile steed and my coat. We didn't even have time to bury the poor bastard and knowing the locals they might do anything including eating him. We landed eventually. O'Connell for once had managed to keep his native wit under control and do something useful. Consequently, neither of us had a clue where we were as we had effectively just headed west until the petrol ran low. We selected a place to land and once the racket from the engine had died down, we collected our thoughts. Petrol was the first priority. Fortunately, our plan had kept us going so far and seemed likely to continue. It was very simple. Land near a town, stay near a road and when a vehicle came past, wave the jerry cans and hope the occupants took us to a supplier. Generally it worked, particularly as we both had side arms and could look after ourselves if absolutely necessary. Well, O'Connell could. My plan in the event of trouble was somewhat different. But none of it was needed. It took some hours to refill the aeroplanes but we eventually managed, had a good nights sleep in a field and woke up to try and work out where we were.

Things improved. We appeared to be near the Italian border and after O'Connell established that Venice was not too far away the biggest dilemma seemed to be which way to go home. Should we skirt around or go over the Alps? In the end, we decided to go around and we set off for Vienna. It just seemed more civilised.

After the frantic heart stopping moments of the previous few days, everything returned to normal. We made our stately progress through Europe passing Munich before we turned more northerly towards Frankfurt and then on and ever on to the coast. We passed through Brussels in late July, and it was here that we got wind that something was up. People were talking about war. None of it made sense though. Apparently the Austrians were a bit fed up that the Serbs had killed their Archduke and had considered having a bash at them but being Germans really they didn't want to risk a fight if they thought they could lose. Therefore, they had tried to engineer a situation so that their German brothers could join in and really teach those rotten Serbs a lesson. This had apparently led to all sorts of jiggery pokery, with the French saying Sacre Bleu, you can't do that otherwise we will slap you, the Russians threatening anybody who would listen and the British in true bulldog fashion letting it be known that any of that sausage eating nonsense and we would invade Belgium and let that be a lesson to you, ha-ha. And you'd better mind out for the Navy as well while you are about it. At least that was how it sounded to me. I thought it was all hot air and told my companions so.

"Well, if it were de Oirish, we'd be on ahr way to Norway by nye," said O'Connell. He sounded like he was serious too, but then nothing he said surprised me anymore, especially once he had a few pints of pig's ear aboard.

"I can't really imagine war over some Duke or other. Good God if we had gone to war over every petty royal murder we wouldn't have anyone left. Hasn't he got a son to take over where Papa left off?" I said. General laughter and good old Flash, rely on him to put it in perspective.

And that was that for the moment. We carried on 'til we couldn't stand any longer and then staggered off to sleep. Last day tomorrow then a hero's welcome at Farnborough. Then these boys would see some fireworks once Flash Harry was at the controls properly.

"Got any experience old boy," they would say.

"Not much. Wrecked a bus taking off from Sarajevo on my way here. Got waylaid by some cavalry you know. Few bruises myself. Other chap had his brains blown out and I had to land it with him half on the stick. Bit tricky what. Nearly spilt my sundowner." With these happy thoughts, I drifted off.

Chapter 6

Farnborough was dreadfully quiet. We landed and put the machine away and ambled into the Mess. Not a soul to be seen. A Mess waiter appeared as if by magic and after serving up some decent grub and a stiff drink we asked him where everybody was.

"Gone to see the King Sir," he replied.

"Surely they've seen the blasted King before," I bellowed.

"No Sir, what I mean is they've gone to see him start the war. Well, in a manner of speaking."

"What war's that old boy?" I spluttered. He looked at me as though I had just arrived from the moon.

"Well, with them huns and wops Sir."

"Which wops are they?" mumbled O'Connell.

"Serbs Sir."

"They're not wops. Slavs, that's what they are." This was the newly arrived adjutant's contribution to the sewing circle.

"Beside the point. Why on earth are we going to fight the Germans? Surely not over Archduke Sausage?"

"Still doesn't tell us where everybody is though." O'Connell again.

"I've bin tryin to say they's all gone up to the palace. Sir."

Typical. Quite clearly, this Mess was no different to any other in its choice of staff. At least he said Sir I suppose.

"Off we go then," I said as I stood up. "This is one party we can't miss."

******

A general hum followed by muttered agreement that we should be where the mob was. It took forever. What we had been unable to see from the air was the congestion in London that night, the 5th August. Apparently, it had been happening all over Europe as the entire continent began mobilising for war. It was a serious business, all too serious as many would soon find out but that night as we left Farnborough by road, we too, even me, the old lily livered cynic, were caught up in the extraordinary excitement caused by impending battle and bloody death. Hopefully not mine. In India, it had been different. Whilst I had learnt to soldier properly and as forecast by my Grandfather, I had grudgingly come to love the place, the thought of pegging out in the Khyber Pass really did not appeal. It didn't exactly appeal now but something about fighting for the Old Country against the murderous hun made one feel protective. At least protective enough to cheer them on from the touchline. We would show them and if some of us had to die, well so be it. They wouldn't do it again once we had shown them the error of their ways. And so we marched on. We had long abandoned mechanical transport and headed north on foot. It wasn't difficult to find the way as everyone was apparently heading for the Mall. As we got closer, the crowds got bigger. Being in uniform helped and slowly but surely we edged closer and closer to the railings. I caught a glimpse from the corner of my eye of one motor car being allowed through by the mob. Led by a policeman on horseback, a glimpse was all I needed to be sure I had just seen my Grandfather. God knew what he was doing there. Probably needed a piss. The main difference was that as he had some influence he had managed to arrange passage through the crowd for his transport.

A huge roar from the crowd announced that an ant had appeared on the balcony.

"That's not the King," someone yelled in indignation. "God save the King," he continued, and it was taken up by all around me.

"Vere 'e is," bellowed a cockney voice at my elbow. The roaring redoubled in intensity and almost assumed a life of its own, reverberating around the Palace forecourt and down the Mall, into Green Park and St James'. It seemed to go on and on. People sang and shouted. The National Anthem too many times to count. The old Boer War songs. Tipperrary, Rule Brittania, the British Grenadiers and so on. It was only when the sky lightened that the crowds started to disperse. The King had long gone. Back to his boozing and cigars or whoever was flavour of the moment.[19] We finally did the same. All of a sudden, it seemed a long way back to Farnborough, which it

---

[19] George V is generally believed not to have taken a mistress, so Flashman is mistaken in this assumption.

was of course. There were no cabs to be had and no trams either.

Approximately one week later, we arrived at a deserted Mess, collapsed into some soft chairs and fell asleep, our walk having taken the best part of the night. We had finally managed to retrieve our transport for the last part of the journey but were exhausted nevertheless. After some hours sleep, we were awoken by the drone of engines. Some of the more enthusiastic residents had gone looking for the enemy, but, having found only clouds, had arrived home desperately disappointed.

"Blast it," said one of them. "Not a sausage to be seen."

"You wait 'til we get to France. Then there will be more action than anyone could possibly want. Even you."

My big story seemed to be entirely superfluous given the current state of affairs so having reported my arrival again to an otherwise totally uninterested adjutant, I found my billet and unpacked. It didn't take long as most of my belongings were fertilising a field somewhere out east. My thoughts drifted back to India and I even, for a brief moment, felt nostalgic for the place, mainly because the weather was better. I then reflected on the boredom and began to wonder if this place would be any different. I even considered visiting the family but decided that that was a stone best left unturned for the present, particularly as they did not know I was back in the Country.

We were ignored for a few days, partly because they didn't seem to have a clue what to do with a newly arrived pair of Tommies to add to the motley collection they already had. Mobilisation may have had something to do with it as well. It didn't last long. Orders arrived for us both to go to Upavon where the Central Flying School had its home, in my case to learn to do something useful. So that's what we did. We arrived to find more chaos and having found somewhere to stay I resigned myself to a long wait.

My boredom didn't last long. Less than three hours in fact when I had a moment to look at a clock. It definitely wasn't like the Cavalry. There didn't even appear to be a drill square. I noticed this as I was led over to a store of some kind to get myself kitted out. His name was Harry. He had just appeared in my billet and announced he was my instructor.

"Got any kit at all?" he mumbled.

"Not a bean." Somehow, my story didn't seem appropriate at that moment.

"Better come with me then. Then we will get cracking."

That was that. Then he led the way. At least by this time I was used to the ton of clothes required to prevent one's freezing to death.

"See you at the hangar in half an hour," said Harry.

"Righto," I replied as if that was perfectly normal.

What on God's Earth was the 'hanger' I wondered and how did one find it. More importantly, what happened when one arrived? In a very short space of time, I had realised how little I knew about any of this. It was all very well not knowing where the Crimea was but I couldn't have named the parts of an aeroplane. I had even less idea how or why it got into and then stayed in the air. Vaguely, I had assumed that someone would enlighten me. I supposed that perhaps as we were now at war you were told only what you needed to know, and that apparently wasn't very much.

Half an hour had now elapsed and I was none the wiser as to where the 'hanger' was. Consequently, I ambled about aimlessly until I found a chap dressed in overalls outside a large shed. I asked him where it was. He lifted his head slightly and pointed towards some aeroplanes.

"Go that way and you can't miss it."

I strolled nonchalantly away with the mutterings of a disturbed fitter ringing in my ears. "Bloody pilots," I had heard him say to no one in particular. "'ow's 'e going to find the blasted boche if he can't even find his machine." The look on Skene's face came back to me. He had a point.

"Got any experience then, old boy?"

"Well," I started. "Yes. Smashed a machine up a few weeks ago in a field near Sarajevo."

"Oh, that was you was it," Harry said, smiling. "Pretty hair-raising I should imagine.

Lucky to be here at all. Sounds like you did a good job though."

"I think there was a deal of luck involved. If poor old Skene hadn't been leaning on the stick I suspect I would have joined him wherever he is now."

"Nothing to be done about it now. Just have to show you how to do it properly."

With that, he mounted up. I could never think of it as anything other than mounting up. I clambered in to the 'Longhorn'. Properly it was a Maurice Farman but no one ever called it that. Harry started the engine and the mechanics hauled the chocks away. Immediately the machine started to move across the field.

"You have her," shouted Harry.

"Me," I shouted back, startled at the thought of doing anything with it on the ground. O'Connell and Skene had shown me many things in the air but on the ground, they had always done it themselves. "Christ," I muttered in a vague appeal to the good Lord. It was becoming a habit, mainly because I seemed to be getting myself more and more regularly into situations that might require the help of the Almighty.

"Throttle's open," said Harry. "When your speed indicator says about fifty pull back gently. And I mean gently."

"Righto." Fifty appeared in an instant it seemed. I did as I was told gripping the stick as hard as I could in case it should try to do something on its own. I realised my eyes were fixed on my hands so I took a peek outside, feeling rather foolish as it occurred to me that it was probably best to know the direction in which one was heading. We were airborne and climbing steadily away from the ground.

"Relax," shouted Harry. Easier said than done. He started giving me instructions on which way to turn and what to head for. Suddenly it seemed quite logical and natural as we floated about the clear blue sky.

"Better head back," he said. "Petrol will be running low."

"Already," I said. "But we have only been up a few minutes."

"What time did we take off?"

"Haven't a clue, old boy."

"Next time, make a note of it. We have been up here about fifty minutes."

I followed him through on the controls as we approached the field and he landed on silk. Afterwards he said that I had pretty much landed it, which was rubbish of course.

"You know, we have lost a few idiots who can't tell the time. Always know how long you have got or you will kill yourself."

Having neatly brought me back to Earth he sauntered off. But I couldn't hide the elation. It was like nothing on Earth. The time business had briefly dented my pride but I soon recovered. I didn't forget though, because I had realised how quickly time, well, flew. In the air, time seemed meaningless, and that was presumably precisely why people killed themselves.

I went to find O'Connell. He was sitting in the Mess looking glum.

"Posting's through," he muttered. "France. Apparently they are desperately short of pilots so Oi will be leavin' tomorrow."

"So we have one last night to create merry hell."

"Aye, ye're right," he said, cheering up immediately. With that, we headed for the bright lights of Salisbury.

Chapter 7

We carried O'Connell to bed as the sun appeared over the horizon. He was feeling much better, or to be more precise, he wasn't feeling much at all. Come to think of it, I wasn't feeling much either. At least he didn't have to fly immediately though. The thought of leaving the ground almost made me retch, but there was no getting away from it. Lesson two was looming on the horizon. I decided to get as much sleep as possible.

Apparently, that was only two minutes. Hawkins, my batman, appeared as cheerful as ever. I told him to go to hell but he ignored me the way these batmen do and continued standing over me with hot water and a towel. He also appeared to have some tea and having confirmed this fact I very nearly became civil. Not quite though. Couldn't have the riff raff getting above themselves. It was nice tea though for all that.

My head was pounding like Drake's Drum with the dagoes sailing up the Thames. Nothing to be done about it though so I shaved, washed, and then heaved myself into my flying kit, which had been very carefully laid out for me. Having consumed my breakfast, which had also been laid out for me, I felt somewhat better. I was beginning to appreciate Hawkins' talents.

I set off for the hangar again. I knew where it was now of course. Much to my surprise there was no one there. At least no one apart from the fitters and riggers and so on. They all seemed

71

preoccupied with the aeroplanes so I left them to it. It wasn't long before one of them tooled round to see what I wanted and if I was going to be in their way much longer.

"Hello Sir. Anything I can help you with."

"Well, as a matter of fact, perhaps you can. I am new to this game. My Instructor isn't here yet, so I was wondering if you could tell me anything useful about all this." I waved a hand airily round the hangar. Quite what I was hoping for I don't know, but one thing I had learnt in the Army was not to dismiss people just because of their lowly status, particularly when they were capable of performing skilled tasks that might just be useful to know about. I also had the feeling that if I was going to get along with this flying business then I would need to know a lot more than my Instructor was going to tell me. I had already heard too many stories in the mess of the deceased. It had nearly put me off completely as I didn't want to die just yet. I had also realised that most of them were dead through their own or others incompetence or lack of knowledge. I was determined this wasn't going to happen to me having already been bitten by the flying bug. Plus, the exuberance of youth, even in me, decreed that it wouldn't.

"Well, Sir, where shall I start? Your Instructor will tell you how to fly it so perhaps I could tell you how to keep it together in the air, and how and why it flies at all."

"Sounds like a good place to start. Captain Flashman by the way."

"Yes sir, I know. McCudden, Sir."[20]

We spent a cheerful half hour with McCudden displaying his knowledge of aviation, which appeared considerable, especially to a heathen like me, until Harry appeared sauntering around the corner.

"Sorry old boy. Got caught up in the excitement."

"What excitement?" I asked innocently."

"O'Connell of course you daft bugger. Just took off for France. Buzzed low over the field. Typical Irish. No brains at all. Brave though. Shouldn't have thought he would last long."

With this cheerful thought, he began to pull at bits of nondescript wire and fabric. At least most were nondescript. Some now rejoiced in names such as aileron, rudder, fuselage and so on, all of which suggested that somehow the blasted frogs had invented it all. Of course, they had invented a significant amount. No one was more upset than the English were when Bleriot[21] flew across the channel, in spite of the fact that there were many guffaws at his landing in an undignified heap. It

---

[20] This presumably is James McCudden. He was based at Netheravon just before the outbreak of war and left for France on 12th August so he could possibly have been at Upavon at this time as it is close to Netheravon. He was a First Class Air Mechanic although he went on to become one of the RFC's aces winning the VC and rising to the rank of Captain before being killed in an accident a few months before the end of the war. Flashman would almost certainly have come across him again in France.
[21] Louis Bleriot made the first channel crossing on 25th July 1909.

all went to show what a load of old rubbish this aviation lark was. "Best stay on your horse old boy," they shouted cheerily. Same thing applied to the machine gun of course.

I dragged myself from these homely thoughts to hear Harry saying that today I would probably go solo. I nearly had a seizure.

"What, on my own?" I screeched in a disembodied voice.

"Well of course on your own. Not a lot of use going solo with me playing wet-nurse."

"But I haven't got the first idea....." I tailed off.

"More than I had. We'll just do a few circuits and then off you go. Hop in."

In I hopped. I was sweating already. Why the hell hadn't I gone to bed earlier instead of seeing the idiot O'Connell get thoroughly plastered? Better pay attention or my going anywhere would be very short-lived without the engine running. With some prompting, I managed to get the thing started with the aid of a young propswinger. It burst into life first time although it was still very vague how this happened.

"Don't forget to check the mags," the cheery one behind me shouted.

I laboriously switched them off and the engine coughed as required and continued running.

Someone yelled "chocks away" which I was surprised to discover was me and off we went. At least off she went. It came quite naturally to refer to this machine as a she.

"Keep your eyes outside then and off we go."

I peeked over the side at the grass below and lo and behold, it was still there. Not really having the slightest clue what else to look for I announced to the world we were off. I think I said tally ho or something equally ridiculous, opened the throttle and steered into wind.

Much to my surprise, it did seem a little instinctive. I glanced at the speed and raised the tail, followed shortly by the nose and bloody hells bells we were flying. I couldn't escape the exhilaration.

"Well turn then," Harry shouted

I realised that despite noting the time of departure I had done nothing but fly straight ahead. Obediently I eased the handlebar down and pushed on the rudder bar. As if by magic, we flew in a continuous arc through one hundred and eighty degrees and there below us to the left was the field. Captivated I think I said earlier. I still was. We levelled off and I flew downwind.

"Remember when you pass the point you want to land on, count to thirty then turn and descend at the same time."

"Righto," I replied counting straightaway as I had all but forgotten the need to land somewhere. I made it seem like I had remembered by counting to forty then announcing that I thought I had overcooked it a bit. He saw straight through me of course but I felt marginally better.

"Don't descend so fast then if you've overdone it."

I know it seems obvious, but you weren't sitting there with Harry, the veteran of hundreds of flights staring into the back of your head.

I opened the throttle. We climbed slightly but that didn't seem to worry him. Then all of a sudden, the ground was rushing towards us. I flinched just before the inevitable crash and we touched the ground, wheels first, lifted slightly and sank down again. We rumbled almost to a halt until Harry said, "What are you doing? Taxi round, take off again and show me a couple more like that."

Right. I will. Like what I wondered.

Three more times I defied gravity and diced with death. Three more times we managed to land without breaking anything.

"Take her back to the hangar then."

For a moment I thought I had committed some cardinal sin and was about to be sent back to India.

"Off you go then. Once round then come and have some tea in the mess. And don't forget, don't climb under forty-five." Harry got out.

I think my hands were shaking. I had to talk to myself so it seemed real. I could not believe what was about to happen, because it still didn't really feel like I was doing anything when we were flying.

"Well I'll show you," I thought in a moment of recklessness. "You can sweep up the wreckage when it all goes wrong. Jesus, no. It can't go wrong. He must know I can do it. How the hell does he know? Can I just get out and run away. The disgrace of it."

I turned into wind and opened the throttle again. The familiar bumps as the tail lifted and then the lack of bumps as the nose came up. We were off. This old bus and me. On my own. I just remembered to turn and head downwind. I started counting as I saw the field go past. Christ, I was still climbing. Seven hundred feet. Crikey, the speed was forty-five. Too late to worry about that now. Nose down, speed increasing. Twenty-five, twenty-six, twenty-seven, lead the turn, whatever that meant, nose down more, cut the throttle, round we go, fifty-five, that's more like it, not far away and here comes the moment of truth. Was it me or was it him. The ground rushed towards me and flinching away the wheels rumbled down. No bounce this time. Bloody hell. Bloody hell. Just like the first time with the loony O'Connell. I switched off the engine and sat there. Sweat poured off me from the late morning heat. At least that was what I hoped they would think. Come to think of it, where were they? The great Harry and co? Didn't the bastard even see me leaving the ugly duckling behind and swooping gracefully down as a majestic swan? No, the bugger didn't and by god was I going to give him a piece of my mind.

"Well done Sir," said a friendly voice.

"Thankyou Sergeant. That's all for today."

"Of course Sir," he replied smiling.

My mood lightened as I walked to the mess. Oldest trick in the book of course. Make him think he can do it and he probably will. Or at least he will believe he can. If not of course then he's more than likely dead in a field in this case. Outcome the same of course. Drinks all round.

******

Drinks all round there were. It seemed to be interminable and resulted in being carried to bed rather earlier than normal. I wasn't complaining as it meant I didn't feel quite so dicky the following morning. Just as well really as after a short trip with Harry I was off on my own again.

"Just make sure you know where there is a decent field so you can land in it if the engine stops."

Round and round I went. It felt like hours but turned out to be only fifty-five minutes. It was exhausting and exhilarating in that order. We stopped for a spot of lunch and it was then that I saw my old pal Gooding. He had apparently caught a boat home shortly after our departure having more or less recovered from his pneumonia but then spent most of the time in his bed with the gripes.

"Made it back then?"

"Yes."

"How's the chest?"

"Oh much better now thankyou. Someone coming to see you later," he replied far too seriously for my liking.

"Who's that then?"

"Can't tell you now, old boy. Strictly q.t. Find out soon enough though. All to do with our friend Skene and whatnot."

Now he really wasn't making any sense. Skene was busy pushing up the daisies so his influence was fairly limited. Who would want to know anything about the whole incident I couldn't imagine. I hadn't actually told that many people as it had all seemed so infuriatingly insignificant compared with the great events across the channel. Apart from that, we had hardly covered ourselves in glory.

I finished my lunch. Harry came flying with me again and this time we ventured out beyond the perimeter of the airfield.

"Basic navigation. Same as advanced navigation really. If you can't see the ground, you are in trouble. If you don't recognise anything, trouble as well. Best to land and ask."

After mooching around for half an hour, we returned to the field. I parked and hopped out. That was the extent of my training. With that, I was awarded my certificate to prove I could fly. Now I just had to practise a bit apparently. I was tempted to ask if Harry knew where the Crimea was but decided against it. He probably did.

"That's it for today," said Harry. "Tomorrow I'll get you to take me to Gosport and land there. Have something to eat perhaps. Best have a quick look at the map. Plan a route as well. We'll take the BE."

Christ, more work I thought. What BE? What map? I hardly knew what the BE looked like, and

I didn't have a map. Stores probably would though. Having acquired the said article I retired to the mess for some tea. It was quiet, as most of the others were still flying, not that I had really got to know any of them yet. I settled in a corner to study.

I was awoken by a short, thickset Navy man prodding me in the chest. "You Flashman?"

"Who's asking?" I replied being somewhat belligerent having just been awoken from a rather pleasant dream.

"Cumming," he said apparently ignoring my remarks. "Are you?"

"Yes I am," now disarmed completely.

"Would you mind having a chat in private? I'd like to ask you some questions about your experience in Sarajevo. Nothing too serious."

How could I possibly refuse? He led the way back to the offices, which were now deserted. He turned along a corridor I had not seen before and opened a door. As I passed through, I noticed with a lurch the words 'Commanding Officer' on the door.

The empty office somehow felt like the Headmaster's study all those years ago. I had a brief vision of my grandfather walking in and almost started from my seat.

"No one will bother us," the short man said, somewhat disturbingly. "Now, I would like you to tell me everything about that trip starting with your arrival in Sarajevo, but before you do, I think I should tell you something of myself. However, there is a condition. Our discussion must not be

80

repeated elsewhere and most of all you must not discuss my identity with anyone. Do you agree?"

My mind was beginning to whirl. What on earth did this old buffer want to know and why? Faced with no choice for a change I agreed.

"My name is Mansfield Cumming. I run a small bureau within the Government. We find things out and put them if possible to some use in the defence of the Country and Empire, particularly now that we are at war on a large scale. You are now part of that bureau."

He let this sink in for a moment and at the point where he thought, rightly, that I was about to protest he continued.

"You won't leave your unit here. You will finish your training and be posted in the normal way. But occasionally when we need skills that you possess, I shall call on you. Now, Sarajevo. You were about to tell me everything."

Shocked? Certainly. Speechless? Temporarily. I had the feeling that my destiny was out of my control, not for the first time. Once I had recovered from the shock of joining the secret service, or rather a secret service as I had an inkling that his wasn't the only one, I told all I knew about Sarajevo. Cumming was particularly interested in Dimitrijevic. Princip he dismissed as a worthless functionary.

"Just like me then," I very nearly said. Instead, I asked who this Dimitrijevic fellow was.

"We don't really know. He has only recently appeared on the stage. Our Ambassadors in Berlin and Vienna were both at a loss when I asked them."

I nearly burst. This was getting out of hand. Half an hour ago, I had been looking at a map wondering how to get to Gosport. Now we were discussing His Brittanic Majesty's Ambassadors and their opinions.

"I think that is all for now. If you think of anything else you can reach me here." He handed me a card on which was written an address. "Perhaps you could memorise it and then, well, destroy it. I will contact you in due course."

With that, he left. I sat in the CO's office for a few minutes to recover from what had just happened. I read the card. 'Rasen Falcon and Co, Shippers and Exporters'[22]. I did wonder if I was still dreaming but it was too far fetched for that. I briefly considered eating the card but that seemed ludicrous so I returned to the mess and collected my map. I had only half planned my route but I couldn't finish it now and with that, I went to bed.

The following morning I was awake before the batman. My head was still spinning from my experiences the previous day. Secret Service. He didn't seem to realise who he was getting involved with. Or perhaps he did. I certainly didn't know one way or the other. I still needed to plan the route or at least familiarise myself with what I would hopefully see. Poring over the map and not looking at my best it also occurred to me why on earth did His Majesty insist on his troops

---

[22] This address was indeed used together with a box number for communication by the Secret Service.

and so forth getting up in the middle of the night when normal people were still in bed. Admittedly, on this occasion, I could blame no one but myself but it was still a valid question. Finally, I had had enough of the damned map and fortunately, at that moment Hawkins arrived with tea. He was momentarily taken aback to find me awake and on my feet. At least I assumed that was what the raised eyebrow meant.

"Morning Sir. Tea. Breakfast Sir?"

"In here I think Hawkins."

"Righto Sir."

He disappeared returning some minutes later with eggs, toast, and such. I gulped it all down, attired myself appropriately for the ordeal to come and wandered off.

"Morning," said Harry appearing from the hangar. "Ready to go?" he enquired of no one in particular.

"Aye aye," I replied feeling far from ready.

At least flying the blasted thing was becoming more like second nature. Within minutes, we were taxiing to the take off point and in short order we were airborne. I simply took off and turned southeast.

"Should have said," shouted Harry. "Always best to climb and turn away from your destination, then with a little height turn back over the field and set course. That way you can time exactly when you started and you get a better view of the landmarks. Your compass will be more settled as well."

So just a few reasons why I had made an utter balls of it within two minutes. Still I was sure there was more to come.

"What's your first turning point?" he now enquired.

"This village, East Chisenbury," I replied.

"Too big," Harry announced in his customary shout. "You need small landmarks so you can navigate accurately. Churches are always good. Railway lines are good if you can tell which way they are going. Villages and towns definitely not because you cannot fix them accurately enough."

Another small lesson learnt. We continued in this vein for sometime until we reached Gosport. After landing, we parked near a row of aeroplanes and went in search of sustenance. The Mess was deserted, but the food was acceptable. After this break, we returned to our steed and set off again for the return trip. Over lunch, we had replanned it Harry's way and it was, as he so rightly assumed, easier to do and we consequently arrived back at Upavon more or less at the stated time.

"Easy as falling off a log, y'see," Harry commented as we strolled back to the Mess again. I had a feeling that it wasn't like that at all. It actually felt like being permanently on the edge of a cliff, frantically windmilling my arms in an attempt not to fall over and only just managing not to do so. Still, I had over nine hours of flying under my belt. Someone, I forget who, had given me a logbook in which I was supposed to record my flying and what I actually did in the air. It currently made desperately uninspiring reading considering the ordeals I had suffered. Of course, these were nothing compared to what the future held.

"Do it again tomorrow. Go to Shoreham only this time, go by yourself."

I recovered from the shock to hear Harry excusing himself and with that, he disappeared. I spent a couple of hours asking for help from anyone who would listen whilst appearing to be calm and collected. I tried to treat it as just another jolly jaunt. I was fast learning that there was no such thing. The only thing that counted was staying ahead of the game. Not for the first time India seemed so simple and civilised. I also hadn't appreciated that, certainly at this stage, all of us were floundering in the dark.

Chapter 8

I took off for Shoreham on a bright cloudless morning. As I set course, the war was coming to the end of the first period of mobile fighting. The next period would come only at the end. After the chaos of mobilisation and a brief lull, the Germans had moved forward into Belgium. The Belgians fought hard for their Country given the inexperience and size of their army. Reports filtered back to England of the atrocities and massacres carried out by the Prussians. Exaggerated they certainly were but some at least did happen. The net effect though was to stoke the fire. Talk was all of how once the BEF got into action it would all be over by Christmas. Farnborough was no exception and the general feeling was frustration at the dim-witted brasshats who were unable to see the requirement for urgency in sending all the best pilots straight out to France instead of leaving them kicking their heels in England. This in spite of the fact that virtually the entire strength of the RFC had flown to France in the first few days. The unlucky(!) ones had been left behind to train new pilots for the expanding force. The fighting meanwhile continued with the BEF indeed giving the Germans a shock. Rapid rifle fire, something the British had been taught about at Spion Kop and elsewhere a few years previously, decimated the attacking Germans. The line of the Mons-Conde canal was held and the British prepared to reinforce and dig in. The French had other ideas and began what was to become a general fighting retreat. The French high command had become disillusioned with the fighting spirit of its troops and decided defence was the way forward. Consequently as the froggies ran for it the British were forced to follow suit. Fierce fighting accompanied them, particularly at Le Cateau, where casualties were significant enough for the British commander, Field Marshal Sir John French, to believe that unless the BEF was taken out of the fighting and allowed to rest it would be destroyed. His worries even encouraged Kitchener, the Secretary of State for War to borrow a destroyer to visit France.

As the retreat continued, the almost inevitable recriminations set in. French blamed the French for withdrawing when he was winning; the French blamed French for leaving a gaping hole in the line by withdrawing the BEF too fast and too far. The Germans, by now only a few miles from Paris then set about their own destruction by allowing a junior staff officer from Moltke's headquarters to visit the lines and declare that they had overextended themselves. Therefore, withdrawal was the answer. They also discovered that the BEF, more or less written off by the Germans and left with a large gap in the German line ahead of it, was not quite dead. Kitchener's visit had forced French to cooperate with the French even if it meant the destruction of his command.

A strategic withdrawal over the land they had fought hard for was the German prize. As they reached the line of the Aisne, Moltke gave the orders that would begin to stabilise the Western Front. The Germans dug in and consequently were able to choose their ground, in the process inflicting heavy casualties on the troops attacking the Chemin des Dames.

But for Moltke it was over. He was relieved of his command and replaced by Erich von Falkenhayn, the Minister of War.[23]

******

Here endeth the lesson. I had no idea that any of this was going on. The Times was very careful when reporting casualties and battles despite the fact that at le Cateau, II Corps under Smith-Dorrien had suffered some 8000 casualties, more than Wellington at Waterloo.

Meanwhile, I continued to float around the sky. I successfully found Shoreham after a frantic search around the coast finally identifying Brighton's Piers and heading west. Going home again was somewhat easier and my journeys around the countryside became more frequent and less erratic as the days flowed by. Every so often, someone would be posted to France and a heroic night of drinking and misbehaviour would follow.

---

[23] Flashman is essentially correct when he asserts that a junior staff officer, Lieutenant-Colonel Hentsch, made the initial assessment that the German's had overreached themselves and in consultation with Moltke and Bulow gave orders for a retreat that established the Western Front. The controversy of a Saxon in a predominantly Prussian Army ordering a retreat has never been adequately resolved, in spite of an enquiry requested by Hentsch in 1917.

I hadn't really learnt anything new for a week when Harry announced his intention to inform the CO I was ready.

"Ready for what?" I almost shouted.

"To go to war," he replied calmly.

"But, well, how?" I asked coherently.

"Who knows? I just teach you how to get up and down again and find your home. What happens then is someone else's department. Best to go and see. Changing every day you know," he said cheerfully as if that was a help.

Realisation was dawning that I would soon indeed have to go and be shot at, assuming someone had decided what I was to do when I reached France. I assumed that was where I would be going and I was right. No sooner had I got my wings to go with my certificate, the posting appeared on the notice board. I was to proceed to St Omer forthwith, accompanied by a brand new machine. I could collect this wood and paper contraption at my convenience from the Royal Aircraft Factory, Farnborough. Harry agreed to fly me there in the CO's private machine, something of an honour I was led to believe. I didn't for a minute think he thought I was going to run away. I on the other hand thought for quite a long time about the prospect of running away. Instead, I decided to visit my family.

*****

I still don't know why. I had hardly been in contact with them since my leaving for Sandhurst some years previously. My Grandfather and Father had both written occasional letters, all of which I had ignored given that it was all their fault. But now it was for real and I was off to fight the boche albeit from the safety of my aeroplane, somehow it seemed appropriate. Even to me.

I found them in Berkeley Square at my Grandfather's house. He had lived there more or less permanently for the last year or so. Shadwell let me in and took my hat.

"Would Sir care to be….. announced?"

I took this to mean that it was somewhat inconvenient just turning up uninvited.

"No thank you. Where are they all?"

"If Sir is referring to the General, he is in the library. If Sir is referring to the Bishop, he is with the General."

"Both in the bloody library," I blurted out without thinking. "I know the way," I said despairingly. I was tempted to offer him a job in the Mess. I pushed open the door to hear my Grandfather saying, "About time. You know I….." at which point the old man stopped. My Father turned to see what apparition had caused paralysis in my Grandfather. It apparently had the same effect on him.

"Jesus Christ," said my Grandfather and earned a reproachful look from his son. Not that he cared. "Thought you were still in India boy. What's that you're wearing?" Sharp eyes this one.

"Wings. For flying. I left the cavalry as it spent too much time sitting on its arse. Even I got bored. Too many flies anyway." What the hell I thought. No point in prevarication. "Just come to say toodle pip and whatnot. Off to France to show these boche who's in charge."

"Well. Well." This contribution was from my Father. It was hard to tell if he was pleased at the prospect or disappointed. "Well," he said again.

"Have a drink boy," said the General to a look of outrage from the Bishop.

"Don't be ridiculous." This was aimed at the Bishop. "The boy is going to fight the bloody Germans not polish their boots. The least we can do is offer him a drink of something stronger than that tea you are forever swilling away. Come and sit down." This last comment was aimed at me and I took him at his word and plumped down next to him in a large leather chair.

"Well," he said again. It was becoming tedious. "I was not aware that you were in this Country. You only replied to one of my letters."
I thought it wouldn't be long before I was in trouble. "Father. I was in India because of you and Grandfather here. I was damned upset about it too. Why do you think I would reply?"

"Well said boy. Leave him alone. By the look of things he has made something of his life already which, if you remember, was the whole point of the exercise. He is a man now. Makes his own decisions. He never replied to me but who cares. I never wrote to my old man once. Mind you, he wouldn't normally have been in a fit state to read anyway." He laughed loudly at this. I noted my Father was equally quiet. "Where's that bugger Shadwell? Ring the bell then boy."

I did as I was bid and magically the butler appeared.

"Supper I think. In here." And so we settled down for the evening. Grandfather proceeded to get loudly drunk and my Father proceeded to get quietly agitated. At last, he could stand it no longer and announced he was going to retire.

"Will you be here in the morning?"

"Yes, but only until I find a cab to take me to the station."

"Then I will see you before you leave. Goodnight."

"Well boy. Just us soldiers left." He let this pronouncement hang in the air for some time. "I always meant to tell you." Another silence. "So much to say though and not much time to say it." Suddenly he seemed utterly sober. "I suspect you are just like me. And before you say how could you possibly be like me when I have done all that I have….. it's just instinct. Let's call it……" He tailed off again and another silence followed. I thought he had drifted off to sleep and was preparing to pour myself another drink when he suddenly spluttered back to life. "Fatherly instinct." He allowed this to sink in. I finished pouring and turned to find he was staring at me significantly. At least that was the only possible description for the look on his face. Finally, what he had said made it through the haze of whisky.

"What on earth are you talking about?" I said as if I needed to ask.

"You've always known anyway. I am just confirming what you have always known. Son."

He was right come to think of it. I had often wondered how I had ended up with the Bishop as my Father. Now I knew. "Yes," I muttered. "I suppose I have. Are you going to tell me the rest of it then?"

"Not all of it. Just enough to be going on with."

We Flashman's had never been much on the family side. Too self-serving. On the other hand, I did wonder how they had kept it a secret all this time.

"Not much to it really. You are my son. I can't tell you who your Mother is for the moment but you will find out in due course. We had to keep the pregnancy secret. Your Grandmother, well, she wouldn't have understood. So we arranged for your Father and Mother to bring you up as theirs. It wasn't difficult to arrange. They had been unable to have another child of their own and you were the perfect solution.[24] Your Mother had to pretend for a while. Other people knew, doctors and such, but their silence was bought. Most people can be bought you know. Money, power or blackmail."

It was all so matter of fact as though every day one discovered a new Father. And a new

---

[24] As mentioned above, Flashman's son Harry Albert Victor had a daughter Selina, age 19 in 1894, and therefore significantly older than the subject of this memoir. The original Flashman papers make no mention of siblings, perhaps because all reference was suppressed and the complicated nature of the relationship and possible repercussions of the knowledge becoming public were too much even for the General.

Mother for that matter. I was speechless again. But what really was to be said. I had never cared much for Bishop Knowall. Now I had discovered we were brothers after a fashion.

"Will you tell Father?"

"Not 'til you have gone. I would suggest leaving early unless you wish to speak to him."

"No. I don't. What would I say?"

"Exactly. Wait until I speak to him. Then, perhaps next time." He didn't suggest when next time would be and nor did I. "One final thing. I mentioned your Mother. My, er, bankers hold many of my more sensitive documents. Don't trust them normally, bankers that is, but these gentlemen are reliable beyond question. You will inherit them when I die. When you do, you can be sure that everything contained within them is true. There would be no point in lying once I am dead. Mind that, son. Everything. All my memoirs are there. Completed them at last. Didn't think I would. Just be careful with them."

I wasn't sure what he meant by all this. I was intrigued by it all and I fleetingly wondered who my Mother was. I would find out in time but as I said, we Flashman's were not much on the family side. Tended to do our own thing. Still, I couldn't help but wonder. And why had he been so insistent that it was all true? I went to bed.

*****

In the morning, I slipped out before anyone was about. Not that I really cared if my previous

Father had met me, I just couldn't be bothered with lying to him anymore. Even I could see that it would be best for him to hear the news from my new Father. I sat in the station reading the headlines. Apparently, the Germans had been severely demoralised by the beating they were taking on the Western Front. Presumably, this was why more and more troops were embarking at every conceivable port in England. Soon it would be Christmas and the war would be over.

Chapter 9

I arrived back at Upavon early enough to see the dawn patrol returning from wherever they had been. Probably nowhere given the fact that the Germans hadn't actually crossed the Channel so far. Harry found me having a late breakfast and suggested we make a start once I had finished. So this was it. I was going to war. I had to go to war. I had even told my Grandfather. I couldn't stop thinking of him that way yet. But war. I couldn't get out of it. I blamed O'Connell and my Father and Grandfather and all the others who now thought I was a natural bloodthirsty son of empire. Just because my Grandfather had the VC and knew the Queen. Why couldn't they leave me alone? On the other hand, I could have grabbed the nearest white feather and left, but I didn't have it in me. Deep down, I had known ever since the last day at school that it would come to this.

"Off we go old boy," Harry beamed as he reappeared. "Machine's all ready."

"Wonderful," I replied with a hint of sarcasm, my only rebellion. At least I enjoyed flying at its most basic level and I wasn't going to be killed just yet. Only other idiots did that by showing off. We took off and for once, I was content to be chauffeured through the skies without having to consider anything apart from the clouds. I was shaken from my daydreaming by some violent manoeuvring initiated by Harry who had cleverly spotted an enormous balloon directly in our path just as we emerged from a cloud. Initially I

96

thought it must be the Germans as they were rumoured to be sending over enormous airships to drop bombs on London.[25] We missed it and having ascertained that it was one of ours, we aimed some curses at it to teach it a lesson.

"I've a good mind to shoot the bloody thing down," Harry shouted "except we haven't a bullet between us." He was right there. I didn't even have a revolver. I guessed from the change to his normal calm demeanour that Harry was thoroughly shaken up by this little incident whereas I hadn't actually had a chance to worry about it. I did resolve to avoid flying through clouds unnecessarily as they quite clearly contained solid objects waiting to send the unwary earthwards in a fiery ball.

"Cheer up," I said having recovered my composure. "They probably thought we were going to attack them, and that isn't a jolly prospect floating beneath all that flammable gas."[26] Harry didn't respond but I noticed his reluctance to fly through clouds continued until we arrived unscathed at Farnborough. Now it was my turn for a shock. After a short interview in the office, I

---

[25] Bombing had started immediately on the commencement of hostilities, but England itself was not bombed until Christmas Eve 1914 when Ltn Karl Casper dropped a bomb in a garden in Dover proving that it was possible to bomb England. The scale of raids increased steadily but there were no airship raids until March 1915 although rumours spread along with the panic caused by insignificant raids.
[26] Airships used Hydrogen gas at this time, a practice that continued until the disastrous Hindenburg and R101 accidents.

was taken to a hangar in which resided a sparkling new Henri Farman, built especially for me by the Royal Aircraft Factory.[27]

"But I haven't flown one of these before," I screeched, staring death in the face.

"Much the same as the Longhorn," replied Harry looking at me strangely. I stared blankly at the machine, knowing I could not refuse it.

Consequently, the Sergeant whose job was to make sure I didn't spoil it with finger marks and so on reluctantly showed me around it as if he was dealing with a spoilt child likely to self-destruct any second. Eventually he allowed me to get in once we had brought it out of the hangar into the elements. Harry then showed me the contents of the cockpit. My training over, he backed away to a safe position.

"Switch off?" the Sergeant bawled as though I was still at Upavon.

"Switch off," I replied in like tones.

"Petrol on?" he bawled again.

"Petrol on."

A pause to suck in some air by dragging the propeller backwards.

"Contact?" he yelled at me.

---

[27] Aircraft production was a haphazard affair at best in 1914. Lagging severely behind the French and Germans, Farmans were being built under licence, BE2's were being built at the RAF, but it was belatedly realised that the RAF was hopelessly inadequate for mass aircraft production. Orders were then placed with civilian firms but not before the RNAS, inspired by the First Lord, Winston Churchill had stolen a march on the RFC.

"Contact," I yelled back, at which point the engine burst into life. Slowly we began to drift across the field. I noticed Harry watching carefully from outside the Mess and wondered for some inexplicable reason if I would ever see him again. Not because I thought I would die, my current predicament notwithstanding, but because he might. I looked away and concentrated on the task in hand. My first idea was to go to Shoreham, which I knew from my endless drifting about the countryside in the name of training. Sweating profusely, terrified to the point of recklessness, I gingerly opened the throttle, rumbled across the field, felt the tail lifting, briefly lifted off the ground, continued rumbling and then as the speed reached fifty, I pulled the stick back and took off. Holding the speed as steady as I could, we slowly staggered away from the ground. I daren't turn, but as I was heading more or less south, it didn't matter too much. Above a thousand feet, I slowly pushed the rudder pedal and rolled the wing down in a left turn. As I turned, and nothing fell off and the engine behaved itself, I started to calm down. I was going to live.

Suddenly on my own again, I felt quite insignificant. Being a Flashman, this didn't last long and having eventually settled into my machine, I spent the best part of the journey staring into space, thinking about my Father of all things. Finally, the field appeared and my mind began to race again. It suddenly hit me that Harry hadn't told me at what speed to land the damn thing. Heart thumping again, I closed the throttle and pushed the nose down. I flew overhead, adjusted my position and hanging on to the controls as though my life depended on them (which it did of course) I glided round to land. I was too low, the trees were too close, the throttle was stuck, I scraped over the top, blinking furiously as the sweat ran into my eyes, the grass came up, I pulled the nose up, floated over the grass, paralysed as the end of the field came in sight, and we touched the ground, with hardly an inch to spare. I taxied over to the hangar and switched off, exhausted. But it was all to do again.

Within seconds it seemed, my machine was filled with petrol and I was setting off on the next leg to Dover where I had decided to spend the night. This time though, the utter terror was replaced with a kind of frantic fear, which also subsided once I was following the coast. As I approached, I drifted over the sea to look at the White Cliffs. They were white. What dawned on me, as I turned inland again was that I had never flown alone across water. I had flown across the English Channel, but that was with someone else in charge.

"O'Connell you bastard," I yelled to no one in particular. "You never told me about this bit. How the hell am I going to find France?" The futility of it struck me along with the more pleasing notion that perhaps some people had in fact performed this feat before. The landing was mercifully uneventful and I thanked my stars again once I was safely in the Mess looking for dinner. It was quiet and I managed to eat in peace until an unruly group of louts came in spoiling for trouble. I ignored them all for some time but inevitably questions were asked and identities revealed.

"Flashman," I muttered in an offhand fashion, as I didn't feel like talking to a bunch of snotty children even if they were pilots.

"Not Harry Flashman, late of the 1st Bengal Lancers and now a member of the lowly Flying Corps. Something of a come down is it not?"

I looked round to see who the owner of the haughty voice was and whether I could safely smash his nose in and get away with it without getting hurt. I decided on the witty riposte.

"Maybe it is," I replied. "On the other hand an almighty step upwards for you."

They roared with laughter, particularly as they were mostly drunk. I received an icy glare for my pains whilst he tried to think of another means to shoot me down, but couldn't. He had to be content with general harrumphing and bemoaning the current state of the Army and how anyone could buy their way in what with Sandhurst and so on. Fortunately few of his little gang were listening having got bored with royalty for the night. I stayed out of his way, and, I noted, he out of mine. One never knew with an HRH. I wasn't likely to be carted off to the Tower but he could certainly spoil my breakfast. It wouldn't do to underestimate him anyway. I thought then that he would make a lousy King and he proved me right in 1936. At the time, he was only twenty and for all his upbringing still needed his arse wiped for him.[28] Or perhaps it was because of his upbringing. Having avoided speaking to Davy again, I sloped off to my bunk. I still needed to find someone to direct me to France but that would have to wait and I would have to trust the Flashman instinct for survival at any cost.

Morning arrived all too soon. I hadn't been able to bring my batman with me, so it was a trifle unexpected when tea appeared at five in the morning. Who he was and how he knew I would be leaving that day was beyond me. Why he thought I needed to be up so early was also beyond me but then no one, as I believe I may have mentioned, has ever satisfactorily explained the ritual of reveille in the middle of the night when it must be plain to all and sundry that the natives weren't revolting and the enemy were the other side of the channel. We weren't in Ireland for God's sake. I hauled myself out of my warm pit and began shaving and drinking my tea. I still hadn't found out how to get to France. Fortunately or unfortunately depending on the viewpoint there weren't too many people around at this

---

[28] Quite why Flashman had such a low opinion of the future King Edward VIII at this particular time is unclear. It is also unclear how Flashman knew the heir to the throne although his Father had a number of links with the royal family. He is right when he says he was 20 at the time having been born on 23rd June 1894. What he was doing in Dover is also unclear but he did visit St Omer at the beginning of November 1914. His subsequent service was all with the Grenadier Guards in France, Italy and Egypt. Then, as now, heirs to the throne were not likely to be risked too far in the direction of the enemy.

uncivilised hour. There was one however, who was worth his weight in gold. My old pal Gooding.

"Flash," he cried on spying my entrance into what passed for a mess. "Well this is a turn up."

For a split second, I looked to see what exactly was a turnip then woke up and said, "Yes, wasn't it just." I managed not to be sarcastic as it occurred to me that his appearance could be providential. "Coming or going?" I enquired.

"Oh going. Only got in late last night. Bit of engine trouble. Almost had to land in the dark."

"Fancy a drink?"

"Well that is very kind. I would as it happens."

"One condition though." His face twitched almost imperceptibly. "Show me the way to France."

"Of course old boy. First time over I suppose."

"Yes and it doesn't appear to be near the Crimea." I grinned at him and received a slightly puzzled look in exchange.

"Oh, Yes."

It was all he could manage.

We found a table and chairs and Gooding spread out some maps he had brought with him. "Very straightforward really," he said. "Just set off more or less south west until we hit land again and once we've identified our land fall we head off for St Omer."

Put like that it was very straightforward. The reality was somewhat different as we had nothing to navigate by, nothing to calculate our drift and at the speeds we were flying at it only needed a brisk breeze and landfall would be somewhere in Spain. Or worse of course, Germany. What a start to a war that would be. This assumed we found land at all. Consequently amongst the limited personal possessions aboard was an inner tube, "to be inflated with the mouth."[29] It wasn't much of an insurance policy but every little helped. We planned a route of sorts and then headed for the aeroplanes. Gooding had a Farman as well. We started our engines and took off into the blue. I was concentrating so hard on following Gooding closely that it was only when I took a brief glance overboard that I realised we were already over the sea. We had climbed to four thousand feet in an attempt to be able to glide across if it all went wrong. My heart missed a beat as I reviewed my experiences with Gooding's navigation concluding that I had no idea if he was able to find the way to bed let alone France. Therefore, I was mightily relieved to see the coast appear. I had no idea which part of the coast it was but I felt sure Gooding had it all under control. As we passed over, he turned northeast. I followed him.

---

[29] When the RFC deployed to France from Swingate Downs near Dover in August 1914, the pilots were instructed to carry a makeshift survival bag. It included amongst other things a water bottle, stove, biscuits, cold meat, chocolate and soup concentrate. They also carried a revolver, field glasses and spare goggles. As there was no rescue service, the pilots were ordered to climb to three thousand feet before setting course, so that if an engine failed they would be able to glide across or back.

We hugged the coast for some time. I forget how long as all my basic rules of navigation such as setting my watch and noting the time at significant stages had disappeared overboard. Quite what I would do if the engine packed up I didn't really know or care to think about. But I did think about it and if nothing else, it passed the time. So much so that I hadn't realised we were now heading inland. We were also descending. The actions were automatic and we drifted ever downwards and joined the circuit at St Omer. I had never seen anything like it. From above it appeared that the world and his wife owned an aeroplane and had brought it to St Omer. Along with a van emblazoned with the legend Houses of Parliament Sauce in huge gold letters. What the hell that was doing there I had no idea.[30] We landed, switched off and strode over to what looked like an important hut. Inside we found some desks with harassed people at them. We announced our presence to no one in particular, loafed around for a little while and then bored with the whole charade went in search of sustenance. There were a few friendly faces but mostly everybody was in a tearing rush to carry a box of pencils from one side of the field to the other only to be ordered to bring them back again.

---

[30] RFC motor transport tended to be very varied at this stage. As a junior corps, they had the last option on government-requisitioned transport and it included the legendary bright red HP Sauce van that was used to carry ammunition and had been a rallying point for all airmen in the retreats of 1914.

C'est la guerre. I hoped that someone was in charge somewhere. As long as he wasn't French.

******

He was of course. French. Not French as in frog but Sir John. He had raced to the channel and arrived at the same time as the Germans, narrowly avoiding falling over the cliffs. Neither side having succeeded in turning the other's flank, there was only one place left where a breakthrough was possible. One of the dreariest places on Earth with people to match, it was to become seared into the collective memories of nations. Ypres. Or Wipers, as the Tommies called it.

The First battle of Ypres, promised as the breakthrough that would allow a resumption of mobile fighting and a swift conclusion to the conflict had begun in mid October when the battered remnants of the Belgian Army, having fought the Germans to a standstill inundated the coastal plain making it impassable. The French to the south tried to thrust into Belgium but were stopped by the Germans attacking, but the real battle was between the remains of the BEF and the German volunteer corps east of Ypres and their regular troops to the south. The Germans attacked with greatly superior numbers but were consistently beaten by the British regulars firing their fifteen rounds a minute. The Germans erroneously believed themselves to be up against numerous machine guns, particularly as their casualties were double those of the British. By the end of October, the German offensive had run out of steam although the fighting flickered on until mid November before stuttering to a halt, both sides exhausted. And the cost of all this? There had been about a million casualties, over half of whom were dead. The 160,000 strong BEF had suffered casualties of more than half, but then these were the regular professional troops and were therefore expected to die. It would be a different story when the great citizen armies arrived to continue the slaughter.[31]

But for the moment, now winter had arrived there was stalemate. No one knew quite what to do. After some deliberation, the answer, apparently, was to dig more holes. This both sides did with gusto. However, the Germans having again chosen where to dig their holes were considerably better off as they held the high ground. Consequently, they not only had a better view of the opposition, they also avoided getting wet as a result of their trenches being above the sodden Flanders plain. The British on the other

---

[31] Flashman's summary of First Ypres is essentially correct. For a more detailed description of the battle and the war in general, John Keegan's history (amongst many others) is a good place to start. The fashionable view of the war these days is of mass pointless slaughter, not a view that would have been recognised by veterans after the conflict, but a more sober and modern view can be obtained from the works of Niall Ferguson, Gary Sheffield, Richard Holmes or Gordon Gorrigan, again amongst many others, all of whom recognise what was achieved, albeit still acknowledging the enormous cost.

hand, had only to dig a couple of feet down to find water, and were forced to build upwards as well. The lines so dug remained virtually stationary for most of the next four years. No one realised at the time that this would be the case as most European troops were trained for mobile warfare. The British Army were in the same position as mostly they dealt with colonial rebellions. The next problem was finding the men to replace those lost already and to create new battalions to repel the hun properly. This was the beginning of Kitchener's call up with his face on hoardings all over the Country. "Your Country Needs You," they loudly proclaimed. Luckily, they didn't say what it needed you for.

******

Here we all were then. Now what? No one knew. Least of all what to do with a couple of stray pilots with no squadron to go to.

"When they need us I am sure they will remember we are here," I said one morning like the prophet of doom. We had been cooped up for all of a couple of days.

"Yes, but we could be of more use now. Even if we weren't flying."

He might be more use I thought. I on the other hand was quite happy being useless for the moment. I had hardly spoken the words of course when a ragtag from the office was heard asking for Captain Gooding and Captain Flashman.

"Over here," we said from our perch in the wintry sun.

"Sirs, your orders are here," the boy stuttered breathlessly. "Well, not here, in the adjutant's office."

"Better go and look I suppose," I replied.

We stirred ourselves into life and ambled, well at least I ambled while Gooding tried to amble and hurry at the same time, towards the hallowed den. We marched straight in as the RFC didn't really stand on ceremony too much.

"Better get your things together. 5 Squadron. Good luck."

And that was that. My destiny was set in stone. After some more ambling on my part, we set off for Bailleul where 5 Squadron appeared to be. A lot of squadrons were still near or even at St Omer after the chaotic retreats of the previous few weeks. Having crossed the channel successfully and grouped on Amiens, they had made themselves useful if not indispensable thus far by artillery spotting and reporting German troop movements accurately and in detail allowing the BEF commanders to stay half a step ahead of their German counterparts. 5 Squadron had also managed to stay half a step ahead and finished up at Bailleul. They had suffered losses mainly through accidents and bad weather but they were still basically intact albeit in the same ramshackle way they had left England. It couldn't last though and from now on, the entire RFC was going to be in the van. Me included.

Arriving slightly dishevelled, we found the correct office and announced our presence and after completing the limited formalities, we headed for our billets and made ourselves at home. I was quite relieved that at least one familiar face was going to be around, mainly as my ability was thus far strictly limited and I knew I would need all the help I could get. Next ordeal out of the bag was to meet the Boss. At first glance, Major 'Josh' Higgins was all 'bum and eyeglass' as the saying went, mainly due to his jutting arse and the monocle. His friends called him 'arsy glassy' although not to his face. The reality was somewhat different. He was highly popular, highly regarded, flew whenever he could and looked after all his men, pilots, observers, mechanics, fitters, every last one of them. He also flew every machine delivered to the squadron to find out its faults before someone too inexperienced, like me, found out the hard way.

"Flashman, you say," he said, fidgeting with his monocle and swagger stick. "Well, good luck." And that was it. And so to war.

*****

It wasn't long before we were in action. The squadron was relatively intact given the ordeals they had experienced so far. All of which I had missed so as the new boy I had a lot of catching up to do. It was different for Gooding. He was a new boy to this squadron but not to the whole game. He already knew most of the pilots and observers and they him so he had no need to prove himself worthy. I had realised very quickly that acceptance into a squadron came with time despite the fact that the squadrons themselves were not that old. Plus for a total novice like me, the need to gain the trust of the other pilots was essential. As an unknown quantity, this also would take time, flying time, and lots of it. It seemed that I had a mountain to climb already. Fortunately, I would not be alone. It was just as well really, as my knowledge of the Western Front at this stage was similar to my knowledge of the Crimea.

I had hardly unpacked before an enormous man with a handlebar moustache appeared in my billet.

"Hello old boy" he announced. "Seems that you're lumbered with me. Or me with you of course. Have to wait and see who's the biggest liability." He roared with laughter at his own joke but I took an immediate liking to him. Lucky really, as he was going to have to trust me to take him into the air and try not to kill us both. His name was Spalding and he was well known round the entire airfield being, in more ways than one, larger than life. Inevitably, he was known as Jumbo. Not very original of course but the best the other pilots had come up with so far.

"Fancy a look at the lines. Get a trip in before dark, what, impress the CO."

"Good idea," I lied thinking all of a sudden that this was only too real.

"Off we go then," and he did an about turn and marched out. I followed him after scraping some kit together. I bumped into Gooding as I left.

"Going for a look at the lines," I stuttered. "Won't be long," I added as an afterthought. At least I hoped I wouldn't.

We set off into the gently darkening sky. The weak wintry sun was behind us as we sailed slowly towards the front. There wasn't much wind aloft which cheered me up no end as Jumbo had spent the time it took to reach the Henri explaining how only recently it had been demonstrated that it was quite possible to fly the bloody things backwards and given that the prevailing wind was west to east, this was not good news.

Airborne again, it seemed a pleasure and I almost forgot why I was here. A swift reminder arrived in the long brown scar as we passed over the home team living in ditches. Moments later, we were over the away team. A loud bang was followed by Jumbo yelling "Archibald, certainly not!"

"What the hell was that?" I yelled back.

"Only the hun gunners having a pop at killing us. Just swerve a bit, they never hit anything." I did as I was told and weaved around a bit. There were a few more bangs and puffs of smoke in the adjacent sky but each time further away.

"What shall we do now?" I asked of my companion.

"Go north a bit and follow the trenches. We'll have a look at Ypres and then go home." I hadn't a clue what he was talking about really but we did exactly that and then returned home. Archie[32] didn't bother us again and we had stayed reasonably high so as not to give the troops anything to shoot at. Ours or theirs[33]. As the sun sank, we miraculously found the aerodrome again and drifted down towards the field. I turned the engine off and sat in the cockpit for a little while as Jumbo busied himself in the front.

"Is it always like that?" I asked.

"Like what?" he said.

---

[32] Archibald or Archie as it became known was initially something of a joke amongst the RFC pilots, hence the amused shouts when it missed. Possibly originated by Lt A.E. 'Biffy' Borton having acquired the phrase from the current music hall comedian George Robey. Skidding on an even keel usually put the hapless gunners off their aim in the early stages of the war but it was only months if not weeks before the Germans aim improved.

[33] A reference to being shot at by one's own side, a frequent hazard in the first weeks of the war. Identification was a problem for troops on the ground as there were no standard markings and the inclination was to shoot first. After a typically understated exchange between the British Dermott Allen who asked a French infantry commander "if he would mind telling his men not to fire at us" as "it puts us off" to which the Frenchman replied that the Union Flag painted on the aircraft looked like the German crosses from below, and the loss of Lt Cyril Hoskins and Capt Theodore Crean in the first of many flamers, shot down by a battery they were spotting for, it was agreed that the RFC would adopt a similar marking to the French red white and blue roundel, reversed from the French marking to maintain national pride. Mistakes were significantly lessened.

"Shooting at us and what not?"

"Oh yes. Just a little taster today."

With that, he hopped nimbly out and together we headed for the mess. You can imagine my thoughts.

After my days experience I returned to the mess to find Gooding and a bunch of others generally regaling each other with stories of derring do.

"Here he is," Gooding called across from a gaggle of young men as I entered. Apparently, I had featured in the storytelling from which I assumed he was telling of my brush with the cavalry.

"How was your trip?" he enquired once I had a drink in my hand.

"Stirred up Archie a trifle," I announced to a roar of laughter. "Quiet really."

And so my induction to this strange world of normality infused with terror began. I heard many stories and many names that evening of which I shall repeat only one and that only because it made me flinch at the time. It concerned one of 4 Squadron's original pilots, Gibb Mapplebeck[34]

---

[34] Gilbert 'Gibb' Mapplebeck went with 4 Squadron to France as part of the initial deployment. He was involved in numerous highly dangerous missions including the flight where he did in fact have the tip of his penis shot off but survived it all to return to England to command a reserve squadron, the policy at the time being that squadron commanders in France had to have commanded a squadron in England first. It was here on the 24th August 1915 that he was killed in what appeared to be a stunting accident but may well have been a crash caused by the structural failure

who, whilst flying over the lines had received what was laughingly referred to as a flesh wound. He had in fact had the tip of his knocker shot off which whilst causing enormous hilarity once the pain had worn off nevertheless made me clutch at my own equipment to check it was still in place. I went to bed smarting from the pain, the laughter ringing in my ears.

Next morning we were up early and off again, over the lines, looking at the Germans both on the ground and in the air. Mostly on the ground as when we saw them in the air they generally saw us at the same time and beat a hasty retreat. A few of the others had got close enough to loose off a few pistol or rifle rounds towards the enemy but mostly we floated round each other looking at the hapless troops below. The limited success had convinced the brasshats of the need for the RFC. In fact, Haig, soon to be in charge of the whole gang was a convert well before the war had started having seen the benefit of effective aerial reconnaissance in India as CGS and then after his return to England being on the losing side in some manoeuvre or other after his opponents outdid him with their aeroplanes. More importantly, Kitchener, when minuted by Brancker[35] that the Armies being recruited would require fifty squadrons to support them simply added the note 'Double this, K' at the bottom. Kitchener was one

---

of the Morane N type he was flying at the time.

[35] This presumably is Major W. Sefton Brancker, one of the major architects of the RFC and aviation in general in Great Britain. He was killed in the R101 disaster in 1930.

of the few realists who knew the war wasn't going to be over by Christmas.[36]

The days dragged on and we were almost bored with the constant repetition but each little piece added to the whole and the efforts of the RFC were being noticed. More importantly from my point of view, I was beginning to get the hang of the whole thing. I knew I could fly after a fashion but making war at the same time was different

The General Staff by now had almost a complete photographic map of the lines, the clock code had been worked out for artillery spotting, still one of the most important jobs, and the wireless flights were slowly improving ground to air communication. The RFC had been reorganised and we now rejoiced at being in the second wing under the command of Pregnant Percy, more formally known as Lt Colonel C.J.Burke.[37] The cold was bitter both on the ground and in the air but even I had to admit we appeared to be better off than the infantry stuck in

---

[36]Lord Kitchener was recalled to take up the post of Secretary of State for War the day after the declaration of war. Best known for the recruiting poster with his likeness on, he was killed when the cruiser H.M.S. Hampshire was sunk by a mine on the way to Russia.

[37] Lt Colonel Charles James Burke, Royal Irish Regiment, was the Commander of No 2 Squadron when it deployed to France in 1914. He was a well-respected Boer War veteran who was promoted beyond operational flying and returned to his former regiment when he heard they were short of officers. He was killed leading his men on the first day of the Arras offensive in April 1917.

their holes in the ground. At least I was warm most days and I hadn't really had a chance to get too scared.

Christmas arrived and it was obvious to everyone that we weren't going home, now or for the foreseeable future, something that made it a rather gloomy affair. Atkins made up for it by beating the Germans at football[38] and with the arrival of the New Year, optimism returned. Plans were being made and we would see the hun back to his lair. For Haig, this meant attacking Neuve Chapelle. For the squadron it meant the end of the comparatively easy life. For me, exposure to some of the harsher realities of the western front. Like death.

---

[38] The first Christmas of the war saw numerous incidents of fraternisation, mainly between the German and British troops. Officially frowned upon, most officers turned a blind eye or took part themselves, justifying themselves with descriptions of enemy trenches, or taking the opportunity to repair their own. Many units used the truce to retrieve and bury comrades. Mostly, the troops exchanged food or cigarettes, although there are one or two well-documented games of football.

Chapter 10

"If you can't fly because of the weather, I shall probably put off the attack." These were the words of Haig to Trenchard before Neuve Chapelle. They had apparently been planning it all for some time and some lunatic optimist or other had said that if the RFC bombed the Germans it could end the war. Consequently, we were all engaged in both spotting for the artillery and once the attack got under way bombing the buggers ourselves. As a new boy, I was still only partly employed, usually doing the mundane stuff, mapping the trenches, registering artillery and being shot at. It was still enough to give one the jimmies but I daren't show it. The rest were all so bloody cheerful even when they saw their friends die. And die they did, especially once the bombing got under way in earnest.

On the first day of the infantry assault, the bombing programme consisted of three aeroplanes from 3 Squadron setting out to destroy the enemy defence headquarters at Fournes and, during a lull in the battle, two aeroplanes were despatched to destroy two targets, the railway junction at Courtrai and another one near Menin. This may sound fantastic. That is because it was. Normally sensible, experienced army commanders had decided that a few twenty-five pound bombs would devastate the targets and prevent German reinforcements arriving thus finishing the war. The fact that the war wasn't stopped in its tracks was nothing to do with the bravery of those concerned. The 3 Squadron force succeeded in setting fire to their target although whether the burning down of the house changed the course of the war is debatable. 6 Squadron's raid was carried out by Louis Strange, by now a flight commander, and his bombs, released from a homemade bomb rack caused local chaos and seventy-five casualties amongst the troops at Courtrai. My own squadron's contribution, and already I considered it my squadron, was equally brave and equally foolish. The junction at Menin was damaged but like Strange, George Carmichael returned in a sieve rather than the aeroplane he set out in having been shot up by troops on a nearby parade ground as well as being concussed by the explosion of his own weapons. It all demonstrated it could be done but for the results to have any lasting effect required considerably more aeroplanes to attack the target.

The next morning 4 Squadron were ordered to have a go much to the chagrin of their commander, Major Charles Longcroft who suggested the raid be postponed. GHQ disagreed and so the three aircraft were launched with torches to help them see through the mist. One crashed on take off and the remaining two were shot down only the irrepressible Mapplebeck surviving. Having burnt the evidence in the form of a BE2a he was helped by the locals including the mayor of Lille to escape via Holland and return to the Squadron after five weeks. For this the mayor was shot.[39] The contribution of the

[39] Mapplebeck was indeed helped to escape by the Mayor of

119

RFC to the battle declined as the weather worsened and the entire battle ground to a halt. What was I doing while all this was going on you may ask? Spotting, spotting and more spotting, but life was about to change again as more and more bombing raids were carried out. And the boche were about to launch a surprise of their own. It was Strange[40] again who was first with the news. He was watching some boche howitzers hammering the trenches below him when he noticed a cloud of green gas form and start drifting over no mans land towards the British lines. Panic ensued and part of the line was abandoned for a short time but the overall effect was limited. Actual casualties were small and most got over the effects quite quickly and returned to their units. The German gains were slight.

I got my first taste of a bombing raid at this time as it was deemed necessary to try and destroy the means of deploying the gas weapons. I had by

---

Lille and some other Belgians. He returned with a German poster offering a reward for information leading to his capture, and death to any who helped him. M. Jaquet the Mayor and three others were shot sometime later.

[40] Louis Strange took his Royal Aero Club certificate at Hendon in 1913 and then applied for a commission in the RFC. He was posted to the sixth course at CFS before joining 5 Squadron on the outbreak of war. He had a colourful war, surviving numerous close shaves. Ever the innovator he conceived the voluntary offensive patrol, low-level tactical strikes at airfields, supply columns or any other suitable target. He was awarded the DSO. He flew right through the war and was one of the few original 1914 pilots to survive. He also flew in the Second World War.

this time changed machine and was now cruising around in a Martinsyde S1 that at least had a Lewis gun mounted to fire forwards outside the arc of the propeller. It was quite fast being capable of 87mph and also able to carry a 100lb bomb. I had followed George's example and cut a hole in the floor so I could at least see what I was aiming at. I had also lost Jumbo but only because the S1 only had one seat. My navigation had improved somewhat through necessity but also because it wasn't particularly difficult to find the trenches.

I watched my bomb being loaded aboard and had a vision of the damn thing going off in the air, which would at least give me the advantage of not knowing anything about the subsequent descent to Earth. Ready at last I climbed aboard myself. It seemed like the whole squadron was going to bomb something somewhere. The engine started and I trundled away over the grass. I watched a few of the others set off and then turned into wind and opened the throttle. The exhilaration was still there as the ground sank below me and I turned east for the front line. Somewhere in the distance, I could see the Archie starting up. I climbed a bit higher. It was an odd feeling being apparently alone in the sky in spite of knowing this was not true. I set my course again for Ypres constantly looking around for enemy aircraft. They didn't seem to want to fight at this stage but that didn't mean they wouldn't take advantage of the unwary. The coward's instinct for survival was invaluable and kept me searching the sky for the first sign of trouble. Most of those shot down either weren't looking out or were hit from the ground. I had no intention of being caught out either way but today was going to be a test as from all I had heard bombing required flying very low over the target and this understandably upset the boche.

I flew high over the front line and finding Gheluvelt set course for my target near Menin. It was quite easy to find really, as the railway line led straight to it. I was helped by some cloud hanging around about a thousand feet up as it meant I could pop in and out to keep the gunners guessing. Archie didn't trouble me until I was well into the opposition half and descending to make my run at the target. Things began to hot up quickly. Several loud bangs announced the arrival of lethal messages from the ground and a few holes appeared in the wings. Nothing major was hurt apart from my nervous system, which was starting to take a battering. Down I went though. Not through bravery you understand, but sheer terror. Unknowingly, or unthinkingly I was hurling my machine about the air in a desperate attempt to avoid being hit and hopefully to put the blasted Germans off their aim. It didn't help being on my own. All of a sudden I wasn't. Another machine, a BE I think, appeared out of nowhere going hell for leather at something or other. He was flying in a straight line with no attempt to avoid the cloud of ammunition ascending to greet him. It gave me a breathing space though and I looked down through my hole and began my run

122

in to the target. I was only about three hundred feet up now and a few seconds from releasing my load. I glanced across at my companion and saw a couple of specks fall away from the machine. The machine carried straight on and I saw the explosions out of the corner of my eye just as I dropped my bomb. I turned immediately and instinctively towards the BE, just in time to see it catch fire. It had lifted away from the blast below but in a strange nose down attitude. Whether the blast had set it alight or not I couldn't tell but alight it was. I could see a figure writhing and I was mesmerised as the aeroplane suddenly pulled up almost vertical before sliding tail first into a short but deadly dive. I climbed away at full power realising I had just witnessed the death of two of the small band of RFC pilots. In the frantic moments following the destruction of the BE I had not even looked at where my bomb landed. I flew in a climbing circle to remedy this and was pleased to see a large hole containing some dead Germans and some very live ones whose barrels were pointing directly at me. I vanished in the cloud before they got too many pot shots in and went home. I didn't stay in the cloud very long as I needed to know where I was, so I popped down to have a look. It didn't seem too hostile so I stayed just underneath what was now a continuous layer until I recrossed the lines. I sat in the cockpit for quite a long time after landing until one of the riggers asked if I was all right.

"Oh yes," I said. "Fine." He knew I didn't really mean it but said nothing. I scrambled out and walked over to the offices where the rest of the squadron were gathering and talking excitedly about the shows carried out.

"How about you Flash?" asked a voice from the crowd.

"Blasted huns spoilt my coat. Look at it."

"Jesus, he's right too," and they all laughed.

"I've a good mind to fly over and drop the bill on them. My tailor will be seething."

I adopted a look of indignation at the cheek of the enemy in attacking my coat and leaving a long burn mark on one side. It covered the look of horror that had almost surfaced when I realised how close the bullet must have been to decapitating me to leave a burn like that.

"What about the bombs?"

"What bloody bombs?" I snarled still examining the material. More laughter followed by a drink pushed into my hand.

"You know, those cylinder things we try and kill the boche with. Any luck?"

For a moment, I had completely forgotten the bombs and without thinking enhanced my reputation no end. They all thought it was a great hoot that I could bomb the Germans and then forget all about it because they had ruined my coat and almost killed me. I assumed a contemplative look.

"Ah yes. Right in the middle of the junction near Tourcoing. Track everywhere. Killed a few and upset the rest."

More raucous laughter as everyone began to tell their tales of the day and the drink began to flow. It carried on well past dinner and into the night before Higgins called a halt.

"More of the same tomorrow I believe," he said.

****

He was right. Off we went again, only this time in little gangs of two or three. I was with another S1 and our target was an artillery battery just behind the boche frontline. Gooding led the way again and I clung to his coattails for grim death. The weather wasn't quite so good. Haze, or more probably smoke hung in the air reducing the visibility. Nothing looked the same as usual and it was made worse with the weak wintry sun peeping through the cloud and getting in our eyes. I suddenly saw Gooding start to weave about and did likewise as several charming puffballs appeared beside and above him. He must have seen the muzzle flashes from the ground to react that fast I thought. I glanced below as I weaved trying to keep sight of the other S1. We were over the frontlines of course so every Tom, Dick and Heinrich was taking a shot at us. I'd rather hoped that our own gravel crushers could tell the difference by now but I supposed the haze and sun were affecting them too. You might have thought the direction of travel would have given the game away. We came away unscathed and almost immediately Gooding was descending towards the jolly old target. I followed him down, conscious now that when he let his bombs go they would be jolly cross just as I appeared for another go. I resolved to get in as close as possible behind him. I saw him wave and looked down through my patent hole in the floor. The battery loomed large and suddenly the S1 was 100lbs lighter. Gooding pulled up to the left and I pulled up to the right. Even I could see that dividing the fire gave us a better chance of surviving the wrath of those below. Not that it had seemed that bad. I supposed that the battery didn't have much in the way of small arms and wasn't particularly suited to engaging two specks in the sky.

We both turned west and flew hell for leather for home with a brief glance at the damage. It looked pretty convincing from where I was sitting I can tell you. After that, it was uneventful. We were both alive and well and remained so until we found the mess bar sometime later. For once, everyone else appeared to be alive too. Higgins was pleased in a relieved kind of way.

Next day the weather was awful. Flying was suspended and consequently the offensive petered out into nothing. Or so the brasshats would have us believe. The truth of course was that the offensive itself, having moved the army forward a mile on a front of a thousand yards, had caused huge casualties and the survivors were exhausted. The French had achieved much the same and had thrown in the sponge as well for the moment. There was a pause for breath and to take stock. The Armies needed men, ammunition and food amongst other things, as did the RFC. Things were changing everywhere. For the RFC, it was the beginning of the Fokker scourge.

Chapter 11

My life was about to become somewhat more eventful, even compared to the previous few months. Fate as always had played a significant part in the form of being in the wrong place at the wrong time. My acquaintance with the S1 finished in a tangled heap when the wheels collapsed on landing. Further investigation revealed that some of the support had been shot away on a routine flight over the lines. I had heard the archie as always and flung the machine around to avoid becoming a victim, but some of it had presumably come a bit close for comfort. The ensuing crash was therefore something of a surprise but at least a short lived one. I had been in the very same situation before of course and my reaction on this occasion was much the same. I opened my eyes praying that I could walk and that the machine wouldn't catch fire and let myself out, dusted down my coat still with its burn mark and sauntered off to the mess. This incident attracted very little comment at the time but was responsible for beginning my romance with the BE2c. And with that came Jumbo. He had seen off my replacement with a stomach full of shell splinters that had apparently bounced off him. The BE was repaired and as I was the only one at the time without an aeroplane I was the natural choice. We also very quickly assumed the role of scout aircraft, designated destroyers of the enemy. This was due to my experience with the S1 and that for some reason this was a newcomers job. It suited me though. It meant I didn't have to go bombing very often or spotting for the artillery. Instead, I could float about high up looking for German's to scare and at that time, they still seemed to scare easily. They very rarely ventured over our lines and so mostly the job consisted of chasing after them in slow motion and occasionally Jumbo firing his rifle. Needless to say, we didn't hit a thing. But it was all soon to change.

Both sides had been getting slowly but surely more aggressive towards each other's aeroplanes and the list of those shot down was growing longer. More importantly, the rifles and pistols with which we had been taking ineffective pot shots at each other were being steadily replaced with machine guns. Lewis guns to be more precise. I had had a brief experience of one in the S1 and they were at once both effective and next to useless. Being air-cooled was an advantage but the oil in them had a tendency to congeal at the wrong moment. The biggest problem was where to mount them. 6 Squadron, with the ever-inventive Louis Strange had mounted a Lewis to fire sideways from the cockpit, which meant having to line the enemy up in a most awkward position. Lanoe Hawker[41], also a flight commander with 6 Squadron and someone whom

---

[41] Lanoe Hawker studied at the RMA Woolwich, learnt to fly at Hendon, and transferred to the RFC in 1913. He arrived in France with 6 Squadron as a Flight Commander and fought on the front for a year before being posted home to take command of 24 Squadron.

I was to get to know very well did the same. They eventually realised that the only real way to fight in the air was with the guns firing forward and so started mounting them on the upper wings above the propeller arc from where the observer could fire straight at whatever the pilot was flying at.

The French and Germans knew this already and the French pilot Roland Garros and designer Raymond Saulnier had effectively solved the problem. By attaching wedges to the propeller in the guns line of fire, bullets could be deflected without damaging the propeller itself. In the space of three weeks, Garros had shot down three German aeroplanes and the French air force started fitting the invention to all their machines. Being frogs, they then committed the cardinal sin of foolishly giving away the secret to the Germans. Garros went on a bombing raid over the lines and managed to get himself shot down. Realising too late that the invention would be useful for the Germans he tried unsuccessfully to burn the aeroplane. Whilst he languished in prison considering the error, the Germans gave the entire machine to one Anthony Fokker.

Rather than copy it, he came up with the interrupter gear that allowed the machine gun to fire through the arc of the propeller. He fitted it to his new E1 along with belted ammunition and the Fokker Eindecker was born.

While all this was going on, Hawker was busily preparing to win the VC. Strange had gone home to form a new Squadron after nearly killing himself trying to change an ammunition drum on his Lewis top mounted in an S1, and Hawker had taken over two flights in 6 Squadron.[42]

I, on the other hand was enjoying the delights of St Omer of which there were many. Wine was available in abundance provided one could pay and the company of women, albeit French women, was a joy. Some discretion was required of course as the cheaper end of the market could result in a self-inflicted wound and whilst not fatal for an officer and gentleman, the treatment would be a source of embarrassment for the victim and no doubt ceaseless mirth from his brother fliers. Fortunately, I was experienced in this area and very quickly became the squadron buyer. I went up in the estimation of some and down in others depending on their viewpoint and resistance to temptation once shown the wares on offer. However, few resisted the purchase of champagne and other luxury items from the locals for the frequent parties and drinking bouts that came with

---

[42] Strange was indeed flying an S1 pursuing an Aviatik near Lille when having fired the contents of the Lewis drum he tried to change it. At best a risky manoeuvre on this occasion the drum jammed. To free it, Strange loosened his safety belt and stood up controlling the aircraft with his legs. He lost his grip however and the aeroplane, still climbing stalled and flicked over throwing Strange out of the cockpit. He was now hanging by the ammunition drum he had been trying to release. His presence of mind allowed him to reach up and behind with one hand for the centre strut and grabbing this he kicked up and got a foot in the cockpit. The other followed and he managed to right the aeroplane and slump back into his seat. The Aviatik reported a certain victory having seen the pilot flung from his cockpit and the Germans spent some time searching for the wreckage.

the poor weather of which there appeared to be no end. Jumbo thought it was all a great hoot and partook with great gusto, which was fortunate really as his life was literally in my hands and mine in his. My command of French improved enormously and I took to spending the evenings discussing the French perspective of the conflict with Madame d'Alprant. I doubt her views coincided with those of Petain or Joffre as she seemed to be of the opinion that the Germans could have Paris, full as it was of stinking French men, and she had heard that the Germans were extraordinary lovers with their jackboots and pointed helmets. At this point, our familiar conversation was punctuated with gasps as I proved once again what she knew all along that only the English were capable of complete satisfaction under pressure. After which I dozed off having had my fill of Madame d'Alprant and her champagne and oysters.

I woke with a start some time later. It was still dark but I couldn't tell if I had been asleep for minutes or hours. I was comfortable which was the main thing and there was no rush as the weather forecast for the next day was appalling and I wasn't required anyway until the afternoon. In the total darkness, I suddenly realised that Madame d'Alprant was not present. The lack of snoring was what finally confirmed this point. I pondered on where she might be hoping that she was perhaps concocting a refreshing midnight feast. My mind wandered back to school where I had taken great delight in breaking up the midnight feasts of the fags and acquiring the cake Mumsy had sent for little Johnny.

I heard voices. Who could possibly be here at this time of night I wondered. Mind you, what was this time of night? I still had no idea. I got out of the bed and looked for a clock. Not so easy in complete darkness I promise you. Just after three o'clock in the morning. Who on earth I wondered again? Nasty thoughts seeped into my mind. How dare they turn up here uninvited and disturb me. Were they uninvited? Suddenly angry at the French betrayal I was unconsciously heading towards the voices. The hair on the back of my neck sprang up like a cat and I wished I hadn't had so much champagne. I stopped to listen, suspicious and now cautious rather than angry. I had been about to steam full ahead and confront the conniving pair until something odd stopped me. I remembered at this point that I was also in my birthday suit. I couldn't hear voices. Only one voice. Only half a conversation.

"Non."

Pause.

"Ah, Non."

Long pause and exasperated sigh.

"Stop worrying. He cannot hear me."

So I wasn't the old cow's only conquest, not that I had seriously believed I was. I stopped myself again from barging straight in.

"No. No. I don't know yet. Why are you so impatient? You know that time will provide the answers. He will keep coming here."

Long pause. I presumed she was talking about me.

"Of course he will. He gives me what I want and in return, I....."

She had obviously been shouted down by whoever was on the other end of the telephone line. I had realised at last that this was what she was doing.

"You guess wrong. Since you ask, quite a bit bigger."

There was a long pause whilst both I and the other gentleman contemplated the import of the last comment, he somewhat more vocally than I.

At last she said, "Have you quite finished? Good, then when I have cause to contact you again I will. Until then I suggest you keep yourself occupied with some young fräulein."

I had just started to creep back to the bedroom having resolved to keep the conversation a secret between the three of us, but the mention of the word fräulein nearly had me springing for the door. Instead, I picked up my pace towards the bedroom and scrambled under the covers. My heart was in my mouth as the implications of what I had just heard began to sink in. What on earth had I been saying? What on earth had I been thinking of? Christ I had been coming here for weeks thinking how clever I was introducing the chaps to Madame d'Alprant's gang of lookers. God knows what I had given away to her and consequently to Hermann. Who was dead because of me? Jesus it didn't bear thinking about but I had to. Here she was back. I had to lay still and I forced out a gentle snuffling snore followed fortuitously by a long fart, a sure sign I was asleep. My heart was pounding like a steam hammer. She slipped under the cover and lay still. My heart slowed down and I began to think rationally again. What a hellish fix. I really had no idea what I had told her but as most of what I said was inconsequential drivel and my experience of the war on the ground was limited it really couldn't be that much. On the other hand, anything might be of use to the boche, even inconsequential drivel. Of course, I could just denounce her to the authorities. I could see the headlines now.

'British Hero uncovers filthy boche espionage scandal' or the alternative 'Idiot officer caught with trousers down admits telling all to brothel madam. Sentenced to be shot at dawn'. Perhaps Le Queux could have written another appalling book about it.[43]

I needed to think clearly and away from here, but I wasn't going to get away that easily. I had to do it without her realising I had discovered her little secret. I turned over to face her and she was clearly just dozing off. Inspired by what I saw and a stirring down below I realised with a start that

---

[43] This can only be William Le Queux, a passionate believer in the threat of German invasion at the time, who spent a considerable amount of time searching for German spies in England and warning all and sundry as often as possible, particularly through his novels. 'Spies of the Kaiser' was the most influential in stirring up spy fever. He had some connections to the intelligence gathering community but mostly he was ignored as an eccentric.

that would be the perfect way to allay her fears if she had any. And mine for that matter. Before she knew what was going on I was aboard and pounding away. Never mind jackboots, all I needed was a riding whip for a perfect finish. After the ecstatic writhing was complete I noticed her wicked little smile as I rolled off and went back to sleep. I couldn't have been calmer. And nor could she.

The morning arrived along with some breakfast. By now, she knew that whilst the French on the whole provide decent food, excepting of course snails, frogs and other garden creatures, breakfast was a truly English preserve. Eggs and bacon appeared all of which was wolfed down with gusto. I resisted the temptation for another circuit of St Omer racecourse and excused myself with a promise to return as soon as I could decently get away.

Jumbo was slumped in the mess when I arrived back. I thought he was asleep until he snorted with laughter.

"Looking a bit tired Flash old boy. Didn't get much sleep last night shouldn't wonder. What was it? Boche found out how to bomb at night?"

I laughed as well, infected with Jumbo's eternal good humour. As it happened, I didn't feel that tired. Possibly something to do with the conversation I had overheard. I still didn't quite know what to do about it. The easiest thing would be to carry on as normal but it wasn't possible. If she was passing on anything I said to the other side, even I could see that was a situation that could not be allowed to continue. I could just stop visiting but she would realise pretty soon that she was compromised and move on to some other poor unsuspecting chap. I could just tell the adjutant if I wanted my career to finish and whilst the thought of escaping the horrors of France was pleasant, the idea of a life in disgrace wasn't, at least not for someone like me. There had to be another way.

"You ready then Flash?"

I realised that all through this Jumbo had been chattering away.

"Ready for what?"

"Christ, you didn't hear a word I said did you. Balloons. Army fed up with them. Got to shoot the buggers down. Just the chaps for the job. You get ready and I will just tell you which way to go."

"But the weather…" I started as I looked out of the window into the bright sun, dappled with white cloud here and there. I hadn't even noticed on my way back and it was no use complaining that I wasn't supposed to be on duty until the afternoon. I went to change.

I hadn't flown an aeroplane for nearly a week and it seemed slightly strange. I started the engine, the chocks were taken away, and off we went. I forgot Madame d'Alprant and concentrated on the job in hand. It was almost pleasant to be in the air again. Jumbo called out the instructions and I flew around with my eyes wide open looking for the boche. We hopped in and out of cloud as we headed for the lines. Soon we were over the Ypres salient, which apparently was where the Germans had some balloons spotting for their artillery. We never normally got very close because they would see us coming miles away and pull the balloon down. Today was different. The cloud was conveniently hanging around about 2000 feet up in long stretches that allowed us to hide quite effectively. Every so often when Jumbo decided we were in the right place, down we would go for a look. I was getting bored with this by the sixth attempt.

"Here," shouted Jumbo.

Down we went again. The cloud was a little lower this time, but we popped out and immediately ahead and slightly to our right was a damned great balloon complete with basket and two observers. I nearly had a seizure.

"Tally ho," Jumbo shouted. "Get in close and give the buggers what for."

I headed straight for it until we were about two hundred yards away then swerved to port. I felt rather than heard the arrival of a few rifle bullets from the basket and then Jumbo's Lewis was in action and he was pouring fire at the balloon and then at the basket. I rolled the BE into a hard right turn and pulled back climbing a little at the same time. Bullets were still flying at us from the basket and now from the ground as well. Holes started appearing in the fabric as I hurtled round for another go. If I had been on my own, I would have been in the cloud but with Jumbo there we had to try to get the thing. I flew at it again and this time sheared off to the right. I heard the chatter of the Lewis and then an exclamation of wonderment from the back. The firing had all stopped so I began the turn again to see what was going on. As we came round, I could see the balloon shrivelling up and beginning to collapse. Underneath I could feel the horror of the two men as they frantically tried to get out. They knew as well as we did that it was too late. The balloon was already on top of them and enveloping the basket. The whole shambles was descending faster and faster. I could almost hear the thud as it hit the ground, just as we reached the safety of the cloud.

"Home I think," I said setting a course to the west. We flew back to the field in silence. We landed without further incident and switched off.

On the way over to the mess Jumbo suddenly murmured, "Got to be done old boy. Otherwise the bastards will kill us."

"I know. Thank God it wasn't us."

The bloodthirsty contingent in the mess were all for it and demanded to hear every detail over and over again. The more thoughtful were consumed with pity. None of us had yet to meet the Eindeckers that would change the view that we were fighting an honourable crusade as knights of the sky.

Me? I had just been the cause of two men's horrific deaths. I thought the buggers deserved it.

Chapter 12

Immelmann. Fearless, daring, chivalrous warrior of the skies. But still a boche. He flew an Eindecker, the soon to become fabled creation of Anthony Fokker, the Dutch aircraft designer. It was the first proper fighting aircraft, designed to attack and destroy the opposition's aeroplanes. The interrupter gear was probably the most important part of the entire machine as it allowed the pilot to aim his machine at the target and watch what he was doing and the result of his actions, adjusting them if necessary to achieve the destruction of the enemy.

The relative quiet of the summer months drifting by had not prepared us at all for what we were about to receive. The fighting around Ypres had dragged on, as had the bombing and artillery spotting. Occasionally there was an aerial dust up with the enemy, but on the 1st August, Immelmann claimed his first victim. An unsuspecting two-seater bomber was blown out of the sky just inside the German lines, according to the German reports. The poor bastards on board never stood a chance. Suddenly, although we weren't yet aware of the fact, the balance of power in the air had shifted decisively east. The only saving grace was that the Germans themselves had not appreciated quite how effective the Eindecker was and consequently only attached them to their front line squadrons in ones and twos. Even so, effective it was and Immelmann's score started to mount. His fame, along with that of Oswald Boelcke started to spread, eventually crossing the lines. Immelmann in particular became well known after his spectacular method of attack using the superior abilities of the Fokker to dive down on his victim then pulling up into a loop and half roll off the top to finish in a clinical killing position. Many witnessed this but not many survived it. Fewer still had any means of countering it. Appropriately it was Lanoe Hawker who probably downed the first Eindecker mainly because he was an extremely skilled and experienced pilot but similar victories were few and far between and the casualties attributed to the Fokker mounted steadily, particularly amongst the BE crews who became the Fokker fodder.

This was partly because it was the most numerous type of aeroplane, partly because it wasn't designed to fight off the Fokkers and partly because increasingly its crews were fresh from inadequate training. The grudging esteem with which the German pilots were held was multiplied by their own newspapers and at home with reports of 'Fokker Scourge'[44] and the like.

---

[44] The British Press coined both the terms 'Fokker Fodder' and 'Fokker Scourge' in response to the albeit brief ascendancy of the Fokkers on the western front. It is hard to know at this distance in time what their intention was although it was probably aimed to some degree at the politicians. At the same time, the press had an almost unwaveringly positive view of even the most expensive minor gains of territory although even this had to change to a more realistic view as the war dragged on with the ever lengthening casualty lists.

I didn't see one at all and unbeknownst to me I was approaching the end of my time in France. I just had time for one more hair-raising ride with Jumbo. The balloon destruction had confirmed our position as the squadron scout pilots and more and more we were sent on designated patrols to find and destroy the German machines. More often than not, they didn't fight us despite generally being on our own. We would sometimes accompany the bombers to protect them from German scouts as well. Usually we were just deployed as an irritant to anyone who happened to be in the way.

It was late afternoon in early September. The sun was behind us, which meant the Germans mostly stayed at home. I had just unofficially, via the squadron clerk, received notice of my posting and the will to survive was strong. We climbed lazily into the air and set off towards the lines in the distance. Jumbo was singing away and we were both constantly scanning the sky for the specks of dust that indicated trouble, the Fokker being especially difficult to see on account of its monoplane build. Nothing. Not a sausage. We drifted about the sky, looking at our lines, looking at theirs and seeing nothing more exciting than the odd bunch of infantry doing very little. It was hard to believe that a vicious struggle was going on at all at times like these. We saw numerous groups of Germans but it seemed mutually agreed that we wouldn't swoop down on them and they wouldn't shoot at us. This continued for some time as the sun got lower in the sky and the ground gradually started to vanish into one continuous brown smudge. A tiny flash caught my eye. So tiny that I couldn't place it for a moment. Then again. Just to the north of us and more importantly over our lines. Could be anyone though.

"Just take a quick look," Jumbo said. "Probably one of ours."

He was right. It probably was. We drifted closer all the time edging west to put ourselves between him and the sun. Whoever he was, he hadn't seen us yet. The sun glinted again on the double wings of an Albatros and then just to confirm it we saw the black crosses loom large on the top wing. Still he hadn't seen us. We could see the observer peering intently over the side. It was Jumbo's idea but I agreed and so we almost turned for home and let him be. Then we saw the flashes down below and realised what the observer was doing. Another bomb slipped over the side to deal out death and destruction to the gravel-crushers.

Jumbo was enraged. I heard him fiddling with the Lewis and somehow knew all I had to do was find a nice position and Hermann was a goner. For once Jumbo's anger got the better of him and despite still being four hundred yards away, he opened fire. We were closing all the time though and it wasn't long before I saw bullet strikes on the German's fuselage. The observer had jerked into life almost as soon as we opened fire. His gun was in the wrong place though and he lost precious seconds remounting it and aiming our way. In the meantime, the pilot had started to weave like mad. I followed his gyrations attempting all the time to let Jumbo get a decent shot at him. We stopped firing and I guess Jumbo was changing the drum. At the same time holes appeared above me and there was a sickening crack. I frantically looked around fearing the worst, looking for the damaged strut that would allow the wing to fall off but I couldn't see it. Jumbo started firing again and I realised that we were diving faster and faster. The German obviously wasn't in the mood to fight us. Bombing troops was his game. Down we went as the wires started to sing their disapproval of the more and more violent manoeuvres I was performing in the effort to keep up. More holes appeared and I started to shout.

"For God's sake kill the bastard and then we can go home."

I don't think Jumbo heard but God did. No sooner were the words out of my mouth then the German's upper wing suddenly folded up and back. The two tips met in the middle as the whole thing detached itself, apparently in slow time. As it departed, it snatched the rudder off with it and the tangle of fabric and wire floated slowly earthwards. Not so what remained. The pilot seemed to have a semblance of control as the remains of his aeroplane continued on in a now shallow dive. Jumbo had stopped firing and was staring open mouthed at the spectacle quite literally unfolding before us. They were brave. The observer we suddenly realised was still firing at us from the wreckage, despite the fact that he must have known his end was imminent. The dive got steeper as the weight of the engine overcame the force of the wing. Still he fired. There was another crack that brought us back into the land of the living. Seconds later the Germans departed from it. The crash flamed briefly in no-man's-land. I pulled up and threw us into a hard turn back towards the safety of our lines. We were still low down and I thought some height might do us good. The wrench backwards was just too much for the old BE though and there was another crunch and the unmistakeable sound of a bracing wire giving way.

"Look for a field we can land in," I shouted.

"You'll be lucky," came the reply. He had a point. There weren't many fields here, mainly trenches.

"Jesus, it will have to be in between."

I turned again, far more gingerly this time as we slowed down sinking closer and closer to the ground. It seemed quite flat. Not that it made much difference, as we didn't really have much choice.

"Hang on," I shouted.

"What do you think I'm doing?"

The wheels touched. I have no idea what happened next.

****

I came to in the dark. It was a darkness crossed with shooting stars though and seemed peculiarly attractive. For a moment, it seemed awfully quiet and I toyed with the thought that I was dead. Then the noise rushed in on me like a steam train. The shooting stars resolved themselves into tracer rounds and I decided to keep my head down. Which way was down though? I gingerly flexed my fingers and then my toes. Everything seemed to be in working order. I seemed to ache all over however and there was a crushing pain I now noticed in my midriff. Exploration revealed I was still in the cockpit, or at least what remained of it. I felt the need to remove myself. I scrabbled around for the safety belt release but when I found it, it was jammed tight. So there I stayed, partly suspended by the belt and partly resting on the wreckage. I studied the racket overhead again and now I could hear shouting and screaming to go with the whine of bullets.

"Jumbo," I called.

No answer. Disconcertingly a bullet pinged off the engine and ricocheted into the ground. Now, for someone of my delicate disposition this was a little too far.

"Jumbo," I shouted again, craning my neck around to see if I could see him anywhere. Nothing. I started flailing around in the hopes that I would somehow get myself free but to no avail. Another bullet bounced off something metal and disappeared into the air. The firing seemed to be getting closer. More of a worry was that it now seemed to be aimed at me. I heard footsteps running nearby and out of the dark appeared the shapes of men with rifles. They flung themselves down in what passed for cover and started shooting into the dark. Needless to say, I couldn't tell whose side they were on. I nearly jumped from my skin when a voice in my ear asked how I was.

"Top hole," I replied. "Never better. I wonder if you chaps could see your way to getting me out of here only my straps are stuck. Jammed solid."

"'ang on Sir. These blasted fritzes"

"I am hanging on old boy."

He didn't reply, as suddenly he had no mouth to reply with. Or head for that matter. As the body crumpled lifelessly to the floor, the intensity of the firing seemed to increase. Now I could hear the crack as rifles were fired in close proximity as well as the whine of bullets passing nearby. I fancied I could hear orders being shouted in German as well as English.

"Blimey," another cockney voice said. "Chalky's 'ad it. Crikey. You bin 'angin' like vat fer a while ven?"

This particular comment was aimed at me from under what appeared to be a wing and accompanied by the click clack bang of a Lee Enfield in action. I didn't answer as the unreality of the situation was beginning to take its toll and my throat was constricting in preparation for a good vomit. As suddenly as it started everything seemed to pass. I was briefly surrounded by men firing, and then they had gone forward. At least I assumed they had gone forward as I had no idea which way was which. I was alone again in the dark and beginning to wonder if I had dreamed it all when I noticed the corpse again. What next though?

"'ere we are," said a voice. "'angin' 'ere. You two get rahnd 'ere. 'ello Sir. 'arf a mo' and we'll cut vose straps."

I was beginning to get a little testy with the constant references to hanging and was about to say so when I wasn't. Instead, I was in a heap in the mud. I staggered to my feet and then returned to a heap in the mud as my legs gave way.

"No good, we'll 'ave to drag 'im."

Without so much as a bye your leave I was hauled off the ground between two soldiers and with my legs dragging behind hurtled off into the gloom. A whistle sounded behind me and I briefly wondered what we were doing at Victoria Station. A couple of times we nearly went down in a crater but we kept going until I was unceremoniously dropped into a trench. I was lying down, barely conscious and not really aware of anything going on around me except that the firing had stopped. Now seemed like a good time to sit up. I dragged myself onto my elbows and peered into the gloom. There were men everywhere, most smoking and sitting down. Some were standing against the wall of the trench staring into the darkness of no-man's-land. Out of nowhere an officer appeared.

"Hello Sir. Moore, Captain Moore, London Regiment.[45] Glad to see you safe and sound. Hell of a fight though."

---

[45] The London Regiment was a unique regiment in the

"Flashman. Glad to be safe and sound. And thanks." Then my coward's instinct and desire to know why they had come to get me forced me to say, "Why on Earth you did that I have no idea." Moore looked offended but not enough not to explain.

"The buggers were dropping bombs on us. At least they were until you settled their hash."

British Army. It was a wholly Territorial Regiment as well as being the largest regiment in the Army. For its first eight years of existence from 1908 it did not form part of any regular regiment. It also did not have a Regimental Cap badge, each battalion wearing its own individual badge. The origins of the regiment can be traced to the raising of the Volunteer Rifle Corps that were formed in and around the City of London in 1859 when relations with Napoleon III were at a low ebb, these corps remaining as volunteers until the creation of the Territorial Force in 1908. At this point, the regiment consisted of 26 Battalions, of which 8 were designated City of London and 18 County of London, most with a further distinction reflecting their previous attachment as volunteer battalions to regular regiments. At the outbreak of the war, all regiments raised 2nd battalions and later 3rd battalions with some raising a 4th battalion. This led to a somewhat confusing numbering system, with for example, 2/22 Bn London Regiment in fact referring to the 2nd Line Battalion of the 22nd Battalion, London Regiment. In September 1915, the regiment was at its largest, consisting of 82 battalions, numerous of which were in France. Flashman has not qualified which battalion he is referring to here and as so many were in France it is impossible to tell which one it is without a more exact location for his crash. In April 1916, the Regiment ceased to exist as all battalions were posted to regular regiments, but the names lived on and many still do as part of the Territorial Army albeit as single Companies or other small units.

"Good God" I cried. I had completely forgotten the dead Germans. "Well, thanks again."

"No need. Other way round really. Least we could do. They've been doing it for days and it gets a bit irritating. Won't be doing it again though."

My memory was now cranking slowly back into action and I finally remembered that I hadn't been alone in the fight.

"Where's Jumbo, my observer."

"He's fine. Snoring away in the dugout. He was thrown out of your aeroplane and knocked out. We dragged him back and he came round fairly quickly. Gave him some rum to put him to sleep. Said he had a sore head. Not as sore as those boche bastards though," and he laughed a deep vengeful laugh. "Come with me and we'll find you a bed."

I hauled myself slowly to my feet, assisted by the owners of this part of the trench, and followed Moore unsteadily. After a few twists and turns, I was totally disorientated. We came to a large hole in the wall and went through it and down some steps. I found myself in a large room lined with planking and with a couple of beds on one side and a chair and table in the middle. The occupant of one of the beds was indeed snoring loudly and had the unmistakeable figure of my observer. He didn't get up.

"Here you are Flashman," and I was handed an enormous tin mug filled with brown liquid. "Rum. All we've got I am afraid. Have to leave you to it for the moment. Get some sleep and we will get you on your way in the morning." With that, he disappeared through the hole.

There was nothing for it. I clambered onto the bed and went to sleep. Not for long though. Yet again, the military determination for everybody to be awake before the birds had me all but leaping out of the cot. I glanced around the dugout and noticed as before Jumbo asleep. Nothing woke him up apparently. No one had been into the place since I dozed off as far as I could tell and there was quite clearly no mess waiter to conjure up a mug of tea. I buried my head under a blanket and tried desperately not to hear the calls of "Stand to," and so on followed by the clatter of soldiers and bits of metal clashing as they prepared themselves for the imminent arrival of the enemy, a thought that sent me deeper under the blankets. All stayed quiet though and I assumed the enemy had not obliged. Eventually I went back to sleep but was almost immediately awoken by the arrival of Moore and his batman with a large pot of tea. I stifled the curses forming on my lips and thanked them.

"Any danger of breakfast," I chortled now thoroughly awake.

"None whatsoever Sir," answered the batman.

"Right I'm afraid," mumbled Moore. "Bully beef and biscuits for a change. Not what you're used to. You get used to the taste eventually."

"Well you've certainly got a way of making friends," laughed Jumbo, now wide-awake, when they had gone. "They probably haven't seen a rasher of bacon since they disembarked and you have the damned cheek to ask for breakfast as if we were in Knightsbridge Barracks.[46]

He tucked into his biscuits as I stared thunderously yet impotently around. I couldn't think of a suitable reply so I didn't bother. I got on with eating the damned awful food thinking mainly of what I would eat when we got back to the squadron. It wasn't long before we set off, walking at first to get away from the front line. Moore said a quick goodbye and we thanked them again for getting us out of what was a potentially fatal scrape. A company runner then led us through a maze of trenches until we popped out on what passed for a road. Nearby was the battalion headquarters. He led us over and announced us to the adjutant.

"Been wondering when you would get here. Gather you showed those blasted boche a thing or two. Clapped a stopper over their antics. Good show. Transport outside. Near the battery. Toodle pip." The one-sided conversation closed and we wandered back outside. Almost immediately, there was an enormous explosion and we both hurled ourselves on the ground. On hearing the

---

[46] Trench food generally did consist of bully beef and biscuits, but it is an exaggeration to suggest that the troops would not have seen a rasher of bacon as once out of the line there was generally plenty of decent food available. For many the diet would have been better than what they were used to before the war. For those with some money to spend, there were eating places available as well. Even in the line, hot stew was generally sent up from the field kitchens at night. Food only became scarce when there was serious fighting with the consequent disruption.

laughter however we stood up and carried on in a pretence that we always did that when our own artillery let fly.

"Ignore them Sir," said the driver as we clambered aboard the truck. "No manners at all. Ignorant swine. Mostly Scots," he said as we chugged slowly away.

"Could you tell us exactly where we are?" Jumbo asked.

"Wipers,[47] Sir."

"Ah," I said in a distracted knowing way. I wasn't able to follow this up with anything especially useful and so lapsed into silence. The ride was uneventful and as silent as it got on the Western Front with three enormous armies constantly trying to destroy each other. It seemed to take an age to get clear of the front lines and all the paraphernalia that was required for total war. Eventually the driver found a half-decent road and we saw grass again. Only then did I realise quite how brown the trenches and their surroundings were. It was a relief to leave it all behind and return to civilisation of sorts.

The mess was quiet as the rest of the squadron were flying. Consequently, we ended up propping up the bar for sometime. The rest of the chaps drifted in slowly and eventually the bossman arrived.

---

[47] Wipers as in Ypres. The British Army have always changed the names of unfamiliar places to suit their own particular accents at the time and Ypres was no exception. It was also immortalised in the trench newspaper that was produced known as the Wipers Times.

"Ah, Flashman," he said. "Orders for you. Home old boy. Flight commander in a new outfit."

"Thankyou Sir," I said. I didn't tell him I knew already, albeit unofficially.

Higgins eyed me suspiciously for a moment, possibly having caught the hint of relief at the confirmed orders in my voice. "Well, those of us that came out at the start and aren't dead could probably do with a rest, although from what I hear it isn't much fun at home either." He turned away with a smile and collared a passing drink. I didn't reply. I stifled the urge to cheer and dance wildly around the room and instead tried to look disappointed. I considered passing some remark about those who were staying having all the fun but given the company I was in, I reconsidered. It seemed a little unreal anyway as I still thought of myself as something of a new boy, but the truth was that the last year had passed very quickly and in that time I had changed from being a terrified, ignorant pilot, to just a terrified one. Most of those who had come over in 1914 were dead. The lucky ones who were still alive had an air of borrowed time about them. The most unfortunate were the real newcomers who were being turned out of flying schools with very little idea of what was about to happen to them and consequently rarely survived for long. Of course, in a way it was only what had happened to me, the difference being I had had a chance to pick things up slowly and my peers had survived long enough and had the time to pass their experiences on. The gaunt exhausted faces filling the mess now hardly had time to change their underwear before being sent off again to fill a new set. Gooding caught up with me.

"Would you take a letter home for my family?" he asked.

"Of course. Where are they?"

He rambled on about a countryseat of some kind and a place in London until I asked him to write it down as the chance of me remembering either was very slim. With that, I sneaked off to bed.

****

My orders were as always to be carried out with the utmost despatch, but I decided that this did in fact include a surreptitious visit to Madame d'Alprant. I arrived at the quiet midday period when very few of the local soldiers had turned their thoughts to exercise and appeared at her door. She welcomed me with open arms. Immediately my suspicions returned from our former engagement.

"Ah, mon Capitaine," she gushed. What was the meaning of 'Ah' I wondered. We rushed into the house and before I knew it really, her expert hands had begun working in my nether regions and my suspicions were once again pushed from my mind by more important issues. The climax passed and we were sitting in the bed smoking when there was a scream that brought all my fears rushing back.

"Ah, Lucy," she mumbled. "You 'aven't meet Lucy 'ave you?" she said in her most attractive English. "She is an expert wiv ze 'orsewhip. You must try someday, yes?"

"How could I possibly think of another woman when I am here with you," I murmured in my best cringing tone. "Anyway, I have to go away for sometime."

She almost burst but recovered in a fraction of a second to mutter some nonsense in my ear about how she would miss me so much. After some few minutes she finally got round to what she wanted to know which was when I was coming back.

"Soon," I said. "Much too soon I suspect," I muttered to myself. She looked pleased and puzzled at the same time so I rogered her again and then left, making sure her last memory of me was a good one. I made my way to the station and waited with a huge crowd of others for what was apparently the only train to the seaside that day. It arrived eventually and with some pushing and shoving and generally throwing my weight around, I finally found a seat in the officers' carriage. I settled down for a sleep.

I woke with a start to find the compartment full of more people than was strictly comfortable and asked where we were.

"We haven't bloody well moved yet," roared a distinctly upset Guards officer. Clearly, he wasn't used to travelling by train. Eventually someone made the engine start and off we went, the Guards officer by now even more upset judging by the colour of his face. It was going to be a long journey.

Chapter 13

It was cold in London. Everyone looked miserable in spite of the fact that they had nothing to be miserable about. Worst of all, the Rag and Famish[48] was full of officers whose units had orders for France. Most of them were drinking but instead of being cheerful about their fate, they seemed particularly morose.

The newspapers had not helped things. Their constant boasting about how the boche was getting or going to get a pasting had slowly but surely changed. Outrage at the sinking of the Lusitania[49] along with their mindless home for Christmas optimism had eventually given way to the reality of ever lengthening casualty lists, and reports of thousands of men giving their lives for a few yards of mud did not sound particularly glamorous. Worse for Asquith[50] was the decline

---

[48] The Rag and Famish, also known as the Army and Navy Club, acquired its nickname shortly after its formation in 1837 when the colourful Captain 'Billy' Duff dismissed it as a 'Rag and Famish affair'. This quickly became the club's nickname.

[49] The Lusitania was sunk in May 1915 with the loss of 1201 passengers, 128 of whom were Americans. The Germans asserted that the ship was carrying arms for the allies, something that turned out to be true.

[50] Herbert Henry Asquith was the Liberal Prime Minister from 1908 when he succeeded Campbell-Bannerman until December 1916 when he was forced to resign and was replaced by David Lloyd George. His period of office was marked by various major upheavals including the rise of the suffragettes, the home rule for Ireland bills and of course the beginning of the Great War.

in the number of volunteers willing to be blown to bits or drowned in mud for King and Country. They had a point really. Nevertheless, I sauntered into the bar and acquired a whisky. I had a couple of days leave having called at Farnborough[51] to find out where I was to go to and when. I buried myself in a corner having no particular reason to advertise my presence but not before an old buffer at the bar had spotted me. He looked significantly in my direction and I looked significantly away. Not significantly enough though as eventually the Colonel invited himself to join me saying, "India was it? Or Sandhurst? Can't quite place you. Too young for the Drift of course." He furrowed his brow while I kept mum. "Got it," he suddenly spluttered. "Sandhurst you old devil. Nearly had you kicked out for setting fire to that boy in 'A' Company. By God, we laughed at that. Different if you'd killed the bugger of course."

I said I supposed it would have been. We lapsed into silence. I was considering my escape when he suddenly came to life again. "What's that you're wearing?" he said pointing.

"Wings," I replied, "for flying."

"Well bless me. Not met one of you yet. 'Til now of course. What's it like? Suppose you spend your time huntin' and so on and then out for a quick bash at the boche, ha ha, and home for tiffin."

He said all this as if he meant it so I came swiftly to the conclusion that he was deranged. I

[51] Farnborough by this time was home of the Administrative Wing of the RFC.

159

had realised by now that it was him I had met on my arrival at Sandhurst all those years ago.

"How's your Father?" His tone had changed abruptly and he had assumed a more serious look.

"The Bishop is fine as far as I know."

"Don't be silly boy. I mean your real Father. How is he? Surely he told you?"

And I thought I was just having a pointless conversation with some old buffer from the past. Apparently not.

"Dead."

"At last," he said firmly. I didn't know quite what to make of this but clearly, he possessed more information than I did on this subject, apart from the fact that my Father, that is the General, had died peacefully some weeks before. The news didn't reach me until after the funeral and no one had rushed to tell me as they all assumed it was in fact my Grandfather who had died. There was no question of leave at the time although I tried my best, I do assure you.

"Some things to give you then," he said. "Can you meet me here this evening, say eight o'clock?"

I nodded my assent and he got up and swaggered off. Once again in my life I was left wondering what on earth was going on. A number of things were puzzling me. First, despite remembering the Colonel from my arrival at Sandhurst, now I thought about it, I didn't recall seeing him again. Second, there was something about him that didn't quite add up although I could not put my finger on it. Finally, my Father had stumped me yet again apparently, even though the old fossil was dead. I left the club in search of a decent meal. I hadn't gone far when I was approached and accosted by one of the numerous overbearing women who had apparently been bred especially for the war. Somewhere in her rant at the military and aeroplanes in particular I discerned her fury at being subject to bombing from those dastardly German's airships. Did we not know in the Flying Corps that England had not been invaded since the Conqueror? I had been fiddling in my pocket all this time as a small crowd grew to witness the spectacle and as she paused for breath, I gave her the contents. She looked at her hand.

"It was all I could find," I said.

"What on earth do you mean young man," she spluttered.

"Boche. After I shot him down."

She stared again at her hand as it slowly dawned on her what I meant. She nearly put her hands to her face but thought better of it as she threw down the scraps I had given her. As she began her descent to the ground, in a condition of swoon as some greasy frog once put it, I began my departure from the scene followed by mutterings of disgraceful and such like. I wasn't sure whether they meant her or me but I didn't particularly care. I was still hungry. Finally, I was seated in a quiet corner of the Savoy Grill and settled down to some decent steak with rather a good claret. I whiled away the time watching the other customers until retracing my steps. I confess

I was intrigued now, helped along by a bottle - or was it two? - of the wine. Altogether, I was pretty well off guard when something fetched me an almighty crack on the head. Stars span around and I gently lowered myself to the floor, also in a condition of swoon.

******

I came to staring at a bright light. I was alone in a windowless room .It was sparsely furnished, in fact, I was lying on the furniture. My head hurt and on closer inspection, I found a large lump on the back of my head. I sat up slowly and looked around carefully. I had no idea what to expect and I was a little disappointed by what I saw. Nothing. Precisely nothing. I swung my legs over the edge of the table and sat for a moment. Gingerly I let myself down to the floor. My legs seemed to work so I took a turn about the room to make sure before venturing on something more ambitious like trying to get out. I walked over to the door and tried the handle. Not too surprising was the fact that it was locked. I put my ear to the door but could hear nothing at all, except my own heart pounding. I paused to consider while panic began to take hold. It didn't take long. I was quite clearly in a fix of some kind.

I ludicrously looked at my watch, which I still had, thinking I'd never make it to the Rag by eight. Then I looked again at the door and went and sat down on the table.

I listened again and still could not hear anything in the corridor.

This was a new experience for me. Confused notions of escape and headlong flight filled my head but first, I had to get out of the room. But was that a good idea? Did I really want to get out of the room? Surely it would be safer to stay put. As I pondered this, other more disturbing questions arose. Who had brought me here and why, as well as whether they were now waiting for me outside. Could they be bargained with? Money I could offer them. But did they want money. Surely they would have asked by now? I walked back over to the door and examined it more carefully. There was a small judas in the door through which I peered. All I could see was a corridor of some kind. I listened again and still could not hear anything outside. I had not learnt the art of patience in this kind of situation yet.

The door didn't look particularly strong and I was a big man but the noise from trying to break it down would surely bring the nosey parker club along at the charge. I tried the handle again to see if it would open. It didn't but as I stared at it, I realised that the whole thing wasn't very strong. There was a larger than usual gap between the door and the frame and through it I could see a latch holding the door closed. I scrabbled uselessly at the gap for a moment and then looked wildly around me for something to force in the gap. My emotions were beginning to get the better of me however and I had to stop myself pounding on the door yelling. As I turned round in frustration, I noticed my tunic was hanging from a nail, which someone had banged into the table leg. I grabbed it without stopping to consider why on earth someone would kidnap me, lay me on a table, take my tunic off and hang it on a nail. I almost turned it upside down but stopped and searched the pockets carefully. In one, I found the knife from my English Channel survival kit. Lord knows what that was doing there.

I returned to the door. The blade fitted neatly into the gap and in less than a second, the door was open. I narrowly resisted the temptation to run and carefully swung the door back. No one directly outside and no noise so I stuck my head out and looked both ways. The corridor was comparatively dark but I could see a door at one end and what looked like steps at the other. It occurred to me that I could be below ground level and that would explain the lack of windows. The door looked forbidding and the steps less so. I crept and rushed at the same time towards the steps, all the time praying that no one would appear. I reached the bottom uneventfully and peered up into the gloom. The steps were wooden. Slowly I placed one foot on the far right of the bottom step. It didn't creak as I lowered my weight on it and so I continued in this fashion, using the edge of the steps. It seemed to take about an hour to climb up and as I climbed, I was conscious that I would shortly be able to see what was at the top, as well as be seen from the top. But there was nothing waiting for me. I crouched and crawled up the last few until peering over I could see another corridor, gloomy and silent but with a door at the end. This door had a window in it and there was light streaming through. I suppressed another urge to run like mad and instead pressed my back against the wall and slid along it. I almost laughed. Here was I, Captain Harry Flashman of the RFC, playing hide and seek in a house in London. At least I assumed it was London. Jesus, what if it wasn't London? Perhaps they didn't need to guard me because there was nowhere to go when one was outside. Christ it was too late now. Why the hell hadn't I stopped and thought about it a bit more. It could be anywhere. As my mind raced ahead to the door and what to do when I got there, I started to review what I had just been doing. It was unbelievable, and if it was unbelievable for me then surely whoever had put me here in the first place realised this also. At this point, I cracked.

I hurled myself the last few feet towards the door, wrenched it open and momentarily checked at the top of more steps leading down into the street. Only momentarily. I was taking them three at a time into a busy street when a loud voice behind me shouted, "Stop thief, stop thief."

A Flashman in full flight rarely stops just because someone shouts and this was not one of those rare occasions. Faces turned towards me and the door from which I had just emerged and at the bottom of the steps, an enterprising young man took a swing at me with his cane. It cracked me on the elbow but I brushed it and him aside despite the agony and barged my way onto the street. Pursued by the shouts I ran like fury along the middle of the street, dodging carts and people and horses. I darted sideways into an alley tumbling an old lady and her basket into the gutter but I didn't look back. I kept running until the shouts stopped and then some. I was free. What from of course I had no idea but I was free. I found a quiet public garden and a bench and sat down to recover. I was breathless and my heart was going like billy-o. I kept a wary eye around me but it was very quiet and the few people walking by hardly noticed me wheezing away. I sat more or less motionless for nearly half an hour in which time my heart slowed down and my lungs stopped heaving. First things first, where was I? I got up and strolled out of the garden looking for a sign of some kind. The first one I saw said I was in Belgrave Square. God knows how I had got there, as it was some way from the Army and Navy and the Savoy. Now I knew where I was what was I to do? The events of the last couple of hours were bizarre to say the least. Who had been trying to incarcerate me and why? For a moment, I even thought Madame d'Alprant had found me out but that was ridiculous. I couldn't answer any of the numerous questions that sprang to mind so I decided not to. Where to go? It seems such a simple thing knowing where to go but I really hadn't a clue.

After some thought I decided to find my way to Berkeley Square and my Father's house. It was doubtful if anyone would be there but at the least, I could perhaps break in. My knowledge of

London had always been reasonable but even so, it took me some time to get my bearings and head in the right direction. It was a long tense walk as although my heart had stopped pounding, my mind was still in a funk. I kept checking to see if anyone was following me in the dark and occasionally I would double back on myself. I reached the square and walked directly across towards the house. As I came nearer, I realised that someone was standing outside the door. Jesus Christ, who was this? I stopped behind some bushes and tried to edge towards the house without being noticed. Fortunately, there was plenty of noise coming from one of the adjacent houses so it wasn't too difficult. I finally peeped around the end of a hedge and saw that it was a policeman guarding the door. I was so relieved I almost stepped straight out and walked up to him until a little voice asked why on earth would a policeman be guarding an empty house and more to the point, an empty house owned by the late General Flashman? Was it because someone thought I might go there? The pace of my heartbeat started to rise again. Where to now for God's sake? Panic was beginning to rise to the surface and I searched vainly around me for something or someone to help. Finding nothing, I crept slowly away from the house again keeping a weather eye on the rozzer and fighting the urge to run like hell. As I did so I realised the answer was a crowd. Somewhere I would be recognized and where no one could clout me and carry me off in the dark.

******

The lights were still on in the club. I breathed a huge sigh of relief as I entered the porch. The porter took one look and started to mutter something about vagrants and pikeys. I glared at him and told him just to open the door as I was going in whether he liked it or not. I could see his mouth working but my obvious authority convinced him opening the door was the correct move. I stumbled through into the hall and headed for the dining room hoping that it was still occupied.

"What kept you?" said a voice from a large leather wingchair with its back to me. The occupant rose slowly and turned to face me.

I swallowed the lump in my throat as the figure came into the light. The Colonel looked me up and down taking in my dishevelled appearance.

"Well Sir, where shall I start? I realise it is long past eight o'clock but I was detained."

"Bugger that Flashman. I do have some things to give you, but I was more concerned about how you coped with our little test."

"Test Sir? What test," I spluttered my imagination beginning to run riot.

"Oh, Cumming and I devised it. See if you've got the right spirit."

"Spirit for what?" I was beginning to get a little cross having spent the entire evening running apparently for my life only to find it was a silly game dreamt up by the Colonel and his daft friends. "Spirit for what?" I repeated when no answer was forthcoming.

"Our….. organisation shall we say." He left the words hanging in the air for a moment or two. "You spoke to Cumming, or rather, he spoke to you. When you got back from your adventures in Sarajevo. He noted you down as someone with the right temperament for our work. You know what we do of course?"

"Attack people in the street apparently and then scare the wits out of them." Well I was furious at being made to look foolish. The Colonel laughed loudly.

"Oh, we do more than that. We abuse them about the Germans bombing London, we arrange for their supper to contain more than expected, we post policemen at likely refuges and then we wait for them to come running back to us."

I was flabbergasted. "All that was your doing was it? You bastards."

"Actually I did know my Father. The point is do you want to know whether you have passed the test?"

"What difference does that make?"

"In your case, two things. First of all, we can go and stay somewhere decent. Second, I can give you all your Father's papers now. At least I can when we get to the Savoy."

I huffed and puffed a little to show my displeasure at the whole charade but the thought of a decent bed was appealing. Oh and my Father's papers intrigued me as well.

"Let's go then," I said.

We stepped out of the club and into a waiting cab which set off immediately, the driver obviously having been warned where to take us. I found the presumption a little infuriating but my temper was dying down and being replaced with exhaustion, physically and mentally.

It didn't take long to reach the hotel. The cab pulled up outside and we stepped down to be greeted by a burly man in an overcoat. Clearly, he wasn't the hotel porter as he showed us through a side door. Once inside we climbed three flights of stairs and passed through another door. Somehow, we had arrived in a corridor of rooms. The Colonel turned and marched off towards the end and when we got there produced a key. With it, he unlocked the door of an enormous suite.

"Get some sleep. We have a busy day tomorrow and then of course you will be off to join your squadron. That is your room," he said indicating a door leading out of the back of the main room. "Your Father's papers are in there," he added pointing at a painting of some flowers. Time enough for those tomorrow."

I had completely and utterly forgotten that the entire purpose of my returning to England was to join a new squadron. I concluded that the painting must conceal a safe of some kind although I thought that sort of thing only happened in books and so I retired, wondering what on earth my Father had that was contentious or dangerous enough to be stored in a safe with these halfwits looking after it.

******

I woke up late to see the sun streaming through the windows. I could hear movements outside the door but I couldn't be bothered to get out of bed for a while. I felt I deserved a bit of a rest after all I had been through. I was trying to make some semblance of order to all that had happened and attempt to add some reality to it. I found it very difficult to believe that all yesterdays events had been some elaborate Boy Scout plan resulting in a large bruise on my head that was definitely still there. Then there was this issue of the papers. What papers? Surely he had nothing of particular importance. I supposed I wasn't to know everything that went on in his life but he had never seemed the type for behind the scenes work. Charging the Russkis was more his style or so I thought. I turned over with the charming thought of going back to sleep and I was beginning to wish there had been a little Dinah alongside when the door opened unbidden and another burly ape appeared carrying a bowl of steaming water.

"Breakfast is on the table," was all he said before stumping out of the room. That was that then. I washed and shaved slowly before getting dressed. I had considered my slightly battered uniform but when I opened the wardrobe, I discovered fresh civvies that fit perfectly. I had to admit that they were certainly organised. I emerged to find the table covered with dishes containing all I could wish for and settled down for a prolonged meal. Glancing around me, I noticed that the painting had been swung right round to face the wall and it did in fact conceal a safe, which was now open. Having settled my initial pangs of hunger, I collected the top file from the safe, sat down again and started to read.

The front of the file simply stated that this was the property of Brigadier General Sir H.P.Flashman VC etc or his heirs. I opened it up and inside was a letter, addressed to me, and with it a thick manuscript. I opened the letter.

Harry,

I know you will be reading this as those whose task it is to deliver it are the most trustworthy men you will ever meet. I say this as one who knows precisely what trust is, and more particularly where its limits are. Here you have my life's work, set down, as far as is possible when one reaches old age, with the utmost concern for the truth. Mark that Harry, everything I have written in these papers is absolutely true. You will find accounts of a life that very few knew of. Those that did are all dead and now that I have joined them in hell, I want you to have it all. What you do with it is your affair. I make no stipulations save one. In here you will find the missing piece of the puzzle created when you were born. You must keep that piece to yourself.

Good hunting
Your old Father,
Harry.

"Good Lord," I said out loud. Truth was I was yet again taken aback by my Father. In the ignorance of youth I had just assumed he was a silly, interfering old buffer that turned up to make speeches and the like having spent his life trying to get himself killed for Queen and Country. Clearly, there was more to him than met the eye. I put the letter to one side and opened the manuscript. It looked like a novel and for a moment I thought that was all there was to it. Until I started to read that is.

******

It was unbelievable, utterly unbelievable. This surely could not be my Father; and yet it was. I knew that it was as he said, all true. It was all there. Rugby, Cavalry, Cardigan, India, Kabul, Piper's Fort[52]. Three hours passed before I got up to relieve myself. I had by this time read large parts of the first packet and skimmed through some of the others all the time discovering new depths to my Father's character, new unknown aspects to his life and history as yet unpublished. What I hadn't found was the missing piece to the puzzle. I assumed it was in one of the manuscripts

---

[52] This must refer to the first published account of the General's exploits entitled 'Flashman'.

173

that I hadn't read. I would have to go through them systematically to find it and judging by what I had read already it wasn't going to be particularly obvious what the answer was and, I guessed, it would only make sense to me. That would have to wait then, as there were eighteen manuscripts of similar size as well as a few miscellaneous smaller bundles of notes.[53] I was about to return them to the safe for the moment when having glanced inside to make sure there was nothing else in there I noticed a box hiding at the back. It was a plain black box with a simple catch on it. I pushed the catch and it sprung open. I lifted the lid and there, nestling in a bed of straw was the largest diamond I had ever seen. I hadn't actually seen that many of course, but this one was like a small egg. I picked it up and held it up to the light. It sparkled and sprayed beams of light on the walls as I turned it over in my hand. I could only guess at what it must be worth. I could also only guess at how my Father had come across it, but something told me the answer was in his papers. I replaced it in its box.

I had a thousand questions racing round my head, but the only person capable of answering them was dead. I sat down again and tried to order my thoughts. The door opened and the Colonel appeared.

---

[53] There are only ten of Flashman's manuscripts in publication as well as a collection of shorter tales, which may be the notes he mentions. What has become of the other texts is unknown.

"I hope you found them interesting." He paused as though for some dramatic effect. "My real name is Sinclair. I knew your Father in Africa." It meant nothing to me but I supposed from the way he had said his real name that it should have done. I kept mum. He turned round abruptly and made for the door.

"Cumming is waiting. Then you must join your squadron."

I assumed this was my cue to leave. "What about my Father's papers?" I asked innocently.

"What about them? They're perfectly safe where they are. You can get them at any time."

"I wanted to take some away now to read."

"Fine. We will be coming back anyway so you can get them then. I just wouldn't leave them lying about." With this, he stalked out of the door. Clearly, he knew more about the contents than I did. I wondered if he also knew about the box. Surely, curiosity would have enticed him to open the box as well. On the other hand, I was judging him by my own standards. Perhaps he hadn't looked at all. I followed him out of the door and down the same stairs that we had come up. Through the unmarked door and we were suddenly out in the Strand.

"This way," the Colonel muttered. "Walking."

We headed towards Nelson standing atop his column and through the square towards Admiralty arch. Before the arch, we turned into Whitehall and continued down towards Parliament. Abruptly we stopped for a moment while the Colonel rummaged for something in his pocket. Then we continued briefly before stopping again in front of a nondescript door. The Colonel slipped the key that he had found into the lock. We entered a dingy corridor that had seen better days. I followed him round a couple of corners up some stairs and within moments, I was utterly lost. There were few lights on and it seemed that we were in fact underground despite an almost continual climb. The Colonel had fallen silent again. I trudged on wondering if this was part of their silly test and if I wanted to be judged a man of spirit and then we were in a brightly lit office with no windows and a woman sitting behind a desk. Without a word, she pressed a button and then carried on working. The Colonel turned to a blank wall and stared at it. There was a creaking sound from somewhere and then I nearly had a fit as the wall suddenly opened to reveal some more stairs. I followed the Colonel into another office that contained a large desk, a row of telephones, heaps of paper and numerous naval models.[54]

"Cumming," he said. "Had a chinwag after the Sarajevo business. Sure you remember."

"Yes Sir, I remember it well."

---

[54] Cumming's main office during the war was situated at 2, Whitehall Court, otherwise known as the Liberator Building. He also had offices in Watergate House near the Strand. Flashman's description of Cumming's office is essentially correct. Major Stephen Alley, one of his agents added that the air of mystery in the office was destroyed by Cumming's secretary occasionally appearing through a hole in the floor.

"Glad you could join us again," he said as if I had some choice in the matter. "I am sure you realise that this war is being fought on many fronts, not just the one you have seen, some more successful than others. We fight our little war behind the fronts." He paused for a moment while this sank in. "Ours, and theirs. We would like you to help us. I know I asked you that question before but to be honest at the time we had little idea of what use you could be to us. It was entirely possible that you would not even survive your training." Nice, I thought. "Now is a different story of course. You could be of immense value to us." He stopped speaking and stared at me. The situation seemed to require a reply.

"That is utter balls, but I assume you are not going to tell me the real reason I am here, so I will have to accept it for the moment." Keep them guessing was one of my many mottoes. Rather unexpectedly, they laughed loudly, Cumming to the point where tears formed in his eyes. I hadn't actually meant it to be funny.

"Well Captain Flashman," Cumming said when he had recovered his composure, "you really are just the thing." I had no idea what he meant but decided that no further comment was necessary. "You will work for us then. There is no need to tell your Commanding Officer. Our authority is significantly more elevated and instruction for you will come from on high. He will be told only what is necessary. I suggest you join your squadron. I am sure you will be able to give them a plausible excuse for being late, if

indeed you are late. Goodbye for the moment."
With that, our interview ended. I followed the
Colonel out of the office and through the maze
back to Whitehall. We turned towards Nelson and
walked back to the Savoy. We entered via the
same staircase and only once I was back in the
room did the tension that had grown on me
unnoticed dissipate, helped by a stiff whisky. The
Colonel disappeared for an hour in which time I
fell asleep. The door opening again woke me and
the Colonel came in carrying my uniform.

"Clean now," he said. "Car outside when you
want it. Safe is open to take what you want with
you. Anything you leave here will be safe, and
you can use this room anytime you require it.
Here is the key for the staircase door. Our friend
here is in charge of the safe." He turned on his
heel and went out. I pondered what to do now. I
had no intention of joining my squadron tonight
even if there had been a way to get there. I
ordered some dinner, read some more of my
Father's enlightening stories although I still
hadn't found what he was referring to in his letter,
then retired. I supposed I would actually have to
set off in the morning or there would be a warrant
out for my arrest. Plenty of time to worry about
that then. For now, sleep in the deep luxurious
bed, while some other poor bugger was fighting
the bloody war.

******

178

Morning came all too quickly. At least it was followed by breakfast. I wondered what my old friend Moore would have made of it if he could have seen it. He probably didn't even imagine it was possible, assuming he hadn't been blown to fragments just yet. I ate my fill once again and then made use of the car. I took some of my Father's manuscripts with me as the more I read, the more fascinated I became. The journey to Hounslow Heath was as dull as it could possibly be. Everything seemed to be drab, including the women, as though the war had declared that no gaiety was allowed. We arrived, the driver disappeared without so much as a nod and I stared at the gate leading into the field. This muddy hole was apparently going to be home for the foreseeable future. I sauntered in amid the familiar noises of an aerodrome, the crack of engines starting, the tinkling noise as they cooled, fitters and riggers hammering everything they could find and armourers stripping and testing all the available weapons. No one seemed in the slightest bit interested in what I was doing there until I came across the great man himself.

"What the devil are you doing here?" he enquired.

"I understand I have been posted to your squadron Sir," I replied in a crawling tone fit for someone who had shot down three huns in one evening and also apparently destroyed a Fokker thus earning himself a VC.[55]

---

[55] Lanoe Hawker's was the first VC awarded for valour in the air, but Flashman is wrong when he suggests it was for

"You must be Flashman. Yes, heard you were on the way. You can take 'A' Flight. Not that there is much to do at the moment as we only have a few old boneshakers fit for the knackers yard if truth be told. Possibly going to give us the night flying. Shoot down the odd zeppelin what?" he said and roared with laughter in a slightly hysterical fashion, which was a little disturbing.

"Of course Sir," I said joining in the merriment.

"New pilots are all very green. Need to train them from scratch shouldn't wonder, especially when we get this DH2. Unstable beast. Needs flying properly. Adjutant's in the mess. Over there," he said, pointing. "Tell him you've arrived."

I ambled off to find him. As I walked up the steps to the mess, I heard a very worrying noise.

"Would ye believe that nye. Cash. Where am Oi going tae get cash? Flashman, ye tell this bluidy man moy credit is as good as... well as yours nye."

"Aye," I said. "It's only when you come to pay for it it's bloody useless. Two large whiskies man."

O'Connell. Yet again.

"I see you're not dead then."

---

the destruction of the Fokker, which nevertheless was probably the first shot down in combat. It was in fact awarded for the triple destruction in one evening. At this time, Hawker was 24 and like so many very young for such enormous responsibility.

"Me. No. Boche'll never kill me. This moight though," he said finishing his drink and ordering another. "What ye doin' here then Flash?"

"Posted. Flight Commander apparently. You?"

"Same. Nivver done it before."

"No, nor have I. Any idea what we are supposed to do?"

"No. Oi expect Hawker will tell us. At least Oi hope so. Supposed to be seeing the adjutant."

"Yes. Perhaps he will come and see us as we are apparently in charge of things."

With a masterly sense of timing, the adjutant appeared.

"Flashman and O'Connell. I should have known of course. MacDonald."

We shook hands and I for one noticed he was wearing wings along with a DSO ribbon. He noticed the glance and immediately explained.

"Och, I don't fly any more. On account of having only one leg," he said. I couldn't help but glance down to where his foot should have been and found it was as he said and he was missing a leg. How much of it was hard to tell but he walked with a stick.

"What happened?" I found myself saying.

"Not much really. Came over with the boss in '14. Had a slap at the boche straightaway. Didn't last long though. Shot down after two weeks. Dragged my machine back over our lines and landed in a shell hole. Silly really. Thought I would have seen it. Mangled the old dancers in the rudder bar. Sawbones

181

had to chop me out before the damn thing caught fire I suppose. I didn't notice at the time as I was out cold. Lucky really." He tailed off. Well if he thought that was lucky I for one didn't.

"What do we do now then? Never been a flight commander."

"No idea, old boy. Never done it myself either. Suppose one just leads from the front. Lanoe's the chap to ask," he replied. That was a lot of help. We carried on propping up the bar. Slowly but surely a succession of boys came in and occupied all the seats. I was beginning to wonder who they were when one of them approached and introduced himself.

"Rutherford, Sir. I believe I am in your flight." Light seeped through the fog of whisky and I realised the schoolboys filling the room were the squadron. Not one of them looked as if they should have left their classrooms. Some would not have looked out of place in a nursery.

"Flashman. How much flying have you done?"

"Oh, over eleven hours Sir."

"Good God." I couldn't have stopped my exclamation if I'd tried. I glanced at O'Connell and I could see the look of horror in his eyes. It looked as if our job was going to be a challenge of the highest order.

Chapter 14

I definitely did not transfer for this. I hadn't done anything like it for years, but now, as a Flight Commander, I had to show willing and do anything the boys could do. This apparently included getting up early and running around Hounslow Heath. It was true there was nothing else to do. The few aeroplanes we had were in such a poor state of repair it was a miracle any of them had made more than one trip. But then the fitters and riggers were virtually all in France continually repairing the shot up wrecks that returned each day from their adventures over the lines.

I staggered into the mess gasping for breath. Of course, the youngsters breezed in as fresh as the daisies and compared performances. After we had recovered, or more correctly, after two of the flight commanders had recovered, we had breakfast. It was a long drawn out affair as although for once I had a flight planned with one of the better pilots, we had some time to pass, as the intention was to defend the City of London for the evening against the deadly threat of the zeppelins. Hawker had been told that as well as preparing the new pilots of 24 squadron for the realities of fighting he also had to assume some responsibility for defending the Empire's capital city. On paper, this meant command of two of the night flying stations northeast of London. In reality, given the dangers for even experienced men flying at night, it meant desperately trying to bring them up to scratch so that they didn't kill themselves too often. All too often for my liking it meant the Flight Commanders having to go and fly around the city in the dark.

The threat of bombs had sent London into a minor frenzy. Not for eight hundred and fifty years had the Capital been under serious threat and the flying corps were just the chaps to halt the destruction of a few chicken sheds and the odd death. Never mind that across the channel millions of men were continually shooting at each other and occasionally rushing forward to grab a few yards of mud from the opposition, the Empire's Capital must be defended. Someone obviously thought it would look good in the Times if a zeppelin was shot down near London. They were probably right but it seemed a waste of time to me and just a distraction from the real war. Not that I minded as whilst it was unlikely that any of us would be able to shoot down a zeppelin, it was probably even less likely that it would destroy us unless one was foolish enough to fly into it.

Darkness fell slowly but surely and Rutherford and myself were to be found traipsing around the hangar checking on a BE. I was going to fly and Rutherford was going to do the shooting and navigating. I hadn't really decided where to go. I thought we might just get airborne and then head for the Thames estuary in the hopes of being able to see something. We didn't. We saw the moon staring at us, we saw the Thames winding and glittering below us as we flew east, we saw St

Paul's, we saw the spires of the city, we saw Tower Bridge, we even saw the Tower, but for a change we didn't see a German of any kind, let alone fourteen of them sitting together in a zeppelin. After floating around for an hour or so getting colder, we chucked it in and flew back across the city, Rutherford taking note of the landmarks in the hope of finding the right place to land. It had been a total waste of time. That at least wasn't unusual.

We spotted the dome of St Paul's again which confirmed we were heading in the right direction, and shortly afterwards I began to drift down. From some distance away, we saw a signal flare and I headed towards it. The hardest thing now was landing without smashing the machine up. I was wondering how to assess the wind when I realised the flares on the field were smoking enough to provide an accurate indication. We were below a thousand feet as I rolled round to line up with the field and we continued down and down. We flew over the edge of the field and the ground suddenly rushed up to meet us. I fought the instinct for a second or two so that we didn't float and then stall before pulling the nose up and letting her settle. The familiar rumble confirmed we were down and we slowed down before turning around and heading for the hangar.[56] As we scrambled out, I realised that for once, I wasn't soaked in sweat, but then nothing

[56] By late 1916, Hounslow Heath was home to three squadrons and was acquiring permanent hangars and buildings as well as tarmac areas.

particularly terrifying had happened. Rutherford however was beside himself.

"Lord, sir, what a pity we didn't find a hun," he said, all eager for destruction. I didn't say anything and left him to rue the missed opportunity alone.

****

I woke next morning late on. I had been excused running after my night-time exertions and so ambled into the mess for breakfast. O'Connell was still there looking exhausted.

"Hello Flash," he muttered. "Got to go flying soon and teach these boys how to survive a bit longer than a week or two." He wasn't joking. We had spent weeks now trying to bring them up to scratch so that they might survive to do the King's enemies some damage as well as themselves. Already two of them would not be going to France, or anywhere else for that matter, which also meant two less machines to train the others on.

O'Connell wandered off to find his charge for the day. Left alone again, I decided to head into London. My curiosity regarding my Father's papers had not abated but until now I had not had any time to do anything more about it. I had finished those I had brought with me and wanted more.

It didn't take long. To get into London that is. The trains still ran more or less on time and so I dozed my way into Paddington. I then got on the underground, something I hadn't done since I was a boy, and made my way by this and other means back to the side entrance to the Savoy. I let myself in and climbed the stairs. Friend ape was there again. I wondered if he ever rested or went anywhere else. The safe was open and I couldn't help sliding the small box out from the back for another look. I still couldn't believe what was in it. I had just finished the fourth packet of papers that dealt with the Mountain of Light and where it had come from. That was incredible enough and it had finished with my Father throwing it to the Governor General having relieved the Maharaja of it, but there the story ended. There had to be some other explanation for how it came now in a safe in the Savoy but so far, I hadn't found one. Perhaps in one of the manuscripts there would be more information. I held the stone up to the window and let the sun shine onto it. The prismatic effects danced on the wall at the other side of the room. I put it away.

After the time I had spent flitting from one packet to another I had settled on reading them comprehensively. The four that I had taken with me to Hounslow Heath I now swapped for the next instalments. It was quite incredible. The pace of my Father's life defied belief. His fortune and misfortune and the rate at which one was replaced by the other was astounding. It leapt from place to place with a series of barely credible events. From watching Jack Gully thrash Bismarck to the denunciation of Lola Montez on the stage of Her Majesty's to the wedding with the Duchess Irma in the Cathedral at Strackenz, his story was simply unbelievable. And yet it was all true. Once more, I simply could not believe that this was the same Father that I had once considered a rather bumbling old fool who happened to be my Grandfather. I had even listened to his rotten speeches on courage. Yet here he was claiming cowardice beyond even my claim to that virtue. I preferred to think of it as a will to stay alive and my Father clearly had it in abundance.

I was beginning to understand the fascination for India. Not much had changed in over fifty years. One thing was very clear from the first and that was that my Grandmother was not and never had been the only woman in his life. In fact, the occupiers of his bed appeared to be legion. The question beginning to form in my mind was which one of this regiment of admirers was my Mother and how the hell was I supposed to work it out if he didn't tell me straight out. A short glance through some of the other manuscripts had suggested that as one of his potentially numerous by-blows throughout the world, I could be related to any one of many royal families or knocking shop madams. I didn't really care to speculate on which outcome I would prefer, but I still most definitely had a hankering to know. I realised that I was going to have to go back to the beginning and make some notes to keep track of it all, otherwise I would never work it out. Surely, you may ask assuming you are familiar with the career of General Flashman, my Mother wouldn't be this far back in my Father's life? Probably not, but if I

188

was going to pin her down so to speak, I needed every available detail, particularly as this was one of the things my Father was good at. Unfortunately, one of the things he was bad at was putting a date to anything. It could be that he had had a fling with a daughter of a previous conquest later in life. Anything was apparently possible in the life of General Sir Harry Flashman VC etc. The only thing I was now reasonably sure of was that with time I would find the answer.

It was wearing into the afternoon and I realised I had not eaten anything. I sent down for some refreshment and it occurred to me that I was in need of other refreshment as well, something along the lines of Madame d'Alprant. A little shudder passed through me as I recalled my last meeting with her and what in fact I had resolved to do about that little situation. I passed over it knowing there was plenty of time for that when I was sent back to France and moved on to jollier recollections. It put me nicely in the mood and I eventually went in search of a bit of fluff for the night. As I left through the secret entrance, I was hit with the happy notion of popping around to the Haymarket and finding a show of some kind. Shouldn't then be too hard to find some after show entertainment. Appropriately, I took a box in the Haymarket. I forget what was actually on the stage but it was at least something lively calculated to tickle the fancy of the troops it was aimed at. None of them were there of course. Only me.

I think I dozed off or at the very least, I was daydreaming when suddenly a spotlight shone directly into the box. I blinked and held up an arm to deflect the glare. I instinctively got up, wildly looking around for an escape route that didn't exist and almost fell out of the box saving myself on the rail in front of me. As I leaned out, I heard someone on the stage saying "gallant defenders of the skies over this great city, one of the heroic pilots of the Royal Flying Corps, Captain Harry Flashman, grandson of the late General Flashman VC, hero of the Great Mutiny and the Charge of the Light Brigade." Applause filled the theatre although I thought he had overdone it and the audience were rather politely acknowledging the conqueror. I put my hand up to acknowledge it myself and then sat down wondering why and how. Eventually he stopped and the show went on. I was dreaming again, when I thought I heard a tapping at the door. Alert again I listened and there it was. The handle turned as I looked round and the door opened enough to let a shapely figure slide through before closing quietly. The figure then hesitated as if unsure what to do next. I decided to help her along, as I liked the brief glimpse I had had and beckoned her to come over. This she did remaining in the shadows. "I don't know what 'imself would say if 'e knew I was 'ere, but I 'ad to come and tell you."

"Tell me what?" I whispered back.

"'ow proud we all are." She stopped as if embarrassed by what she had just said.

"Well now, that is very kind of you," I said slipping an arm about her waist and gently lowering her into the chair beside me. She wriggled slightly and her breasts brushed against my face as she sat down. From that moment she was not going to get away unsullied. She giggled and muttered something about "ooh you mustn't" as my mouth closed on hers and my hands went to work beneath her costume. There was a brief but unenthusiastic struggle and then she was astride my chair, moaning with pleasure. I had only just managed to get my breeches undone and in the same stroke released the voluptuousness of her bosom which was now caressing my face as I delved deep in all senses of the word. Obviously, this wasn't the first time a conquering hero had been assailed in the box. I wondered whether the whole spotlight thing had been arranged as well. Only briefly though as both the action on the stage and in the box were reaching their respective climaxes. There was a sudden silence and then a tumultuous round of applause rang in my ears mingled with sobs and screams from my companion. At this point, the chair cracked and we subsided onto the floor without a break and completed the business there, not that it took more than a few seconds. The applause was dying away and I was aware that the gasping coming from the box was getting proportionately louder. She seemed quite content on the floor and my appetite now quenched for the present I decided that prudence dictated an early departure. I buttoned my breeches again and straightened out the rest of

191

my uniform as far as possible in the gloom, wished her a goodnight, slapped her backside for good measure and left.

The mob hadn't started to depart yet and so I escaped from the box without further recognition. I considered retiring to the bar but decided I could do without all and sundry telling me what a wonderful chap I was and asking about the zeppelins and when I was going to shoot one down. I found myself outside and drifting towards the Rag and Famish again. There at least I knew I could get drunk in peace. But no, the bloody Colonel was there waiting for me like the grim reaper.

"Job for you," he said in a matter of fact tone as if I was about to be sent to the shop for some eggs. "Cumming said you were just the chap. Wants to see you pronto."

"How did you know I was here?" I said, covering my horror at this news and also instantly suspicious and indeed wondering how on earth they appeared to be aware of my movements all the time.

"My job. I am…. your guardian angel, shall we say. I should have thought you would have realised that by now. At least I am in this country. God knows who it will be in France. Then perhaps you have no need. Depends on how long you expect to stay alive I suppose." By Christ, he was a cheery one and no mistake. "Are you coming?"

"You could at least let a chap finish his burra peg."

Off we went again, threading our way across the square where I looked Nelson squarely in the eye again wondering if he really meant it when he said he "didn't need a bloody blanket as love of his Country kept him warm."

"Ah, Flashman. Just the ticket. Need you to go to France for us. Government are concerned about the losses of pilots and the supremacy of the Fokker. Trying to match it of course, as we can't have the blasted boche beating us in the air all the time. Doesn't look too good don't you know. DH2 on the way of course but those fly chaps in the Ministry are worried it may be out of date already. E1 is quite a different kettle of fish. Need you to get one and bring it back for us to look at and compare. Don't worry old boy, we will square it with Hawker. You can go as his advance guard. Perhaps take someone else with you, at least as far as St Omer."[57] I think the matter of fact way he had said I was to go off and pinch a Fokker from under the Fritzes noses and calmly fly it back for them to look at had elicited an involuntary squawk accompanied by my habitual sign of fear. Apparently, he took this to mean I was worried about what Hawker would think. Nothing was further from my mind. Red faced I stared in disbelief. I didn't have time to say anything before Cumming added, "Of course we naturally thought of you and your talents in this direction. Sarajevo springs to mind, ha ha." The triumph in his voice had to be heard to be believed. What the hell

---

[57] 24 Squadron were posted to France in February 1916 with their DH2s. This dates Flashman's journey early 1916.

crashing a box of string in a field with the brains of my erstwhile companion on my coat had to do with all this God alone knew.

The Colonel now entered the fray with some more helpful advice, suggesting I brush up my German as he thought they probably had instruments in their aeroplanes that were German. This revelation was nearly enough to send me over the edge but instead I screwed up my face in a thoughtful way and muttered something about the right man for the job. They both looked up and I continued. "Of course I would jump at the chance to deal such a blow to the enemy but I was worried about leaving my boys (ha, I was only twenty seven myself!) to the mercy of the Germans midway through their training and the chance of being first to nab a zeppelin and my German was quite rusty. A more experienced man maybe…"

They nearly fell off their chairs.

"What do you mean a more experienced man? You are the most experienced man we have for this kind of thing. Good God man you are ideal for the job. You aren't……" He didn't finish his sentence as he had just stabbed himself in the leg with his knife. I suppose he wanted to see me flinch, but he reckoned without the nerve of a Flashman, especially one who had just discovered that the old bastard had a wooden leg and this was all part of the show.[58] He tailed off and my nerve

---

[58] In October 1914, Cumming lost his lower right leg in a car accident in France that also killed his son, an officer in the Intelligence Corps. He apparently used this technique to

now failing me I took the opportunity to jump in saying, "Of course not, I just wanted to be sure you had the right man. My boys will have Hawker and O'Connell of course." This last with a thoughtful glance to the ceiling to reinforce the idea that it was only my concern for them that made me hesitate. They fell for it anyway.

"Dead to rights old boy. Hawker will look after them never you mind and when you get back, they will be raring to go and give the Germans what for. Right. What else? Ah, yes. Take someone with you. Drop you off and so on. Parachute might be the best way. Have you tried it? Maybe not then," he muttered seeing the aghast look on my face. "Well, up to you I suppose how you get there. When you get to St Omer, speak to Baring. He will help you out. Good luck."

My interview terminated I was shown the door by the Colonel. He had to lead me back through all the passages again as I still had no idea where I was. Finally, he left me outside in Whitehall.

"Good luck," he added as well.

"Sounds like I shall need it," I replied and turned on my heel. I had had enough of their ramblings as though they had arranged for me to get the train to Brighton and I could take my best chum along for the ride. I made my way back to the club and proceeded to get drunk, my original intention you will recall. I had decided to stay

---

weed out unsuitable agents, stabbing himself with either his dividers or a paper knife to see if they flinched.

there and be damned to Hawker for the night. I could explain it all tomorrow.

******

Here I was again. We were climbing above Dover to gain the height necessary to cross the Channel again. I was extremely cross that my sojourn in England had been cut short. I had taken readily to the easy life again, excepting the morning runs of course. Reading my Father's stories was fascinating but that was going to have to take a back seat for the moment. I had considered bringing them with me but the diamond persuaded me not to. The risk of losing them or someone seeing them who shouldn't really was too great. It was infuriating nevertheless. I wanted to know what on earth it was and why it was there. I was deeply fascinated by it all. I suppose that was at least part of my annoyance at finding myself over the channel again. For once in my life, I had a purpose other than pure selfish indulgence. The more I read, the more I thought about it, the more I wanted to solve the problem and here I was being dragged away on a crackpot chase around the sky in the hope I might be able just to acquire an Eindecker. Oh and dicing with death at the same time no doubt.

We turned southeast for the last time and set course across the sea. The sky was cloudless and even at seven thousand feet it was relatively warm. At first the sky and sea were apparently empty. But, as we drifted lower we started to see more aeroplanes making the same crossing, and below us, small dots slowly hardened into ships going both ways, troops going over for their first taste of the trenches and those coming back, either in one piece or more for the not so lucky ones. The least lucky weren't coming back at all of course. At least there was no archie to contend with. It was almost jolly. Rutherford thought it was absolutely top-hole and no mistake and kept exclaiming about if the boche could see all this they would pack up and go home. I didn't reply. I didn't have the heart to disillusion the poor boy on his first day in France. He would find out soon enough what it was really like down below. Then perhaps he would see that any sensible man would not even be contemplating what we were doing.

The crossing was uneventful and we slipped over the French coast unnoticed. I showed him the front lines by way of an excursion, carefully avoiding the chance of being blown to bits by archie and then we landed at St Omer. It was dusk as we stopped the engine and clambered out, looking for sustenance. Fortunately having been here before I knew just the place and we were soon comfortably propping up another bar. I must admit I didn't see the point of searching out Baring that night. There was time enough tomorrow to see to the details of my lunatic mission. I decided to go to bed. At the same time, the bloody artillery opened up. I knew I was back in France all right.

Chapter 15

Baring[59] was a tall, shambling man with penetrating blue eyes. He had the vague air of a schoolteacher and reminded me of James, which put me off straightaway. I had no need to be reminded of Rugby, particularly as it was easy to blame the place indirectly for my current predicament. I had no choice but to see him.

"Flashman," I said, looking him in the eye and hoping he had never heard of me.

"Ah, yes," he replied looking right and left in that ridiculously English way of keeping a secret. If he had tapped his nose and got out a false beard to go with his huge moustache, he could not have told anyone nearby more effectively that something odd was going on. "Follow me," he beckoned. He ludicrously looked past me to make sure the Germans weren't hiding behind a hedge and I equally ludicrously looked over my shoulder to check the same thing. As there was fortunately nobody to be seen, I followed him into the small

---

[59] Wing Commander the Hon. Maurice Baring, fourth son of Lord Revelstoke, born in 1874 into the Baring banking family, educated at Eton and Cambridge, joined the Diplomatic Service before resigning to become a foreign and war correspondent. Scholar, poet, novelist, linguist and unlikely driving force behind the RFC, he was throughout the war Private Secretary to its senior officer, a post held for the majority of the time by the then Colonel Hugh Trenchard. In 1920, Baring published Flying Corps Headquarters, one of very few personal accounts of the RFC in France. It is essential reading for anyone wishing to study the RFC in the Great War.

chateau, along a corridor and into what was presumably his office. The ludicrous conversation we had had outside now continued. He looked left and right again before speaking.

"Between you and me," as if it was going to be between anyone else, "the Fokkers are shooting down far too many of our boys." I was about to make a schoolboy remark about the Fokkers but was dissuaded by the serious look on his face. Humour, particularly of the more banal variety, clearly did not form a part of his day. He continued. "It has to be stopped. Trenchard is clear on that." Well good for bloody Trenchard seeing as it wasn't him who was to do the stopping. "We must have an Eindecker!" Very royal.

He rambled on for some time about the way the Fokkers had been destroying everything with apparently very little to do about it if one happened to be on the receiving end. Hawker had shot one down some time ago and others had followed but so few as to be entirely useless in finding out why our lads didn't stand a chance, particularly as the wreckage was always on the German side or out in no-mans land.

"Perhaps it's the lack of training," I added helpfully. I received a stare that clearly stated that this was not the case, at least not at HQ.

"Parachute is the best way to get you over. It is an excellent means of delivery, much safer than landing and Woodhouse[60] is just the chap for the

---

[60] Presumably Lt Jack Woodhouse DSO who had indeed been specialising in unusual operations for some time. He

job. He will be arriving here tomorrow and weather permitting you will depart tomorrow night."

Well, that was nice. I had thought.... well a number of things really. First of all, that once I got to St Omer an opportunity to get out of this caper would present itself, secondly that perhaps someone else would fortuitously acquire an Eindecker, and thirdly that if anyone suggested going by parachute they would have to find someone else, as I would have resigned my commission. In the event I stood, open mouthed as Baring continued with the hair-raising plan for dropping me into the sky from a coffin like construction on the wing of a BE12a, beneath which would be a parachute that would open automatically as my weight detached it from the aeroplane. Sound incredible? It certainly did to me. It also sounded impossible. And dangerous. And completely barmy. I could take it no longer.

"And what the bloody hell do I do then, assuming I have survived my ride in a coffin, my plunge to the ground and my arrival on it, eh? Eh? What then?"

It was Baring's turn to look open mouthed. He didn't say anything for a moment or two. When he did, it was utter rubbish.

"Coming from anyone else, I would assume they were afraid. But with you I know it is not

---

had dropped numerous secret agents behind the lines as well as spent a considerable amount of time practising flying at night by chasing zeppelins, a highly risky business.

fear, only a thirst to be at the enemy, to stifle their aims and destroy their intent."

Now we were both speechless. Baring recovered first. "Now then, where was I? Ah, yes. Woodhouse. He will be here later. Have to meet him of course. Expert at this sort of thing. He will explain the details. Best at night of course. Don't want to be caught floating down in the daylight do you now, ha ha!"

Ha bloody ha yourself. Stupefied by his response to my outburst, I was still wondering where on earth he got the idea that I wasn't scared out of my wits at the thought of what I was about to receive. On the other hand, it was hardly a reference if he did think I was scared, so perhaps best that way, assuming I lived to tell the tale. Cowardice wasn't a popular state of mind given the present state of affairs.

"Better get down to details I suppose. Not much else to tell you though. Woodhouse will fill you in on the flying side of it. Obviously, you will know how to fly the machine. Really, it is just down to me to tell you where to go to get one. I have a map here…."

And so it went on. Why he thought I would just know how to fly the machine was beyond me. No one had ever seen one of course. Well, apart from over the shoulder whilst under attack and that didn't really count as it didn't generally last long and more often than not one did not live to tell the tale.

"Any questions? No. Good. I will send for you when Woodhouse gets here and leave you two to take it from there. Splendid."

Any questions! Plenty really, most of them impossible to mention. I took my leave and returned to the mess. I sank on my bed in the depths of despair, mainly as there was no getting away from it now. All the way, I had nourished hopes of some other fool solving their problem or a cancellation of the plan or crashing and having a broken arm and having to go home, but it was not to be. Shortly, a maniac would turn up and take me up over the trenches of the western front, and throw me off into the darkness. I formulated a number of useless plans whilst staring at the ceiling, until I really was resigned to dying in a thousand foot fall to the ground. I supposed I would know nothing about it as in the dark I wouldn't be able to see the ground approaching. So far, I had not even considered the possibility of surviving. This illustrates my faith in the parachute.[61] I sat for some time with my head in my hands. I was disturbed with a message that my presence was required on the aerodrome. I made my way to the office indicated to find Baring. This time he was accompanied by a man about my size, dark haired and apparently in the grip of some sort of fever.

---

[61] Parachutes had been used since before the war and had numerous limitations, but with careful use were in fact reliable, something that many balloon observers would attest to.

"Woodhouse," he boomed, "Flashman I take it. Excellent." Clearly, there was no need for me to speak. "Got the old girl all rigged up as usual. Come and take a dekko and I will show you how it works. Fantastically simple. Ha." This as he was leaving the room in his presumably normal state of frenzy. I followed him outside to where a BE12a[62] was sitting quietly in the sun. At first glance it looked much the same as every other BE I had ever seen or flown. Until that is we walked round to the far side where there was indeed a coffin attached to the wing.

"There," he announced loudly. "How about that. Warm as toast. Quite comfortable. Best bit is here though," and with that he crouched down and peered underneath the fuselage. "Parachute goes in here," he said pointing to a bag nailed to the underside, "and the harness is attached to you of course. All automatic. As soon as you jump off your weight pulls the parachute away and it opens by itself and down you go."

He was beaming with pride at this fantastic innovation. He didn't notice the look of horror on my face and nor did Baring as he seemed utterly convinced of the marvel before his eyes. I managed to soften my look to something near the expected gape of incredulity required.

"How many times have you used this successfully?" I asked wanting to puncture the balloon a little.

---

[62] The BE12a was a single seater with a 140hp RAF engine. Woodhouse's aeroplane had the wing root strengthened to carry an agent in a prone position.

"Oh none," he replied cheerily. "Worked with a sand bag though." I pondered this and realised that he neither knew nor cared whether his cargo survived the descent provided he left the aeroplane with the parachute. He was far too impressed with his contraption.

I managed to suppress the urge to run like hell and never come back. "When are we going then?" I asked next.

"Just after dusk. Don't want too many nosey parkers to see us leave. Mum's the word and all that." So much so that we had just stood outside Flying Corps HQ with Woodhouse loudly pronouncing how his contraption worked to all and sundry. Presumably, the HQ was immune to leaks of information. I looked at my watch.

"Better get some tea and my kit then." I stalked off to the mess leaving the two of them discussing the finer points of the suicidal drop into oblivion that I was going to have to make. Neither of them had ever done it of course.

******

I still hadn't decided what on earth to take with me. I had asked for and been refused Baring's map of the lines on both sides as this was too sensitive to be carried about with the chance of it falling into the wrong hands. In the end I settled on a revolver, not that I had any great resolve to shoot my way clear, if necessary, well bowled Sir, here's my bat was more my style, but it could still be useful for threatening the natives although Cumming had assured me they were mostly friendly and would most likely assist me. Presumably, he had been there and asked them all what they thought. Very reassuring. I had almost told him about Madame d'Alprant but decided against that just yet. Her reckoning was some way off, assuming I was around to do it. Some chocolate, money provided by Baring, and a flask of brandy. Oh and a torch and box of matches. I have mentioned that I was used to travelling light but this was bordering on the ridiculous. I wasn't going to ask Woodhouse or Baring any more questions so that would have to do and I at least had had the sense not to spread around exactly what I was doing by asking advice from the locals. Even Rutherford thought it was just some preliminary work to do with the squadron's imminent arrival in France.

I paced around restlessly waiting for evening. I packed and repacked my pockets although that hadn't taken up much of my spare time. Eventually the sun started going down and Woodhouse appeared.

"Ready old boy?" he enquired.

I got up and followed him to the door. It seemed strangely quiet outside for so early in the evening. That was the only real advantage of winter. Fighting after dark was almost as dangerous for the pursuer as the pursued and consequently to be avoided, the occasional adventure over London in the dark notwithstanding. Landing was quite literally a black art and not to be attempted unless absolutely necessary.[63] Exceptions were the complete maniacs of whom Woodhouse was one. We walked over to the BE12 and Woodhouse began checking it over. I waited until he was ready to get aboard before squeezing myself into the box over the wing. The less time spent in this contraption the better. I made myself comfortable. How, I hear you ask? Quite. The familiar chatter with the ground crew resulted in the engine starting and immediately I was engulfed in the wash from the propeller, which got worse as he increased the power to move away. Fortunately, I had foreseen this during my inspection of the machine and I was wrapped in everything I had been able to find. I had even swiped Rutherford's kit as well. He would find out eventually and it seemed like an insurance of a kind knowing I would have to return it. I found the most comfortable position was to rest my head on the wing itself and try to ignore what was going on around me. The experience must have been similar to that of a blind man being taken for a ride. My senses told me we were accelerating and then we were up and climbing away. It was appalling. The feeling of helplessness was almost overwhelming. I was at the mercy of the machine, Woodhouse and God help us if archie saw us and decided to say hello.

---

[63] Night flying was still in its infancy although the problems mostly occurred in attempting to land. Woodhouse, in between his spy dropping exploits, was able to bomb targets at night that were impossible to attack during the day, although he still tried to land after daybreak. The advantages were obvious but it was some time before the problems were adequately solved.

Admittedly this was unlikely it being extremely dark now, but I was prepared to consider any possibilities. As we climbed and time passed I almost grew used to my predicament. The engine note dropped as we levelled off and settled into the crossing of the lines. Woodhouse had at least reassured me a little by telling me that he was going to climb up to about four thousand feet before turning on course so that we wouldn't be spotted straightaway. He was then intending to take me southeast of Ypres and drop me about five miles behind the rear German line, far enough behind for it to be quiet, but not too far from where they kept their aeroplanes. This seemed logical. At least as logical as the whole operation was likely to get. We had scrutinised the map carefully and selected the landing zone. This of course was where in my view logical thought and the operation parted company.

I thought at one point I could see Poperinge and shortly afterwards Ypres itself. In no time at all, I heard the engine note dropping again and felt the beginnings of descent. At the same time, I felt the rising of my gorge as the moment of truth approached. We glided steadily down for an eternity of at least two minutes and then Woodhouse was giving me the signal to go. I have it on good authority that later on in his career Woodhouse was not averse to helping reluctant passengers off his aeroplane. I am not sure quite whether he helped me or not but I had let go of everything attached to the machine when he pulled up. The result was that I slithered backwards cursing him for the swine he was and how could he throw an almost innocent man – me – to his certain death. A few seconds later, I was swinging gently back and forth beneath a C.G.Spencer parachute shouting into thin air. I heard the engine pick up again and although I couldn't see him had the impression he was turning back to a nice warm mess at St Omer. The realisation that I was alive for the moment was something of a relief. As my senses recovered from the ordeal so far, I suddenly felt what sailors call the loom of the land. I looked down but couldn't see a thing. I just had time to bend my knees as Woodhouse had said when the loom became reality and I hit the ground with an enormous thump. I must have knocked myself out briefly as I came round with a splitting headache, but fortunately, after gently flexing each limb nothing appeared to be broken. I removed the harness and rolled up the parachute itself. Having done this I realised that I had no way of getting rid of the damned thing and nothing with which to bury it. I couldn't leave it behind, as that would be a sure way of announcing my arrival to all and sundry. I didn't want to take it with me, as that would not help my cover story of a shot down pilot wandering the countryside trying to get home. I had decided on this aspect as no one else seemed to have thought about it at all and the prospect of being shot as a spy did not appeal. I considered burning it but having decided a fire was probably a good way to bring down the local constabulary I rejected this plan as well. I was going to have to carry it and hope to find some way of disposing of it later.

My next consideration was exactly where I was. My eyes had grown accustomed to the dark but that had revealed nothing except that I was apparently in the middle of a large field whose edges were indistinguishable. Furtively looking around me, I set off. I had no idea in what direction I was going, as there was nothing with which to navigate. I had not brought a compass as this was also an unlikely accompaniment for a downed aviator and instead I was going to rely on the sun and divine inspiration. Without a map, I would need it. I reached what I took to be the edge of my field and found bushes and trees and generally thick undergrowth. I pushed my way as far in as I could and hollowed out a space where I could at least lie down. I was sweating profusely with the effort and the general tension but at last, I managed it. Lying on the ground curled up around the stems of whatever bushes were above me I fast began to cool down again. Soon I was thanking my stars I had brought the 'chute along with me as it made a very convenient blanket. I spread it over me and possibly with the reaction setting in went to sleep.

I woke to the sounds of rustling nearby. Frozen in fear I daren't move. I still had the blasted parachute, which hardly looked innocent, and somehow in my sleep I had managed to wrap it around myself thus restricting the view. I listened, as the rustling got nearer. Then I heard little snuffling sounds as well and realised it was some sort of animal that was going to get an almighty fright when it discovered what I was. Unintentionally I moved. The rustling stopped for a moment or two, and then I heard the sound of a hasty retreat. Quietly I now fought my way out of my shroud and peered around. It was dawn, light enough to see but still quite dark in my refuge. I crawled back to the edge of the undergrowth and peered into the winter morning gloom. It was not very encouraging. At least I didn't appear to be in the middle of a boche position, which would have been somewhat of an embarrassment. I sat still for about half an hour to make sure I was alone. I had some of my chocolate to quell the pangs of hunger that had replaced those of fear and considered my next move. Everything really relied on my finding an aerodrome nearby. My difficulty was going to be finding the aforementioned in the first place. I could tell roughly which way was north and so on simply by looking at the sun. Which way to go was another problem. I supposed it didn't really matter. At some point, I was going to have to ask the locals if they could help and the first thing to ask was where I was exactly in the desperate hope that Woodhouse had managed to drop me somewhere near the arranged point. If he had then life would at least be a little simpler. I scrambled back under my bushes and, deciding that wherever this was seemed an unlikely place for the Germans to visit in the foreseeable future, did my best to conceal the parachute. It had seemed pitifully small when I was trying to sleep under it but since I had fought my way out of it, it seemed to have doubled in size. One final boot and I scrambled out again, took a good look around me and decided to go north. There was no reason for this apart from a gut instinct and more cover.

The sun climbed higher in the sky and even with the temperature low as befitted autumn I was soon sweating. It was hard to believe that not far away there was a large war on. I could hear distant rumblings of thunder and knew they were the incessant music of the artillery, but apart from that, I could have been out on a Sunday morning stroll. The ludicrous nature of my position made me laugh out loud and then furtively look round to make sure no one had heard. Impossible of course as my only companions were some cows chewing happily in a field. I briefly wondered what they made of it all.

The further I went the less cautious I became, mainly as there was not a thing to be seen. Everywhere was quiet and I was beginning to wonder where Woodhouse had really dropped me and whether it was anywhere useful. I suspected not and as I reflected I thought of him sitting with his feet up in the mess at St Omer, probably telling them about another successful clandestine flight completed. As I was daydreaming along following the hedge, I came upon a road running more or less southeast to northwest. I looked both ways for some time and then decided to follow it northwest which would hopefully bring me into contact with civilisation so I could then get on with my task of escaping with the machine or, if not, then I would eventually find the coast.

Somewhere in between I was rather hoping to find some lunch as I had already missed breakfast and my chocolate supply seemed to be dwindling rapidly to the point of inadequacy.

I turned a corner and there was a village. A tiny, sleepy village. I almost followed my first instinct, which was to arrange for something to eat but decided swiftly that whilst this course of action was highly desirable, having a scout around first for Germans would be sensible. This I did and it became obvious very quickly that the Germans were nowhere to be seen. I therefore followed my initial instinct and walked straight into the village and up to what appeared to be the most important house in the place. This was to be the moment of truth then. The reaction of whoever opened the door would see me either on my way home or possibly running for my life. I hesitated for a moment to allow my nerves to settle, knowing that I had almost certainly been spotted already, and then hammered on the door. Nothing happened for a few minutes but then I heard rustlings inside and then the unmistakeable sounds of bolts sliding back. The door swung open creaking as it did so and there stood a vision of beauty. In an instant, I took in the long black hair, the full red lips, the undoubted hourglass figure with its all-important top hamper and in another instant, my identity changed.

"Enchanté, mademoiselle. Capitaine Gilbert. My aeroplane rather let me down and I had to land in a field last night. I have since slept in a hedge, hence the unpleasant odour assailing your delicate nostrils, and I have walked far."

I left this sentence hanging in the air and dropped my eyes to the ground in submission.

"Mon Capitaine, mon Capitaine. Entrez, entrez."

Now this was promising. I stepped past her into a small room and she glanced around outside and shut the door behind me. I thanked the Lord that the French were so much more sophisticated in these matters. Had I been in England I could have easily seen myself being thrown out onto the street with a stream of accusations following me. Now the question was where exactly do we go from here? I decided to launch immediately into my story which I had prepared earlier but now required some adjustment to take account of my new identity. She showed me a seat and flapped around fetching wine and food, which was altogether welcome. Amongst this activity, and between bites and gulps, I explained how I had been on a raid over the lines when my engine had started to splutter. At this point, I made little spluttering noises at which she laughed coyly. Continuing I told her how I had tried to turn for home but had not made it, the wind being too strong for the little power my engine had left. I had landed my aeroplane in a field in the gathering dark without being spotted by the hated boche and destroyed everything useful but hadn't burnt it, as I didn't want to attract unwanted attention. I had then had to sleep under a bush and now I was filthy and hungry, well not so hungry now that mademoiselle had kindly provided all this wonderful food. Judging my moment, I then explained how I had to get back to my squadron, as they would think I was dead and obviously, I was itching to have another slap at the enemy.

She looked downcast at this news and as I thanked her for her hospitality and made preliminary moves to leave she suddenly leapt from her chair and grasped my arm tightly saying "surely one night would not hurt, tomorrow was another day and rest and a warm bed would help me recuperate so much the better."

I looked blank for a few moments as if I was thinking deeply and then launched on part two of my simple plan that I had formulated on the jildi[64] so to speak.

"Perhaps I should stay. The morning would be better. Do you know...?" I started and then faded away. "No, I shouldn't want to compromise you," I said looking pointedly at my feet.

"How can you possibly compromise me," she retorted.

"Well, when you put it like that. Do you happen to know if there are any German aerodromes near here? And where exactly is here? You see, if there was one, I could save a friend from an appalling job and steal an aeroplane that was shooting down so many of our Countrymen." I explained in some detail, missing out that it was in fact the English who wanted the aeroplane and tailoring the entire story to fit the situation I found myself in.

---

[64] Jildi. From the Hindustani jaldi meaning quickness

"Yes, I think there is," she replied. "I see them," she spat with contempt "flying over here and sometimes they come into the village to buy things, these swaggering Germans who think they rule the World." A fine temper she had on her and I realised I had hit on just the right note in occupied territory. "Come, I will show you the bath."

I sat in the luxury of a warm bath singing away, the Marseillaise seemed appropriate given Mademoiselle's patriotic disposition, helping myself to more of her appalling wine and wondering what the hell Hawker would make of this. And Cumming more to the point. Without realising it I stopped singing to ponder on these and other questions before finally clambering slowly out thoroughly refreshed and wishing I were somewhere more civilised with proper entertainment for exhausted officers.

"Ooh, mon Capitaine," she gasped. I nearly jumped out of my skin when I realised she had come into the room. Her hands were clasped firmly over her mouth and her wide eyes were staring straight at my loins, which were showing appreciative signs that she had clearly noticed.

Carpe diem,[65] that was what Cumming had said at one of our little chats. So I did although I doubted very much that this was what he had intended. At least not in a bath behind the enemy

---

[65] Dum loquimur, fugerit invida Aetas: carpe diem, quam minimum credula postero. Horace: While we're talking, envious time is fleeing: seize the day, put no trust in the future.

lines. Fortunately, she was as enthusiastic as I was and having thoroughly soaked her clothes, we finished the job in her boudoir. Lying exhausted for a moment, I foolishly wondered if I could simply stay indefinitely and forget all about Fokkers and war and such like. Then it occurred to me that her husband was probably at this moment fighting for his life in some hellhole on the Chemin des Dames or Vimy Ridge[66] and that whilst a little Flash 'nuitamment' was something for her to savour, hanging around too long afterwards probably would not be quite so popular with the village hero. Assuming he survived of course.

I awoke alone, still in the same prone position. For a moment, I thought I was back with Madame d'Alprant and that she had somehow found me out. I started to climb out of the bed before remembering that I was somewhere else entirely, with someone else, at which point it dawned on me that I had no idea what her name was. It was becoming something of a habit, but probably a safe one.

"Capitaine Gilbert," a little voice was calling. I briefly looked round for him in my stupor and then swiftly assumed my character again.

---

[66] Like much of the Western Front, Vimy Ridge was fought over again and again, the French coming to grief in late 1915, before the British and Canadian armies took it in 1917. The Chemin des Dames, the road built for the pleasure of the daughters of Louis XV was the scene of numerous costly battles for the British and French and hosted the disastrous offensive in 1917 that precipitated the French mutinies.

"Oui, ma chérie," I replied. Well it didn't hurt.

"I have made you some breakfast." She had as well and there was coffee and the usual display of rubbish that the French believe constitutes a hearty start to the day. And they have the cheek to criticise the English. However, this was not the time to be lecturing them on their many and varied shortcomings and so I tucked in with relish, showered Marie (I had now found out her name) with compliments in between mouthfuls of grease and generally tried to ingratiate myself further. In spite of the food and my thoughts on the location of her husband notwithstanding, I was now busily considering how I could put off leaving for another year or so. The fact that I was in enemy territory seemed an insignificant problem. The more I considered the facts, the more I was determined to stay where I was, perhaps not for a year, but surely another day was acceptable. I just had to find a plausible reason for not leaving immediately. I guessed it was already well into the morning and I still had no idea where I was. With small talk, I managed to make the refreshment last for at least an hour. This was promising as it suggested that Marie was also not in a particular rush to see me out the door. With this in mind, I ventured on the subject of our location.

"Oh la la, mon Capitaine. You must not rush off so fast. You still need a rest before you can return to the war." Now this was more like it. "Come, I have a small favour for you."

Eagerly I followed her through the house to a yard in which stood a pile of metal. I surveyed this with some trepidation as I was clearly about to pay for my breakfast. She smiled at me and I knew that unless the pile of metal deigned to spring into life then all my efforts so far would be wasted. On the other hand, if it did behave itself then perhaps I would be thoroughly rewarded. No further conversation was necessary. I smiled back and set to work praying only that the problem was something obvious. She smiled again and turned on her heel. If only the Colonel could see me now. Perhaps he would have reconsidered my suitability for the job. I wandered aimlessly around the machinery looking for anything vaguely familiar. A faded brass plate stated that it was made by Clayton and Shuttleworth of Lincoln[67] which was vaguely comforting. I peered underneath to see if that helped at all. It did not. I stared at some dials wondering how to get out of this fix. Perhaps all Frenchmen knew how these things worked and this was a test, failure resulting in denunciation to the boche, or her husband. I almost put my head in my hands and cried. Here was I, Harry Flashman, hero of the London theatre, destroyer of German balloons and

---

[67] This suggests that the machine here is a portable engine, widely used in farming in the 19th and early 20th centuries. Clayton and Shuttleworth built their first engine in 1845, subsequently building thousands of portable steam engines both in England and Europe and exporting worldwide. They could be applied to numerous tasks normally being connected via a belt to threshing machines or any similar appliance.

aeroplanes, agent of the Government, staring at a blasted engine of some kind in occupied France without a single idea how to get back to my comfortable bed and decent food and plump women and proper whisky and…. well a thousand other things. If Woodhouse, Baring or any other of my legion of irritants had appeared at that moment I think I would have murdered them with my bare hands.

"Monsieur?"

I jumped out of my skin again. Standing beside me looking up was a boy of about ten. He was clearly wondering what on earth I was doing with his Mother's contraption. There was no doubt about his parentage from where I was standing.

"Hello," I replied with a large grin, trying my best to look innocent. "Gilbert," I said crouching down to his level.

"Edouard." He grinned back. "Are you the pilot?" Clearly well informed, I agreed that I was. "I bet you have killed many of the Germans haven't you," he continued. I admitted that I had destroyed a few of them, fortunately restraining myself from an account of going home to England to get some better aeroplanes. "How come you got shot down then?" The implication that I was a fool was not very well hidden. In a flash of inspiration, I said, "I wasn't shot down. But don't tell your Mother." This in what I imagined to be a conspiratorial whisper. I let him dwell on this for some time in which he suddenly raced around the yard with his arms outstretched before landing back where he had started.

"Why not?" he said once he had come to a halt. I waited for him to complete another circuit.

"It is a secret. A big secret. Everyone must think I was shot down, but really, I crash-landed deliberately. Over there." I pointed vaguely in the direction I had come from the day before.

"But why?" he asked, now properly interested in this strange man.

"Ah," I said, tapping my nose. "If I tell you, you must promise not to tell anyone, even your Mother."

"I won't, I promise I won't, please tell me."

"Well, if you are sure you can be trusted."

"Yes, yes, I can, I can," he pleaded.

"I am a spy. I have come to steal a German aeroplane which is causing the English many problems."

By now, he was goggle-eyed and his mouth had dropped open and left him speechless.

"A.... a spy."

Before he could turn tail, run off and tell his Mother I said "I need your help."

"Me.... help.... you..."

"Yes, that's right." Warming to my task, I continued saying, "you must be an observant boy living here with your Mother and helping her to help us win this war." I didn't mention how she was helping to win it. "You must have seen the Germans flying over and I bet you know where they keep their aeroplanes."

"Yes, yes I do, I do, not far away from here, lots of them with crosses on them, and they have machine guns, and sometimes they wave and I poke my tongue out at them, I hate them."

Well this was just the ticket. He was frantically pointing in what seemed to be north or thereabouts. He took off at that point and for one moment I thought he had cracked completely and my plan, pathetic as it was, was about to take a terminal turn for the worse. Fortunately, it was just another bigger circuit of the yard before returning to me and trying to drag me off to go and steal one of the aeroplanes now before I changed my mind or they disappeared in a puff of smoke or something equally mad.

"No, I have to fix this thing first for your Mother."

"That's easy." He now looked sheepishly at the floor.

"Good," I replied. "Come on then." He didn't move. "What is it?" No answer but more sheepish looks in the direction of a small shed. I jumped up and made off towards the offending building, thoroughly mystified. Edouard immediately followed before darting ahead to go in the door first.

"This is my workshop," he said accompanied by more guilty looks. "I was trying to help Mama after Papa went away." Lying on the bench were clearly pieces of engine, recognisable in that despite being steam driven, many of them were similar to my own favourite RAF1.[68] I silently

---

[68] The RAF1 was the Royal Aircraft Factory designed aero

wished I had paid more attention when we had been looking at the bits and pieces that drove us through the air, and then began picking up the pieces and examining them carefully. Presumably, Edouard had taken them apart and therefore must have an inkling of how they went back together. Between us, surely we could fix the damn thing. I of course had the added incentive of a grateful Marie providing another bath time romp.

"Ah," I murmured. "Um." I doubted a Frenchman would ever say 'um' but Edouard appeared not to notice. I held each piece up in turn to the light, turning it over and over in my hands simultaneously hoping for divine inspiration but none was forthcoming. I tentatively tried to fit two pieces together and was rewarded with exclamations of "Ah, non non," from my diminutive friend. Perhaps he did know, so I handed him the pieces and nodded in an encouraging way. He immediately started to assemble them deftly and I was beginning to wonder why he hadn't done this before to get the damned thing going when we came across the stumbling block. There was a lever or rod, which as far as I could tell should have been attached to one of the pistons, and it was jammed tightly in a small gap where it had no right to be. Edouard pulled at it ineffectually and there was the problem in a nutshell. No one had the strength to free it. He banged it hard on the bench with no

---

engine produced for the BE2. The pre-war shortfall in aero engines was filled by orders from the French and so many BE's had Renault engines.

effect. He hit it with a hammer, something he had tried before no doubt and nothing moved. He offered me the hammer and I waved it away. I assumed my thinking position, thumb firmly in nose. Brute force was not the answer. I examined it carefully, wondering at the same time how it had come to be in this position in the first place. A theory began to form. Somehow, whatever it was attached to had come adrift under tension and in so doing had released it to wedge itself neatly in the available gap.

"Ha, that's it," I announced to no one in particular. Triumphantly I held the offending piece aloft and stared at it again. "Well, at least we know what happened," I said. Edouard nodded and described the day when the machine had stopped with a loud bang, just after Papa went away and how they had no money to fix it and then the Germans had come and he had tried and so had his Mother but all the real men in the village were fighting. I listened and nodded before returning to the job in hand. Leverage was the answer. But how? I needed to get a proper grip on the rod and pull it back in the direction it had come and at the same time hold the body firmly. I began looking around and Edouard helped although he didn't actually have a clue what we were looking for. I went outside and the answer was staring me in the face. The engine itself. How, you may ask? Well, simple really. I remounted the loose pieces and it immediately became obvious. All I needed to do was apply the correct force in the correct direction and bob's your uncle. As I said, it was just a matter of positioning and leverage.

******

I came to staring up into the sky. As my vision cleared, I realised there were two faces staring down into mine. I lay still trying to work out where I was and opened my mouth. It was too late to stop myself asking the question. In English.

The faces staring down now exclaimed as well. I didn't quite catch what they said but whatever it was, it most certainly wasn't a lament for Capitaine Gilbert. My worst fears were realised when I received a couple of slaps around the face. The staring continued. I groaned as the pain in my head asserted itself, and struggled to get up. Immediately I was assisted to my feet and led groggily inside the house to a seat near a fire. I sat down heavily and began trying to make sense of my changed circumstances. Marie was fussing around and suddenly produced some scalding hot coffee.

"What happened?" I said in French, expecting I knew not what.

"You fell and hit your head on the wall and knocked yourself out. At least that is what Edouard tells me. Drink your coffee and I will prepare some dinner."

"Thankyou." What else could I say?

"You are English?" I nearly spat my coffee on my lap. I knew she knew of course but one shouldn't blurt out bad news without a second thought.

"Well, yes, in a way, I am. Flashman. Captain Flashman at your service, Madame."

"And you are a spy?" I looked around for the traitor Edouard.

"Well, in a way."

"Oh, you English are so funny. I don't care. You are my hero tonight. My engine is fixed and we will survive the winter and plant new things for the summer."

"Jolly good," I replied. At that moment, there were mechanical noises from outside followed by a clattering and in came the traitor.

"It works, it works, it works." He looked my way with what I can only describe as awe.

"Marvellous," I added by way of encouragement, still not entirely sure of my position.

"Come, have your dinner."

We all three sat down and ate. It wasn't bad in spite of being smothered in garlic, and having recovered somewhat from the fall I was grateful for food of any kind. We ate in near silence.

"We will help you find your aeroplane," said Marie. "Tomorrow." She got up and cleared the table and Edouard dragged me to his room where we played with some toy soldiers. The Germans, looking suspiciously like Blucher's mob at Waterloo, were positioned on the floor and the heroic French were on the bed, from where they hurled missiles at the Germans until they were all casualties. Not one frog was lost. It was almost as one-sided as the real thing. Finally, Marie came in and Edouard was packed off to bed, much to his annoyance. He shot me a look as I went out which said as clear as a bell that much as he thought I was a decent chap when it came to fixing machinery and shooting Germans, he didn't approve of what he imagined, and I hoped, was about to happen.

Two glasses of red wine were waiting in the kitchen. I drank mine in a gulp, as it was, as I expected, tasteless. Marie sipped hers more politely, as least she did until I decided enough was enough, darted swiftly round the table, caught her up in my arms, stifled her protests with my mouth and deposited her on the bed, where without further ado I popped her assets out, extinguishing the candle with my other hand. This time I used every trick in the book to tease her into a frenzy, and being French and a natural born whore we galloped away for what seemed like hours before I finally collapsed exhausted and more than satisfied with my unmasking as an English spy.

I had clearly made an impression and spent my time wisely since arriving in Marie's house, as in the small hours I was having a wonderful dream in which I was trying to steal the engine in the yard and tow it away with an aeroplane, but the lever in my hand kept swelling up so that I couldn't until I realised that the lever in question was actually in her mouth. This was something I had never tried before that was certainly worth repeating.

Morning came all too swiftly. Breakfast was the same and I found it oddly irritating. Perhaps it was the imminent departure promised the previous evening, maybe the food or possibly the thought of giving up a decent billet just to pinch an aeroplane and save a few lives. I managed to keep my temper in check though. Any outburst of anything other than gratitude could quickly lead to being shoved out the door on my own and I didn't really fancy that option. The time would come of course and it had also crossed my mind that the Germans had occasionally shot those who helped the enemy to escape and the thought of a woman whom I had loved pushing up the daisies so some squarehead could pretend to be a hero didn't bear thinking about. Of course, if it came to her or me, well that was a different kettle of fish altogether. That bridge we could cross if it ever hove into view.

She daintily cleared the table and I collected my belongings. Having used up twenty seconds doing this I was ready. I thought it better to reassume my identity as Gilbert and Edouard laughed. I almost kicked him as it would only take a schoolboy giggle in the wrong place and we would all be in trouble. I had disguised myself a little, as it also seemed wrong to walk about with Marie dressed as an airman, but I also did not relish the thought of being shot as a spy. In fact, I didn't relish going out of the door very much at all. I kept this to myself.

Marie opened the door and stepped out. Edouard followed and then I nonchalantly stumbled out, conscious that the entire village was probably watching. They had nothing else to do in this flea bitten pit. It was bitterly cold suddenly. The sun was still low in the east but at least it was showing its face and it wasn't raining. We walked through the village heading vaguely north, a most unorthodox conspiracy. I could hear Edouard occasionally stifling giggles and receiving reproachful looks from his Mother whilst I tried to keep an eye all around for anything threatening, hide in the shadows and look casual. It wasn't easy, believe me. Several times an animal of some description nearly had me diving through the nearest window, but mostly nothing happened. Not a living soul appeared to disturb our progress.

After about three hours on the Flashman scale and ten minutes on my watch, the buildings started to peter out and fields take their place. About a quarter of a mile past what was apparently the last building in the village, Marie pointed at and then passed through a gap in the hedge. The road had started to sink but now we climbed up onto a footpath that led away from the side of the road into some rough land that was clearly no good for riding horses on. Well not at the charge anyway. We were a silent band now, and I for one was sweating in my part aviator getup. I had to stop and get my breath back and I mentioned this quietly to Marie. She waved me on and I began considering plans for bringing the Mother's meeting to a close. Abruptly she turned off the path, walked into some trees that I had hardly noticed preoccupied with my feet and body temperature as I was, and sat down on a stump. I was surprised to discover that over an hour had passed since we had left the village. I was even more surprised to find that Marie had brought lunch on our ramble in the countryside.

Edouard had run off into the woods with a stinging rebuke not to attract attention ringing in his ears whilst Marie and I tucked into her idea of a sandwich. What the Earl would have made of it God alone knew. I ate it, as I had nothing better to offer, munching away in the silence punctuated by the occasional squawk from Edouard. We finished with some water from a tiny stream, brushed the crumbs away and set off again. All the time we had been heading more or less north but now, we turned more north west. I was beginning to get jumpy again having relaxed when we first left the road. We must be within a few miles of the front and as the thought formulated in my head so I made out the distinct crump of heavy artillery. All three of us flinched. Our pace had noticeably slowed as the afternoon wore on.

Without any warning, we were saying adieu. Marie suddenly started gabbling away, so fast that initially I couldn't keep up to understand, but slowly the thread started to emerge. Apparently if I carried on for about another mile I would trip over an aerodrome, they had aeroplanes, I could steal one from there and then…. at this point the French emotion started to reveal itself. Even Edouard started to blub while I put my hand on his shoulder and entreated him to look after his Mother until his Father returned and more rubbish in a similar vein. What I really wanted to know was how Marie was going to explain my visit to Jean Paul when he returned, assuming he did of course. The entire village must have known what was going on. Maybe they were all at it. French of course.

Swiftly reaching the end of my compassion, I announced that I had to go and they had best bugger off as well before someone heard them. Eternally grateful, send a card at Christmas and whatnot. I grabbed Marie by the shoulders and she looked into my eyes fearfully. I think she thought I was going to shake her. I kissed her full on the lips and lingered long enough to feel a little squirm of the tongue. A picture passed through my mind of the previous waking but it was not possible to repeat the experience right now. I turned on my heel and walked away into the gloom that was descending. I glanced back once and saw them hugging together. Edouard was waving at me. Then I was on my own again. All I had to do now was find the damned aerodrome and then hope the boche had one of what I was looking for, pinch it, fly it home for tea and eternal thanks. Simple really. I briefly considered turning round and eloping with Marie. Very briefly, as she had far too much spirit for me to keep in check. I carried on instead.

My watch said it was nearly four o'clock and it was getting quite dark now. The trees were thinning and I was creeping along all the time looking to stay in cover. The eerie silence was suddenly shattered by an aeroplane right overhead. I dived into the nearest bush fumbling for my revolver. How the hell had they spotted me? Quaking, I slowly peered up and round the bush. In the distance, I could hear the noise of the engine and then it stopped. Some freak of the wind brought laughter into the woods and then I realised how close I was to the aerodrome. The dusk had blended the field into the edge of the woods and I had nearly stumbled straight out onto my intended victims. Once my heart had slowed to a more normal pace I crept out of my hole and crawled to the edge. There, laid out before me was a German aerodrome. I could tell it was German as even in the dark I could see that everything was laid out in nice tidy lines and the aeroplanes were anchored down identically with a three feet gap between wingtips. It would never do in the RFC.

I slunk back into the trees far enough to be entirely out of sight even for the most inquisitive and set about bedding down for the night. I wanted to think through my plan of action so that I at least had a better than even chance of arriving home in one piece.

Chapter 16

Morning came after an uneventful night. I had slept fitfully, whereas I am sure my enemies had slept soundly in their beds. The crump of the artillery had periodically woken me and I cursed all of them on both sides. Stiff and cold I stretched out and breakfasted on the parcel Marie had given me. It was all the food I had and I considered I really only had two nights to make the attempt. In my waking moments, I had crawled up to the edge of the wood and examined the aerodrome hoping for inspiration. Nothing had moved and this was in itself good news. Our aerodromes always seemed to be crawling with extraneous people. The boche did not run their show that way apparently.

I made myself a small hideout from where I could observe the goings on during the day without being seen. I watched and watched and it was all jolly exciting stuff. First of all Hermann came out and he was soon joined by Fritz. They had a chat and wandered about, occasionally pointing at things on their aeroplanes. Others joined them and the story ebbed and flowed with abandon. I still hadn't seen an Eindecker, which was very disconcerting. However, after a small meal with a glass of Chateau Marie et Edouard, the jackpot was well and truly hit. The doors to a large shed opened and a bunch of riggers pushed out the monoplane shape of an E1. After much fussing around it, the squadron hero no doubt clambered into it. Someone swung the prop and it burst into life. He waved the chocks away and off it went. It didn't occur to me at the time but that probably meant the end for someone or other on our side. I waited and watched and dozed off from time to time. It finally returned. The men on the ground filled it with petrol and checked it over and then much to my horror wheeled it back into its shed. There was no way I would be able to get it out of there. I flopped back onto the ground contemplating utter failure and a damned long walk home assuming I could get there at all. I sat up again and stared at the shed until my eyes hurt. The sun was beginning to go down again when I was startled out of my wits by another aeroplane flying right over the top of me and landing in the field. It rolled over towards the shed and stopped. My heart was thumping as I had noticed instantly that this was also an E1 and if they could fit two in that shed, I would eat my hat. If I had one. What mattered now was that they followed what appeared to be normal procedure and filled it with petrol. It seemed like an age before a petrol truck appeared and I breathed a sigh of relief. Why you may well ask. I still had to acquire it from under their noses.

I had instantly decided that tonight was my best chance, providing no lunatic decided to go off flying at night. I buried what little evidence there was of my camp and moved into my forward bush for the last stage. If I was to survive at all I had to pinch the thing then fly it back over our lines in the dark and position myself so that I could find a friendly aerodrome without being shot down by dawn at the very latest. All this had to be timed to perfection so that I didn't run out of petrol in the dark and finish up filling my own crater. Still, one thing at a time old boy. I decided that five o'clock would be a nice time to take off. Half an hour to get over the lines in the dark. An hour or so loafing around and then another half hour to find somewhere suitable to land, preferably St Omer so that I could present the thing direct to the horses mouth.

I tried to sleep but what little I had was punctuated with dreams of disaster and fear of waking up as the sun rose. By four o'clock, I could stand it no longer and even the Flashman instinct pushed me to get on with it.

I stood up slowly, looked all around and then set off down the gentle slope onto the field. There were no lights anywhere near me and so I walked fairly briskly for the first ten minutes or so. The field hadn't seemed so big from my vantage point in the wood, but the dimly lit shapes steadily resolved themselves into buildings and aeroplanes. I was now crouching down low and moving much more slowly. I was trying to keep the E1 I had seen land between me and the light over the door of what was apparently a mess of some kind. Certainly all the pilots had seemed to vanish through the door and not emerge again.

I was surprised when I looked up and found myself virtually beside the beast itself. I froze for a moment, wondering what to do next and straining for any sound at all. Nothing. In a trice, I was beside it on my knees. It seemed very low and very exposed compared to the comforting structures that normally surrounded an aeroplane. Staying on the less exposed side, I stood up and peered into the cockpit. Completely black until I remembered my torch. I slithered stealthily over the side, or at least I did in my imagination. Muffled curses accompanied cracks and bangs as parts of my anatomy made contact with parts of the machine. Eventually I was in the seat with my head poking disconcertingly out of the top. There was a tiny windscreen in front of me and that was it. No rigging to hide in, no upper wing. I pulled the back of my coat over my head and as far forward as possible then switched on my torch. There were more switches and instruments than I was used to but to my immense relief nothing that I couldn't identify. Baring was at least right in that respect. All I had to do now was fly it. And start it of course. But for once in my life, experience in the field turned out to be useful. My tour as prop swinger and dogsbody, attached HM extraordinary mission to Archduke Ferdinand (deceased) now came flooding back to me. My hands seemed to know what to do without a conscious thought. I had just jumped to the ground when the reality of what I was about to do reared its ugly head again. The noise of an engine this early in the morning might disturb someone, maybe even the guards and there had to be some. I paused to collect my thoughts. I had done this before, swinging my own prop but it was tricky and I only had one go once the engine fired. I ran through the sequence of events in my head a couple of times. Finally, I took a deep breath, checked my watch, quarter to five, and heaved on the prop.

It was always a surprise and this was no exception. I stood for a second amazed before hurling myself under the wing and popping up to control the throttle. I grabbed the chock ropes and hurled them out of the way. Instantly the E1 began to move and stumbling against it, I caught my balance and leapt onto the step. Getting in was going to be tricky without upsetting the engine, my greatest fear being the damn thing cutting out, but it didn't. I was seated at last, opened the throttle and drove away from the other aeroplanes. I had no idea what was going on elsewhere. I just assumed that the racket would have woken them up by now and so I careered off trying to give myself enough into wind space to take off. I had no idea how much space I needed but I couldn't go far wrong if I went to the edge of the field.

I turned into wind and opened the throttle slowly, not wanting to strain anything too much. The E1 started to move faster and almost immediately, the tail rose behind me. I held the machine down as we accelerated, faster, faster until I could hold her down no longer and we lifted away. I didn't glance back at all. I had no wish to know what was going on below me. I climbed away at full throttle for a couple of minutes until I was pretty sure I was out of range of any guns on the ground, corrected my course to something north of west and climbed steadily up to what I guessed was about four thousand feet.

The German instruments were much the same as ours, the major difference being the use of metres and kilometres per hour. My only fears now were cloud, petrol and finding somewhere to land without being shot down, preferably on our side of the lines and not in the sea. I needn't have worried. There was hardly any moonlight or cloud but navigation was simple. The two armies stood out easily enough. I hadn't thought to look on my way over, being a little preoccupied, but no mans land was clearly visible, and the muzzle flashes from countless guns kept the night bright, albeit in a kind of hellish maelstrom.

I shone my torch on my watch and then the petrol gauges and decided I had gone far enough. I was well behind our lines now and I fancied I could see the sea in the distance. I flew in a large circle, using up time until there was light enough to see the ground, and then tried to work out where I was. With a jolt, I suddenly realised that the petrol gauge was desperately close to empty. I hadn't much time left but as the light improved I realised I was overhead Merville. There was Hazebrouck, and shortly after that, I saw the familiar field at St Omer. However, it really was starting to lighten now and I decided I was best off on the ground before I ran out of petrol or some over zealous dawn patrol took me for a lost boche and sent me packing. That would be an injustice too far.

I circled around the field and tried to gauge my descent. I really needed to get this right first time as once they were well and truly woken up they might object to a boche aeroplane swooping around and once the shooting started…. well it didn't bear thinking about. I gave myself plenty of room and came in lower than I would normally, and probably faster. I eased the throttle back and slowed down to what I imagined to be about fifty miles an hour. Slipping over the fence, the controls were still responding normally and I sank towards the grass, easing the speed back further until we touched the ground, bumped off briefly and touched again, at which point I cut the throttle completely. I rolled over to HQ and switched off. An open-mouthed sentry simply stared. I jumped down and swaggered over to where he was still looking as if the man in the moon had just arrived and said, "Get that bugger Baring out of bed and tell him I have his new toy."

"Yes sir. Any name sir?"

"Flashman. And I could use a cup of char."

I sat down on the step as my legs suddenly felt like jelly. Just behind the seat of the E1 was a neat row of four holes. Where the fifth and sixth etc were was a mystery I did not care to contemplate too long. I closed my eyes and leaned on the post. There was a clattering behind me and a suppressed exclamation.

"Well done sir, well done." Baring.

"Thankyou. Where's that bloody sentry with my tea?"

"Right here Sir, right here," and he was. Nothing could have been more welcome, unless it had been Marie herself presenting the mug.

"Well, I am off for a sleep if you don't mind."

"Of course, of course." Other spectators were beginning to appear and I decided my best bet was to disappear for a few hours before emerging triumphant as the saviour of the RFC.

******

It was short lived. My triumphal return that is. Trenchard and Baring saw to that. The E1 was spirited away that same day, while I was asleep. When I woke up, I was invited for an interview with the great men themselves. Looking a little more like Captain Flashman again, I ambled into the waiting room. I had hardly sat down when a secretary of some kind ushered me into the presence.

"Well done Flashman. Perhaps get an idea of what we are up against now. Not too done up? Good. Need men like you back at your squadron. 24 was it? Yes. Hawker. Good show."

He shook my hand and returned to the stacks of paper on his desk. All the time Baring had been alternately beaming at God and me. "This way," he said and led me out into another office. "Busy man," he mumbled for want of something intelligent to say. "Yes," I replied. "Very."

"I am sure the mess will find you some lunch. Car whenever you want it to take you back."

"Good. Looking forward to it," I said with just enough insolence to attract a frosty glance. And that was that. Far from a hero's welcome with wine and women and a fast boat back to Blighty, I was going to be plunged straight back into the fray. I sulked in the mess for about an hour. I didn't even feel hungry despite having not had a decent meal for some time. Worst of all, there was no one to take my temper out on. Finally, I left, noisily knocking the furniture around as I did so. The kitchen cat briefly interrupted its wash to examine this spectacle, quickly deciding it was of no interest. I continued sulking in the car.

It was about seventy miles to Bertangles[69] and we arrived at the field in the late afternoon. My spirits had lifted a little at the thought of seeing the maniac again, and he was virtually the first person I saw.

"Tank God ye're back," he said. "Oi've been losing at de cairds and de barman says he wants cash again. Jist takin' moy machine up for a test floight. See ye in a tick."

With that, he wandered off. As I watched him settle into the DH2 that looked for all the world like just another useless contraption and no match for the E1, I wondered how he had managed to get in debt already as they could only have been here a matter of days. He lifted off and climbed away from the field. I watched him for a moment and then went into the squadron office. I emerged again after about ten minutes to see a small clutch of men looking skywards. I glanced up to see a DH2 flying overhead. I looked away my mind

[69] 24 Squadron were based at Bertangles, just north of Amiens, from February 1916 until December the same year.

returning to my own set of problems and carried on past. A collective gasp made me turn round. The DH2 seemed to be motionless. Nothing new in that of course. What I hadn't seen was the manoeuvre that led to that state. I watched for a moment as one wing dropped, and then suddenly it was on its back. It flipped round and for a moment, I thought everything was all right. Almost instantly, it was over again. It started to turn round and round as if it was descending around a vertical pillar. Down and down it came while we all watched transfixed. I clenched my fists tighter and tighter. I had seen plenty of aeroplanes stunting but this was somehow different. I was willing whomever it was to pull up so that we could all laugh at what a fine pilot he was, and it struck me just then. O'Connell was taking up the first DH2 flight in France. It was O'Connell. And he was about to die. I knew it. All our eyes were following the spectacle downwards and there were seconds to go. Apparently in slow motion, the ground drifted up and met the DH2 coming down. It subsided rather than crashed. The wings sank around it and it seemed to stay upright. I was running before it hit the ground. Other people were around me but I hardly knew they were there. The mass arrived at much the same time to find O'Connell sleeping in the seat. However, there was no waking him.

I walked away, back to the mess, shocked by what I had just seen. I couldn't believe the dopey mick was dead. He wouldn't need the cash now anyway.

The evening was a sober affair. Even Hawker with his habitual cheer could not lift the gloom. The loss of a flight commander on the first flight made it that much harder for the boys of the squadron.

It was three or four days before the mood began to lift. Then it happened again. This time an inexperienced pilot was over the field again and got into a spin. I didn't see what happened but it sounded appalling. As he descended faster and faster, the aeroplane caught fire. The pilots who saw what happened said they could see him writhing trying to beat the flames off. The crash was a merciful end. It was almost the end for the fighting spirit of 24 squadron. The pilots were already calling it the spinning incinerator and immediately a reluctance bordering on insubordination became apparent. They had a point really and I agreed in spite of my lofty position. Action was needed and in Hawker, there was a man to provide it. He took a machine up and spent hours spinning and stalling it from all angles. He came down and calmly explained how it was done. He made sure everybody, including me, knew exactly what to do to recover from any of the many available methods of entering a fatal dive. He then invited all of us to take a machine into the air to try it. I had to go first.

My face was burning red in the hereditary Flashman reaction to terror, but I dare not show it. I was shaking like a leaf under my thick clothes and sweating enough to fill a bath. My hands automatically roamed around the cockpit. My head was frozen. The engine started and I began to roll over the grass. Faster until I lifted off and began climbing. I had resolved to go up as high as possible before I started the show. Hawker had privately insisted I perform my antics over the field to inspire confidence. I had wondered how much confidence the sight of another heap of flaming wreckage would inspire and he laughed, telling me what an old cynic I was and how he would stand me a bottle provided I survived, ha ha.

Here I was. Twelve thousand feet above the aerodrome, shivering. I had already put the moment off as long as I dared. It still looked hesitant. I throttled back and pointed the nose upwards. Almost immediately, the controls felt sluggish and then without warning, the left wing dropped away and I was falling out of the sky. I had no idea which way up I was or where the ground was and the bile was rising in my throat. I could see O'Connell and the other poor bastard on fire. I had to get a hold of myself. I couldn't see the altimeter, but I could occasionally see the ground. Finally, I cut the motor. Centralise the rudder and push. I fought the instinct to pull as hard as possible and pushed, bowels dissolving, my streaming eyes virtually shut with terror. Suddenly it stopped. The rotation stopped. I opened my eyes, glancing at the instruments. I was in a steep dive but the speed was manageable and I gently pulled up until I was flying level again. The noise diminished, my muscles relaxed, I was alive. More importantly, it worked and was simple. I did it again. Not for pleasure you understand, but so I could see myself, and so they could all see. See that I could survive, because next time I might not be at twelve thousand and I might have the boche on my tail. Four more times I did it, each time losing less and less height, and recovering quicker. It still brought the pit of my stomach up to visit my throat, but that was a minor problem. I circled round the field and landed. As I dismounted, the other pilots surrounded me. I could sense Hawker in the background, so I got straight to the point.

"Simple," I said. "Just like the Major said. Forget which way up you are, centralise the rudder and push. Forget your instincts and push." The clamour increased for a moment and then suddenly dispersed as they rushed away to try it. The air was filled with the noise of Gnome engines as the entire squadron set off to exorcise the devil. Not long after, the first specks plummeted earthwards and recovered. I think they were enjoying it, God help them.

The mood in the bar that evening was incredible, as though a weight had been lifted. Fear had evaporated. Only war could produce a situation where two men died terrible deaths one day, followed by euphoria and a belief that the cause of them had been solved the next. Of course, we then had a drunken binge and finally the next morning we went back to the serious business of war.

The emphasis had changed since the last time I had flown in France. Trenchard's order in

January had said that all reconnaissance missions over the lines were to be escorted by fighting machines as otherwise, they were too vulnerable to attack and the attrition rate was too high. He had a point. The squadrons were dropping bombs and spotting for the artillery, but on a much bigger scale and the Fokkers had taken to hanging around just inside their own territory and massacring RFC formations trying to penetrate the German lines, largely because our motley collection of aeroplanes, including the so-called fighting machines, were too old, too slow and just not up to the job.

The arrival of the DH2 and FE2b was to redress the balance. At least that was how it appeared to me. I just wasn't sure that the DH2 was actually up to the job given the reputation of the Fokkers, particularly as so far we had lost two without even seeing the bloody Germans. A vivid picture of O'Connell presented itself, just sitting in the cockpit, pegged out. At least he wouldn't have to worry about credit with the barman any more. Credit with a higher authority maybe.

It wasn't long before we were flying all the hours in the day, training for our new offensive and protective role. We had been told we were working up to a big offensive that would surely break through the German line and win the war. All we had to do was float around above and do our bit and it would all be over. The youngsters were all for it. I thought we were all mad and said so. Unfortunately, the Germans refused to comply with the wishes of the high command and decided instead to smash the French army to pieces before lording it over the British and laying claim to being the Masters of Europe. They thought the best place to do this was the ancient fortress of Verdun. On 21st February, much to the consternation of those in charge, the boche roared over the hill and after some vicious fighting, took the first of the fortresses at Douaumont a few days later. For once, the crapauds thought this part of their country was worth saving and Petain, their new chief poured more and more troops into the area. Von Falkenhayn did the same for the Germans. Slowly but surely they edged forward and the forts began to fall. The British were worried. Not only were the frogs being beaten, they had started giving up bits of their line to the British so that we could hold it instead. This of course meant more and more work for the pilots and fatigue started to take hold.

Every available machine was thrown into the fray and every day the RFC were up before dawn, taking the battle to the Germans and desperately attempting to comply with Trenchard's order. This was easier said than done. Even with a fixed rendezvous, it was all too easy to arrive late, miss the BEs we were supposed to escort, float about for a while, cross the lines looking for them, get shot up by the Fokkers then go home for a jolly lark about it all. I felt like I had been in France for years.

One particular skirmish nicely demonstrated what we were up against. Our orders were for two flights to take off at 0700 to meet a squadron of

BE's near Arras. Seven of us arrived at 0720, Winfield having returned with a dud engine. We climbed up to eight thousand feet and circled round looking for a friendly face. There was no sign of anyone let alone an entire squadron of BEs. We flew up and down for about half an hour. I was on the point of giving up and going home. Some flight commanders in this situation attacked anything to hand to claim something useful had been done. Personally, I thought this just stirred up the trenches unnecessarily and my old friend Moore thought so too. I was in the process of attracting the attention of my gaggle of friends when one of them, Rutherford I think, waggled his wings and turned northwest in a dive. I soon saw what he had seen, a flight of assorted stragglers returning over the lines. Behind them and catching up fast was a little gang of Fokkers. I knew we were too far away. Almost immediately, flames appeared from one of ours and it headed for the ground. I couldn't tell whether it was under control or not and I lost it against the trenches. The rest had scattered and were now being followed by the German machines. Another machine, an RE5 I thought, appeared to disintegrate in slow motion and disgorge it's occupants into the air where they plunged to the ground in a manner too terrifying to contemplate. There was another machine on fire and then we arrived. The Fokkers didn't appear to have noticed us until we were on top of them. They suddenly broke off and turned straight towards us, presumably thinking here were some more lambs for the slaughter. I frantically pulled up and over the top of them to give myself some space and try to get behind them out of the way of their guns. The others did whatever came naturally and suddenly it was every man for himself. There were machines everywhere. I seemed to spend most of my time trying to avoid hitting them. I did fire my guns at one point as a Fokker drifted through the sight and had the delight of seeing him jump out of his seat. I didn't do any damage though and lost him in the melee. And then it was over. The Germans were heading east in loose formation above us and we were checking around to see who was still alive. Everyone apparently was, not counting the poor devils in the RE and the other stragglers whose machines were probably now smouldering in no-man's-land. We huddled together and I motioned west, home time. The rest of the flight was uneventful. We all landed and I reported what had happened. Then I went outside, sat in a deck chair, and smoked while the riggers, fitters, and armourers prepared the machines for our next adventure.

God help us. Or at least God help me. The Fokkers had appeared to swarm all around us even though we outnumbered them. We had fired enough ammunition to keep an entire factory busy and yet they had still gone home intact when they were bored with trying to kill us. It was highly disconcerting.

There was nothing to be done about it though. A couple of hours later we were off again protecting another apparently aimless raid. At least we found our charges this time, flew above them over the lines as they slowly drifted towards a railway junction near Bapaume, and proceeded to destroy it. At least for today anyway.

Archie joined us as we returned home and one of the DH2s got a bellyful of splinters but for once, that was the only damage. No empty chairs either.

Arriving at the mess, I flung myself into a chair after a debriefing chat with the adjutant and stared into space. I had neither the energy nor the inclination to do anything else. The youngsters were involved in a game of something or other that seemed to involve shouting loudly at frequent intervals and drinking no doubt. Hawker was shut away in an office somewhere with the other flight commander. That just left me. A new flight commander was due to arrive to replace O'Connell, but the problem was a severe shortage of experienced men. Most of the originals were either dead or already commanding flights or squadrons. Some were back home instructing and Jack Salmond had been sent home with the specific task of reorganising the training schools so that they sent out pilots with a chance of survival and consequently also a chance of damaging the enemy. One other had resigned and become an MP and was now in the Commons haranguing the Government and anyone else who would listen about the shortcomings of the training methods. I think he even called some of the RFC brasshats murderers particularly with reference to the number of fatal accidents in training. He was right of course.[70] The training schools were even ahead of the Fokkers when it came to disposing of pilots.

It was something of a surprise then when Gooding walked through the door, said "Hallo Flash, busy as usual," threw his belongings on the floor and collapsed in a chair.

"What the hell are you doing here?" I replied cheerily.

"Heard you needed some professionals. Sorry to hear about poor O'Connell though."

"Aye, well it was only a matter of time I suppose. He always was a daft bugger. Doesn't owe the barman £4 any more though."

"Suppose not. What's this DH2 like then? Heard it spins of course."

"Aye, it does that very well. One needs to take it up and try it until you get it right."

"That's all very well but how does one extract oneself exactly? The only survivors I have heard of have been lucky and didn't know how they managed it."

---

[70] Noel Pemberton-Billing was an RNAS officer who after a short distinguished career resigned his commission and returned home where he became an MP. He then spoke as an expert on aviation with some authority, suggesting the creation of a single force, attacking the over-ordering of the BE2c claiming the pilots themselves had stigmatised it and suggesting that the RFC itself was murdering quite a number of its officers. It was true at the time that more pilots were being killed in training than at the front although this was already being addressed as Jack Salmond had been sent home to reorganise the training of RFC pilots. Pemberton-Billing's charges resulted in a judicial enquiry that began the process of amalgamation of the two services.

"Simple really, just the last thing one would think of as you span towards the ground." I proceeded to explain the mystery of the spin and how to get out of it if it happened. It still seemed pretty odd to me to push the stick forward when what appeared to be required was to yank the thing out of its mounting. Having done this at length we parted company, he to his quarters and me for a customary drink. I joined the youngsters briefly for a brandy and laughed along as they slated Winfield for leaving them to it twice in one day with a dud engine. Mercilessly they ragged him and constantly referred to feathers and how white they were. Finally, he had had enough and after a brief skirmish, they all divided into two teams and destroyed the place. I kept to one side and refereed, fining all minor misdemeanours with shots of brandy until they ran out of steam and stopped to rest. It didn't last long. Rutherford stood up suddenly and suggested an excursion into Arras. There were plenty of volunteers and without so much as a by your leave we were in the tender and on our way.

It was only eight o'clock but the darkness and the light headed feeling of having drunk too much made it feel much later. More than once, we stopped for some unfortunate to be sick on the side of the road, if you could actually call it that. Having had plenty of practice I was able to keep mine down and instead led them in the singing. After confirming that it was indeed a bloody long way to Tipperary, we moved on to Lilli Marlene who had been transformed from Fritz's sweetheart to a brothel madam who spent much of her time scrubbing the floor and being taken by surprise, much to the amusement of the younger pilots who in their brief time in France, and in their all too brief lives had no idea what a brothel was and what the madam actually did. They were all very willing to find out though. It had struck me many a time that many of these boys would die without ever knowing a woman, even a French one. At long last, the driver pulled up near the Abbey Square[71] and disgorged his now relatively sober but shaken passengers. They piled into the nearest estaminet and a round of drinks appeared. Within ten minutes, they were as raucous as before and attracting the stares of a number of Army officers, a few of whom had staff tabs. I had detached myself from my charges and was making enquiries of Lucille as to where those who wanted to could find some proper entertainment. It was a long shot but I was also curious to find out if she knew the whereabouts of my old friend Madam d'Alprant, but she didn't seem to. I guessed she didn't want any lucrative business disappearing out of the door as she had rightly guessed that I was nominally in charge of the drunken gang who were her most likely customers at the moment.

"Ah, Captain. Your men…." He left it hanging in that stupid English way of assuming that whoever you are talking to has a sixth sense and will be able to work out the rest of your sentence without a word being said.

---

[71] Presumably St Vaast.

"Yes they are," I replied being deliberately obstructive.

"They, well, they are representing the King of course."

"Is he here then?" I countered looking around. He was momentarily flustered.

"What, er, regiment are you?" I had foolishly thought that everyone recognised the uniform of the RFC with its distinctive maternity jacket and forage cap, not that we all wore it. I still wore the insignia of the Bengal Lancers.

"Do you mind? I am negotiating with this young lady." I turned away knowing full well that he would now explode.

"Well Sir, indeed Sir. This is a matter for the provost. Maybe even courts martial. How dare you turn your back on me." He had well and truly boiled over. I turned back to face him. Of course, our little contretemps had gradually attracted the attention of all and sundry and a hush had fallen over the place, broken only by a shout of ecstasy from upstairs. We all pretended we hadn't heard.

"Where, exactly, do you do your fighting?" I asked him. "Upstairs?" My charges roared with laughter, as did a number of the other groups of officers. He was braver than I was really though as he stood his ground despite now being at a moral disadvantage. He huffed and puffed a bit still smarting from the accusation. Not so long ago he would probably have challenged me to a duel. In a flash, I thought of my Father deloping. He tapped his boot with his whip, something I hadn't noticed until now and for a heart stopping

253

moment I thought he was going to slash me with it. Then they would all have been treated to a display of Flashman courage and no mistake.

"South Africa mostly. Boers. Zulus." He turned on his heel muttering disgraceful under his breath. He picked up his drink, finished it and left. I watched him go and then had another drink thrust in my hands while all and sundry slapped me on the back roaring "good show," and the like as in their view I had seen off the red tabbed enemy. In my view, I had just made a red tabbed enemy. I resolved to avoid him at all costs.

The party continued as did the negotiations and slowly but surely the pilots disappeared upstairs for some exercise. When they returned, they all looked flushed and flustered. I had guessed correctly that for most of them this would be a new experience, not having the advantages of a Flashman upbringing. They now carried on where they had left off with the local wine. Most of the other officers had eagerly joined in the games, both upstairs and down. A few hadn't bothered and I guessed they were the older married men who were simply blocking out the horrors of war with drink until they were forced to return to the front. Me? I kept quiet after my incident with the staff colonel, continued my negotiation with Lucille and eventually received what I had been after all along, a romp with the chief trollop on the house.

Chapter 17

More importantly, I had eventually extracted the current whereabouts of Madam d'Alprant. By chance, one of Lucille's girls had only recently changed employer having moved from St Omer and it seemed the d'Alprant operation was still in full swing. She had been a little reluctant to reveal her location on the grounds that I might take my young brood there to get a bit of fluff instead of spending their hard-earned cash in her Café. I reassured her in a number of ways that it was a purely personal matter, vaguely hinting that it might put d'Alprant out of business. Quite how she thought a simple RFC Captain could do this I am not sure. She believed me though. Or at least she wanted to believe me. My dilemma now was what exactly to do? Did I just breeze in, give her a thorough reminder of the qualities of the English lover and then hand her over to the pigs? Would they even believe me if I did that? And how could I explain how I had come about this knowledge. There were altogether too many questions to consider and I decided to put off visiting her until I had come up with a proper coherent plan, one in which I was the unblemished hero and not some fornicating lout.

In between bouts with Lucille, (I was as good as my word knowing that I was on to a good thing) I had to fly as well. Hawker had us at it from early morning until last light, both training and operating as Trenchard was still having forty fits at the losses being inflicted by the Fokkers and he still had too few machines to counter them properly. The success of the E1 had bred the E11 and the E111 and the Germans had finally realised that if they sent them out in large groups or entire squadrons they could massacre any undefended groups of inferior aeroplanes they found. Singletons didn't stand a chance. I thanked the Lord on a daily basis that someone somewhere had seen fit to give me an aeroplane that might be up to the task of fending off the Germans. Perhaps my Father was looking down on me from on high. Perhaps not, given the likelihood of his ascending in the first place.

Slowly but surely we became an efficient fighting squadron. The youngsters learned to survive, something that the unfortunates posted to the BE squadrons often did not have time to do given the desperate inferiority of their machines. Consequently, we had very few evenings with an empty chair to remind us of the frailty of our existence.

The DH2 handled correctly, and once the mysteries of the spinning incinerator were a thing of the past, turned out to be quite a good machine and in fact superior to the E1. We just did not possess anything like enough of them to escort all the raids and spotting and photographic missions being flown over the front. Trenchard was still promising the Army everything and insisting that we keep the initiative and fight in enemy territory. The French meanwhile were presenting the British Commanders with more and more of their line to defend while they carried on feeding troops into the mincing machine at Verdun. Apparently, the pressure for the British to go on the offensive was tremendous with Haig being continually harassed by Joffre and Petain who regaled him with useful statistics like the number of Frenchmen being killed every day and the likely length of time that they could hold out in the remaining forts. It must have made for a cheery time all round. The truth was that Haig was doing all he could. The New Army battalions were coming, but nothing could change the fact that it took time to train infantry to an even barely acceptable level before they could be flung into the campaign. All this of course was going on at some distance from where I was going about my business and no reference was made to my ideas on how to win the war despite my being related to former members of the staff.

I applied for leave. I felt like I had been in the thick of it since the beginning, and the truth was that I was exhausted. Fatigue was a new idea although some of the more original commanders in the RFC had realised how nerve wracking continual flying was and had begun to recognise the signs that someone was near the edge of breaking down and sent them on leave at opportune moments. My leave was granted without question. Gooding was the senior flight commander anyway and Rutherford was able to deputise for me. Being an officer meant I could go home in relative comfort, and as the proud possessor of a house in Berkeley Square that I had now inherited, I actually had somewhere to go.

The journey back was uneventful and tedious with the usual hold-ups along the way. Eventually the train arrived in London and a cab took me the rest of the way.

"Hello Sir, welcome home. Allow me to take those things." I gratefully handed over my valise and greatcoat. "Fire in the library, Sir and cook 'as just this minute set to making some dinner." It was all very civilised and I allowed myself to be pampered and fussed over. I supposed as the new owner that Shadwell and Co had a vested interest. I had collected my thoughts during the interminable journey back as I didn't actually have all that long once the travelling days were discounted. The system was nonsensical of course and made no allowance for where home might be and so if one lived in the wilderness north of London, the chances were that by the time one arrived home it would be nearly time to go back. My plan was therefore to attend on Cumming like the decent chap I was but not until the last day before I was due to return. No point in spoiling my fun straightaway. Mostly though I intended to read my Father's documents and try to find answers to the host of questions he had posed. Oh and I thought I might visit my former Father.[72]

---

[72] Leave rotas were instigated very quickly on the Western Front for officers and men. It was generally assigned in one week blocks although initially at least, no allowance was made for where one lived, which made it virtually pointless for anyone living too far north to attempt to get home. This was soon rectified. When their turn came, men were issued leave warrants that enabled them to get to Calais to catch a leave boat, continuing their journey by train from

The latter being only marginally less disagreeable than an interview with Cumming I decided to get it over and done with.

My half brother seemed distracted when I turned up. The reason turned out to be a relation of my Grandmother's who had appeared and was now staying for the duration. She was a Morrison through and through, with all the grasping, striving desperation to save a penny that that entailed. It pleased me intensely that I was not related to them at all and could treat them with the devil may care attitude I reserved for those who had no hold on me. It infuriated her no end although she never publicly berated me. Clearly it infuriated my brother as well but being the holier than thou prig he was he daren't say anything. Plus he was a relative. I assumed that she didn't know the truth about my parentage and I toyed with telling her just to see if I could make her faint but I couldn't be bothered in the end. My brother didn't mention it at all, as if the subject was now closed forever, but he did actually support me on one occasion. I had just been on the receiving end of a complaint about eating too much as the poor boys doing the fighting didn't get proper meals and I was hardly sympathetic when from the corner of the dinner table a voice

Folkestone to Charing Cross or Victoria. Travelling accommodation was not especially comfortable. Officers travelled in passenger carriages. Men travelled in trucks with the telling label that there was space for forty men or eight horses. The most frequent complaint was that officers got home more often than their men did, and this was certainly true of senior officers and generals.

said, "What do you think he has been doing since the beginning of the war Grizel?"[73] Silence descended.

"Well, I have never heard such impertinence and you a man of the cloth. I shall retire." How my Father put up with it for so long I will never know. On the other hand, my Grandmother, his wife was clearly not like that at all. And old Morrison did appear to provide the money.

After a day and a half of such enjoyment, I took my leave of them all and returned to London. I immediately went to the Savoy, spent a couple of hours making notes on the half dozen manuscripts I had already read and then removed a pile of documents from under the nose of the resident ape and returned to Berkeley Square. He protested, as he knew I was home from the front and I eventually had to promise to return them before I left the country again. He clearly wasn't as stupid as he looked and the more I read the more I realised it was probably prudent to leave them in a much more secure place away from nosy servants anyway.

I hoped to get right through all the remaining manuscripts, especially as I had been forced to temporarily abandon my studies months before to go gallivanting about behind the lines.

There were some obvious non-starters in my notes already. Judy I could probably rule out and Gul Shah's charming lover, Narreeman. Apart from anything, I wasn't part sambo. Duchess Irma

---

[73] Presumably, this is Grizel de Rothschild, General Flashman's youngest sister in law.

was out as she would have been in her late fifties when I was born; the same applied to Mrs Leo Lade who he was squiring at much the same time. Susie Willinck was unlikely and Cassie had been a possible until I discovered she already had a bastard son, the only one mentioned in the papers so far.

As I progressed, so the list of women grew but most went on the definitely not or unlikely list. I dismissed the Russian Valla and her interesting Aunt. I doubted somehow that it was a Chinese concubine or an Indian Rani, but each dismissal left more questions. Most of the scripts referred to events in the forties and fifties and chronicled women who were foreign and even if my Father had impregnated them, would most likely have remained in their own countries. There were some yawning gaps though and I guessed that these would be filled later on. There was one revelation that made me sit up though and that was his encounter with the Austro-Hungarian Emperor in the eighties. I suddenly recalled the reaction of the Archduke when my name was mentioned shortly before his death. It was an odd connection with the past.

I seemed to be getting closer though. His entanglement with Princess Kralta was not long before I was born and she could definitely go on the possibles list. Along with Lily Langtry whose name leapt off the page at me. I felt my heart beat faster as I tried to match up times and places. I had been beginning to think it was a hopeless waste of time.

Langtry.

He had mentioned her to me in passing some years ago, almost with affection. I struggled to remember exactly what he had said but it was buried deep. His time with her didn't quite match up but so far it was the best I had, and the more I read and the more candidates I dismissed, the more it seemed she was the leader. Perhaps one of the unopened packets would shed more light.

******

It was in a peculiar frame of mind that I returned to the Savoy a few days later, carefully inserted the manuscripts back behind their picture frame, took another look at the Koh-I-Noor, shut the door and left. I walked down the Strand to Trafalgar Square and continued into Pall Mall and then to the club. The Colonel was waiting for me as appointed.

"Good show. Cumming impressed. Have a drink boy." He offered me a large whisky, which I took and gulped down.

"Steady on."

I ignored him and ordered another. "Will you join me?" I asked.

"Of course I will. Just don't want to be staggering in on Cumming do we now."

"No. I won't be." I downed the proffered glass.

"How is France?" I looked up, as he had never asked a question of this sort before.

"That depends. You've seen enough to know it isn't a picnic. Boys come and die like men. And sometimes like animals. Probably no different to Waterloo or Balaklava or the Drift. Living in trenches can be appalling. But they get plenty of food, plenty of time at the back, plenty of women available, plenty of beer. What more do they want. I suspect it is hardly worse than some of the seedier parts of London."

"Lice. Never get rid of the buggers. Hate them."

"Yes. Can't say I like them myself. We don't really have that problem in the air, and the messes we live in are somewhat cleaner than the trenches. Not quite living like kings, but then can't have everything, can we?" I replied, with a hint of sarcasm.

"No, I suppose not." He finished his whisky and placed the glass deliberately back on the counter.

We didn't say another word until we were in the Admiralty. Apparently, this was just a temporary home for Cumming's office, but it was still as forbidding as the last time. The man himself was sitting at his desk scribbling away at something. When he saw who it was, he stood up, hobbled round the desk and shook my hand whilst staring straight into my eyes, something I found a trifle unnerving. "Well done," he said at last. "I knew you were the right man for the job. It won't go unnoticed."

He didn't say by whom it wouldn't go unnoticed. I suspected that an awful lot of people wouldn't notice that I had stolen the German's pride and joy from under their noses.

"No sir," I said with a glance at the Colonel who was examining his fingernails.

"I take it you have been on leave?"

"Yes, I am on my way back to France now," I replied in a downcast way, hoping that he was about to invite me to stay and work in London away from the war.

"Well, keep up the good work. Be in touch if we need your talents again, what." He said this with a great grin on his face as if I should be delighted that I might be called upon again to risk my neck in another of their mad schemes. Not for the first time I wondered how I came to be here. "Right, let's get on with it then."

I didn't have time to wonder what 'it' was before Tweedledum and Tweedledee were leading the way through more passages, up and down staircases, through dusty dark rooms past dusty dark and anonymous people until suddenly we stepped through a door into the arch leading from Whitehall into Horse Guards. A Life Guard in his long scarlet greatcoat stared rigidly at us as we made our exit. It seemed fantastic that a cavalryman was here guarding me and only a hundred odd miles away... we hurried past the guard who was entirely unmoved by our departure and climbed into a cab. Briefly, I wondered why we should be getting a cab to the Savoy, but then I supposed Cumming didn't like walking too far.

The cab turned the wrong way down Whitehall and passed Downing Street before skirting round Parliament Square into Great George Street and thence Birdcage Walk. I was still staring blankly at my surroundings when we drove through the Palace gates, the same gates that I had watched my Father drive through, was it only a year and a half before. The next minutes were simply a blur as flunkeys swished delicately around us and dispensed useless advice on how to approach His Majesty and gang. I ignored it having learnt from my Father that none of it actually mattered and the trick was to make him feel like your best friend and confidante.

Doors opened and some other hanger on announced our presence. I was slightly taken aback by the stare from the Prince of Wales whom I had last seen in Dover. Perhaps he was as surprised as I was.

I approached the King who smiled through his beard, halted before him, saluted and then stood more or less at attention.

"So like your Father," he laughed. "He once told us that we should have to keep a weather eye on you." He laughed again.

"He certainly did, Sir." The King's eyebrows moved a fraction skywards as he tried to work out whether or not I meant I agreed or that he had in fact kept an eye on me.

"And how is life in France? David has been across, said it wasn't too bad at all. With the Grenadiers of course." Of course.

"Well, I should say it was pretty terrifying. Frog food and so on. But at least we have something to do to get away from it all. Get up in

265

the sky and find some Germans to take pot-shots at." It was lost on him, but not apparently on Davy who I could see out of the corner of my eye was glaring at me. Eventually after some more witticisms and laughter and finally stabbing me with an MC[74], I retreated to where Cumming was trying hard not to do himself a mischief and the Colonel was trying not to roar with laughter.

"You young pups, no respect at all for your betters." This was Cumming.

"Rubbish," chimed in the Colonel, "he's just treating it the way he treats everything, with contempt." I left them to their discussion of my character flaws and attacked the lunch that had clearly been provided for our consumption, trying to eat as much of my 30d in the pound as I could.[75] My assault was curtailed by the arrival of Prince Davy and his acid tongue. Cumming fortunately engaged him in polite conversation but I knew there would be no escape.

"Ah, Flashman. One's exploits are being well rewarded. Whatever next? It must be difficult for a man of your singular talents to remain on top form. One imagines it is hard for you, ah, gentlemen of the flying corps to avoid all those

---

[74] The Military Cross was instituted in December 1915 for officers of the rank of Captain and below.

[75] Flashman appears to be referring to the income tax rates. The rate of income tax rose from 6% in 1914 to 30% by 1918. Income tax has been used to fund wars since the time of Napoleon. It is annually renewable by act of parliament and a number of Prime Ministers have promised to abolish it entirely, never quite managing to do so as the circumstances at the time have precluded this course of action.

beastly Germans in the air, especially if one has been at it constantly. But then not as hard as it is on the ground of course. Cumming says one has just had some leave and on one's way back to the front. Well, good luck old boy. Keep at it and we will soon have this business over with."

He knew of course that I was unlikely to be rude to him in his own house with Papa presiding over proceedings and so he felt quite safe slating the corps and me, although why he thought I cared what he thought of the corps defeated me. I replied with a barely civil bow and thanked him for his kind words. Sarcasm was lost on him, as it was on the entire German race. That concluded the formalities. As we were leaving, I almost knocked down an attractive woman running through a door. I humbly apologised in my bluff manly fashion reserved for those who may have the pleasure of occupying my bed and she blushed before making off at a slower pace, peeping over her shoulder, her heart beating significantly faster, and not through exertion, I might add.

"Who was that?" I enquired of my fellows.

"Princess Alexandra[76]," replied Cumming. We continued in silence until we were inside another cab.

"Where would you like to go?"

---

[76] Presumably Princess Alexandra, 2nd Duchess of Fife, Granddaughter of Edward VII. Born in 1891, she married Prince Arthur of Connaught in 1913. Photos of her indeed show an attractive young woman. What she was doing in the palace is unknown but she did serve as a nurse at St Mary's Hospital, Paddington during the war.

"Anywhere except the Reform," I replied. They didn't even smile. "Berkeley Square then."

And so another long day in the life of Captain Harry Flashman, RFC late 1st Bengal Lancers, drew to a close. I reflected on my Father's first visit to the Palace, which I had read about only days previously. I was sure he had taken a fancy to the Queen. Quite what she made of him was another matter.

******

Now what? I couldn't put it off any longer as even I could see she would be up to mischief and possibly causing the deaths of our men. The dilemma was how to broach the subject with Cumming. But of course there was no need. I could tell the Colonel and he could pass on the glad tidings, by which time I would be on my way to France. With this more or less happy thought, I tooled round to find him in the club in his usual place. He was a little surprised to see me.

"Thought you'd gone," he growled.

"Something to tell you," I replied using the same tone. "Last time out, I spent a night with a woman called d'Alprant."

"Well bully for you, I don't want to know what you get up to in the night. Might arouse the old jealousy again."

"Eh?" I was speechless for a moment wondering what the devil he meant, but recovered quickly and said "It's not what I get up to in the night you need to worry about. D'Alprant is a madam in St Omer. I suspect thousands of troops have passed through St Omer and a significant number have passed through Madam d'Alprant's door where they have been plied with drink and shown how French women are brought up. When they compare it to their life in the trenches and the possibility of extinction at short notice, I suspect that the unwary are quickly led up the garden path and encouraged to talk about everything they know, information which swiftly travels through the lines and finds its way to her opposite number." Now it was his turn to be speechless. He finally spoke.

"Bloody frogs, useless allies. Always the same. Better off fighting them than the Germans. At least you know where you stand. Grandfather fought the buggers at Trafalgar. Father suffered them as allies in the Crimea. Now here we are again." He actually gnashed his teeth at this point. "Useless, utterly useless. Well what are you standing there for?" Foolishly, I had assumed that he would now convey the news to Cumming but this was not to be.

Here we were again.

"How the devil do you know this woman is passing information on?" spluttered Cumming. My story suddenly seemed awfully thin, which of course it was. Plus I hadn't thought through how I was going to extricate myself from the less glorious aspects, having decided in a rush of blood and in the aftermath of the visit to the Palace just to get on with it.

"I heard her."

"When?"

"A few weeks ago. It didn't occur to me at the time that she was passing on information." Christ it sounded weak.

"Why ever not? How the devil can it not occur to you? Either she is or she isn't. One doesn't hear a woman talking about troops and ships and whatnot and think she is referring to the staff or her latest purchases or, or...." He tailed off in a fury. I thought it best to say nothing further just yet. "What the hell are you going to do about it?"

"Me Sir," I spluttered although why I had for a moment thought I would not be involved I really didn't know.

"You got us into this mess. You can now extricate us." Note how it was now us who were in a mess but it was only me who was to get us out of it. "The sooner you are back in France the better. You had better start watching this d'Alprant woman and find out what is going on. Who do we have as a liaison?" This to the Colonel.

"There is a staff sergeant on Baring's staff, former policeman, totally reliable. Name of Holmes. He is the man."

"Good. Contact him and let him in on the secret." He turned back to me. "Flashman, get out of my office and get this little mess sorted out, or it will be an iron cross in Berlin as your next decoration." He sat down with a thud. I thought he was being a bit high and mighty about it all, but before I could steel myself to say anything, the Colonel dragged me out of the room.

"Don't say a word. He will calm down shortly and then I will be back to reassure him everything is all right. As long as you don't make a balls of it. You won't will you?"

"If you say so. How the hell was I supposed to know? She didn't talk about troops or anything like it. It was just an impression that formed later." He didn't need to know the actual details of the conversation.

"I know that, and soon Cumming will know that. I will go back and remind him why we recruited you in the first place, and give him a better impression of how you found out. Don't worry, your reputation will be intact. I will contact you through Holmes and vice versa. Just find out exactly what she is up to for the moment, and then we will decide what is to be done about her." With that, he turned about and headed back towards the Admiralty, leaving me at the end of the Strand. I continued on towards the Savoy and went up to the room. I wasn't particularly concerned at my reputation as it was unlikely to suffer, at least not where it counted and that wasn't with Cumming. I was more concerned at the chance of my suffering at the hands of Madam d'Alprant. The thought of what she might be capable of left me cold, particularly in the light of some of the more interesting women I had discovered inhabiting my Father's life. I was a rank amateur with the fairer sex compared to him. And why did I have to deal with her? Clearly, they had other people working for them in France, and Holmes sounded a likely lad. He would be far better equipped to solve the problem.

I returned to my other line of research, but I couldn't concentrate and went to bed, helped by some decent whisky. I had to leave the next morning anyway, before the provost arrived with a reminder.

Chapter 18

The scourge was over. It hadn't lasted that long and if it hadn't been for the Germans initially not realising their advantage would have been far worse. As it was, the Fokkers, the first real fighting aeroplanes, had killed numerous crews. My part in it was completely forgotten as some other joker had captured an E1 intact and this was the one used to evaluate it against the DH2 and other machines.[77] By the end of April, its ability to outfight and out fly the RFC had evaporated. More were being shot down and the Germans had relapsed into their previous scared state. I suspected this was only temporary, as they no doubt were dreaming up some new machines with which to attack us.

It was a tremendous relief, to me at least, that the machine I was flying was probably the best available at the time, and having acquired, through no fault of my own I might add, a healthy dose of experience, I felt relatively secure. The flight virtually ran itself, Rutherford was a good deputy and Hawker was a good boss. It was said, though by whom I don't recall, that 24 Squadron had not lost any of its sheep when escorting them over the lines on their spotting missions, though I could vouch personally for some close run things, as the Duke once said. I hadn't actually accounted for any of the enemy but I had been close enough

---

[77] Flashman is correct that another E1 was captured as well as a new E111 that was flown over the lines and landed accidentally at a British airfield.

to be riddled a couple of times. It was highly disturbing. My coward's instinct was useful for spotting the buggers, but that didn't stop my colleagues then going after them like billy-o and a general melee developing. Once this had happened there was little time for anything other than hauling my machine around the sky hoping not to hit anything with it, occasionally letting off a burst in the vain hope of hitting a German. How we didn't shoot each other down I will never know, though truth be told we probably did on many occasions. I doubt anyone would have admitted it at the time.

May drifted into June but it stayed cold.[78] The morning mists were rarer though, and the days lengthened. This meant more flying. The French were still getting a pasting, both on the ground and in the air. Some genius at their GHQ had complained that the troops never saw the Aviation Militaire over the battlefield, only the boche, and that they were consequently being bombed all the time and what a disgrace it was to the Mother Country and more tripe like this. No one stopped to consider whether there was a logical reason for this and slowly but surely the pressure on du Peuty[79] to defend the troops properly mounted.

[78] June 1916 was on average one of the three coldest June's of the century.

[79] Presumably Commandant Paul-Fernand du Peuty. Du Peuty's tactics were similar to Trenchard's in many ways, not least in his insistence on dominating the enemy's air space or he would dominate yours. As always, political pressure required him to bow to the wishes of the Army and concentrate his machines over the French lines. The casualty

Eventually he agreed and at once surrendered the initiative to Boelcke and friends who seized the opportunity to give the French troops a hammering. The good thing about it was it kept them away from us. I mooched up and down the lines north of the Somme for days and weeks on end hardly seeing a German aeroplane. It was almost fun. Very occasionally, we would catch some straggler and destroy him. This reinforced my conviction that luck had put me in the right place to survive.

The natives were getting restless though. Rumour had it that Haig was planning an offensive. The rumour solidified into reality as the build up of troops continued, along with the arrival of more and more artillery. Our orders dropped a very unsubtle hint that German aeroplanes, especially reconnaissance types, were not to be allowed to cross the front line at any time. The build up seemed to go on forever and speculation mounted that this would be the big push to get out in the open again, drive into Germany and finish the war. I could not help but think of the same lunatic optimists who thought it would all be over by Christmas.

We carried on, plodding up and down, up and down searching the skies for the hun and rarely finding him. I took to examining the trenches in

rates climbed steadily as the Germans realised their advantage and bombed and strafed the troops and destroyed equipment and installations, until on his own authority he reverted to his previous plan proving he had been right all along.

some detail, if only to relieve the thorough bore of flying over the same ground again and again. It was clear to me that we were preparing something on a grand scale. The worst of it was that I would no doubt be up to my neck in it.

Something else I was up to my neck in was the problem of Madam d'Alprant. A couple of days of bad weather had meant excursions away from the aerodrome for those who were interested. Many weren't but I was the first in the truck to visit the lines. Hold on though I hear you cry. Flashman heading for the front where the bullets and shells were? Well yes. But not too near. My Father had taught me many useful things. He probably could have taught me many more if I had stopped to listen, but one I had not forgotten was his saying knowledge is power. He didn't mean the rubbish I learnt at school, most of which I had forgotten instantly anyway. He meant useful knowledge. Like the location of artillery batteries, whether they were capable of identifying friendly aeroplanes, how high their shells flew across the lines and so on. So I never lost an opportunity to visit them. It wasn't lost on Hawker either who also encouraged the younger pilots to come with me. He was all for them learning their trade properly, particularly as most of them arrived without the faintest idea of what they were letting themselves in for. Very few had more than ten hours flying to their names when they arrived in France. For far too many of them, their eleventh hour was their last, although the arrivals at 24 squadron had the advantage of both a decent machine and a capable man in charge.

We spent a cheerful enough day touring a reserve area of Fourth Army somewhere northwest of Fonquevillers. We visited a couple of batteries of artillery and a Kitchener battalion of infantry. I couldn't help but think they looked like what in fact they were; civilians sent to war, without much notion of what that entailed. Just like the boys with me really. The Officers seemed cheery enough, and greeted us warmly allowing us to help ourselves to their meagre stores of drink and food. It was all very democratic and a far cry from the Mess of the 1st.

The final treat, and on this occasion my real reason for leading the whole party, was dinner in St Omer. I found the place I was looking for just off the cathedral square. It had seemed a jolly wheeze right up to this point, but now it seemed just a trifle nerve racking. We entered. I was not leading the group and I can't remember who was, but I recognised the voice as she offered us a table near the bar and sent a couple of girls over with wine. I stopped behind her as she watched proceedings and had the pleasure of seeing her nearly jump out of her skin when she turned round to face me. She recovered her composure quickly enough though.

"Ah, Capitaine, so you 'ave come back for to take me away from 'ere?"

"Of course not. I have come to remind you of what you have been missing."

"What would zat be zen, mon chéri?" She coyly looked down at this point avoiding my lascivious leer. I had forgotten quite how wicked she was and the thought of giving her a knee trembler had me panting. Gone were all thoughts of Holmes and his sensible advice about observing from a distance and developing the contact.

"A big dose of Flashy in the night."

She was as desperate as I was but I, even in my heightened state of awareness, wanted to play her along for a moment or two. I needed to be sure I would get invited back. At this, I turned away and sat down at the table, a certain tightness below my waste informing me that the moment had arrived and further delay could only lead to embarrassment.

She couldn't say much now as I joined in with the raucous crowd at the table. The wine had started flowing immediately and already one or two of the real youngsters had flushed faces. Food appeared and was engulfed and I lost count of the bottles as they came and went. The party was in full swing when I slipped out of a back door for some air. I took good care to let d'Alprant see me go whilst appearing not to notice where she was. A few minutes later, the door opened and she appeared, looking around her uncertainly. I immediately stepped up behind her and convinced her I was there. In one swift move, her tits were in my hands as I gripped her from behind. She gasped but there was no effort to get away, so taking this as my cue I pushed her up against a low wall, hauled her skirt up and set to partners without further ado.

When the job was finished, she turned to me, adjusting her attire and said "I 'ope you are intending to pay me for zat," and stalked off.

I stayed where I was for a moment watching the stars and moon, wondering whether I had done a good job, or just made a complete balls of the whole thing. Then I decided that I didn't care very much right now, and Holmes could shove his plan down someone else's throat. I would deal with this my way and be damned to Cumming and the Colonel and co.

I sauntered back in to the dining room. I wasn't surprised to find a couple asleep, a few gaps where some of them had gone off to sample the other available entertainment and the rest pretty well oiled. Rutherford was still there, though judging by the state of his uniform I guessed he had been upstairs and returned already.

"Take the tender when you are ready old boy. I think I will spend the night here. Make my own way back tomorrow."

"Jolly good, Sir." He belched and for a moment I saw the enthusiastic youngster aching to shoot a zeppelin down over London, before he reverted to the hardened battle weary man he had become. I slipped away, arranged to settle the bill with one of the girls and then went upstairs.

She was waiting in her boudoir. Almost immediately I came to attention as the reflection in the mirror showed her ample bosom which was barely covered with a flimsy garment. She got up as I approached and turned to face me. Unable to contain myself any longer, I was disrobing on the run and picked her up on the way to the bed. In seconds, we were pounding away like old times. The climax took longer to arrive on account of our previous exertion but after satisfying her desires again, I rolled over and lit a cheroot I had brought with me for precisely this reason. She didn't particularly like it and pulled a face. I just ignored her. Smoking meant I didn't have to talk, and I wanted her to open the batting on that score.

"Soon you will be dead," she said in a sulky way. Charming I thought.

"What makes you think they can kill me?" I retorted. "They're only a bunch of sausage eaters." Good old English stuff you see, worth two of any foreigner.

"Zey know you are coming. Everyone knows zis."

"Well, I don't."

"Zen you 'ave your eyes shut. Zey will be waiting for you."

"How do you know all this anyway? Don't tell me, the Kaiser pops in for a nightcap and a tactical appraisal every night."

"You do not take it seriously, you English. And ze French, pah, zey are fit only for zeir mistresses beds, and zen only so zey can cower underneaf." She spat this last out in utter contempt for her countrymen.

"But what about Verdun?" I asked puzzled. "They aren't beaten there."

"No, not yet, but soon zey will give up. Unless ze English rescue zem."

I suddenly was at a loss as to what to say. Like a simpleton, I had been answering her questions because she was sulking. She had been asking them to collect even small snippets to add to the general picture and I had just helped out without a care in the world. Perhaps Holmes was right. I could picture it all so easily, the sated infantry officer on a break from the grind of the trenches, her moaning in pleasure one minute and then apparently moved by imminent death and destruction, followed by reassurances that all would be well, the British Army would soon show those blasted boche how to fight, oh and where might that be kind sir? I had to get out of here and work out a better plan. In my ignorance, I had been outwitted by a whore. A damned good ride mind you, but still outwitted.

"Well I don't know what they are going to do. Who cares anyway? I just want to stay alive so I can continue with our jolly night entertainment." It was pretty lame I grant you, but I was struggling to think of something to say that would not incriminate anyone, least of all me. She seemed to accept that I was uninterested, at least for the moment. I wondered if I could be brought to the mark for a third time in one evening, and decided that the best course of action would be to suggest Marie's little night time trick.

So I did. It was hard to tell if she enjoyed it as much as I did, but it did confirm one thing, and that was that she was willing to go to some length to keep me in favour.

In the morning, I left early for the long trek back to the Squadron. I arrived to find the place in a bit of a flap. Rutherford cornered me and told me that Hawker was having a squadron briefing in about fifteen minutes and everyone was to be there. Quite a number of the pilots were not in a fit state for much, let alone a briefing from God. He rushed off so I strolled over to the briefing room. A few minutes later, there was a flurry and the great man appeared. Standing in front of the squadron notice board with its large motto 'Attack Everything' staring at us, he began by surveying the room, no doubt taking in the bloodshot eyes and general squalor of his pilots.

"Right, I have just been informed of the latest German success. They have taken the forts at Vaux and Thiaumont and are consequently very close to breaking through the line completely. Should that happen, we are in trouble." He let this sink in for a moment before pointing behind him at the board. "We have to redouble our efforts to try and provide any relief for the French and that means attacking everything. Guns, troops, wherever they are, shoot them up, bomb them, destroy them. Above all, we must shoot down any huns we can find and that means going looking for them and fighting them in their own lines. Starting now. Good day to you all, and good hunting."

He abruptly turned and went out. There was a scramble of sorts to get up and then a general clamour started. I assumed that Hawker would want to see Gooding, Jock and me and so we presented ourselves in his office.

"Glad you have come," he said, as though we had been invited to the village fete. "Trenchard is quite explicit in his orders. We are to fly as much as possible and shoot up anything that moves. No German is to be allowed to cross the lines, and if they should, they are to be destroyed before they can return home. Jock, take your flight to Bapaume, Gooding, you can take your flight up towards the Somme, Flashman, you can head for Lens. Good luck."

We took off, the warmth of the afternoon sun replaced by the chill of altitude. Still, it was an effective cure for the night's excesses. We climbed to about ten thousand feet, heading east all the time and crossed the lines south of Lens. About five miles behind, we turned north and followed the scar, keeping a weather eye out for boche, but we saw none. As we neared Lens itself, we began descending in a loose formation. The endless blue transfixed me and I fancied, not for the first time, that I could see the North Sea in the distance where the sky merged with the early summer haze. I drifted into daydreams of picnics on the rolling hills of England, drowsy with drink, dozing in the sun with a wicked pair of satisfied trollops on hand for my every need. A loud bang returned me instantly to the present and I craned round looking for the archie, but there was none to be seen. There was a smaller bang and a disturbing clatter as I realised that the noises were a bit closer to home, in fact not three feet behind me. I stared frantically round again looking for my assailant but the sky was empty, apart from my companions who were still gliding serenely downwards, but now seemed to be pulling ahead.

I forced my racing mind to consider things in a more sensible fashion at the same time as the clatter of metal on metal started again. This time it did not stop although it was not as loud now, and I finally realised that the Gnome was not behaving in the approved fashion. I was now dropping back from the formation and my instruments reinforced this view of declining speed. Out of the corner of my eye, I noticed Rutherford had dropped back and was waving furiously. I waved back, signalling that I was all right, but with my innards churning at the thought of a solo voyage home without the benefit of a gang of roughs to escort me in my reduced state. He rejoined the others and suddenly I was in fact on my own, over the lines, with an engine that if not entirely dud, was definitely not at its best.

I turned west, I still had plenty of height, just a question of finding a suitable friendly field and not breaking my neck by landing in a shell hole. I experimented with the throttle and discovered merely that the volume of the clattering increased the more power I applied and vice versa. I found a happy medium that meant the noise wasn't too disturbing and the descent was not too alarming. As my descent was now fairly slow I decided it was possible to get somewhere near home. This would save me an awful lot of bother and I turned more southwesterly back towards Lens initially. It meant being over the lines for longer but in spite of my jolt I was still in a jolly frame of mind, it was sunny and the war seemed a long way off and for the moment at least, I didn't have to take part.

Lens was passing slowly underneath as I drifted inexorably towards the ground. I was now about seven thousand feet above the town and I peered over the side to get a better view.

My sightseeing tour was abruptly interrupted by the sound of bullets passing by. Instinctively I ducked at the same time knowing this was entirely futile and by the time I came up again, I was surrounded by a furious melee of machines. This was not a pretty sight and I was now gibbering with terror at the suddenness of it all. Unable to achieve anything by manoeuvre, I just kept on in my steady glide southwest. I think I had my mouth open. As my mind dragged itself from its state of lethargy, I began to identify those around me. There appeared to be about a thousand Fokkers and two FEs. And me. As I looked around, I noticed the owners of the FEs were flinging them around in a desperate struggle to stay alive in the hornets' nest they had found themselves in. The Fokkers were trying to catch them by equally frantic flying and actually appeared to be getting in each other's way more than anything. In amongst this demented aerial dance I realised that if they wanted to the Fokkers would finish me off in seconds if they stopped to think about it, as my engine would be very unlikely to outperform them in its current state. I continued with my glide, still not knowing what to do or able to do much anyway.

The FEs appeared to be holding their own for the moment and I just prayed that the Fokkers concentrating on them would continue to ignore me. However, it was clear that if they succumbed it wouldn't take long for the boche to find a new adversary. No sooner was the thought in my head than I saw a Fokker out on my starboard wing pull into a steep climb. I watched fascinated as I had heard much about the celebrated Immelmann turn. In no time at all the Fokker was vertical and pulling over the top of a loop, when he suddenly half rolled from his upside down position and turned upright. I was inwardly impressed at this stunting, clearly a perfect example, when the Fokker suddenly stalled, dropped almost vertically downwards and then let fly at the bewildered FE crew. I say it let fly, but I didn't see or hear it. I just saw the result, which was the destruction of the FE. In a few seconds, it had gone from a fighting machine to a tangle of rags and wires with two men engulfed in the whole. It dropped away and I followed it down for a moment. I glanced back to the scrum which was now dropping steadily behind me to see what had become of the German destroyer only to see him pointing straight at me, albeit a few hundred yards away. He was levelling off presumably to look for his next victim and in an instant I realised he had found him.

The bile rose in my throat as I realised at last I was going to have to fight for my life in earnest with my crippled machine.

When terrified, apart from turning red, the Flashman family are generally not slow in making up their minds. I rolled right, hauled the stick back and nearly pushed the rudder bar through the nose. My machine reversed its course and I was all too quickly head on with my adversary. At this point, panic took over and I pulled the trigger letting fly with my Lewis. I could see the tracer arcing away towards the Fokker but descending below it as it lost its impetus. I didn't stop though. I just held on to everything until the gun stopped. I cursed it with every vicious expression I could think of for jamming at such an inopportune moment, not realising of course that it hadn't jammed at all. I had just used up the entire drum of ammunition. I glanced up at my foe weighing which way to go, only to see him pull up in an odd fashion as the last rounds went underneath him. I hauled my machine round again diving at the same time to get some speed back and as I did so it dawned on me that he hadn't seen me until my fire went a bit close. The sun was low behind me, and once I had got past the melee, I was in it and virtually invisible. I had probably given him a bit of a surprise. As I completed my turn now cursing my delay in making myself scarce, I realised that he was now receiving another surprise. As I peered up and behind in the hope that no one was following me, I saw an FE letting fly for all he was worth. Clearly, he had been following him when I had turned towards the Fokker, and his instinctive reaction pulling up had slowed him temporarily and put him nicely in the FEs sights.

The firing stopped and the Fokker continued his shallow dive. He was slowly overtaking me and for a minute or two, we were flying parallel. I didn't get too close as I had no desire to be shot at by the troops who would no doubt let fly at any opportunity, but then his machine started to break up. If he wasn't dead already, he soon would be as the wreckage was now plummeting earthwards. His friends had all scarpered.

I didn't see him hit the ground as I was far too engrossed in my own drama as all my turning and descending had left me without much room for manoeuvre, and I was frantically searching for a suitable landing place that was not pitted with shell holes and also preferably with the home team. Finally, I spotted a track of sorts running east to west through what had once been a farm. I lined myself up, realised I was far too high, 'S' turned like mad to lose some height and finally thumped the machine down more or less on the track and rolled to a stop.

I sat for some time reflecting on the last few minutes. I looked at my watch. A whole twelve minutes had passed since the finish of my tour of Lens. I undid my straps and clambered out. I picked myself up from the mud where I had measured my length, a not infrequent occurrence after prolonged exposure to the cold or the Germans or both in this case. I surveyed my surroundings, looking for anywhere where I might get some sustenance and find some transport home. I set off down the track to the only visible signs of civilisation, stuck my head through what passed for a door to find a couple of soldiers sitting drinking tea. They looked up suspiciously as I entered.

"Can we 'elp Sir?" one of them asked between great slurps from his mug.

"Hope so. Just landed my machine on the road outside. Need to contact the squadron and get some transport pronto."

"Well, come to the right place then Sir. Which squadron would you like to speak to?"

By some minor miracle I had walked into the local telephone exchange and the two Corporals of Ally Sloper's Cavalry[80] running it passed on my message immediately. They also whistled up some gunfire and before long, I was regaling them with my exploits of the afternoon.

"We thought something was up. Sergeant went up the road to see a Fritz what crashed not long ago. You could catch 'im up."

I finished my tea and decided to do just that. I don't know why. Morbid fascination with my adversaries I suppose. I had plenty of time. It would be hours before the tender arrived to carry me back.

---

[80] Ally Sloper's Cavalry was the nickname for the Army Service Corps. Created in 1873 by C.H.Ross under the name of Judy's Office Boy, Ally was a wide boy with a big nose and sloping forehead.

They pointed me in the right direction and I hadn't gone far when I saw the rising smoke that probably indicated the scene of the German's demise. As I approached the smouldering wreckage, I could see a motley crowd of onlookers. I could hear the laughter and the ribald remarks and see the pointing and crowing over the dead German. I suppose that this scene should have disgusted me, and as an officer and a gentleman, I should have dispersed the mob and arrested the more unruly, but I didn't. I examined the wreckage in front of the now hushed mob, noted the numerous bullet holes around the tailplane and the control wires and supports all shot through, looked in the cockpit at the lifeless figure, hard to tell what had finished him off, walked away and said "serves the bugger right."

The mob agreed. It was something of a novelty to see a crashed aeroplane containing its owner and they rightly had little sympathy with someone who not long before had been trying to kill them or their friends. There was no animosity, just a cavalier disregard for the niceties of life during total war. It was no different to the soldiers shaking the hand of the corpse buried in the side of a trench.

"Did you get 'im Sir," asked one of the men.

"Not really. Might have helped a bit though. Certainly made him jump with my Lewis." I did nothing of the sort. It wasn't the Eindecker that I had tangled with briefly, but some other biplane. I didn't hang around but returned to wait for the tender.

******

Hours later, I arrived in the Mess. A bone shaking ride had left me severely out of sorts and desperately hungry. I stalked in looking for trouble. The mess was full but very quiet. The atmosphere was odd, and I was wondering who was dead. For a minute, I thought it was Hawker, or Gooding, or an entire flight but a quick check round assured me that this was not the case.

"Ah, Flashman," Hawker said. "Heard the news old boy?"

"It would appear not. Have we lost the war?" A brief titter faded into silence again.

"Not as serious as that. Immelmann is dead. Shot down over Lens. FE got him. Probably get a cross out of it." It took some time for the implications of this to sink in. My face turned white and I had to lean on the bar.

"Did you see anything? You were near Lens when Rutherford last saw you."

"I did. I saw him head on." There was a collective gasp and there was nothing for it but to tell them the whole tale. I told it as only a Flashman could, with plenty of pauses and wondering statements like "so that was Immelmann" thrown in for good measure. I played my part down so well that I left them thinking I had outfought him with a dud engine only to have the glory stolen by a damned FE from 25 Squadron, a pilot whom I praised as magnificent. We finished by toasting the mighty fallen, more or less including those that were partly fallen in the process, like myself.

The German's didn't like it one bit. Their own fault of course. They had made him out to be some sort of flying Charlemagne and so his demise had left them with some explaining to do. Before long, a story had crossed the lines that he hadn't been shot down at all, his interrupter gear had failed and he had shot his own propeller off and this must be true as no English pilot was good enough to beat the great Immelmann. Well I was there, and he was beaten fair and square because he didn't see me in the sun and when he did, he made a mistake that the FE pilot was good enough to exploit. So there. The Germans didn't believe it either as within a few days Boelcke had been withdrawn from the scrap although we didn't know this at the time. Presumably, they were worried he was going to shoot himself down too.

Chapter 19

"I wish those blasted guns would stop for a moment," shouted Rutherford. "I can hardly think."

"Good God man, I can hardly hear them," replied Hawker appearing from the office door.

"Just thank God you aren't firing them," I added.

"And that you aren't on the receiving end," Hawker continued.

Rutherford looked crestfallen.

"And when they do stop...." I let this statement hang in the air for someone else to continue, but no one did. Not that it needed saying. We were all exhausted from virtually continuous flying over the lines, bombing or shooting up the troops, occasionally attacking a German aeroplane although they were still few and far between and spotting of all kinds, spotting them and spotting the results of our bombardment. Then the fog came down.

On the first day, it was confidently assumed that it would lift and before long, we would be off for another dose of terror, but as midday came and went, we realised that we were staying on the ground. The second day was the same and I approached Hawker with a proposition for disappearing into Arras. I tried to sell it as an educational visit, which of course it was, just not related to the current subject. He refused point blank. He didn't enlighten me beyond a raised eyebrow, which I guessed was meant to say something was up. Now terrified with the thought of what was to come, I prayed constantly for fog. I was rewarded with another two days of pea soup, which I spent hanging around the aerodrome, occasionally chatting with my crew to make sure my machine was at its best in case I had to go, but more often than not cringing in my bunk wondering what on earth we were in for. A raised eyebrow from a man like Hawker meant that even he thought our chances of survival were limited.

The guns continued throughout with hardly a pause, and as I waited, my train of thought modified itself, thinking about the destruction being wrought on the German side. From here, it wasn't far to a situation where the German lines were so badly destroyed that the sight of the combined might of the British Army with the gallant RFC overhead had the survivors running for their lives as we triumphantly took over with hardly a shot fired. I guess that this is what the optimists on the General Staff thought as well.

"It's lifting," Rutherford said from his seat in the mess. I peered round to see that he was right. The mist was thinning and the setting sun was beginning to peep through and I muttered something about getting used to this idleness. At which point Hawker appeared and asked if we wouldn't mind rounding up the troops for a briefing, let's say in ten minutes.

Ten minutes later the entire squadron was sitting ready for their briefing. Hawker came in with a shuffle of chairs and grunts and what not before everything settled down.

"Gentlemen," he began. "I think you have all heard the bombardment that has been going on over the last few days. It is the preliminary to a major assault that will allow us to break out of our lines and take the war to the Germans." He let this sink in for a moment or two. I don't know what he was expecting but it wasn't the silence that descended. I suspect the realists among us had told enough tales of woe for this sort of cheery talk to be treated with the suspicion it deserved. He continued. "Tomorrow morning, the assault will begin at 0730. We will be in the air before then carrying out all our usual tasks. The Army will be carrying red flares, which they will set off at stated intervals. It is not our specific task to identify them but I would suggest that if you see one you make a note of its position and the time and report on landing as this will aid the progress of the advance." He rambled on with more details about how and where we were going to be and what exactly our tasks were to be. Mainly we were to protect the BEs who would be doing the cooperation work, spotting for the artillery, bombing and recording the progress. Poor bastards.

He finished at last and we all retired to the mess for dinner. The atmosphere was subdued. We had known it was coming but the reality of tomorrow's jobs for everyone was that for a lot of men it would be their last night on earth. I prayed to God it wouldn't be me. Well, any port in a storm.

I slept fitfully. It didn't help that the bombardment continued all night. (It had done on the previous nights as well, I just hadn't noticed being preoccupied with my numerous other problems.) Reveille came with a steaming mug of tea and I struggled into my fancy dress feeling rotten. The tea helped a little but the sight of breakfast nearly had me heaving in a corner. There was no mist to speak of and by the time we were ready to go, it had gone.

Mechanically I wandered round my machine, checking that all the required pieces were there. I passed the time of day with the rigger and fitter and they reassured me that all was well. I mounted up.

"Switch off?"

"Switch off."

"Petrol on?"

"Petrol on."

"Contact?"

"Contact." The propeller swung and the engine burst into life. I waved the chocks away and began to roll over the field. Behind me, Rutherford and the rest of the flight were going through the same motions. Whether they were in the same state as me was hard to tell, but I doubted it. I hadn't actually witnessed a large battle from the ground let alone the air, but I had seen and heard of the outcomes. The continuing contest at Verdun was a case in point. With these happy thoughts, I took off. We formed up in a loose gaggle and turned east and as we did so, climbing all the time, the sun peeped over the horizon. As usual, it was right in our eyes effectively hiding anything directly ahead. We continued climbing, now a few miles southeast of St Omer where no doubt the d'Alprant operation was in full swing. I swallowed hard wondering how much she had passed on to Hermann and what the consequences of that might be.

My fears subsided as we found nothing to do except cruise around the sky. We had no specific task other than protection although we were expected to go behind the lines looking for trouble. However, the Germans weren't up yet, sensible chaps. We hung around for a bit longer before drifting back towards the lines and descending to see what was going on. In the distance, we saw some aeroplanes heading east. Given our lack of progress so far, I waved at the others to follow me. They were clearly intent on some important task and as we neared them, I was relieved to find they were on our side. I waggled my wings crossing above and ahead of the leader and he did the same. I looked down to check our position finding we were over the gap between the two lines, near to what looked like Pozieres, but I couldn't be sure. One stretch of mud looked much the same as another and the smoke from shells bursting gave the whole area a hazy blurred look.

Something in the air caught my attention. I frantically searched the sky but couldn't for the life of me see anything hostile. I looked round at the rest of the flight and I could see them all searching the sky as well. Whatever it was, we had all sensed it. I looked down at the BEs and they were holding their positions more or less, flying in organised circles. Then it struck me. The guns had stopped. Even through the racket of the engine, we had been able to hear the continual thump of shells, but suddenly it had stopped. I looked at my watch. It was 0730.

I heard whistles. Or I imagined I heard whistles. Or perhaps I just remember them because someone told me they were used. Who knows? What I do know is that at 0730 on the 1st of July 1916, I was over the battlefield in my machine, watching the start of the day's tragedies unfold. As we scoured the sky for German machines, I kept looking down at the trenches and the no mans land in between. Within seconds of the guns stopping, groups of soldiers began scrambling out of their lines and moving over the open ground. On the opposition side, there was no movement at all. For a brief moment, I thought the optimists were right and below us, the end of the war was in sight. Then, slowly but surely, small figures began appearing in the German trenches. More and more of them. The brown troops below me were heading east, some were walking, others were running and stopping, some crouching, even some waving at us. What they weren't doing was advancing as if they were on parade as the popular belief is these days.[81]

---

[81] Flashman's phrase suggests that it was written in the late twenties or early thirties when the idea of victory in the Great War had faded to be replaced by the slumps and

Rawlinson wasn't a complete fool.[82] I glanced again at the German lines and already there were more of the bastards crawling about. The silence was shattered as the artillery started up again.

"Too far," I yelled. I guessed that they thought the Boche front line was done for, perhaps the BEs had already been telling them that, but clearly, they weren't, and as the thought crossed my mind, I saw the Tommies stagger, as if they had all been hit at the same time with some enormous hammer. Of course they had, only it was called the machine gun. The soldiers seemed to lie down side by side. A few carried on a little further before succumbing, but in seconds, it was over. To my horror, I then saw another wave clambering over the trench parapets and I believe I screamed. Transfixed I watched as they came forward, uncertainly as if wondering what had become of those that went before. The first men reached the line where the previous wave had foundered, and here they suffered the same fate.

"Good God," I shouted. "Somebody tell them to stop." Utterly pointless. As I said it though I

depressions that afflicted many countries including Great Britain. This was when the conduct of the commanders came under serious scrutiny and led to the vilification of many. Gary Sheffield's 'Forgotten Victory' is an excellent recent addition to the debate. See appendix.
[82] General Sir Henry Rawlinson was commanding Fourth Army when the Somme campaign started. A career soldier, born in 1864 the son of an English diplomat, he served in India, Sudan and the Boer War before the Great War. Raised to the peerage in 1919, he died in 1925 whilst at the head of his profession.

realised that someone was diving down towards the German lines and we all followed. For once, and possibly the only time in my life, my terror was replaced with a terrible fury and I dived with the rest of them.

As we pelted down through a thousand feet, a shell hit whoever was leading. Hard to tell if it was one of ours or one of theirs, but it didn't matter as it ploughed straight through the centre section and exploded blasting the DH2 to tiny pieces which fluttered past all of us as we flew through the wreckage of machine and man.

No time to think about it though as the new lead aeroplane started firing and so did I. I pulled my nose up as I did so aiming it at any figure I could see, screaming as I did with the fear and hatred mingling uselessly into one long burst of fire. When the Lewis stopped I pulled hard away craning my neck back to make sure I wasn't about to fly into someone else. I climbed hard using the speed I had gained to put me out of range of the German guns. Slowly we assembled above the scenes of destruction below.

There were only two of us returning to Bertangles. True to form, Winfield had been the unlucky recipient of the high velocity shell, and the new boy, Parsons, had just flown straight into a German trench. No one knew why, but he had been firing to start with.

Hawker looked shocked when I told him what had happened. He didn't say anything. But then there was nothing to say. All of us were quiet while the armourers reloaded the machines, the fitters and riggers checked them over and they were filled with petrol again. It was only just past eight o'clock.

By half past, we were in the air and by nine, we were over the lines again. The battle had clearly only just begun. The air seemed to be full of machines now, and the ground was a heaving mass. Shells were exploding all over the shop, presumably both theirs and ours. Every time I went down low I could see gaggles of soldiers, some very much alive and firing at anything they could see, but many were dead, dying or badly hurt. I thanked God again that it wasn't me lying in a shell hole at the mercy of fate because in that maelstrom of bullets, shells and bombs there was little chance of someone coming to get you out.

Our orders had been to protect the BEs in this sector of the line but if we didn't see any, to do what we could elsewhere. We most definitely were not to sit on our arses and wait to see what happened. We saw plenty but none apparently in trouble so after another twenty minutes of circling the mess below without contributing we moved a bit further north. I hadn't seen one flare.

By this time, we had split up into pairs to patrol specific parts of the line. I had been given another new boy, Leggett, as my companion, as Rutherford, the only other surviving 'A' Flight member, was needed elsewhere. The idea was that we would wait for a relief pair to come along at the end of our time, go home to rearm, refill, take a piss, and then go and relieve someone else. The DH2s were well spread out now as the primary

301

fighting machine and at least a couple of other squadrons had joined the fray. (I believe it was 29 and 32, 32 under the mad Welshman Lionel Rees.) Disappointingly, it was about this time that the German flyers woke up from their nightly exertions with their 'kleine mädchen' and came to take part in the show. For once, they didn't seem content to mooch about behind their lines and came over hunting for BEs. I suppose they had realised that this wasn't just a skirmish.

The first ones we saw were a pair of Aviatiks. They were no match for us and therefore perfect targets and with a glance upwards to make sure they were not the bait in a trap, I waved at my number two to follow me. My heart moved steadily into my mouth as we manoeuvred above and behind them and at the perfect moment came tearing down on them out of the rising sun, just what the buggers generally did to us.

Three hundred yards, two hundred, another few seconds and then I let rip with the Lewis. Leggett did the same. I took the left machine, Leggett the right. They pulled up and away from each other as the tracer streamed past them, but not before I had sent quite a lot through the machine itself. I saw it falter and start to trail smoke, so I gave it another burst having slowed down to stay behind him. I could see pieces breaking away and then the unmistakeable glow of flames. I cringed at the thought of it but still watched as the machine fell away in a dive that became uncontrollable as more pieces fell off. For once, it had been like shooting rats in a barrel.

Looking round I saw the other Aviatik fighting for his life and he was holding his own. Leggett was doing his best with his limited experience but the German was wriggling closer and closer to the lines and looking for a way home. He was getting lower and lower and didn't see me immediately, but when he did, I could almost feel the despair. Or perhaps I was feeling how I would feel if the situation was reversed. He tried to escape by feinting west away from the British lines and dropping down to ground level. He was good, I'll say that for him. He was almost flying in and out of the shell holes and it was difficult to get a shot at him without doing the same. Leggett was trying from directly behind him by flying in a curious wave pattern up and down, not daring to get any lower, occasionally letting off a burst until he suddenly realised our own rear lines were approaching fast. I saw a few rifles pointed upwards as we flashed past the men below. I slid out to a position about three hundred yards off his starboard rear quarter letting Leggett carry on with his pursuit. Trenches flashed underneath and I saw a hail of bullets ascend at the same time. I just hoped they wouldn't shoot up Leggett too. He had to make a move soon, and I had seen what he apparently hadn't in his desire to live. Directly ahead and to his port side was a long row of poplars, so carefully planted by Napoleon. How they had survived the shellfire, God alone knew but he had to go over them or turn towards me, and if he turned I had him, if he climbed hopefully Leggett would get him. He only had a few seconds left.

I saw his nose come up and for a moment, I thought he was going to climb, but he didn't. The nose came round in a tight arc and the gap between us rapidly closed. He aimed his machine straight at me and my heart almost stopped when I realised he intended to try to crash his machine into mine. I was sure whose nerve would crack first and my grip on the Lewis tightened with fear, the magazine emptying itself in what seemed like only seconds. I didn't have time to reload so I hauled the stick back in an attempt to pull it out of its mounting, turning left at the same time. I was fumbling with the drum but my fingers did not seem to work. I was also desperately looking around for the German but he wasn't behind me. I banked tighter continuing the turn back towards my head on confrontation and there, glory of glories was the Aviatik rolling on its back and sliding down towards its doom in the mud. I guessed that Leggett had followed it round the turn and probably with a tighter turn radius had managed to get inside him and give him what for as he lunged towards me. Either way he was finished and my heartbeat slowed again as the Aviatik dug its own grave.

I couldn't take much more of this. My nerves were in pieces and it was only the middle of the day. I silently thanked the Lord when the relief pair arrived before we had time to find any more action, particularly as I was low on ammunition again and the thought of defending myself with insults and rude signals appealed less than doing it with a gun.

When we landed, Hawker was there again. He had apparently not moved from the last time I saw him a couple of hours previously. No doubt he was itching to get in the air and fight. Well he could go in my place and I could do the standing and worrying about what letters would have to be written later.

"Got a pair of Aviatiks," I said with a forced grin. "Leggett here got the second. Good pilot too. Almost got away." I would let Leggett tell my story later on. But Hawker wasn't interested.

"Casualties are heavy on the ground," he said looking shaken. Well I knew that. I had seen them lying on the very ground he was speaking of. "Better get on, eh?"

I wanted to shout. I had just been fighting for my life with a couple of Germans, one of whom had had the temerity to try to ram me, and all he could say was better get on. I ask you.

"Of course, Sir," Leggett said as Hawker turned to go inside again. I wanted to follow and give him a piece of my mind. I stood rooted to the spot and fumed instead. What exactly was I going to say? I was alive and thousands of the gravel-crushers weren't. I spun on my heel and marched off to find out where we were going next, telling Leggett on the way not to worry, I would make sure he got the credit for his victory. I had no doubt at all that he would return the favour.

The adjutant greeted me cheerily as I entered the briefing room. Clearly, the slaughter had little effect on him. But then he wasn't going to join in of course. He limped round the desk and pointed to his map of the lines.

"Thiepval.[83] Irish doing well it seems. Not much luck either side though, so we need you to go and patrol while the BEs check what is going on. Should be a pair from 32 at this northern point." He pointed to a village the size of a flea called Beaumont Hamel. "You are to relieve them. When Gooding's flight come back I will send a pair to relieve you and that should be your lot for the day. Good luck."

I stared at the map for a moment or two, memorising the likely landmarks and the position of the lines, hoping I would wake up from a dream where someone had just said that one more trip to hell would be my lot.

"Shall we go then, Sir?" Leggett said. "Machines are ready."

"Yes. Seen the map?"

"Yes Sir. Going near Pozieres again."

On the one hand, it was like going to a tea party at the vicarage, on the other a kind of nightmare where people did normal things whilst trying to kill each other. I staggered through the routine again, climbing away from the aerodrome and heading east. At least the sun was behind us now and gently slipping down the sky. We groped

---

[83] Thiepval, where the 36th Ulster Division attacked, was where the furthest advance was made on the first day of the Somme. Of the 100,000 men who advanced that day, roughly 20,000 were killed and 40,000 wounded. It remains the biggest tragedy in the long history of the British Army.

our way in the gathering gloom below us, suddenly struggling to identify what were familiar places, eventually finding the remains of Beaumont Hamel. We turned a little southeast to fly over Thiepval and see what we could see. Which wasn't much at all.

We descended through a thousand feet, no sign of any BEs or enemy, continuing down to five hundred feet.

Everything was eerily still and we floated around aimlessly looking for someone or something to tell us what was going on. As we got lower, I could make out more detail. I wished I hadn't. The paddys had obviously managed to get this far but they certainly weren't here now. At least the live ones weren't. Plenty of dead ones though. The passage of tracer rounds returned me to my senses and I realised we had come under fire. A moment of frantic searching confirmed there were no boche aeroplanes so it had to be coming from the ground. I was already climbing and the German gunner didn't have a great deal of enthusiasm for his task as it stopped as soon as I was pointing upwards. Leggett followed me and we climbed up to about three thousand feet and drifted back towards Beaumont Hamel.

When it became clear that no one was going to relieve us and the dark was beginning to envelop us, I waved at Leggett and we went home.

Chapter 20

It was over. That first nightmare day. The squadron survivors sat silently in the mess, some smoking, some drinking, hardly anyone with an appetite for dinner. We had lost four machines, an entire flight. Three pilots were certainly dead. Gooding was at best a prisoner. There was nothing to say.

Even Hawker was downcast. He had sent us out to help the troops win the war. Instead, we had achieved very little at a huge cost. At a squadron level, four out of twelve was a pretty big casualty rate, something that was a new experience for us. BE casualties were worse by all accounts. No one dared to think about what was left of Kitchener's new army as night fell. Plenty of them were still lying out in no-man's-land, injured, conscious, unconscious, dead. We weren't to know the extent and it wouldn't become apparent for some time just how bad it had been. The first day on the Somme would not be forgotten, mainly because it was the worst day the British Army had ever experienced.[84]

Possibly the worst part, at least for those of us still alive, was that it was all to do again tomorrow. And the next day and the next. It seemed to go on and on. How I or anyone else survived the next two weeks was a miracle. Not for want of trying on my part. It needed a steady

---

[84] The First day on the Somme is rightly remembered as a tragedy, when Kitchener's New Army was decimated. See Appendix 4.

nerve and a will of iron to keep myself clear of trouble. How the troops stood it beats me. They must have known what had happened to their comrades, but still they went over the top, again and again. Different regiments, different battalions, mostly the same results. There were occasional successes as the Commanders had seen the folly of the long bombardment followed by the infantry assault. One particularly spectacular success occurred on the 14th July when a surprise assault in the half-light succeeded in capturing a large part of the German first and second lines on Bazentin Ridge. Successful did I say? Only up to a point. Communications were as poor as usual and so the breakthrough wasn't exploited, reserves were in the wrong place and the Cavalry were most likely hunting foxes.[85] But overall, it seemed like a continual nightmare battle of attrition. The Germans suffered as well as for some reason they counterattacked in much the same way and consequently suffered similar casualties. After the 14th, the attacks petered out into sporadic attempts at taking the German lines and generally keeping up the pressure. The

---

[85] The Cavalry were perhaps the most misunderstood arm of the British Army in the war, largely because they were viewed, mostly with hindsight, as obsolete and an anomaly in a large modern army. In fact, they performed many varied tasks – but the poor communications and the wariness of the higher commanders prevented them exploiting breakthroughs where they could have made progress. Unfortunately, without a modern Charge of the Light Brigade to their name, most of their exploits went unnoticed.

casualties mounted steadily as each raid cost hundreds if not thousands of lives. The spotters noted the continual movements of German troops from the south thus achieving at least part of the stated aim of relieving the French at Verdun before they cracked and gave up. Unfortunately for us, the movements provided nice targets to drop bombs on and the bombing flights needed some protection from marauding squareheads. Hence, my nerves were in pieces as time passed merrily by.

Salvation came unlooked for when Hawker called me into his office one day. We had not flown all day as it had poured with rain again from low thick cloud and the ground was too churned up for us even to try to get airborne. It was bad enough watching the weather from the mess windows. Lord knows what it must have been like to live and fight in. I had just beaten Rutherford at billiards again when the message arrived.

I didn't know what to expect when I entered the presence but it wasn't leave.

"You need a rest Flashman. Couple of weeks should do the trick. Can't stay a flight commander for the rest of your career, what." This with another of his significant glances. His eyes seemed to bore into my mind seeing my innermost turmoil – joy at the thought of getting out of this disaster on my own feet rather than feet first, horror at the thought of being given a squadron. Oh yes, I sought promotion and favour and credit with the people that mattered. Leading a squadron was a horse of a different colour entirely. I might be found out. I knew I wasn't a Hawker or a Rees.[86] Time to worry about that when the time came.

"Report back here on 2nd September. Good luck old boy."

Dismissed, I didn't waste any time with pointless chatter. Rutherford had set the balls for a return match as he had just lost a couple of nicker. I simply waved and shouted cheerio as I passed on the way to get my kit.

"Look after my flight."

"What....," was all he had time to say before I disappeared to pack. In a daze, almost, I clambered on the tender and rumbled off towards the coast. I was alive and I was going to live for at least another two weeks. You will note of course that even my certainty of troubling the world for decades had diminished to weeks and that only when I wasn't required to fly. I could almost feel my heart slowing down from its now normal breakneck pace.

I slept most of the way to the Channel. It was a sleep born of total exhaustion. It revived me though and when I went aboard the tub that was taking me home, I was ready for the dinner that was offered and fortunately, the channel was millpond like so I would probably be able to enjoy it. It occurred to me then that these Naval Officers were perhaps in the luckiest position of all

---

[86] This is presumably the Welshman Major Lionel Rees, commander of 32 Squadron awarded the VC at the beginning of the Somme battle.

compared to what I had just witnessed on land and in the air, Jutland notwithstanding.[87] As senior service, they knew it as well.

Dinner lasted most of the way across and within a couple of hours, I was standing on the docks at Folkestone looking for transport of some kind. I sent a telegram to say I was coming home on this occasion, mainly to avoid the looks of disgust at the return of the prodigal, and hopefully so that there were at least some comforts waiting for me. As it was when I reached Berkeley Square, the only comfort I needed was my bed. Alone.

I slept again for something near fourteen hours waking in time for lunch next day. Ownership of the house hadn't really had a chance to sink in as I had only been there briefly since the death of my Father. I had been a little surprised to benefit at all from his will but the house was a very pleasant London residence complemented nicely by the Leicestershire estate,

---

[87] The Royal Navy's role in the war is regularly reduced to the Battle of Jutland, despite continual engagements throughout. Dogger Bank, Heligoland Bight and Coronel were all costly engagements and the submarine war in the Atlantic, which at its unrestricted height was sinking over 800,000 tons a month came very close to defeating the Royal Navy. Jutland itself was at best a draw. Three major ships, Indefatigable, Queen Mary and Invincible blew up when hit by German shells, although the main reasons for blowing up were poor procedures allowing too much ammunition to be accessible and design flaws in the armour. The Rules of the Game by Andrew Gordon is a superb work on the battle. Over 6000 British sailors died at Jutland along with over 2000 Germans.

neither of which was much frequented by the Bishop as he had his own place provided by the Church.

Having tucked in to a large breakfast of kippers, eggs, bacon, coffee and much more besides, I pondered on what to do and in what order. Holmes had collared me when I passed through St Omer and gave me a letter for Cumming. "Just a brief summary," he informed me. I wondered whether to tell him to go to hell but he was too much of a cool hand to dismiss lightly. I briefly considered steaming the letter open to see if he had commented on my contacts with d'Alprant but decided against it. If he had, I could explain it away one way or another and surely he wouldn't have given me the letter if it were too damning.

It could all wait until I was ready. I had nearly two weeks to loaf about and generally make a nuisance of myself, and I wasn't going to waste a moment of it.

"The Times Sir." Shadwell dropped a copy on the table beside me and I glanced at it to see the headlines. Usual uninspiring stuff about some minor advance through the mud at the cost of only hundreds of casualties. Whoever wrote it clearly had not been there at the time. Of course, on the 1st of July they had mostly talked about Roger Casement[88] as though anyone cared a damn. They

---

[88] Sir Roger Casement was an Irishman who spent most of his life working in consular posts, notably in the Congo Free State where he exposed the inhuman treatment of the population by the Belgian rulers, and again in Brazil, where

did mention a battle in passing on the third just to say it was going well, casualties were believed to be light and the enemy lines had been overrun everywhere. Fifteen hundred prisoners had been taken. This shows you how much it was worth relying on the Thunderer for information. I idled my way through the morning, not giving the squadron or any part of the western front a second thought. The release from the strain was most satisfactory.

It was in this relaxed state that the days post arrived. I had already waded through a great heap that had been waiting since my least leave, most of which was rubbish, demands for money, subscriptions, you know the sort of stuff. There were six letters, all of which I swiftly consigned to the fire, and one telegram. I opened it without a thought.

"Imperative you attend palace immediately stop Avoid embarrassment stop Legh stop"

I read it again to make sure that I was not dreaming and at the same time, I heard a carriage pull up in the street. For a moment, I considered running for the back door on the assumption that I was guilty of some misdemeanour and the rozzers

---

he completed much the same task for which he was knighted. After retiring in 1913, he returned to Ireland and took up the Nationalist cause. He sought help in America and then in Germany. In 1916, he attempted to ship rifles to Ireland but was arrested after landing from a German submarine in County Kerry, three days before the Easter Rising. The arms were intercepted by the British. He was imprisoned in the Tower of London and hanged for high treason.

were here already, but I instantly changed my mind. This wasn't some banana republic,[89] I was in my own house for God's sake, and anyway, what could I have possibly done wrong that concerned the Palace. More likely, it was the other way around. The Prince of Wales had probably done something disreputable and for some bizarre reason he wanted me to help him sort it out, although why he thought I would willingly help him out of whatever fix he was in was beyond me.

"Major Sir Piers Legh,[90]" Shadwell said as he showed him into the room.

"Major Flashman, may I be the first to congratulate you," and he marched up to me, grasped my fin and pumped it up and down whilst

---

[89] This phrase was coined by the American writer O. Henry with reference to Honduras.

[90] This must be Sir Piers Legh, known as Joey, later Lieutenant Colonel, second son of the 2nd Baron Newton. He was educated at Eton and commissioned in the Grenadier Guards. He was a military secretary in the war and was mentioned in despatches. In 1919, he became an equerry to the Prince of Wales until 1936 and then King George VI. He remained an equerry until his death in 1955. In 1941, he became Master of the Household. Whilst in Canada as ADC to the Governor General of Canada in 1920, he married Sarah Polk Bradford who was related to the 11th US President Polk. His ancestral home was Lyme Park in Cheshire, the main hall of which was built in 1541 on the site of the medieval house which itself was given to Sir Piers Legh for rescuing the standard of the Black Prince during the 100 years war. The chapel was built in 1442 for Sir Piers Legh who fought at Agincourt in 1415 and later at Meux in 1422 where he was fatally wounded. Sir Piers' role in Flashman's case must have been unofficial.

beaming at me. "I believe it was gazetted this morning."

Well this was news to me, and being inordinately wary of strangers bearing gifts I wondered again what on earth I had done. I didn't say anything at all, as I was interested in where this was leading. Legh hopped from one foot to the other for a few seconds; clearly, he was as embarrassed as a knight of the bath could possibly be. He studied his feet, then the ceiling and finally with a sort of strangled cough he cleared his throat and began.

"The Prince of Wales requests your presence to discuss a matter of some delicacy. I have brought a carriage..." His speech concluded he returned to studying the décor. He didn't leave though so I had to assume that we were meant to go straight away.

"What on earth could His Snottyness believe I can do to extricate him from whatever mess he is in?" I said in the hopes it would provoke some sort of explosion and possibly an explanation as well.

"I am afraid I am not at liberty to explain. My instructions are simply to, er, accompany you to the Palace."

I have heard many veiled threats in my time and the guarded language could not hide the fact that I was to be escorted to the Palace and no mistakes. I racked my brains to think of what this was about but nothing came to mind. Having failed to upset Legh I resolved on taking my time before going with him. I had no choice of course but I wanted to think. After all, what could happen? It was only the Palace.

Half an hour later, we were clambering into the carriage. I had changed into my Lancer rig, as I knew it would get up His Walesship's nose and he wouldn't be able to say anything as it would appear churlish.

Buoyed up by thoughts of what the stupid bastard had been up to, I settled into the carriage for the short drive to the Palace. I ignored Legh and he returned the favour. We didn't go through the front gates this time. Presumably, my visit had less public interest than my previous sojourn as I think we entered through a tradesman's entrance, clattered to a stop and Legh leapt out. He didn't wait and I was left considering his rear view. Well two could play that game so I adjusted my dress carefully for a moment, grasped the rail and stepped out, looking around me as I did so for some sign of welcome.

Legh appeared again, torn between shouting at me for holding him up and cajoling me into doing just as he wished. He almost found the time to be pleasant but not for long. It was like having a spaniel on hand, one minute leading and sniffing around yards ahead, the next hanging round your ankles trying to make you hurry.

I continued to saunter along behind Legh and eventually I was lost in the twists and turns of the Palace corridors.

One final turn and Legh stopped at a nondescript door and composed himself. He was slightly out of breath, but then he had covered twice the distance that I had. He knocked, paused briefly and entered. I followed, and suddenly I had that chilly feeling that all was not well. If you have ever dealt with royalty, you'll know what I mean. They make uncomfortable company at the best of times, but now, after all that had gone before, I was ready to make a bolt for the door. You may say I should have smelt a rat long before. But you weren't there. And how many times have you walked straight into the jaws of doom whilst believing you were on the way to a tea party?

It was all jolly enough. Legh turned to face me and I looked past him to where the Prince of Wales and another man I did not know were standing with their coattails raised by the fire.

"Major Flashman. Good of you to come so promptly. This is a rather delicate matter."

Now of course I was really suspicious. He had never spoken to me in this way before and I wondered what exactly could be delicate that had anything to do with me.

"We have been considering how to, er, bring up the coincidence that brings you here now. There is a remote possibility we may be related."

He let this sink in for a moment, time I spent gaping at him, my mind in sudden turmoil. An hour ago, I had been reading letters and the Times, now, well, now I appeared to be related to the biggest fool since Yorick.

"Jesus Christ, you mean.... you mean you are a bastard?"

Furious looks all round accompanied this remark, mainly I suspect because I had not addressed His Royal Highness correctly. Clearly it was true though. I'll say this for his high and mightiness, he kept his cool remarkably as there was obviously more to be heard on the subject before stumps.

"Possibly. We are not the only one of course. There is plenty of doubt surrounding the constitutional issues that may or may not arise when we ascend the throne of our Empire. Which we may say, we will do as any that do arise will have been, ah, taken care of long since." He hadn't taken his eyes off me for a moment and I felt the pressure boring into me as I gaped about looking for allies and finding none. The emphasis on 'taken care of' sent a chill down my spine as well. As I mentioned before, how often have you gone into a children's tea party only to have your bones frozen to the marrow. You may take it from me that that is what I was feeling.

"So, Major Flashman, what is to be done?"

I was beginning to feel a little inconvenient and in no state to answer this presumably rhetorical question.

"We are not sure how much you know about your parents. We are sure that somewhere in your Father's effects exists proof that you are not quite who you think you are. Of course I mean General Flashman when I refer to your Father. We take it you are aware of that connection at least."

I nodded my assent, as that was a harmless admission.

319

"Good. What we must next establish then is what you know of your Mother. What, exactly, do you know?"

Good question. Although my Father had promised answers in his papers I had not come up with any hard evidence so far, only vague ideas and a few possible candidates. It was entirely possible that these clowns knew more about the subject than I did myself, but I did not want to let on my ignorance. Clearly, I could dismiss those with no relation to any of those in the room. My mind was working furiously to come to some conclusion from what I knew but I was struggling badly. All I could think of was a passage somewhere where he had counted up all the women he had known and reached a monumental figure. The silence was beginning to tell against me and I had to force myself to think. I deliberately looked at each of the men in the room in turn.

"Your Royal Highness, gentlemen. You have me at a disadvantage. You clearly have definite information on a subject where I do not." I could almost feel the relief flood the room. "I have narrowed my search to a small number of candidates, but without the proof that you have, I feel it would not be fair of me to mention names which might enter the public domain and give a false impression." The tension returned.

"You need have no fear of any name mentioned entering the public domain," Legh muttered.

"That is as maybe, but unless you are prepared to reveal your information, then I see no reason to reveal mine."

There was some gnashing of teeth and Princely murmurings and I found myself wondering for the thousandth time how on earth I arrived in these predicaments.

"We would prefer it of course if this matter were resolved amicably, some accommodation arrived at." A pause. "Major." The emphasis on the word Major was slight but definite. The atmosphere was threatening now. They were looking at me expectantly, waiting for me to give them the information they wanted which I knew I could not give, as I didn't know.

"Sir, really, I do not know the answer to your question. If I did I would tell you." That was true. I had swiftly realised that they were if not desperate men then at least severely perturbed and therefore had boots to be licked right through if necessary, my distaste for his highness notwithstanding.

"In that case," the Prince of Wales hissed, "Major Flashman may wish to remain here to consider his position more carefully." So there. Before I could utter a word, he stormed out of the door, which crashed shut behind him. Legh and the other man remained.

"I think that indeed we need to carefully consider the position we find ourselves in," he said quietly. "His Highness has an aversion to the less glorious chapters of life, particularly as he and his family are scrutinised constantly by an ever increasing mob of, well, undesirables." I wondered for a moment if I was included in this mob. "Since the beginning of time speculation has surrounded the succession and numerous of our monarchs have had, how shall I put this, a rogue parent. A number of bastards, as you term it, have had to legitimise themselves through conquest, war, diplomacy or other more extreme measures before climbing onto the throne. Of course no such problem lies before the current heir." Of course not. We were here for the aforementioned tea party. I was also wondering what was more extreme than war for obtaining legitimacy. "However, it is important one remembers that rumour travels fast and can assume disproportionate importance before one has the chance to correct any misconceptions." He smiled at me. "Drink, Major?" I shook my head. "So, you see I return to the subject of parents, and in particular, your parents."

Well he wasn't making sense to me at all. I knew the General had covered a lot of ground and that the chances were I wasn't his only by-blow, but how the hell did this concern friend Davy?

"Your Father was a regular at Balmoral in the Old Queen's day," he began.

"Good God, surely he didn't, surely not..."

"Pull yourself together man, of course he did not cause Her Majesty any concern," he spluttered, clearly disturbed at the thought of a Flashman cavorting with the Queen Empress. "At Balmoral he became part of the then Prince of Wales set." He said this with his nose raised to the ceiling as if just the mention of Bertie the Bounder was enough to turn the air fetid. "His Highness and your Father shared a number of vices. Drink, horses and women." He paused to let this momentous news sink in. "And I mean shared." I was thinking how jolly it must have been when the emphasis on shared finally struck home. At the same time, I recalled a throwaway line in my Father's documents. "Anyway, I was aboard Lily Langtry long before Bertie the Bounder."

Silence descended on the room, broken only by the ticking of a clock on the mantel that showed it was now early afternoon already. I had not even been offered any lunch, which just goes to show.

"Ah, lunch. I have some business to attend to. We will continue our conversation shortly." With that, he and his silent companion went out. I thought about making a run for it and be damned to the lot of them but I didn't have the nerve and pressing my ear to the door, I could hear the dull conversation of at least two apes in the corridor.

Was it definitely Lily Langtry? What was the connection then? Was she my Mother? How did all this connect me to the Palace? What did they want to know? All these questions raced through my mind as I sat nibbling the chicken and sipping the Margaux. But what did it matter if the General had boarded and taken Mrs Langtry? All the world knew about the royal mistresses despite the pretence in the press that this sort of thing never went on. Perhaps she was my Mother, but how did that affect the Prince of bloody Wales? There had to be more to it, and perhaps there was more in the unread documents.

My Father's papers? Perhaps they knew about them, perhaps they had seen them or knew what they contained. Perhaps the General had teased His Bounderness with the contents, perhaps a thousand things, and what was the damned Koh-I-Noor doing in the box? I wanted to blub at the mess I was in and I believe I did for a moment or two. Then I fell to cursing my Father and the royal family and all those who had conspired to push me helplessly into this particular corner.

The door opened and Legh returned. I peered up at him from my chair and half-eaten meal. I was beginning to feel desperate, desperate enough to wish myself back to the front. I kept mum, mainly because I didn't know what to say. At no point had my interrogators told me exactly what it was they wanted to know and I was pretty sure that whatever it was I did not know the answer. Yet.

"Well Major Flashman, I think we will need to continue this interview another time. His Highness has further engagements and I am required. The matter we have spoken of is both delicate and of national importance. I would advise you not to speak of it directly with anyone. When we need you, we will summon you again. Good day Sir." He disappeared through the door and was replaced by a flunkey who waved me to follow him until we reached a side entrance where a cab was waiting.

"Berkeley Square," the flunkey told the driver. I climbed in and sat in silence pondering the day so far. The temptation to run away, far, far away and never come back was almost overwhelming

Chapter 21

The following morning I resolved to finish reading the remaining papers before I returned to France. I was up and out before eight o'clock and on my way to the Savoy. I decided to walk. The morning was cold but clear and busy already with people going about their business, oblivious as ever to the war. I stopped briefly to see the headlines and as I turned back to continue on my way an odd movement caught my eye. I daren't look round but in that instant I was sure I was being followed. It seemed that everybody was on a mission to catch Flash Harry by the essentials. Well let them follow me. I wasn't going anywhere interesting anyway. At least that was what I thought until I considered the whole situation, the documents I was going to read and the events of the previous day. Perhaps it wasn't such a bright idea to let whoever it was follow me and give away the location of my hoard. Even friend ape would not be able to keep prying eyes with royal backing out of the safe for long. I took a detour to collect my thoughts, now somewhat ruffled by this latest problem.

My subconscious brain steered me towards Pall Mall, St James's and the Rag. I suppose I was subconsciously hoping to meet the Colonel who would be able to advise on the best course of action, on the surface I was just heading for somewhere familiar that provided a refuge from danger.

"Mornin' Sah," said the porter. I stopped and stood outside for a moment or two. My instinct for survival now charged to the fore and I said to the porter, (who was an old veteran of Omdurman[91] and consequently assumed, presumably having considered my ancestors, that I was also the sort who would charge anything I was told to) "I am being followed. I know why but I don't know by whom. In a moment, I will enter the club. Anything you can find out will be of great interest to me, and financially rewarding for you." I strode immediately into the club and took a seat.

About ten hours later the porter finally found me, shivering with nervous anticipation.

"Ah give 'im the rightabout sah. Said 'e was wiv a member but ah wasn't 'avin' any of 'is ole sauce. 'Ard to tell what 'e was sah. Not army and not a grass'opper." I was about to berate him for failing me in a simple task my Grandmother could manage when he came up trumps. "Still, might tell you 'oo 'e is in 'ere," this as he presented me with a brown leather wallet. " 'e won't miss it straightaway and when 'e does 'e won't connect it wiv me. See ah larned my trade....." His voice faded away as I stopped listening to his undoubtedly fascinating story of life as a dip in turn of the century London. A suitable pause brought me back to the present and I gave him a sov for services rendered and made sure the barman put two bottles by, one for each of them.

---

[91] Omdurman was one of, if not the last, recorded full-scale cavalry charges of the British Army. Present was the young Winston Spencer Churchill.

It crossed my mind that they could all be in this together but I instantly dismissed this as unlikely. Anyway, they knew me and thought I was a bit of a scoundrel like them and turning a rozzer or at least the equivalent out of the door appealed to them.

More importantly, they would keep me posted, provided I smoothed the way so to speak.

Left alone for a moment I opened the wallet. Nothing obvious to start with, just some scraps of paper, some money and oh yes, a tiptop letter saying nothing in particular but with the fouled anchor of the Admiralty in the corner. It was a short deductive journey to naval intelligence, a misnomer I realise. It made sense though. Davy and his ancestors were navy through and through despite the Grenadiers connection. They had all been to Brittania and finished up in charge of a minor ship. Personally I would not have let any of them take command of a rowboat on the Serpentine.[92]

Having identified my pursuers the next question was what to do about it. Not for the first

---

[92] Flashman seems uncharacteristically muddled here. The Royal Family have a long history of service in the Royal Navy, but 'David', the future Edward VIII served only in the Grenadier Guards although he did, as a boy, attend the naval college at Osborne on the Isle of Wight with his brother, the future George VI. George served in the Navy after attending the Royal Naval College, Britannia at Dartmouth, and was aboard HMS Collingwood at Jutland. Their father, George V served on HMS Bacchante as a cadet with his brother, the Duke of Clarence, and continued to serve in the Navy until 1891.

time the best option appeared to be to run away and never go anywhere near these people again, but I knew it wasn't possible. What I really needed was help from someone I could trust. Immediately I thought of Cumming. Immediately I remembered his office and the ships in it and his career in the Navy. Immediately I dismissed that idea as nonsense. On the other hand, the Colonel was a safe man. And thinking about it more, Cumming had never mentioned my Father or his papers and only the Colonel had been present at the Savoy. If the Colonel was on the other side, he had had plenty of opportunity to sell me down the river. But he hadn't and he had clearly read some if not all of the papers. I was beginning to wonder who was in fact on whose side? Had Cumming recruiting me been the accident I thought it was? Was he deliberately employing me to get to the treasure? Who employed him?

The morass deepened steadily as I thought of all the possible combinations. Only one thing was clear and that was that the Colonel was, if not on my side, at least sympathetic to my cause. Why? I had no idea although I suspected there was some other connection to my Father that I did not know about.

"Good God Flashman. Even your Father didn't start this early." The Colonel had arrived.

"Perhaps he just never got the chance," I retorted.

"What are you doing here anyway? On leave again?"

"Yes as a matter of fact. Hawker said I could do with some time away from the front. Not that being away from the front seems to make life easier." I started to regale him with my morning's tale. He sat silently and motionless.

"I can't say I am surprised. I thought something like this would happen eventually. Naval intelligence? More like naval incompetence. Picked his pocket you say? Useless." At this point, he took a great swig of his glass, spluttered, and swore under his breath. "Cumming does not know about your Father's papers. They were entrusted to me and are a separate affair. Separate to…. all this. He is not involved as far as I know. If by some chance he were, then he has not told me."

"What about our friendly guard dog?"

"He is a safe man."

"Who else…."

"No-one else knows where they are or what they contain. Before you ask, yes, I have read some of them and I certainly understand less than you do. Your Father told me many things, a lot of which make no sense to me. But they will to you."

We paused again.

"What the hell do I do now? Our naval friend won't give up because he's lost his wallet and presumably he knows which side his bread is buttered."

"I suspect they have something on him which would finish his career overnight if it got about in the right circles. Plus the vague promise of a knighthood to smooth his path would be the least of it. For starters, though, we need to get you away from here. Preferably far away. France is ideal."

I nearly fell off my stool. "Not bloody likely, Hawker gave me two weeks to recover away from the front. I am not going back before my time."

"Who said anything about the Front? We still haven't got to the bottom of this d'Alprant business. A little intense work should see progress. Holmes tells me it is going to be a difficult nut to crack." I noted that Holmes didn't say why it was going to be so, but he hadn't split on me. "Yes, the more I think of it that would seem the obvious solution. Get yourself back to France and finish this d'Alprant business. Holmes will help you. It would be nice if we could control her ourselves and perhaps feed the Germans some nice scraps. Unlikely though. We will need to get you away from here without being seen though. They will have covered the doors by now. You won't be able to remain unseen for long but a couple of weeks incognito would help. Judging by their recent performance it will take them that long to find you again. Not much they can do in France I suspect."

He stood up and wandered towards a door at the back of the room that I had not noticed. "Are you coming then?" he said to me as I hadn't followed. I sprang after him. The room was empty apart from the two of us and I got the feeling that this particular situation was not new. He unlocked the door and we both passed through, carefully locking it behind us. I followed as the Colonel led us down some steps and then along a dark passage lit intermittently with electric lights and which was punctuated with sharp ninety degree bends every so often. As far as I could tell, we walked in more or less a straight line until I nearly walked into his back when he stopped suddenly and opened a door in the wall. I had lost track of the distance when I gave up counting my paces and, after climbing some more steps and peering through a hole in the door we arrived at, was surprised to find myself in an underground part of Charing Cross station. Neither of us was wearing uniform so it was easy to mingle with the travellers and shortly we were back in my old room in the Savoy.

"Stay here today and we will arrange for your passage out tomorrow," the Colonel said. "Best not to contact anyone." He turned and left again. I silently thanked the Lord that he was on my side and that our opponents were rank amateurs in comparison. I had a chuckle at the interview which I was sure would follow from my shadow's inattention to his subject and settled down for the rest of the day.

By now, I had amassed about forty sheets of paper, each with a potted history of various women who may or may not have been my Mother. I read them all through again attempting to rank them in order, but I knew already that most of them were non- runners. Recent events had convinced me that the field had narrowed somewhat. Prime candidate for the coveted position of Flashy's Mother then was Lily

Langtry, entirely probable given her apparent taste for men. And when I considered it, it was not implausible. So far, I had no cast iron evidence, but there were still three packets unread.

I drifted from thoughts of Langtry to Bertie the Bounder and the persistent rumours surrounding his less than scandal free eldest son, Albert Victor, Duke of Clarence and Avondale, Eddy to his friends and also apparently known as Victoria in the Hundred Guineas Club.[93] Despite his penchant for dressing up, I recalled that he was briefly engaged to the daughter of the Duke of Teck, Victoria, otherwise known as May. Fortunately, they were not too deeply in love as after his early demise she swiftly became engaged to his brother, the significantly brighter star George, the same George who stabbed me with my medal and whose son seemed so suddenly interested in my parentage. May was already twenty-six when she married him.

Albert Victor, according to popular belief, had fathered a bastard with a commoner after which one Inspector Abberline of the Metropolitan Police had joined him in his daily routine, ostensibly to protect him. No one asked whether it was to protect him from himself or

---

[93] The Hundred Guineas Club was a transvestite establishment apparently frequented by the young Prince. It would appear his lifestyle alternated between the duty and rigidity of the Royal Navy and the bohemian lifestyle shown him by his Cambridge tutor. After leaving Cambridge, he also served unenthusiastically in the 10th Hussars and was allegedly a high profile participant in the Cleveland Street scandal.

outsiders. If he had fathered one, then the chances were there were more lying around somewhere, and if any one of them could prove their relationship, they would be a threat, albeit somewhat unlikely, to the succession.

Thoughts of bastards inevitably led my mind back to my jaunt to the Palace and the conversation there. Why had the Prince been so concerned about his accession?

I began to feel sick. What if the General and the then Prince of Wales had been getting their greens from the same woman at the same time? What if it was Langtry and what if there had been a child? What if someone, and Christ knows there was only one candidate, had been passed off as a Flashman when he was in fact a Saxe bloody Coburg and now they thought this Flashman might have inherited information to prove it and wanted to sit on their damned throne? Oh my God, surely they couldn't believe I was a threat to the succession. After all, this wasn't some mediaeval court, was it? It occurred to me that although the Prince had alluded to my Father as being the General, he had not definitely stated it. He had then gone on to question my knowledge of my Mother. Suddenly I felt just a little lost.

But, and now I was getting myself even more confused, if the General wasn't my real Father, he obviously thought he was or surely he would not have gone to all that trouble with the letter and papers and so on.

And then, just to add to my mounting confusion, I came across the papers again that dealt with the Baccarat Scandal.[94] Lily Langtry had surfaced again, but more importantly, so had my Grandmother. Back in 1859, Good Prince Bertie amidst the clearly debauched atmosphere at court had apparently made a beast of himself in the potting shed at Windsor with her when the General was out of the Country. What if that, or any subsequent encounters, had led to something or someone inconvenient? What if my Grandmother had had a son by the Prince? Could she conceivably be Mother to Albert Victor who was born around that time and who conveniently kicked the bucket in 1892?[95] Or someone else entirely? Or was Albert Victor my Father? Good God, none of it sounded too far-fetched the more I thought about it. How on earth, I mused, had whatever the truth was been covered up?

Well, if there was one thing I was certain about, it was the involvement of Brigadier General Sir Harry Paget Flashman VC etc in the burial of the true story. Now he was dead of

---

[94] Published as Flashman and the Tiger.

[95] Albert Victor, Duke of Clarence and Avondale was born in 1864. This would suggest that either Flashman's Grandmother was not his Mother, or that she had an ongoing relationship with the Prince of Wales. He died prematurely in 1892 of pneumonia, an event that has also attracted much speculation, not least because much of the documentation on the life of the Prince has been destroyed, mislaid or kept secret. How Flashman knew so much about him is unclear, but it is likely he learnt much from his Father/Grandfather who was close to the then Prince of Wales, Bertie the Bounder. The Prince's reputation has suffered enormously over the last century. Why it should have done so is a difficult question. See appendix.

course, the other interested parties had descended like flies to head off his appointed heir at the pass and make sure he didn't have the damned effrontery to let any of their secrets out.

This same General had said I was a chip of the old block. I looked like him, or so everyone said, and I thought like him judging by his writings. But who was the old block? And what if it was an old royal block?

The thought of King Harry had a momentary pleasant ring to it. I considered my Father's experiences with royalty, notably his time as Crown Prince of Strackenz and the idea appealed. The run of the palace, crowds of adoring women, food, drink and entertainment to suit an eligible bachelor, all of which had me in a fine fever. In the same moment, I recalled the drainage system of the Jotunberg, the Sons of the Volsungs and the lunatics that seem to swarm round royalty like bees round a honey pot, and I changed my mind. At least the King Harry bit. But I still wanted to know the truth. It had occurred to me that at the very least, I held the key to some embarrassment that the royal family wished never to be made public, and if I could not turn a profit from that, I really had lost my touch.

I forced myself back to the present predicament, which was bad enough in itself. I decided to leave the three unread packets for another time when I had got some order into the whole business and that would have to be in France. Bugger the risk, I would take them with me and get to the bottom of it there.

For the moment though, I had to stop thinking about it or I would go mad. My head was aching from the whirl. From a port of some certainty, I had suddenly slipped my cables and drifted off into the unknown.

******

I awoke with a start as the door opened and the Colonel came in. He looked tired and dishevelled.

"Get your things. We are going now." He barked this as if to some pimply subaltern but I wasn't in a position to argue over forms of address. Meekly I picked up my few belongings and followed him out of the room. "Cumming is in a terrible state. Until now, he was unaware of the situation, at least that is what he told me. However, someone at the Admiralty or the Palace, and it doesn't really matter which, has enlightened him. He is aware that you are in the Country and he thinks I am trying to find you, a position I am content to foster for the moment, not least because it disconnects us. It was only by chance that any connection between you and Cumming was made. I am not sure what Cumming expects me to do if I find you. Let's just make sure that little scene does not arise or we are both done for. Fortunately, he trusts me enough not to have me followed. For the moment." As he said this, we left the building through a tradesman's entrance that was invisible from the Strand. We stopped briefly while the Colonel and my big friendly

337

guard dog surveyed the lie of the land. Then it was collars up and keep moving swiftly, the Colonel beside me and Fido a few yards behind. Time had clearly flown by, as it was almost dark. None of us spoke as we marched through the gloom. I mastered the temptation to keep looking behind me. What I really wanted to know was where we were going. I was quickly lost as the Colonel kept changing direction and darting down deserted tiny streets. Suddenly we turned a corner and there was a bridge directly ahead. We crossed the road onto it and started to cross the bridge itself. I was trying to identify it when we stopped momentarily, passed through an iron gate, descended some steps and came to a door that led into the bridge itself. We entered and immediately descended again. I presumed we were below the river now. We reached the bottom of the winding stairs, rounded the end of the wall and came into a station.

"It has never been used. There are a few of them around underneath the city. Most people have forgotten or never knew they existed. They are however very convenient for leaving the city unnoticed." Well that was very nice but I wondered how. Surely a steam train wasn't going to appear just for me, as that struck me as a way of attracting plenty of attention. We stood on the platform, the Colonel staring into space while I peered into the tunnel. I thought I heard a squeaking noise coming from the other direction and I was right. Suddenly out of the dark, our silent friend appeared on a small truck with a pump handle on it. He was pushing it up and down and by some more or less invisible means, it drove the little truck along. He rolled to a stop just in front of us.

"Well get on then," the Colonel said. "You take the other side. We haven't got far to go." Without further ado, I climbed aboard, grasped the contraption and at a signal from the other end we started pumping. Slowly at first but then picking up speed, we rolled off into the tunnel. The Colonel lit a cigarette and as he blew a stream of smoke into the air that trailed behind us, I laughed at the unreality of it all. We hadn't been going for more than a few minutes when I felt the pace of the pump slow down. I followed suit and we rolled into another station where the Colonel and I disembarked, clambered onto the platform and through a doorway, up some stairs and out into the cold night air. We walked about a hundred yards before I saw a motor car loom out of the dark. The Colonel opened the door, I stepped in, and he poked his head through the window.

"Holmes will meet you in Etaples. You know what to do." This to the driver. As we moved away in the darkness, I peered back through the rear window but he was gone already. I sat in silence as we drove through the night. I fell asleep at some point but it was not very restorative.

Dawn was breaking as we arrived in a small port. I didn't recognise it at all, but moored to a jetty was a small grey fishing boat. The motor car stopped beside it and the driver motioned for me to get out. He immediately drove off leaving me nervously fidgeting on the dock.

"Major Flashman?" The voice came from the boat. "Come aboard Sir. We have some breakfast here for you." Kippers, bacon, toast, eggs, it was all very appetising and I ate heartily, regretting it within half an hour as we set off into the Channel which was having a rough day. Having heaved my guts over the side like the seasoned sailor I was I went below and found a more or less comfortable place to lie down, assisted by the cheery Captain whose name I still hadn't found out. Perhaps he hadn't told me.

After what seemed like days but was in fact only a couple of hours, the engine note diminished and we slowed down. I came back on deck to find the coast passing down our port side, and shortly a small port hove in view.

"Etaples," the cheery one said. It was less than inspiring. We drifted slowly up to the dock and stopped.

"Thanks," I said to the Captain unenthusiastically, who smiled, waited until I was safely ashore, started his engine again and began the journey home.

I stood like a lost soul hoping for inspiration but none came for over an hour when another motor car pulled slowly onto the dock and Holmes appeared.

"Well Sir, shall we go?"

"Where to?" I asked.

"St Omer, Sir." I nearly spat my teeth out.

"What, you mean I have come all this way in secret only to drive into St Omer in broad daylight?"

"Not quite, Sir, we have a small place in Lumbres for you to stay in, well out of sight of prying eyes, Sir, just the ticket for springing our little trap on Madame d'Alprant. After that, Sir, well yes I suppose it will be back to your squadron." Marvellous. I wished I had never set eyes on any of them, Cumming, d'Alprant, O'Connell, the Colonel. Not for the first time I even wished I was back on the frontier.

Chapter 22

I spent the first whole day back in France in my room, trying to straighten out all that had happened over the last few days and reconcile it with what I knew about my ancestry. I had brought the remaining unread papers with me as well as my summaries of the rest.

As far as I could make out, the Royal Family, or more particularly the Prince of Wales, for whatever reasons, believed I was related to him. He was not entirely sure how but was worried that my Father was the same person as his Grandfather, Bertie the Bounder, and I was not a Flashman at all. Alternatively he thought my Father was his Uncle, the Duke of Clarence, either of which would indeed cause a constitutional problem if it were generally known and could be proved, leaving aside the minor point of legitimacy.

I, on the other hand, was more or less convinced that my Father was General Flashman and was more concerned about finding out who my Mother was and I was now almost sure it was Langtry. Mathematically it was all possible.

My other major concern was what the Prince of Wales meant by taking care of any constitutional problems arising. I could only presume he meant me if I was foolish enough to start jockeying for position. All of which had me reaching for the brandy.

And suddenly there it was. The answer I had been looking for in front of my very eyes.

"I blame Kipling who was editing the local rag at the time. All I did was to suggest he put some of his versifying into a book and before I knew it, there it was, plain as a pikestaff to anyone with half an eye, incompetence and corruption on show for all to see.[96] I was on the boat home at the time. He had dedicated it to me in an oblique fashion, at least the first edition was. This didn't last long though once it reached jolly old England. At first I thought it something of a wheeze having punctured so many puffed up balloons in my time, but this one came home to roost, quite literally and in a number of unconnected and unexpected ways."

And so it did. Here is a summary.

It seemed that following his adventure in Austria with the Emperor, the General had been shanghaied into Gordon's debacle in the Sudan culminating in the fall of Khartoum. Having escaped this disaster, he found his way to the civilisation of India where he met Kipling who was the editor of the Civil Military Gazette in Lahore. Shortly after arriving in India, he left again without saying what he had been doing there at the time. He arrived home and swiftly found himself in another of his familiar dilemmas. He had been rogering La Langtry around society and having a whale of a time possibly as a reaction to the recent shocks he had endured, when she discovered she was with child. At first, he didn't believe a word of it particularly as he

---

[96] This is possibly Departmental Ditties, a volume of satirical verse published by Kipling in 1886.

was nearly seventy at this time but she persisted and of course, eventually evidence started to appear. Denial seemed a pretty good rope to haul on as dear Lily was no shrinking violet but she was adamant that the General was the Father. However, before any real scandal took hold, Lily miscarried and the crisis was past. At least for the moment. It seemed opportune to be rid of the attention of Lily altogether and as she was an avid climber of the social ladder, she jumped at the chance of sharing the bed of Bertie the Bounder. She was only one of a legion of occupants of this particular bed but entranced him for some time; at least until Babbling Brooke appeared on the scene.[97] However, that is to jump ahead.

In 1887, the Princess Kralta, a former acquaintance was in England and the General, having renewed his intimate friendship with the Princess, was introduced to numerous of her circle in England. This circle of the German Upper Classes, most of whom were related to each other as well as the British Royal Family, included one Victoria Mary Augusta, daughter of the Duke of Teck, Teck being a tin pot duchy near Stuttgart. Victoria Mary Augusta, in her early twenties and young enough to be his granddaughter, took up with the General for a time. Long enough to find herself in the pudding club. Vidi vici veni as they might have said in Rome.

There was only one possible Father who, in time-honoured fashion, arranged to abscond

---

[97] Daisy Brooke, mistress to the Prince of Wales after Lily Langtry and later Countess of Warwick.

finding himself caught up in the Usuthu rebellion in Zululand.[98] Having escaped with a relatively whole skin he returned to England to find Victoria ensconced in the house of his legitimate son and his wife and daughter, Selina. Somehow the ménage a six worked. Quite how the General squared all with Lady Flashman is not mentioned, but one can only assume he managed it somehow. Perhaps her own infidelity played a part.

Shortly afterwards, the baccarat scandal exploded on a goggle-eyed public who followed it with fascination as the principals in the action damned each other to hell and back. The Prince of Wales, amongst others, was made to look foolish but the General was as a consequence of his assistance brought back into the fold, as a result of which, Victoria Mary Augusta, May to her friends, made the acquaintance of the Duke of Clarence and Avondale, second in line to the throne.[99] (At this point in my reading, I began to hear alarm bells the size of Big Ben). Without as

---

[98] During the Scramble for Africa, the British, fearing other colonial powers annexed the reserve territory and the rump of Zululand, sparking off rebellion when they replaced Dinuzulu with the collaborationist Zibhebhu. It took several engagements lasting most of 1888 to subdue the uSuthu. Flashman's part in this has not so far been documented.

[99] The Tranby Croft affair, otherwise known as the Baccarat scandal took place in late 1890. Sir William Gordon-Cumming was accused of cheating and the Prince of Wales was forced to appear as a witness in the subsequent court case. Flashman's role is documented in Flashman and the Tiger. Given Flashman's claims here, it is quite possible that May was introduced at this time to the Prince of Wales' circle and consequently his son.

much as a bye your leave, they were engaged. Given the Duke's unconventional tastes, it was soon pretty clear that whilst they had much in common being German, they had little in common as a future husband and wife, let alone King and Queen, but the dice were cast and there was no question of breaking off the engagement as May was likely to be a steady if dull influence on the wayward Prince. Besides, the Queen Empress approved and so there really was nothing to be done about it.

In the meantime, the baby was turning into a little boy, the clergyman and his wife were content to bring him up and May paid less and less attention to her son.

It was now, in 1892, that one of the most secret deals in the murky history of the Flashman family was done.

Clearly, the Duke of Clarence was unfit to sit on the ancient throne but the equally ancient laws of primogeniture could not be dismissed just because the heir was a transvestite[100] halfwit. Some other solution had to be found.

First in the plot were the proposed spouse and her former lover and Father to her child. Next up was the Prince of Wales. It was a secret, known only to the three principal agents and the occupants of the Prince's bed. The obvious answer was to do away with the Duke somehow. It had been done before, but hardly in a civilised society. This notion was dismissed but not before

---

[100] The term was coined in 1910 by the German Dr Magnus Hirschfeld.

346

the suggestion of having the Duke confined as mad had surfaced. The General in his usual fashion took great delight in proposing ever more risky schemes including one in which the Duke undertook a royal progress to the dominions and where at some convenient point he was simply confined and told he had to remain where he was forever and change his identity, to Victoria if he so wished, but could never reveal his true ancestry or return to his home country.

The plotting continued for some months, with none of them able to make up their minds what to do. Someone even suggested involving Salisbury[101] but this was vetoed.

Of course, as with all secrets the fun is in the telling and it was no surprise that the household started to get wind of something afoot, not least because both General Flashman and the Prince of Wales were sharing the same woman again, Babbling Brooke, Countess of Warwick to be.

Then the Duke died. Pneumonia apparently. But of course, rumours soon began circulating that he had been done in by at least a dozen different parties. Denials were issued by some of them only adding to the feverish speculation and not helped by his former betrothed getting hitched to his brother, the damn sight more acceptable George.

Where was I? Growing up with my parents, the vicar and his saintly wife, none the wiser. I was sent to Rugby at the appropriate time, made a

---

[101] Robert Gascoyne-Cecil, 3rd Marquess of Salisbury was Prime Minister almost continuously from 1885 to 1892.

nuisance of myself, found myself ejected and in the Army, and now here I was, Major Harry Francis Alexander Flashman, MC, Royal Flying Corps,[102] son of the renowned fighting General and the Queen Consort of the United Kingdom of Great Britain and Ireland.

No wonder the buggers were after me.[103]

******

Next morning I sat and stared at the manuscript again, not sure what to think. I had gone from the virtual certainty of knowing my Mother was the old King's former tart to the total uncertainty of knowing she was in fact the present King's Queen. It was a terrifying uncertainty at that. The Family were definitely not keen on this little snippet making it into the public arena and my deductive powers had led me to believe that Prince Davy was quite willing to go to extraordinary lengths to prevent it, hence the Navy shadow. I also had the feeling they were aware of the true nature of my Father's character. A true blue hero would not dream of using this sort of information in an inappropriate fashion.

---

[102] Flashman does not mention it but Francis Alexander were the Christian names of the Duke of Teck, his maternal Grandfather.

[103] There is no available evidence apart from the unpublished Flashman manuscripts that the Queen Consort did in fact have an illegitimate child. She was certainly living in London at White Lodge, Richmond Park, at about the right time and her family was apparently no stranger to debt having fled abroad in 1883 to avoid their creditors.

But then of course a true blue hero would not have a son by the monarch's wife.

I wondered what they would do. Did they know the whole truth though? If they did, why had they dragged me into the Palace? Intimidation? I didn't know. Whatever it was, it certainly wasn't for my welfare.

I was still staring at the manuscript when Holmes appeared.

"Ready Sir?"

"Eh, oh yes, I suppose so." I gathered up the papers and stood up. At least for today's excitement we had a plan. Holmes had told me all about it on our drive through the countryside.

It was pretty straightforward really. I was the bait and Holmes the line. Madame was the old boot. I hadn't seen her for sometime and it seemed to Holmes that if I dropped in unexpectedly, expressing my undying devotion, I could soon be talked into letting slip an agreed nugget of information that she would just have to pass on to Hermann tout suite. I would either depart the premises or be asleep when Holmes, having listened in to the conversation with his prearranged phone tap, arrived, presented Madame with the evidence of her treachery and invited her to work for the British or swing on the end of a rope. So, all I had to do was act out my part without overplaying it and hurrah, all would be well.

It was only as we approached St Omer that I started to get the jimmies.

"What if she isn't there?" I enquired.

"She is. I have checked."

"Oh. What if she won't see me? What if she throws me out for abandoning her? What if she suspects something? What if she makes a run for it? She keeps a blasted pistol under her pillow," I babbled now thoroughly out of sorts and ready to jump ship.

"She will not do any of those things."

"How the hell do you know that?" I shouted. I received a stare that bordered on the contemptuous.

"Because you will not let her do any of those things. Why on earth should she suspect you? Only if you balls it up. Besides, if by some mischance she should try to escape…" He let the words hang in the air for a moment. "I will be waiting. She will not go far."

"What, you would shoot her then?"

"Of course I will bloody shoot her," shouted the now irritated Holmes. For a moment, he had forgotten he was talking to a senior officer, although I decided that now was probably not the moment to remind him. "She is an enemy of the state and is to be dealt with accordingly," he continued. "You had better walk from here. There is no need for me to be identified until she has decided what her fate is to be." I clambered disconsolately out, trying to look discreet, straightened my uniform and turned to find the plan in tatters.

"But 'Arry, why are you in such an 'urry?" she cooed as I virtually knocked her down.

"Ah well, you see, look here," I said. My mouth continued moving but nothing came out. Out of the corner of my eye, I could see the great Holmes disappearing around the corner. Fat lot of good all his observation had done. He hadn't even spotted her. Nor had I of course, but then I had never claimed to be anything other than an unsuitable player in an exceedingly complex and dangerous game.

"Where are you going, my big 'Arry?" This was accompanied by a lascivious stare at my nether regions and a hand on hip stirring of the rump that finished all chance of sensible conversation until something was done about it. Of course, the other advantage was that it steadied me. I slipped her arm through mine and we set off to find a convenient location to transact our business.

An hour or so later, I was sitting in her bed, sipping champagne with a satisfied smile on my face and her pair of exquisite bouncers gently bobbing as she brought me up to date with the war as seen through the eyes of Madame d'Alprant. The French were still appalling apparently and the English only marginally better, with the exception of yours truly. She didn't mention the Germans to begin with and I saw no reason to bring them into the one sided conversation. Having recovered my strength and my composure I was wondering how to drop my little grenade into the proceedings when I realised she had stopped wittering on about nothing. I glanced up to find myself looking at the business end of a Lebel. I could tell it was a

Lebel, if only because it resembled my own service pistol and had the characteristic swing out chamber.

"What the hell...." I said before I had appreciated that silence was probably the best immediate policy.

"You 'ave a decision to make," she said imperiously. "We both live, or we both die." Quarter of an hour ago we had been rutting like possessed rabbits. I gaped at her in disbelief.

"You fink I am stupid, you English and your games. What is it to be?" I knew the answer of course but it wouldn't have looked very heroic, leaving a brothel prisoner of the Madame, presumably, once she had escaped, to return to HQ and pass on the glad news that I had botched up the plan and the fox in the chicken house was gone. I needed to think fast. There was no time for fear so I passed straight to bluster.

"How did you know?" I exclaimed. She threw her head back and laughed.

" 'ow did I know?" She paused to scoff again and shrugging her shoulders said "I knew from ze moment you mounted me in ze middle of ze night, I knew you 'ad 'eard my conversation. I knew when your spy kept turning up 'ere and buying 'imself a drink and not a woman, I knew when you did not ravish Lucy wiv 'er 'orsewhip." She was wrong there. I hadn't ravished the pupil because I wasn't finished with the teacher, and as for Holmes, if he hadn't played the King and Country act so hard and behaved like a normal human being, she might not have guessed. "I was sure when I saw you get out of ze car today. Lucky for me I did I sink."

I was having trouble knowing where to look and I defy anyone to tell me that he would have looked her directly in the face. There were three other objects of far more interest. In the absence of some other influence, I stared at her left tit. We sat in silence contemplating the next move. She was a little agitated. I was a lot agitated although I dared not show it, particularly as her initial comment about both living was still fresh in my mind. I don't think she was sure what she was going to do next. Even getting dressed was going to be tricky as presumably she thought I was the sort of desperate fellow who would do anything to escape. We continued to contemplate each other.

"You must dress first." I slowly climbed off the bed and collected my attire, without taking my eyes off her. I assumed she was looking for an opportunity to clobber me with the pistol and provide a chance to dress herself. Clearly she hadn't thought the whole thing through, but then that is so often the way. I finished dressing wondering what she was going to do next.

"Out, froo ze door over zere." She waved the pistol at a door in the corner of the room. I walked backwards over to it, felt behind me for the handle and opened it. I reversed through to find myself in a closet of some kind. I turned to see what exactly I was walking into and she took her chance, lunged for the door and tried to slam it. It hit me in the shoulder as I turned back and for a moment, I was off balance and almost measured my length.

As I fell, I grasped at thin air and then my hand snatched at a metal fitting on the wall. I felt it give but it didn't come away and it spun me round again, my right foot giving the door an almighty kick as it went past. There was a momentary look of disbelief on d'Alprant's face as the door hit her square in the face, breaking her nose, and she fell back. There was an enormous bang and I felt the passage of a slug that buried itself in the wall near my hand. Maybe it was an accident, maybe not but I was not going to hang around to find out. I recovered my composure first and vaulted over the bed. She was still sitting slightly dazed on the floor, blood pouring from her nose and that gave me the few seconds start I needed. I flung the bedroom door back and was out in the upper hallway. I bounced off the rail in my haste to get away, and ran headlong for the top of the stairs. The post gave me both a hold to change direction and a sound knock on the ribs as I passed which winded me a little. I took the stairs two at a time stumbled halfway down and crashed in a heap at the bottom. The little things that save your life! A second shot had accompanied my fall and had I not, it was possible that she would have hit me given that I was still only a few yards away. I dived around the corner in the flight and glimpsed her leaning over the rail to take another shot but I was moving too fast to take more notice than that. Anyway, the more she lingered the better my chances.

Unsurprisingly the commotion had started to attract attention from other quarters. The house was big and on four floors with Madame's room being at the very top. It provided plenty of suitable accommodation for this business and even at quieter times of the day, there were still a few clients tasting the wares. Gunfire had brought the braver ones out of their rooms. Why it had that effect beats me, as I have never been someone attracted by that particular sound. Of course, in so doing the Flashman escape route was becoming a little crowded. I rounded another corner, barged a squealing trollop out of the way and came up against her suitor. It was hard to judge the look on his face as an enormous Kitchener style moustache obscured it and I would hesitate to say even now if he was English or Frog, but the plain fact was he was in my way. I smashed my right fist into the now astonished owner, barely hesitated as I leapt past the falling body and made another bound for the steps. Shouting was now accompanying my flight both from above and below and a further gunshot echoed round the stairwell. I descended the last flight into the hallway, crashed heavily into the wall at the bottom and squealed in terror as I was suddenly presented with a view back up the stairs and there she was leaning over again. I howled in pain as the bullet ripped into my shoulder, but I knew I couldn't lose consciousness. I had to keep going. I dragged myself up and made for the open door that led out into the street and there I collided with another of those idiots who seek sorrow and we rolled down the steps into the road itself at which point there was another loud bang in my ear. It was swiftly followed by two more and in that moment I resigned myself to dying at the hands of a French trollop and thinking what a splendid headline that would make for the stuffed shirts in Whitehall, Cumming among them, to read.

I came round lying on the pavement.

"Wake up for Christ's sake," a voice was saying from far away. Something slapped my face. "Get up, get up, we need to get away before the coppers get here."

"I can't, I'm hit, you'll have to carry me," I replied, the mention of the provosts at least reinforcing the urgency of the predicament.

"Hit, Christ, you're just scratched, get up will you." There was an edge of panic in the voice now and I focussed on its owner to see friend Holmes.

"What….."

"For God's sake, now is not the time, get up and let's get out of here."

I struggled to my feet at last, Holmes bullying and helping until I was able to stand and follow him. I glanced at the doorway and wished I hadn't. D'Alprant was laying asprawl down the steps, face down, naked and obviously dead. I followed Holmes across the road, turned into another street and saw him snatch open the door of the car. I climbed in and turned round to see what was happening behind us.

"Get out, you'll have to crank it," shouted a severely shaken Holmes.

I hopped out again, vomited against the wall as shock set in and ran round to the front, grabbed the handle, flinched as the pain from my injury reminded me to use the other hand, cranked it furiously and was breathing a sigh of relief as the engine started. Terror replaced this as someone let fly with a pistol again from the end of the street. I flung myself in through the open door and Holmes accelerated away from the scene of the crime. Less than ten minutes ago, I had been congratulating myself with champagne on a job well done.

"There's a first aid station not far away. We'll go there first and get that shoulder looked at. Then we will have to get away from here. Even the frogs aren't likely to overlook murder without a decent explanation."

******

It was shortly before midnight when we arrived at the aerodrome. Baring was there to meet us as somehow Holmes had passed on the glad news.

"Ah, Flashman," he said as if I was something the cat had dragged in. "Hear you have had a somewhat exciting day." He chuckled.

"That is one way of describing it I suppose," I replied, really in no mood for civil conversation. All I wanted was to go to bed, but no, first I had to explain at length how the hell I had made a hash of the operation and why we had last been seen leaving St Omer in a car with a corpse in the doorway. I went through it all in detail leaving out some of the juicier parts but on the whole sticking

357

to the truth. There was no other explanation really and it wasn't as though Baring was going to arrest me. Wrong again.

"For your own safety, Major," I heard him say. "A formality, no more." I wondered if the King had been at him.

I had seen worse of course. The hardest thing was the boredom. Holmes had looked in briefly and apologised again for my incarceration. There was obviously more to Mr Holmes than met the eye. For one thing, Baring had been somewhat in awe of him despite his lowly rank. Secondly, he wasn't sharing my cell, despite his role in the demise of Madame d'Alprant. He also advised on the procedure for courts martial.

I languished in my 'room' for a week. The food wasn't bad, the bed was comfortable for a cell, but my temper had become doom laden as the week passed by.

"At last, Sir." Holmes had appeared. "We have the officers assembled. Only three as I mentioned Sir. Need to keep it under our hats as well as appease the frogs eh Sir."

He opened the door for me to leave the room. It seemed very quiet, but then I supposed that Baring had arranged it that way. We walked along the corridor until we came to a nondescript door. Holmes knocked and a voice from within bellowed 'Enter'. I took one-step through the door and stopped. My head swam and I swayed. Holmes grabbed me by the arm muttering "this way Sir," and guided me to a chair in the centre of the room. I looked up at the three officers sitting behind the table. A Brigadier General no less, a Staff Colonel and a Major. I knew only one of them. His name was Legh.

Chapter 23

I am told there were other people there and looking back there must have been. Apart from the three officers, there was a judge advocate, a civvie lawyer of some kind to make sure the thing was more or less fair, a greasy frog to represent the deceased no doubt and some kind of clerk. Oh and a prisoner's friend. Holmes had declined the offer, as he could not be recognised so I was stuck with some staff walloper who I didn't know either. I had been 'advised' to avoid someone from the squadron as the whole affair was to be kept secret.[104]

"Gentlemen," boomed the General "I declare the trial open." At least that is what I remember him saying as if he was opening the village fete. Then it passed in something of a haze. Legh hardly said a word. I was called on to explain my actions, beginning with why on earth I was in France when I had been given leave. Heaven knows what I said but as the charade continued, I realised that it didn't actually matter. Holmes had advised me to avoid all reference to Cumming and his organisation, which of course made it difficult to explain anything at all, but apparently, I managed it.

---

[104] Flashman's trial was almost certainly a Field General Court Martial, universally used in the war for officers and men on active service. It could sit with three or even two officers. The Judge Advocate was originally an adviser on points of law, but the role slowly transformed over the centuries to equate more or less to that of the judge in civilian court.

After a tortuous hour or two of explanation, we finally arrived at the day in question. I had already admitted that I had carnal knowledge of the deceased but on the spur of the moment, I decided to pretend that it was someone else that had overheard the conversation with Fritz and they had then come running to me in a dither about what to do. I had taken it upon myself to investigate further and having done so I had decided to have it out with the Madame. At some point, the General asked whether or not I had thought about reporting the matter further up the chain of command, the clear implication being that as a Major I was not paid to think, only to respond to the will of my superiors. I replied that it had never crossed my mind and the devil in me prompted me to add that my Father had never thought like that. If he had, all manner of disasters would have befallen the British Army and I believe I mentioned the Charge and so forth. The General looked pleased with himself and muttered something about having the right spirit.

Now we reached the crux of the matter. I explained that I had come across the Madame deshabille but being furious with the situation, it had not crossed my mind to do anything other than follow her to her room and have it out with her. When I had mentioned treachery she had pulled a gun and fired at which point I had taken cover. I had been unarmed as I wasn't the sort of cad who took a loaded weapon into a lady's boudoir. There was some barely concealed sniggering at this remark. When the second shot was fired, I had decided the time had arrived for reinforcement and sounded the retreat. I briefly explained the descent to the street and then I was snookered. I hadn't actually thought about how I was going to explain away the final act. I stared around the room for inspiration noticing a satisfied smirk on the frog face and then lamely said I believed the fatal shots had come from across the road. Why? I had no idea m'lud.

After that, events moved quickly. The Colonel summed up the evidence so far, I was sent out of the room for about half an hour, and then recalled to hear my fate.

"Gentlemen, Major Flashman has been charged with manslaughter. We hereby find him guilty as charged." There was a gasp from the centre of the room. "The court will now be cleared for sentencing."

The frog made protesting noises as he was led away. Presumably, he wanted to hear the despised English pig sentenced to hang and see his reaction, which would be to plead for his life from his knees pissing with fear at the thought of the rope and the drop. But it wasn't to be. Once the extraneous people were removed the General returned to his theme, but not before the defendant had made a short speech, possibly from his knees, in which he pleaded with all and sundry present, including God Almighty to spare him as it wasn't his fault and he was only doing his duty and if it hadn't been for that dozy bugger Ho...

"Major Flashman. Control yourself." The General stared down from his perch, slightly bewildered at his own sudden intervention as it was possibly the only time in his life that he had uttered an unambiguous order. He paused while the defendant resumed his seat.

"This is a most singular case, the most singular I have ever heard. I have been instructed to sentence the defendant to one week's confinement, which I understand has already taken place. I am also instructed to expunge the record from your personal file and take all notes and documents from this courtroom directly to London where they will be held in secret. In which case, Major Flashman, unless the other members of this court have anything to add, you are free to go."

The General beamed around the room as if to say what a wonderful job had been done.

"I do have a short statement to make," Legh said loudly. He stood up and the General sat down somewhat deflated. "The King wishes me to make it known that this officer has hitherto had an unblemished career and performed numerous acts of bravery whilst in the service of His Majesty, resulting in the recent award of the MC." I doubted all that but I wasn't going to complain. "Furthermore, he understands the predicament the Major finds himself in and hopes that his intervention will allow the Major to continue in his career. He does however stipulate that some things are best kept secret and that ANY information the Major may or may not be in possession of would better remain so. The consequences of this information entering the public domain could be very serious." He just managed to change the 'would' to 'could'.

Now I knew what it was all about of course. How they had found out was beyond me but having done so, they had framed me up and no mistake. Any suggestion that Prince Davy was not the rightful heir and I would be hauled in to answer for it. There was no doubt in my mind they had set up the whole charade. But they weren't silly enough to let me hang for a murder I hadn't committed. They had just made sure that the waters were muddy enough to discredit anything I said as well as making the trial look silly. No doubt, someone somewhere could claim I was let off and review the sentence. If 'new' evidence suddenly came to light, they could possibly retry me for murder. I was sure that it was not possible to be tried twice for the same crime but there were plenty of ways around the law. I had just seen them in action.

The officers collected their papers, shuffled their chairs under the table and left the room. I was still sitting in the middle. Legh did not even give me a second glance.

It suddenly occurred to me that the General's speech about secrecy wouldn't wash. What about the damned frog? He was bound to blow the gaff and it would be all round the Army in days if not hours. I held my head in my hands. I must have been there some time.

"Flashman?"

"Who the devil wants to know?" I replied, thoroughly sick of the whole business.

"I do." It was the Colonel.

"Where the bloody hell were you when I needed you? Do you know what they have done to me?"

"Yes I do, and before you start damning us all to hell, there is some explaining to be done. First of all, I could not appear here, any more than Holmes could. He is outside now, making sure we are not seen. Come with me and I will tell you the position. And there is no need to look so damned glum about it."

I followed him out of the room. Holmes was at the end of the corridor and as we appeared, he waved to us to follow him. A minute later, we were in another motor car and leaving the scene.

"First things first. We are going to a little estaminet I know where we will have a decent meal. You will then stay there until you are due back at your squadron when you will arrive fresh from your leave as if nothing has happened."

He was right. The meal was excellent, apart from the distant thunder of artillery to remind one of the ongoing disagreement. For once, it wasn't soaked in garlic and it was accompanied by numerous bottles of Chateau Lafite and followed by Havanas and Hennessy Cognac. Blissful silence descended through the smoke. At last the Colonel spoke.

"I think we owe you some explanation. You see, there is more to this than you think, even considering your, er, disagreement with the palace. We have known about d'Alprant for some time. Holmes here was watching her before you arrived on the scene. Cumming knew nothing about her and doesn't need to know. She has been ensnaring young officers almost since the beginning of the war and very successfully, I might add. She benefits of course from the fact that many of those who unwittingly passed on their information are now no more. We did not get wind of this until about eighteen months ago, about the time of Neuve Chapelle, when she became so confident in her own ability she also became careless. That was when she started using the telephone to pass her messages. Initially she coded her information but when nothing untoward occurred, she started transmitting clearly. That was when we knew we had to stop her. A lot of what she passed was innocuous enough but all of it helps the wider understanding of the enemy. The decision was taken to terminate her arrangement. That was where you came in. Having stumbled on it quite innocently (here there was a strangled squawk from one of us) we realised that you could be used to break in and confront her without compromising any of us."

"But she knew," I said. "She told me that she knew you were spying on her, she knew someone had been going to her place and buying drinks but not women."

"Well someone else knows more about this than we anticipated then because it wasn't us. We are not amateur simpletons. This is a deadly business. As you found out." He could say that again.

"What about this trial then? I'll be staggered if that doesn't get about within days."

"It won't, I promise you. Legh is your business but my guess is that he arranged to be on the board for some other reasons that need not trouble us just now and that he will not want the details leaked out. We know who he is of course. We tried to veto it but a higher power than even my superior was involved. The General and the Colonel have been instructed from on high to keep their mouths firmly shut if they wish to retain their commissions and were chosen for precisely that ability. Your records will not even show that you were involved, far less guilty of anything. As for the clerk, he works for me indirectly and the Frenchman is paid by me also. He will report the result of the trial without naming anyone. He will hint at an appropriate sentence for murder and then disappear and the citizens of St Omer will go about their business as usual. After a week or two, it will all be forgotten and d'Alprant will hardly be missed. She had no relations in the town and so far, we have been unable to trace anyone that even knew her. We think, although this is mere conjecture, that she may be from Alsace."[105]

And that was that. God forbid I ever got on the wrong side of this lot.

---

[105] Ownership of Alsace-Lorraine has been disputed by the Germans and French since Charlemagne. It had been under German control since 1871 after the Franco Prussian war. Alsace contains mainly German speaking people while Lorraine is predominantly French speaking.

"What did my Father do that has kept you in his debt for so long then?" He wasn't expecting that.

"You Flashmans never cease to amaze me. But I think that perhaps the time has come. First, I will get the bill, and then we will talk. Garçon, l'addition s'il vous plait."

There was a long pause.

"It was a long time ago. I was at the Cape station." He glanced at me to see my look of horror at the revelation of his being in the Navy. "My naval past has no relevance here, so you needn't worry. I volunteered for service inland suppressing the Zulu. It was a brutal campaign as fighting John Zulu always is. I am sure your Father would have told you that, being one of the few survivors of Isandlwhana. But I didn't meet him until Ceza Mountain. The uSuthu had just handed us a fearful licking and in the aftermath, I was wounded. I was also trapped outside our lines when a lone horseman appeared in the nick of time, galloped straight through a gang of blacks who were creeping about finishing off the injured and crashed over the wall behind which I was lying. He rolled out of his saddle as the horse was all but done and collapsed beside me. He was all in as well, but I grabbed one of his guns and set about the blacks. I thought I had driven them off but two of them had in fact sneaked around behind us. They leapt out of their cover screaming and my companion shot one dead instantly, but the other was on him like a tiger. They fought and rolled roaring all the time until there was an

368

appalling scream and a knifepoint appeared out of the back of the attacker. I dragged the dead man off as the rest of the gang had scarpered, and my first thought was that my saviour was dead as he was covered in gore. But then he spoke. He said 'Any idea where the General is old boy? Message for him. Flashman by the way.' So you see, your Father saved my life."

My Father told it a slightly different way. I recalled quite clearly the passage in his notes. The horse was wounded and out of control and careered through the gang before unceremoniously dumping him behind the wall. He thought for the thousandth time he had had it, but a wounded man who he did not identify grabbed a gun and blazed away at the enemy, driving them off or so it seemed. He was set upon by two others, but they gave themselves away by screaming, a hastily fired lucky shot did for one of them and he had no option but to fight the other, screaming in fear until he managed to turn his assailants own weapon on him. Realising swiftly that it was over and thanks to the unknown man he would probably live himself, he reassumed his air of nonchalance, enquiring after the General. I thought that this was best kept to myself.

"Of course, your Father tells a different story." I managed to keep a straight face by biting my tongue hard. "Who knows? Fear, courage, selfishness, selflessness, all just different sides of the same square. I don't care why he did what he did." He paused to throw back his whisky, before unsettling me again. "But why, you may ask, do I

369

feel I owe you anything, just because your Father saved my life?" I looked up to see both of them staring at me.

I glanced around and realised that we were entirely alone. Not a soul. Silence. And expectation. My throat was dry but I could feel a bead of sweat breaking out on my forehead. I felt sick. I had to say something. A disembodied voice croaked, "I have no idea."

"Have you heard of the 'Order of the Poor Knights of Christ'?" I looked blankly at them, as it was the last thing I was expecting to hear. "Well, yes or no?"

"Yes. The Knights Templar. My Father told me.... when I was a boy....." I tailed off.

"I am sure he did. I am equally sure it meant nothing to you then, and it probably doesn't now. However, you are a Freemason amongst other things and so I can enlighten you. Up to a point anyway. Generation after generation of St Clairs, and more recently Sinclairs, have guarded the secrets of the Templars, some with their lives. But there are few of us now who know the truth." He looked at me again, noting I presume the terrified expression. "The truth about the royal blood. You see, some of the Royal Families of Europe have spent considerable amounts of money and time in protecting their own particular bloodlines, desperately trying to ensure their legitimacy. The papacy has done the same. On the other hand, some know they are descended from one man, one very important man, a man who some believe to be immortal, a man the Church believe was not a man at all, the husband of Mary Magdalene, a man whose line yet lives and will never be extinguished while there are men like me to protect it." He paused again. "Jesus."

"So what the hell were you doing in Africa if you were supposed to be protecting this bloodline?" I said before I could stop myself.

"I was protecting it. I was looking for your Father. Only he found me first."

The import of what he had just said seeped slowly into my reeling mind. It was simply too much to comprehend. He continued.

"I realise this is a significant revelation, but I think you need to know, if only so you appreciate what you are up against. You see, Christianity, in its current form is a deception. The Roman Catholic Church has manipulated us for centuries. They are not alone. The Church of England is hardly innocent despite its formation being a blow to the Roman Church. But it all goes back to the Pharaohs and in particular Akhenaten, otherwise known as Moses."

He then proceeded to tell me the most incredible tale I have ever heard. It started with Moses, proceeded to King Solomon and his mastery of so many arts, Jesus and how he was a royal and priestly descendant of David, had married Mary Magdalene and had children, how at least one of those children, Josephes, had had his own children in Europe. It jumped back to Constantine the Roman Emperor and his conversion to Christianity and his Council of Nicaea where the church was hijacked and turned into the eventually powerful Catholic church, the suppression of the female lines and Mary Magdalene and her children, the slow conversion by Paul of Jesus into a divine being instead of the man he was. Returning to Europe, he spoke of King Arthur who was descended from two lines of Jesus' family and thus extremely important, the rise of the Merovingians, their overthrow by the Carolingians and the church, the crusades and the Kings of Jerusalem, the Knights Templar and their eventual destruction and flight to Scotland with their secrets. He spoke of the Ark of the Covenant, Bannockburn, the rise of the true royal line in Scotland and its merger with the English royal line under James I and then Charles I, the civil war and the execution of the King. He dismissed Cromwell and friends as puritan maniacs, and lamented how after the restoration, parliament still managed to get the upper hand by deposing James II and imposing a monarchy that would eventually reside firmly under the dead hand of parliament. He finished with the true heirs in the line of Bonnie Prince Charlie whose history and family had been suppressed.

"They are still at it of course. Nothing will stop them. It is only twenty-eight years since the 4th Count of Albany, a direct Stuart descendant and therefore a direct descendant of Jesus, was due to come to an exhibition in London to celebrate the Stuarts. Our friends the Hanoverians put a stop to that though and the Count was found murdered in Italy. The following year a celebration was held for the bicentenary of the deposal of James II. Its patron was Victoria, and it was used to recover yet more documents from the Stuarts."

Silence descended, broken only by the ticking of a clock. It was dark outside and I realised I had been listening for nearly two hours.

"Your Grandmother's Grandmother was a Stuart. I presume that is what you wanted to know."[106]

He looked up. I opened my mouth to speak but nothing came out. I closed it again.

"Somehow despite all our efforts to the contrary, your friend Legh and his sponsors have got wind of the fact that you are a descendant of a branch of the Stuart family, albeit a very minor one. There are lots of you, but most do not know anything about it. When we find them, we do our

---

[106] Flashman's story here could easily be dismissed as pure fantasy – except that since the discovery of the Dead Sea Scrolls, historians and theologians have taken a long hard look at the bible translations and other related documents and realised that the errors are numerous. As more and more documents are translated and come to light, alternative views on Christianity itself have been put forward, many of these views being more likely than the accepted Church version of events. To use just one example, December 25th is accepted without question by the majority of Christians as the date of the birth of Christ. In fact, Jesus was more than likely born on 1st March 7BC. His birthday was moved to December by the Emperor Constantine to suit his version of Christianity and combine it with other more ancient beliefs, December 25th being very close to the Solstice. For someone to have known any of this at the beginning of the 20th century would only have been possible with knowledge handed down through the ages. See appendix 6.

best to protect them. One day, the true Kings will be restored."

And that was nearly that. My Father's talk of the Templars flooded back. I had dismissed it as rubbish at the time, the meanderings of a drunken old fool, but now I had realised that I was in a very serious and apparently deadly game.

"What the hell will they do now?" I whispered, suddenly realising that they weren't interested in who my Mother was.

"Do? Why nothing of course. They think they have got you just where they want you. They know nothing of me, and they will assume, at least for the time being, that you know nothing of your ancestry other than what they want you to know."

"But what the hell do I do now?"

"You. Do nothing. Don't encourage them. Let them think you are satisfied with knowing your Mother was the Queen consort. Let them think you are indeed terrified of their Sword of Damocles. In short, return to your squadron when your leave is finished.

So that is what I did, at least I did after a few more days of delicious idleness. At first, I had turned the events of the previous weeks over and over, but then realising it was a waste of time and only led to the bottle I gave up. I had no wish to mention any of it anyway as it was hardly an edifying spectacle and it seemed that Legh and Co really had concluded their investigations provided I didn't shoot my mouth off. Well I didn't intend to. Not yet anyway. The time would possibly arise. They didn't know I was the possessor of the Koh-I-Noor. And when I thought about it properly, particularly the remarks about extreme measures to ensure the succession, I realised that if they knew that I knew, they would have hunted me down and exterminated me. My knowledge was nothing but dynamite.

******

Back in Bertangles once again, Hawker was apparently pleased to see me. There was some good news he said. Gooding was alive and well apart from a broken leg and being held prisoner. Only one other pilot had been lost since I went on leave. I wasn't sure why he told me that as it only invited comparison to the casualty rate when I was around and the disturbing conclusion. Nevertheless, he didn't dwell on it.

"When you have settled in come and see me," he said.

I did. The next hair-raising job on the list was to fly around our own lines at night making as much noise as possible. I nearly asked what for but as it didn't seem to involve anything chancier than taking off in the gloom and possibly landing in the dark I fairly leapt at the chance to stay alive a little longer.

I had a day or two to get in some practice at landing in the dark, which I duly did. Initially it was a trifle difficult, beginning with flying circuits of the aerodrome in the dusk and landing between the makeshift lighting. This really was the hard part as the darker it was, the harder it was to make out any sort of horizon or reference point and so landing became a lottery until one got the hang of it. I had a few bumpy landings and one particularly exciting moment when having taken the ground by surprise I soared back into the air applied full power as we sank again and climbed away for another go, praying the whole way round that I hadn't broken anything important underneath. I flew a couple of shows over the lines during the day but they were quiet and it seemed as if the whole area which had just witnessed a titanic struggle for supremacy was cowering, waiting for someone else to make the next move. I couldn't fail to notice that so many of the casualties from the offensives were still lying where they had fallen. I was glad I couldn't see them at close range.

After much speculation, Hawker called us together for a briefing.

I glanced around the room before he began and wished I hadn't. A few familiar faces, Knight, Saundby, McKay, Rutherford, who had now taken over Gooding's flight and been promoted to boot, Jock. It was only then I realised that apart from Hawker, Rutherford and Jock were the only ones left from our runs round Hounslow Heath. I shivered and tried to attend to what Hawker was saying.

"Our show tonight and for the next few nights is very different to what we are used to. The scientific sorts at home have come up with a secret weapon to break through the enemy lines."

There was a collective groan at this. Hawker ignored it. "It is known as a tank." Guffaws and catcalls of derision about what sort of tank it was and whether it would contain water or whisky. He ploughed on regardless. "These tanks are to be brought up to the front line over the next few nights and in so doing will create a singular noise which may attract the attention of the enemy. To avoid this we will fly overhead the routes and assembly areas being used to drown out the noise and distract the enemy. Each flight will fly two nights in succession until the movement is complete beginning with your flight Flashman." He nodded at me.

The detail was left to me and it seemed prudent for the whole flight to take a look at the routes these machines would be taking in the daylight and try to pinpoint some markers that might be visible at night. It was like Piccadilly Circus. Everyone assigned to this task had decided to do the same thing. It occurred to me that if we were all up in the dark at the same time then it was highly likely that we were going to run into each other although I presumed that not everyone was covering the same route at the same time.

We landed again an hour later and had some dinner before donning our kit again in readiness for the night's excitement. It turned out much as Saundby had predicted when he said, "It will never work, it'll just be another bloody shambles."

The first shift arrived at the rendezvous in the gathering gloom. We had been assigned a five-mile strip of track on which we were to maintain a constant patrol from ten o'clock until dawn. There was no sign of any movement below when we arrived and it stayed that way all through the long cold night. The next night was more eventful. When we reached the same place there were some oblong metal objects parked side by side and as we watched, smoke started to belch from one or two of them. We assumed our patrolling pattern and it was just possible to make out some movement before the dark enveloped everything. From then on, all we could see were occasional sparks as the metal monsters lumbered up the track. When dawn broke, the objects had moved about two miles nearer the front.

"When's the attack?" laughed someone. "Christmas?"

The laughter was tempered with Jock's description of the inevitable mid air collision they had witnessed. The fireball had lit up the sky for some time until it crashed. Luckily, it wasn't any of our DHs.

They must have made more progress the following nights as we were not required to perform again and instead Hawker briefed us again on the forthcoming offensive for which we would be reprising our role of aggressive protection for the BEs.

Early reveille and breakfast had us ready to take off at the appointed time of 0600. As we climbed over the lines, we could see the smoke from the barrage falling on the German trenches. It was unusual in that the barrage had left wide lanes where no shells were falling, presumably so the mud wasn't too churned up for the tanks. Eventually we saw them, lumbering slowly through the gaps.

Fortunately, this was to be the offensive to end all offensives. The tanks would storm across no mans land, the infantry and cavalry would follow, the Germans would run away in terror and we would look on from above for all the world like Zeus or Ares inspecting the Greeks before Thermopylae. The staff were presumably hoping for a better result though.

We took off and flew in pairs towards the lines. I glanced around periodically and the sky seemed full of aeroplanes. Below I could see a flight of BEs, presumably loaded with bombs, on their slow way to join the fray. All it needed was the Navy to show up and we would have a full house.

We descended as we approached the lines, as much as anything through curiosity at the new monsters that were to win the war today. From five hundred feet we were rewarded with glimpses through the smoke that seemed to surround the entire operation. The artillery had been pounding away as usual creating a thick haze and the tanks themselves appeared to be pouring out smoke as they made their way forwards. We swept over the top climbing again to reposition ourselves for the arrival of the German scouts. I noticed as we climbed that the infantry were pouring out of the trenches only they weren't advancing in open order. Mostly they were taking cover behind the machines and good for them. Anything to avoid the deadly machine guns. It crossed my mind for a moment that we might really be on the verge of something here. Perhaps the P.B.I. would at last have the advantage.

Still, I wasn't about to find the answer as above the racket of my engine I heard the rattle of a machine gun nearby which brought me hurriedly back to our own particular task. The bile rose in my throat as we were instantly plunged into a furious melee. Everywhere I turned my head were aeroplanes and more aeroplanes. I had never seen anything like it. It seemed that the entire RFC and German air force had arrived for one last battle. The noise was incredible although why I noticed that I have no idea. My hand was gripping the stick as if to let go would allow me to plunge to the ground. My other hand was on the Lewis although so far I hadn't fired a shot. Aircraft shot across my bow so fast it was almost impossible to identify friend or foe. I kept craning round to see my tail and make sure no hun was about to attack it. McKay, my sidekick had disappeared in the mass. I could see a couple of pillars of smoke that registered the demise of someone and then I had a perfect target in front of me. I hesitated for a moment picking my spot as I turned onto his tail. As I did so he opened fire on a BE in front of him. I saw splinters of something and the BE observer frantically trying to get a shot at the German. I had seen the markings now and I squeezed the

Lewis trigger. The tracer arced away and I must have hit him because he suddenly pulled up almost vertically out of the stream. I tried to follow him but the DH2 did not have the guts for that sort of manoeuvre. The BE rolled away left in a descending turn, presumably trying to escape the battle. I stopped my climb and looked around for my adversary. Suddenly I was on my own. I seemed to have flown right through the fight. Then I saw the big German pulling out of a stall turn and heading my way. Plainly, I had upset him and now he was looking for revenge. There is only one thing for it of course when this happens and that is headlong flight. I pointed the nose down to pick up some speed and applied full throttle in the opposite direction.

Within seconds, I was back among the scrap. I hadn't even seen them ahead of me as I was concentrating on the location of friend hun, but here I was again, frantically heaving the stick all over the place to avoid collisions and very occasionally letting go the odd burst from the Lewis.

The noise of someone throwing stones on my engine nearly had me giving birth and something hot struck my cheek at which I howled in agony. I opened my eyes again to see a BE directly in front of me collide head on with a German. Oddly, there was no fire or explosion, just a tangled mass of wreckage, which floated momentarily before starting to descend. I heaved back in the nick of time and felt rather than heard an appalling bang, which tipped my nose forward. For a few seconds

I thought I was a goner, but the DH carried on flying. It felt odd though and I briefly wondered if my wheels had hit some of the wreckage from the collision. I daren't look just yet. Suddenly it was all over and I was among friends. The Germans seemed to vanish, including my opponent. I breathed a sigh of relief and closed my eyes for a moment.

We were above a large patch of cloud but moving slightly north we could see the battle below again. The BEs were regrouping and descending to a more suitable level to drop their bombs and we reformed above them. Someone was missing but I couldn't tell whom. There were at least five columns of smoke gently drifting away now.

Below I could see quite a lot of what was going on. We were directly over the German trenches now but there was very little fire coming our way. Looking west our troops were advancing in skirmishing order and quite quickly too. The tanks were spread out all over the place. A few seemed to have driven straight through the wire and over the frontline trench and around these were concentrations of troops moving through the gaps, exploiting what was clearly a local victory.

A glance forwards showed the BEs turning having laid their eggs and it seemed like a good time to go home ourselves. Apart from anything, I was low on ammunition and I suspected that everyone else was too.

We formed up loosely and I noticed Rutherford slide up beside me and wave and then point at my wheels. I had forgotten and now I peered over the side to see my starboard wheel was missing entirely. Port side looked battered but was at least still there. The jolly prospect of breaking my neck on landing presented itself and stayed with me all the way back. I was last to arrive, the wreckage underneath evidently holding me back. I flew overhead the field, my reluctance growing with every moment.

I circled the field once more, screwing up the necessary courage for this once only landing. As I flew past again, I noticed a little gang of onlookers, presumably waiting to see the Flight Commander come unstuck. I pushed that thought to the back of my mind and began the shallow descending turn onto my final approach. I wanted to be as slow as possible and with the breath of wind slightly on my port side. Two hundred feet and the controls started to go a bit sloppy as the DH approached its stalling speed. A little power to arrest the deceleration without gaining any height. Down, down, fifty feet and the fence marking the edge of the field flashed underneath. Twenty, ten feet, five, I pulled back a little and I was ploughing through the grass. The port wheel touched as I rolled ever so slightly to the left. I tried to close the throttle beyond the stop but there was nothing else I could do now but await events. I felt the starboard wing start to sink, and then the remains of the wheel touched the ground and all hell broke loose. The crowd of spectators described it accurately to me afterwards. Fortunately for me there was an afterwards.

Apparently, the remains of the starboard wheel dug into the ground sending the DH into a sharp turn to the right. The nose dropped down, the Lewis dug into the ground and the pilot was launched like a mortar shell when his harness mounting broke, possibly damaged by the earlier collision. I woke up surrounded by my colleagues and mumbled something about not being in a circus to which the obvious remarks about human cannonballs were made.

I had an appalling headache for the rest of the day that had not gone by the morning. I didn't fly the next day either and thanked my stars for it as that was the day the tide turned against us, not that I knew this at the time.

It wasn't until late afternoon in the mess that I walked in on a conversation describing what had apparently happened.

"4 FEs and 6 BEs. Less than ten minutes. All destroyed." Jock sounded utterly offended that this could happen at all.

"I heard it was 6 FEs and 8 BEs," added Saundby.

"Good God. Poor bastards."[107]

"They didn't stand a chance against those machines." This was Rutherford. He turned towards me. "Twin machine guns firing through

---

[107] This sounds very much like an action that took place on 17th September, the first for Jasta 2, which had only arrived on the front the previous day. Four of six FEs and two of eight BEs were destroyed by five Jasta 2 aeroplanes, including Richtofen and Boelcke, although other aeroplanes from both sides were involved later on in the action.

the propeller. Outperformed everything we had. Very aggressive. Not your usual hun." He gulped his whisky down and ordered another.

******

The offensive season was nearly over. The failure of the tanks to make any appreciable difference to the direction of the battle was disappointing but even so, promised much in the future. The rain had begun in earnest and everything was turning brown as the mud found its way into every crack and crevice. The Germans had failed to destroy the French at Verdun, helped by the British offensive that had caused such huge troop movements north and now with the Germans left in Verdun exhausted, the French were steadily retaking the lost forts. Douaumont and Thiaumont fell to the French before the end of September. Haig consolidated what little gains had been made and relative quiet descended. Relative only from a distant perspective though. From where I was standing, it still looked appallingly dangerous and now it was cold and wet again. The worst bit was now the troops had effectively suspended the offensive, we foolishly imagined the let up would apply to us as well. But no, not if air superiority was to be maintained to Trenchard's liking. We found ourselves flying every day provided the weather allowed us to, and it was always over the lines to attack the hun. But they had their new Albatros and Halberstadt machines and the DH2 was no match for either of them. Consequently, the losses started to mount up particularly amongst the newcomers who were still arriving with hardly any experience at all let alone enough to start fighting against superior enemies. Those of us who did have the experience tried desperately to pass it on in the limited time available, and a fortunate few survived long enough to learn for themselves the best way to stay alive. But mostly it was depressing for the squadron returning every afternoon to find another boy was missing. I say for the squadron, as for me, as long as I came back in one piece, there wasn't too much to be concerned about.

The only real success that came our way was through a combination of luck and tenacity on the part of those involved. Including me.

As usual, we were trying to do too much with too little and so Knight and McKay disappeared off towards the lines on an offensive patrol. I took off shortly after with another new boy whose name I cannot even remember. We were to go to the adjacent sector and for most of the transit to the front, I could see them, a couple of miles ahead. We climbed high above them and positioned ourselves slightly to the south.

The Germans were waiting for us. They had even come across no mans land. Five of them to start with. I saw my companion start waving frantically and pointing and saw Knight and McKay break away and start weaving and diving. The Germans were virtually queuing up to destroy them. We had no choice but to turn towards them and try and assist, but I was further terrified by the sight of another six Germans appearing from our side of the lines to join the melee. A burst of premature gunfire from my companion had the tight German formation scattering looking for the attacker and the temptation to shout 'It wasn't me' was strong. We passed through what would have been the centre of the six and dead ahead were the other five jostling for position behind the DHs both of which were manoeuvring like mad to get away. I rolled hard right and pushed into a descent aiming to go as low as possible and hopefully get some assistance from the ground, something that had not happened for a long time, and as I did so, I saw two machines ahead and above both in steep dives. One was marginally steeper than the other was because they were both heading for the same target and as they caught him up, I realised that the two huns had not seen each other, so intent on destruction were they. Almost in slow motion, I watched fascinated as the top aeroplane sank onto the lower one. The wheels struck the upper wing and a few pieces flew off. They separated instantly as they realised what had happened, and then for a few long seconds, both appeared under control.

It seemed as if everyone was transfixed with this unfolding drama and I don't remember hearing any gunfire at all. A few more seconds passed and I was about to breathe again when the top wing folded backwards and broke off floating in the air behind the now stricken craft. In that moment everyone knew the occupant was a dead man. What the Germans knew and we didn't was that the occupant was the great Boelcke.

Top wing missing and all strength gone, it started to break up. The engine was now a dead weight in the nose and dragged it down. The speed increased, the lower wings started to fall apart. I had seen it before of course. I lost sight of the wreckage as I suddenly remembered the present but the sky was clear. The Germans vanished in shock. Knight and McKay were long gone too having apparently out flown their adversaries. I looked around for my attendant and found him sitting patiently by my wingtip. We turned round and headed back for our sector and after an uneventful patrol returned home.

Knight and McKay were already back and I remember walking into the mess and finding the beginnings of a huge party. I questioned someone about the reason for this and was told it was because we had got the great Boelcke. Other people since have told me that there was no way the news would have reached the squadron that quickly but who knows. I just found a place at the bar and joined in. It took my mind off the fact that my aeroplane was now obsolete with precious little sign of anything new to replace it.

I led the dawn patrol the next day, as I was one of the few who were not hung-over from the nights excess. It was quiet though and the Germans seemed to be brooding over their loss. Someone suggested dropping a wreath and it was duly despatched and dumped on Boelcke's aerodrome.[108]

Hawker went on leave. He needed it. It was Guy Fawkes when he left and he missed another monumental binge when the squadron attempted to re-enact the destruction of parliament in the form of a small hut, which once emptied of various spares turned out to be fiercely combustible.

I borrowed his office and for a couple of weeks I was introduced to the problems of squadron command. I knew already what they were of course, but knowing and doing are two entirely different things. The most difficult part was writing letters to tell someone that their son was now spread over France or had been incinerated in a seven thousand feet fall from the sky. I lied as well.

I also found sending them out again and again without going myself strangely difficult. The thought that I wasn't going to be shot to pieces was exhilarating but even with my ability to shirk, I still felt it necessary to accompany a couple of the raids. It was all very wearing and overall I was glad when Hawker returned.

Leave had not been an uplifting experience for him though and in a rare moment of openness, he told me about a night in London where he had been unable to find anyone he knew because they were all dead. I sympathised with him but it seemed pointless telling him about my experience of leave. He decided the best cure was to fling himself back into the fray. Another couple of

---

[108] The inscription read, 'To the memory of Captain Boelcke, our brave and chivalrous foe.'

months and he would be promoted and going home anyway.

Next day, along with Jock and Saundby, he took off on an offensive patrol. Over Bapaume, they found what they had set out to find and Hawker dived on some two seaters. Jock and Saundby followed him but they were themselves being pursued by Albatros scouts covering the decoys below. In short order, Jock's engine was hit as was Saundby's but both of them saw the Major holding his own against the boche. Here Hawker's story came to an abrupt end.

I heard long afterwards that a couple of the cabbage eaters had described the aerial duel as a 'fight between first rate champions of the air' as they watched the outclassed DH2 hold off the far superior Albatros. It was unfortunate that the Albatros pilot was a man soon to become feared by the RFC. The fight was drifting further and further into German territory and Hawker must have known that he was going to have to run for it. He surprised the Albatros with a sudden dive to low level and zigzagged furiously towards home. He was almost there when with its final burst of fire, a bullet from the Albatros hit Hawker in the head killing him instantly. He crashed fifty yards short of the lines.[109]

---

[109] This is an accurate description of Hawker's last flight. It also confirms the identity of Jock Andrews, a highlander who was indeed one of the original pilots posted to Hounslow Heath and R.H.M.S. 'Bob' (or 'Sandy') Saundby, who went on to be deputy to 'Bomber' Harris in the second world war.

In the macabre way that only a German would consider, the pilot arranged for the DH2's machine gun to be dug out of the ground so that he could hang it on his wall like a pair of antlers. His name? Baron Manfred Freiherr Von Richthofen.

Chapter 24

It was a gloomy squadron now that the boss was dead. He had seemed invincible, not only to the boys that appeared every few days but to the experienced hands as well like me and Rutherford or Jock and Saundby. We eventually heard the whole story and how close he had come to getting away and it just seemed unfair for him to die this way. Not that there was a better way in my opinion. Plenty of worse ones of course.

The routine of squadron life carried on though. Dawn patrols, morning patrols, afternoon patrols but at least that was the end of it with the shortening days. None of us wanted to take over the squadron and so we took turns at running it. It wasn't too difficult to do as Hawker had instilled a good routine that continued more or less of its own volition. Flying was becoming more difficult as winter set in. Mist and fog regularly kept the squadron on the ground as well as torrential rain and cloud so low it seemed you could reach up and touch it. But we did fly occasionally and Trenchard still insisted on keeping the upper hand. The main offensives had finished and it seemed that the general view of the war was that we were now waiting for the spring to come along and help us finish the job.

It did not seem like it at the time but it was generally accepted after the event that the Somme offensive had at the very least stopped the frogs from throwing in the sponge, something that would have probably meant losing the entire war.

From an RFC point of view, we had maintained superiority over the lines but at an enormous cost in lives and machines. The difficulty now was that our machines were virtually all outclassed by the new German scouts and whilst there were not that many of them in comparison, whenever they pounced on an RFC formation, almost invariably it was destroyed. It did not help that the new pilots arriving in France were still as poorly trained if not worse and very few squadrons had either the time or the right people to both fight and train at the same time. Yet in those that did manage to train new pilots in aerial tactics and give them some time to find their feet before they ventured over the lines, the survival rate was much improved. In many ways the scout squadrons, with DH2s, FE2bs and Nieuports, fared worst because the new pilot was extremely vulnerable and had little idea of what to do when attacked. On the other hand the BE crews, although far more exposed in terms of the shortcomings of their machines, at least generally had one experienced member aboard as well as having to complete some training to establish the necessary routines for photographing and spotting.

However one viewed it, it was not funny. But it had to go on.

For me it had been going on far too long but having just had leave, albeit disrupted by unforeseen events, I could hardly claim to be in need of a rest especially without a squadron commander.

I took off in a foul mood. Christmas looked like being a total washout. Rutherford was due home and probably about to get a posting as flight commander somewhere, as were Jock and Sandy. I could see it now. My earlier promotion meant I was as likely to get the squadron as anyone but without any of its experienced pilots, and I had witnessed the toll this had taken on Hawker. I was somewhat preoccupied as the four of us set off towards the lines, myself, Rutherford and two newish boys.

The sun was low in the sky and what light there was emanating from it was directly in our faces. The wind seemed fairly set in the west as well meaning the familiar long haul home later. You will note here my optimism that there would be a journey home. We reached Pozieres without mishap and loosened our formation to allow us to weave when the archie started. But it didn't and we crossed the lines unmolested. There was no sign of the BEs we were supposed to be protecting but that wasn't unusual. We circled at the rendezvous for about fifteen minutes without anything happening at all. Periodically I stared down at the trenches and it seemed that both sides were dozing fitfully, not wanting anything to happen to disturb them from trying to keep warm in the bitter cold. As I thought about it I realised I was having trouble feeling my fingers in spite of my many precautions most of which were pointless. I felt sure there was ice forming in my gauntlets.

I shivered at the thought just as a burst of gunfire brought me back to reality. One of the DH2s seemed to rear up, smoke starting to trail behind it. A few pieces floated away and a red aeroplane shot past in a steep descent. Instinctively I rolled towards it and pushed forward frantically looking for the rest of them. They never seemed to hunt alone if they could help it. Typical Germans really with their sledgehammer approach to everything. I was not disappointed. In a few seconds, I counted eight more of them. I had rolled out of the descending turn, as now it was just a fight for life like many others previously. If I managed to shoot up a German, well so be it but my main concern was to escape with a whole skin.

As I craned my neck round I noticed more and more aeroplanes joining the fight. Some Nieuports had appeared from nowhere along with some BEs although God knows why they had joined in. At least some of the huns were obvious with their brightly painted craft although this smacked of a supreme arrogance to me. The sky was now full. Everywhere I looked or turned was a mass of aeroplanes buzzing around like a swarm of bees. There were bullets everywhere. I felt a couple pass through the cockpit, one grazing my gauntlet, as well as seeing a few new holes appear in the fabric.

I fired a burst at a weirdly multicoloured aeroplane but it carried on as if nothing had happened, weaving through the mass where I lost sight of it as I heaved backwards to avoid another machine that appeared to come at me from nowhere. I rolled hard left before I lost my speed entirely, and as I rolled level again another German reared up in front of me providing a perfect target and I let fly with a long burst finishing the drum of ammunition. For a moment, I thought I had wasted the whole lot but as I turned again I noticed the German machine suddenly roll over and burst into flames before beginning the long spin to the ground. I didn't have time to watch it as the fight was still developing and self-preservation had pushed itself to the fore again. I desperately wanted to change the drum but I had no chance as the manoeuvring got more and more violent in my attempts to avoid destruction. I had fleeting glimpses of aeroplanes of all shapes, some looking a little the worse for wear, some on fire, as well as an apparently continual cloud of ammunition. Half of the ammunition was friendly of course although it didn't realise it. There was an appalling crash and a random piece of floating wreckage bounced off the nose, hit the underside of the top wing and was shredded in the propeller, narrowly missing my head as it passed through. The engine note changed. Clearly the propeller was now unbalanced and the vibration threatened to shake the machine apart. I daren't throttle back too much or I would just make myself a sitting duck. Equally, if I left the engine running so fast it would destroy itself anyway. I considered this dilemma for a fraction of a second deciding that the only answer was to get out of the way as fast as possible. I rolled into a descending turn and was immediately forced to pull up to avoid a collision with a burning wreck. The sudden change of direction and the declining power available was too much for the DH and it suddenly fell over. At least that was what someone told me later was the cause for what happened next. For a few seconds I had no idea what had happened. When my brain caught up with the situation I realised I had seen this view before. I just hadn't seen it from quite so low. A picture of O'Connell sitting in his cockpit dead flashed before my eyes and spurred me into action. I pushed the rudder hard against the opposite stops and forced the stick forward and the ground stopped spinning round. I balanced the rudder again and pulled the stick back. I could feel every wire straining against me but the nose came up and nothing fell off. I was letting out a sigh of relief when I saw a flash of red out of the corner of my eye. I knew I was done for instantly.

In that moment I died another coward's death as I imagined the bullets ripping through the fabric and setting fire to the machine, whereupon it would roll over and drop to the ground with its occupant writhing in agony as I had seen so many times before. I found myself mumbling pleas to the almighty for it to be over soon. At the same time I was descending as that was the only way I could maintain any sort of speed, as well as weaving around the sky in the vain hope that the owner of the red machine would go away and leave me alone. But he didn't. He could see I was in trouble and he was deliberately shepherding me away from the safety of our lines and I knew that the moment I tried to run for it would be when he shot me down.

Lower and lower and further away and this was my last chance. I hauled the machine round, felt rather than heard something give way, ducked instinctively as a long burst played on the fuselage and the tail, realised it was futile and looked for somewhere to land. We were so far from the front line now that there were numerous empty fields. I picked one and concentrated on aiming for it. Slowly the ground rose up to meet me, and the machine subsided onto it, gently tearing itself apart as the wings collapsed and the fuselage broke. I can't say I really noticed any of this at the time. I think I may have been concussed at some point during the landing and it was in this state that I found myself walking towards another machine that had landed waving a handkerchief that I had found and bawling "Kamerad, nicht schiessen," or something equally foolish.

I nearly walked into him in my bemused state. He stared at me quizzically and I looked down my nose at him. This was because I was alive, English and a good foot taller. And he was just a squarehead of course.[110]

---

[110] It is quite possible that Flashman was taller than Richtofen although a foot seems excessive. Photographs of the Richtofen brothers show Manfred as being shorter than his brother Lothar who stood out in a crowd, and probably shorter than average. Flashman in common with his family was a big man and would have appeared to tower over Richtofen although the actual difference was probably a few

"Richtofen," he announced as though I should have known.

"Flashman," I replied in the same manner.

"I sink you are from ze same squadron of Major Hawker?"

Immediately I knew that this was the bastard who had shot him down and killed him.

"Afraid I can't tell you that old boy." I glanced over at the wreckage of my machine hoping it would catch fire on its own.

"Of course, of course. Vee go and have dinner now and zen in ze morning your var vill be over." He laughed at his own joke. I smiled thinly before following him to where a horse drawn cart had appeared. He motioned at me to get in which I did.

The ride was at least short. We rumbled slowly up to an aerodrome which for a heart stopping moment looked like the one from where I had stolen the Eindecker but wasn't. Not that anyone would have recognised me but it was as well not to publicise that little episode.

Their mess wasn't so different from our own. The pilots all looked the same age. They all looked suitably scruffy in a tidy German kind of way, smelt of oil and cordite, and shortly they would smell of alcohol. In deference to me, those who could spoke in English, and the conversation was virtually the same as their opposite numbers just over the lines. Initially I said very little, preferring to listen and size them up. It was hard to tell for certain but I was getting the impression

inches.

that this was some kind of elite squadron. They called it a Jasta.[111]

I was starting to lose interest in the proceedings, not least because I was decidedly hungry now and the Germans were starting to get drunk and noticeably louder. They had toasted all and sundry with schnapps, including the Kaiser, the Fatherland and most importantly themselves. I had remained on the edge and it was only as I was staring into space that I suddenly noticed what was hanging on the mess walls, just above eye level. Instead of the usual dreary decoration, they had gone for something slightly unusual. The remains of a number of our aeroplanes with serial numbers were nailed up. I didn't recognise any of the numbers but it was still very strange.

"You do not approve?"

I glanced at him and smiled but made no comment.

"Goering. Hermann Goering."[112] He held out his hand and I shook it.

"I wouldn't give any of it house room myself." I looked up again.

He chuckled at what he imagined was a joke but in fact was a simple truth. I took the opportunity to study him. He was a big man, his height accentuated by his immaculate riding

---

[111] Jasta, short for Jagdstaffeln or Hunting Squadron.
[112] Hermann Goering had recently returned to the front after being shot through the thigh. He was posted to Jasta 26, so in this instance must have been visiting Richtofen who was commanding Jasta 2.

boots. He was the picture of the German aristocrat with the associated air of arrogant superiority.

"You prefer Turner perhaps? Or Stubbs?" I wondered if I was supposed to be impressed with his knowledge of my drawing room walls although Hogarth was more to my taste.

"Cranach." That raised his eyebrows. "One of your lot I believe. Renaissance," I added just to confirm his ignorance.

"Pah, then it is just the usual weak minded rubbish. None of them had the vision to see that their supposed greatness was in fact a mirage, an illusion, a deception of the highest order." Clearly, I had touched on a nerve. "Take your average wop, now." I am sure he said something like that but my mind was beginning to wander as he launched into a detailed description of the shortcomings of the French and the Italians and even the Austrians, followed by a summary of the virtues of being German. He mentioned the English in passing but obviously felt it would be rude to put them down too much in the presence of the celebrated Major Flashman, former colleague of the late Major Hawker. I only listened half-heartedly because there was in fact nothing else to do as dinner was delayed.

"Albrecht Durer of course was one of the most important of the gothic artists, the teacher perhaps of the lesser men." I could see the eyes of a fanatic and was beginning to wonder how long I would have to endure this harangue.[113] I had only mentioned Cranach to score a point and

---

[113] Hermann Goering spoke little or no English.

demonstrate the advantages of a public school education where one could stare at women's tits all day long provided it was possible to claim that one's mind was being improved in the process.[114] Providence finally got bored as well and announced that dinner was about to be served. I noticed that quite a number of the Germans were staggering slightly, though neither Goering or Richtofen were among this gang. They entered the dining room first. Goering motioned to me to join him and Richtofen at the top of the table. There was little ceremony and shortly the locals were punishing the drink again. I sat mute merely absorbing the picture. The same young faces, the strain etched on them, the bravado and slightly false over confidence. The conversation had reverted entirely to German as the alcohol consumption increased and mine was not good enough to follow all of it but I could feel the general drift. They had new orders to go on the offensive and use the superiority of their machines. There was also some talk of concentrating the Jastas and using them to clear a particular part of the front line of enemy machines to allow observations for their own side, presumably in preparation for an attack. I thought I caught some discussion about the relative

---

[114] Lucas Cranach the elder was a German renaissance artist of the late fifteenth and early sixteenth century. He specialised in portraits, including many of European royalty. He was a friend of Martin Luther, painting him on numerous occasions, as well as a leading protestant of the time. Flashman presumably knew him for his numerous nudes, many of which concentrate on Adam and Eve.

strength in numbers and was surprised to learn that they at least thought the RFC had about double the number of German machines. I had no idea this was the case, assuming they were right of course.[115]

Suddenly I realised they were talking to me.

"Tonight you stay here but in ze morning vee have to send you to prison. Too many of you escape from us eh?" at which he chuckled as if to reinforce what a jolly game it all was. "Of course you vill not escape tonight, no?"

"Not tonight," I replied. Not ever if there was a way to spend the rest of the war in a comfortable place away from the bullets and shells and death and destruction. A plump mädchen to liven up the evenings would complete the picture. I would soon find out of course what exactly was in store and whilst I was not under any illusions, I guessed it would not be too arduous. The brandy had arrived and some rather good cigars and soon the table was wreathed in smoke. Tiredness was creeping up on me. I had had an interesting day of course. The last remark I heard was Richtofen as he said, "Vee vill make sure your friends know you are here," after which I must have fallen asleep in my chair.

---

[115] Essentially this is correct. The RFC strength was roughly double that of the German Air Force, but the German machines were of a superior quality and also included far more scouts. As a result, Hindenburg ordered an unequal distribution of squadrons allowing occasional local air superiority for German observations of the British lines or to deny the opposite for a period.

******

Shivering woke me up. At the moment of waking, I couldn't see and for one appalling moment, I thought I was blind. I was in a cell and it was as black as pitch, so much so that I could not actually see my hand when I held it in front of my face unless I was virtually touching my nose. I decided it must be dark outside still. Someone had taken my watch. I sat up on my bed and in so doing, realised it was a hard slab. So much for a comfortable night.

Even as my eyes got used to the dark I could not make out anything in the cell. I stood up and gingerly moved around to assess my latest prison. I had hardly moved when my outstretched hand touched the wall. I turned to my right and took two steps before encountering another wall and having done the same behind me, I quickly realised that the room was no more than the size of a large bed and apart from the bed, there was nothing in it. Scrabbling around underneath I found a bucket in which I was clearly meant to perform.

Having explored the cell I returned to the bed and lay down again. Getting up had demonstrated that I still had too much alcohol aboard. I lay pondering my situation. It was a pity the soft part was over but then Richtofen had been right when he mentioned the ease of escape from the Germans, regularly helped by the locals. I presumed they had learnt their lesson.

I could not tell whether it was hours or minutes that had passed. I assumed the former as my head had stopped hurting. There was the sound of a key rasping in a lock. I couldn't tell which end of the cell it was, as I had not even found a door handle. A door was flung back on my right and the light was blinding. I recoiled into the wall covering my eyes. Slowly they adjusted to the light and I focussed on the two figures in front of me. They simply stood and stared down at me. I returned the favour by staring at the door.

"Major Flashman?" It was posed as a question.

"Who wants to know?" I replied insolently thinking I was safe. There was an almighty slap followed by an almighty wail as the quiet man smashed the back of his hand across my face.

"Major Flashman?"

"Yeth," I moaned through my red-hot cheek. I carried out a small survey on my teeth with my tongue and decided they were all still there and in one piece.

"My master wishes to see you." They turned round and marched out. I took it that I was to follow. A guard fell in behind me and the little procession continued until we reached a closed door. It was opened from within and we all marched in. The chief saluted the back of an enormous chair and announced the arrival of one Major Flashman.

"Good, good," said a voice.

A man stood up and came round the chair to stand directly in front of me.

"Yes, we have met before," he said in perfect English. "Of course you remember me." It was a statement rather than an enquiry, but he was wrong. I didn't remember him at all and I was making it all too obvious that this was the case. Even if I had, I doubt I would have been able to speak. Perhaps he recognised the terrified stare of the helpless animal. He laughed.

"I will help you. Over two years ago. Sarajevo." My mind filled instantly with a picture of Skene and the terrifying end of his last flight. "Dimitrijevic. Colonel Dragutin Dimitrijevic." He paused and let me continue to stare. I very nearly said how jolly nice it was to meet him again after all this time but something stopped me. Perhaps it was the tense atmosphere. Finally unable to hold his stare any longer, I turned to look around the room at the other occupants, all of whom were staring at me.

"It is very fortunate that we found you at all. A chance meeting and a chance mention of your name. Hermann was most obliging." I had guessed that much, but whether it was fortunate or not remained to be seen. "You see, we have so much in common, so much to talk about. Your Father..." He let this comment hang in the air for a moment whilst I wondered if he was another bastard with an axe to grind. "....was temporarily employed by the rulers of the empire. It is even mentioned in your strange book, Who's Who. Personal bodyguard to H.I.M. Emperor Franz Josef, 1883." I wondered where this was going as I could recall the whole episode in my Father's papers and if read in the original was yet another adventure with some less than glorious moments. More to the point, which side was he on, and which side did he imagine I was on and what did he propose to do about it. These reflections did not, as you may imagine, allay my fears.

"I thought it was strange when you were presented to the Archduke that he reacted as he did. I noted it as something of interest but little practical value at the time. As I am, or was, only tolerated in his circles, it took me sometime to find out why exactly he recognised you, or your name. Needless to say, I did find out the answer, but you and your friends were long gone. And the Archduke was dead. In case you are unaware of the connection, I will enlighten you, so you can at least appreciate the situation in which you find yourself. The people I represent have long resented the rule of the Austrians over people they neither like nor know anything about. They are dedicated to changing this by any means available. I am sure you know something of the history of the Habsburgs." He paused his lecture to investigate the, I assure you involuntary, snort of derision that issued from the centre of the room. He had been pacing around restlessly and getting more and more worked up but now he stopped. "Can I assume that you are not aware of the nature of this family?" I nodded my assent. He let out a sigh, a strange sound emanating from this particular man, but he continued. "These people have oppressed us for eight hundred years, but their time is finished. This war will exhaust them and their power will be broken. Serbia will throw off the shackles and rise up as the phoenix from the centuries of darkness." I thought he was mad but I didn't dare to say so. "We have already removed the original heir, the Empress and the replacement heir. Of course, you were present at the demise of the Archduke Ferdinand. The old Emperor has just died. All that remains is to remove the new Emperor, and our victory will be complete." Somehow, I knew that yours truly had been accommodated in their plans. Why? I didn't know, but I could hazard a guess.

"You are wondering why we have chosen you for this enterprise. Firstly, it removes the debt you owe us." My mouth opened in disbelief at this statement. How could I possibly be in debt to this band of lunatics? "Your Father prevented the assassination of the Emperor long ago and it is fitting that his son repairs the damage. Secondly and more practically, you are the only one who can carry out this act. You are effectively unknown to the Emperor but have a name that can only be revered by him. You are English and therefore not given to murder and assassination as a political tool. Finally, you are a proven man of resource." (He was wrong there on many counts!) I looked up at him in wonder at this point. "Ah yes, we know all about your antics with the German aeroplane and your connections to the secret service. There is no point in denying this." He grinned at me in the way a wolf would grin at a cornered sheep.

"I can't. It is impossible." So far so good. I was managing to keep my nerve and think quickly. "Yes, I have worked for the secret service. But I was only the errand boy. I am not trained for close quarter fighting or assassination. Besides, I am a prisoner of the Germans and they won't...." I stopped and looked around the room.

"You were a prisoner of the Germans. But Hermann is more than a little sympathetic to our cause and was delighted to allow us to borrow you for a few days. Of course once we have finished with you, we will return you to the Germans."

"You can't bloody well do this to me. I am protected under the Geneva Convention. I am a prisoner of war, not an assassin. I don't care about your bloody Emperor and I am not going to kill him for you. They know I am not dead. They will make enquiries. This is too much." I held my head in my hands and blubbed.

"Just as we suspected. Take him back. We must begin the preparations." For a delicious moment I thought they had realised they were mistaken about me but as they filed out of the room, I heard someone say, "We cannot use him Colonel, surely?" only for Dimitrijevic to reply, "You are too easily misled Kratky. Men like him are trained to use any method available. His Father was a master of pretence at being a coward and it has been passed on. You have read the papers on the affair."[116]

---

[116] For more detail on General Flashman's service for the Emperor, see Flashman and the Tiger.

I was dragged unceremoniously back to my small cell wailing most of the way. Surely, the fools could see I wasn't up to it. They flung me through the door and it closed behind them. Total darkness returned. The cell was filled with what the Celtic brethren would call a lament. Then I cursed the swine until I was hoarse before crying myself to sleep, something I hadn't done for weeks or even months.

******

I awoke in darkness. It could have been night or day. I had no idea how long I had been there. I had no watch. Occasionally the door would be thrust open and amidst the blinding light, food and water shoved wordlessly onto the bed. There was no sign of Dimitrijevic and his deranged ideas and I briefly felt hopeful that he had been persuaded to drop the whole mad scheme. But as time went on, I realised that was a vain hope. There was no point in keeping me cooped up if he didn't want me to do something unpleasant. My mood swung erratically and I started to both crave and dread the appearances at the door. I tried shouting at the assortment of people who brought the meals, I tried shouting out of the door, I tried sitting in silence and kicking the servant. Nothing made the slightest difference.

I began to feel exhausted. It seemed to me that they were waking me up from deep sleeps every time the door opened. I started to have vivid dreams and hallucinations.

The worst had me trapped upside down in a burning cockpit and falling slowly towards the ground. Each time the fire came closer and closer, and I desperately tried to get further away, waking and finding myself bundled into a corner of the room. I could hear Skene and his last cry and it seemed I would wake and still be able to hear it. It was only just this side of real torture with thumbscrews, iron maidens and other cheery paraphernalia but it broke me just as effectively.

"The BE2c is my bus I shall not want.

He maketh me to come down in green pastures.

He leadeth me astray on cross-country flights.

He maketh me to be sick.

He leadeth me where I will not go.

He taketh me along and thou preparest a crash before me in the presence of thine enemies.

Thy RFC anointeth me with oil and thy tank leaketh badly.

Surely to goodness thou shall not follow me all the days of my life; else I shall dwell in the house of Colney Hatch.[117]

Forever."

The pilot's psalm. Perhaps it was just the thought of Colney Hatch that made me think I was beginning to go mad. Finally, I could stand it no longer.

---

[117] Colney Hatch was an infamous Victorian Lunatic Asylum.

"What do you want me to do?" I wailed the next time the door opened. Dimitrijevic appeared as if from nowhere.

"Ah, Major Flashman, you have seen the error of your ways at last. This task will not be as, er, difficult as you imagine. Our plan is very straightforward."

Chapter 25

Flashman scholars will know exactly the position I now found myself in. My blasted Father had contrived to get involved in a scheme to rescue the Emperor's halfwit brother and had been awarded some medal or other and earned the gratitude of the imperial family. For reasons that were far from clear, Bismarck, another German and sometime acquaintance of the General, had contrived to shanghai him into trying to foil a plot to kill the Emperor by turning up unannounced at the Imperial hunting lodge and accidentally on purpose killing the assassins. What Bismarck had failed to appreciate was that his right hand man was not only in on the plot itself but was the assassin. By a stroke of luck, my Father discovered that his gun was loaded with blanks and realised the meaning of that. He attempted to attack the assassin only to find himself clobbered in the process. The British Secret Service was involved as well and it was their shadow that saved him from another early demise.

The Emperor lived on, almost entirely unaware of the goings on in the dark and how close he had been to having a steel spike in his gullet, but the name of Flashman would live for evermore in the more unsavoury chapters of the Habsburg history. The startled rabbit reaction of the Archduke all those years previously made much more sense now I had all the facts to hand. No doubt he wondered why I was there, and if he knew too much he probably had the palpitations.

If he had looked even harder beyond the spectre of a Flashman at the ball, he would have seen the reaper ready with his scythe.

But I digress.

Dimitrijevic filled me in on the missing details. "The new Emperor has been informed of the dangers of his position and the existence of groups that do not have his welfare at heart. He has also been informed of the rumours circulating of a plot to kill him. It is believed to include some Frenchmen, an Englishman and some Hungarians. He understands that his secret police are doing all in their power to get to the bottom of the plot, including consulting all known sources. This happens to include your own secret services. It also includes my occasional employers." He didn't say who this employer was but it was obvious that he was double-crossing either them or the Emperor. I was also surprised that our own hapless mob was involved. I suppressed a grin when I thought of Cumming receiving a request for help from this lot. But then the more I thought about it, I realised that it would not have been quite that simple. He was speaking again. "Of course a strange coincidence has been brought to his attention. The presence of one Flashman, intercepted on a mission for the British Secret Service, attempting to prevent an assassination that could, if presented correctly, destabilise the entente, perhaps enough to conclude the war but for the wrong side. The Emperor is naturally intrigued by all this and has, of course, requested to meet this Flashman, not least because he recalls a heroic deed that saved his Uncle many years ago." He paused for effect, pacing slowly round the room until he stopped and turned to face me, catching my eye and holding it, all the time gauging what I made of his clever plan.

Well the answer was bugger all. I didn't understand how the Emperor could be made to think any of this was normal and what the hell he thought I was going to tell him at our little tea party was beyond me as well. Of course, I wasn't actually going to tell him anything. I was just going to make the fictional mission a reality and bedamned to what everyone else thought about it. Perhaps it would destabilise everything. Perhaps someone would eventually let me go home and never be called upon to do anything dangerous ever again. Perhaps, but it was not going to be Dimitrijevic.

"Well Major, I think you understand the position. We must go southeast from here. We have to go to Vienna and there you will meet the Emperor. Once. For now, you will eat, sleep, and in the morning, we will leave.

It didn't take long to pack. Now I was one of the gang, I had been provided with the essentials having lost all mine in the crash all those days ago. Or weeks was it? Now I thought about it I didn't know and no one had seen fit to tell me. I wasn't even sure if Christmas had been and gone. I certainly had not had an appropriate dinner.

Dimitrijevic breezed in full of the joys of spring. He seemed to think we were off on a Boy

Scouts jaunt in the woods and that I couldn't wait to begin.

"I am sure it has crossed your mind that our journey may afford ample opportunity to disappear. I wish to assure you that should you attempt to break our bond, then you most certainly will.... disappear."

The threat alone was enough to set my innards quaking. I ignored the statement and studied the horizon, which was grey and forbidding. Like all journeys, it promised to be utterly tedious and devil the sign of a woman for company. Dimitrijevic was obviously one of the more abstemious of his race. I was pretty sure my history lessons had included much about the old royal courts in Vienna and so on, and they had been pretty debauched places. Of course my own Father had first hand information on the nineteenth century version, but presumably their own incarnation of Victoria had put paid to all that. Just like at home of course. Except for Bertie the Bounder and his set who had tried hard to keep the family traditions alive and well, ably assisted by General Flashman and Co.

I clambered aboard a comfortable looking coach and settled into a corner. If I had to go, I was definitely having the best seat in the house. We shuffled off as it started to rain, slowly at first becoming heavier as the time passed. Shortly after consuming the contents of a hamper that Dimitrijevic conjured from under the seats, we arrived at a station. It hardly mattered but I think it was Oudenaarde. If not it was definitely somewhere that the French had received a thrashing. I was highly displeased to find that train journeys in occupied Belgium and Germany were as bad as those in France. There was one slight difference and that was that as we were officers, the average squarehead shifted out of the way mighty fast once he realised. Perhaps they thought they would get a flogging if they didn't, who knows, but everyone knew their place and kept to it. I could just see that working in England.

We sat on the train for the best part of the afternoon and it didn't move an inch. Dimitrijevic was on the verge of having kittens as presumably he thought this would be as good a time as any for me to slip my cable. How he thought I was going to disappear amongst hundreds of German troops disguised as a British officer, God only knew.

As always, I had slipped into an optimistic appraisal of the position. First, I did not have to risk my life three or four times a day in a flimsy aeroplane. Second, I was warm and reasonably comfortable. Third, I wasn't hungry or thirsty and there was a decent bottle of whisky stashed in my valise, something I had insisted upon and had been granted with no more than a grunt. Finally, there was plenty of time for the whole plan to fall apart before I ever had to consider actually carrying it out. Then it would be back to the chokey of course, but that was no hardship. No prison could be worse than Rugby.

As darkness fell, a whistle sounded, a great scramble started to get back on the train and a few minutes later, it moved with a great clanking and grinding, slowly picking up speed as it headed for the German border. I wondered where all these troops were going. Leave probably to spend Christmas at home. I had discovered that Christmas was not for another couple of days, so these were the lucky ones. I brooded on that and my misfortune at spending Christmas here until Dimitrijevic told me they were heading for the eastern front and were jolly upset about it as it was about ten times colder there. It was their own fault of course.

The swaying motion of the train and the dark soon had me feeling drowsy and I drifted in and out of sleep. Dimitrijevic relaxed a little, realising that I was not going to attempt to jump from a speeding train, and sat down.

It was hardly a refreshing journey even in the better part of the train. Too many stops, interruptions, and sudden braking for proper sleep. At least my host could not blame it on the bombing of railway junctions. He could, however, blame it on the necessity to move troops around to cope with the damned British, and unceasingly did. His relaxed state had not lasted long and he was now primed to go off.

"Where do you think I am going to go? We are deep in German territory now and my chance of escape must be limited."

"Ah, yes. But a man of your resource." He jumped again as we crossed some points unexpectedly. And then it occurred to me. He was more worried about being found out himself than me vanishing. Of course, there were more than a few factions in the German hierarchy. There were plenty in the British but on the whole, they tended not to kill each other. They sat in parliament instead.

Perhaps Richtofen and Goering were conniving at something without the knowledge or approval of their masters. Perhaps they had some longer-term aims. I didn't know but it gave me a small chink in the armour of my captors. Not everyone would see things their way.[118]

The journey ground on and on. At some stage, Dimitrijevic announced that we were in Munich. I started from my seat, peered through the windows, and saw nothing whatsoever that set Munich apart from any other station I had ever seen. It was odd though. Places and people kept cropping up from my Father's past. What I had done to deserve this I could not fathom at all.

We had to leave the train here. Dimitrijevic did not explain why but we set off for somewhere called Rosenheim, about twenty-five miles southeast of Munich. The full force of winter showed itself as we drove. There was plenty of hail and rain and very little to ward off the effects. My bottle was all but empty and my requests for more had been met with stony silence. I had contemplated refusal to continue under these

---

[118] Hermann Wilhelm Goring was a typical Bavarian officer, educated at a cadet college and officer's school before joining the German air force and serving throughout the war. He showed no apparent inclination for politics until he met Adolf Hitler in 1923.

conditions but decided that in doing so I might inadvertently play my ace card too early. So I sat in the corner, shivering uncontrollably.

It was evening by the time we arrived. The cart in which we had travelled rolled into the front of a gothic pile, which with the black sky and occasional flash of lightning to silhouette the buildings could easily have come straight from Stoker's pages. My unease was not helped when we entered the main hall to find an entire Company of infantry taking their ease. They studied the newcomers for a minute or two before returning to whatever was previously occupying their attention.

An enormous servant appeared and shepherded us away from the mob and into a smaller suite of rooms where at last there was a fire. I stood directly in front of it for an age before I felt really warm again.

"We rest here for two nights, maybe three. The servant will provide everything you need." Dimitrijevic muttered a few sweet nothings to the servant before disappearing through the door. I heard the sound of bolts sliding into place and knew that they would be watching my every move.

I did nothing, at least nothing to excite any suspicion at all. I ate, slept, paced the room occasionally and bided my time. Three nights turned into four, and I was just getting ready to retire when I heard a commotion outside the door. There were some raised voices, orders were barked and then I heard the bolts sliding back and the door was thrust open.

"It is time to leave Major. Fifteen minutes." He spun on his heel and marched back through the door. Well, we would see about that. The servant appeared with my valise and fifteen seconds later, I was ready to go.

It was another forty minutes before Dimitrijevic returned. I was really quite fed up with all this now and I foolishly let my guard down and called him a bloody peasant, which of course he was. His fury was a sight to see. How he never struck me or pulled out his pistol that, too late, I had noticed he was wearing, remains an unsolved mystery. He eventually calmed down enough for us to embark on the final leg of the mission. You can imagine how my feelings changed once he had informed me of this.

Another freezing ride found us in another station and shortly on another train. This one wasn't of the military variety and it occurred to me that a denunciation might be in order. He had told me we would disembark in Vienna itself and surely some of the locals might take exception to someone who was coming to kill the Emperor. Except there weren't any. It was the middle of the night when we arrived and the locals were all in bed being kept warm by someone else's wife.

We left the station, the carriage wheels making tracks in the thin snow as we ghosted along in virtual silence. Dimitrijevic was keeping a close eye on my every movement now, almost as if he expected me to do something desperate. I daren't move a muscle. We pulled into the front of a house with dark windows. One of our accompanying crew opened the door and we filed in, Dimitrijevic last in line. At the back of the house, a small room had been prepared for our arrival. Food, drink and a bed. I slumped down and removed my boots.

"Now bugger off. I want to sleep."

"Yes. And in the morning, we work." He stared at me for a few seconds and convinced that I was not about to evaporate or explode, he left.

******

Morning came and work we did. Dimitrijevic was not available as he was out assessing the situation. Spread out on a large table were maps of the city, some enlarged to show particular routes to and from the palace at Schonbrunn. This I gathered was to be the setting for the crime. The palace itself was about three miles southwest of the centre of the city. I didn't know where exactly we were but it would be useful to have some reference points once I found out. Kratky was a hard taskmaster. I was to learn four different routes to the palace each one beginning at a different point in the city. There were also four escape routes, again each finishing in a different place. I had to memorize them, particularly the landmarks I would come across on each one. On top of this was a detailed map of the palace. This also I was to commit to memory, at least the route from a particular door to another door into the Emperor's suite.

Kratky would talk me through each route in turn, leave me for half an hour studying before returning to interrogate me on the exact details. It was exhausting, repetitive and did not reassure me at all about the chances of success on my part. Midway through the afternoon, Dimitrijevic returned.

"It is ready. We are ready. Tomorrow night. The eve of the New Year. That is our time. You," pointing to me, "must know all this information by then. Tomorrow I will explain how you are to proceed once inside the palace." You will note that I was just to carry out a procedure. Nothing as frightful as a murder. I did not reply and Dimitrijevic disappeared again. The rest of the afternoon was spent studying. There was nothing for it. I had to know these routes as I suspected my life would depend on it.

After we had supped, I spent the rest of the evening alone in my room, alternately rehearsing the routes to the palace and gnawing at my fingers in the hope that I would have a revelation. I didn't of course and the decisive moment drew ever closer. I watched it minute by minute throughout the night and by morning was thoroughly out of sorts as well as tired. There was no let up and I yawned my way through more of Kratky's dull lectures.

About three o'clock, Dimitrijevic appeared again. He looked thoroughly pleased with himself.

"Excellent, excellent," he began. "Everything is in place. Now then Major, to business. It is better than even I had hoped. Where shall I begin?" He was talking somewhat at random in his excitement. "We can dispense with the route into the palace. I have procured an invitation, a personal invitation from the Emperor for the Major to the palace tonight for the New Year celebration. He is delighted that the Major is in Vienna and hopes his incarceration will be enlivened by the ball." I raised my eyebrows having experienced the Germans at a party far too many times for it to be an enlivening experience. "So far so good. Now here is the clever part. My friends and I have arranged a disturbance for a little after midnight. To most people it will just appear as part of the fun, some peasants trying to muscle in on the rulers, but to the Emperor's personal guards it will be a trial. Imagine. The history of assassination in the family is long and they will jump to the correct conclusion that the Emperor is in danger. Consequently, they will attempt to remove the protagonists immediately and preferably execute them. In so doing, their direct presence with the Emperor will be virtually removed, particularly as I have arranged for certain of his staff to be taken ill. However, at the moment of crisis when the guards are trying to contain the problem amidst the hordes of drunken guests, a perfectly sober Major Flashman, son of the renowned protector of the Habsburgs will offer his services as close guard to the Emperor. In their relief, they will accept immediately and allow the Major to escort the Emperor to his chambers where he will be safe. You see my friend? It could not be easier. And once the deed is done? Well, you will guard the chamber where the Emperor is sleeping having retired suffering from exhaustion, until such time as the guard returns and relieves you, at which point you can leave on your designated escape route."

Having escaped by wandering out of the palace, I would be met by the Queen of Sheba and Uncle Tom Cobbleigh who would then arrange for passage back to England in the royal train, attended by an army of amazons ministering to my every whim.

It was therefore with some trepidation that I began preparing for the nights excitement. I was to be told the escape route at the last possible moment. Someone slipped into the conversation that there would be other of Dimitrijevic's people mingling at the ball to keep a protective eye on me and make sure I carried out the required act. I had assumed that this would be the case but having it spelt out that unless one carries out a murder then one is likely to become the victim of one is a sight more unnerving.

Dimitrijevic and Kratky wolfed down an enormous dinner and I noticed that Kratky in particular, beneath the bravado, punished the wine with relish. I ate nothing at all. All too soon, the time for our departure arrived. I was not in uniform as that seemed a trifle antagonistic so some appropriate civilian wear had been acquired. It had an excellent cut to it and I wondered where on earth they had got it from as it fit perfectly. I say so myself but I cut rather a fine figure as I stepped out of the carriage at the front of the palace.

"Herr Major Fleshmann und Herr Oberst Dimitrijevic." Two things surprised me, first that I had been announced first and second that the Colonel used his real name. I dismissed it as of no consequence and applied myself to charming the horde of appalling women who swarmed briefly round the newcomers before returning to the task of reducing the mountain of champagne to nought.

Fortified with my own minor contribution to the task, Dimitrijevic steered me towards the Emperor's gang of toadies. Exclamations and before I knew it I was standing before the man himself. I bowed graciously which seemed appropriate in the circumstances and then before I had the chance he grabbed my fin and pumped it up and down as though by doing so he would be ensuring my protection. He smiled and muttered something unintelligible at which the whole crew roared with laughter.

There were a few more pleasantries and then some other supplicant was in the firing line. I drifted away to where a table was laden with delicacies of all sorts and tucked in, feeling ravenous suddenly. Time dragged by particularly as the Germans got drunk in the approved manner. I couldn't even talk to the women much as my usual method was useless, as I was required to stay at the ball.

It was a quarter to midnight. The talk now was all of the fireworks that were to accompany the end of the year and there was a general drift onto a large veranda. There were some loud bangs and after the initial surprise, everyone laughed and said how dreadful that someone had let off a firework too early. Whoever it was would find himself in the dungeons shortly. But then there was murmuring near the rail. Some shouts came from below and the report of a rifle firing. There were some gasps nearby and the women started to look frightened. The men, bar one, started to assume protective positions and look round for the source of the outrage.

I could see the Emperor's party near the doors into the palace and guards had started to appear from the woodwork.

An exchange of shots caused more consternation and guards were moving to the rail and crouching behind the pillars.

"Now is the time," a voice said in my ear.

I found myself being steered towards the Emperor's party. Just to add to the confusion, the fireworks began. I heard a brief snippet of conversation.

"Yes your majesty. The guards are needed in the garden."

Bang, crackle, bang.

"At once, your majesty."

Bang, bang bang.

"I will find him now," bang.

"Here he is your majesty."

Someone shoved me forward.

"Perhaps I could be of some assistance," I found myself saying over the growing noise below.

"Yes, Herr Major. This door is the only way from here to the royal apartments. Perhaps a guard…" Whoever was speaking tailed off as His Majesty's attention had been grabbed by someone I recognised and who was clearly now dissuading him from posting me as sentry on the door.

"Would the Herr Major consent to escort His Majesty back to his apartment, there to mount guard at the entrance until these rebels are rounded up?"

"What a splendid idea," I replied. Someone shoved a weapon into my hand, which I pushed into my waistband.

"Lead on your Majesty," I shouted above the din. Chaos was fast approaching.

We twisted and turned through the palace, some other servant leading, the Emperor in the middle and yours truly bringing up the rear. I kept a good lookout behind, as I wanted to know if anyone was following, particularly if he was called Kratky or Dimitrijevic.

Not a soul. Suddenly the lead man stopped at an ornate door. He heaved it open and went in. A few seconds later, he reappeared and ushered the Emperor through the door. He motioned me to wait outside but I ignored him. If he thought I was hanging around in the corridor, he was wrong. He glared at me as I followed them and no doubt cursed me for a blasted foreigner. The Emperor had hardly said a word through all this and was content to be taken sheep like into his apartment. He passed through an inner door that I imagine led to a bedchamber and the other man returned. I had stayed by the outer door wondering what to do next. Because now of course, the moment of truth had well and truly arrived. What exactly was I going to do next?

Out of the corner of my eye, I saw the raising of the barrel and heard a slight click. I dived out of the door and rolled against the farther wall, frantically groping for the Mauser in my pocket. The double report of the pistol was loud in the otherwise quiet room but was accompanied by an instinctive and anticipatory cry of pain. The two shots flew through the door and hit the wall. I heard steps across the room and by some stroke of genius from whoever decorated the room, I saw him, or at least his reflection, a moment before he saw me. That and my wail of agony saved me. He thought I was dead, dying or disabled, but I was none of those and in the split second it took him to realise that I fired. He span round with blood soaking his shirt just below his right shoulder and sank to his knees. He wasn't done for by any means and I saw him try to transfer the gun to his left hand, but his reactions were too slow with a 9mm slug in him.[119] I kicked him in the shoulder and he collapsed to the floor, writhing in agony, his weapon slithering across the floor behind him.

I was breathing hard now. My adversary's cries had reduced to a whimper as I stood over

[119] The Mauser C10 and C96 pistols were as commonly used as the better-known Luger was.

him wondering who he was. Dimitrijevic clearly was not the only one who wanted the Emperor dead. But why try to kill me in such a noisy fashion. If he wanted to kill the Emperor, he could almost certainly have done it quietly and then just calmly walked out. I would have been none the wiser.

At that point, I realised that it was quite possible that the Emperor was in fact already dead. Leaving the now quietly groaning heap on the floor, I looked out into the corridor again. There was no sign of any imminent arrivals so I walked back into the apartment, stepped over the body and through to the Emperor's room. He was standing stock still in the middle of the room.

"You will be caught. I have misplaced my trust I find. Make it quick if you must kill me." I wanted to laugh at the ludicrous nature of the position. Here was I, desperately trying to think of a way out without doing anything of the kind when some Austrian lunatic tries to shoot me and finishes up ruining His Majesty's carpet with his gore. Meanwhile, His Majesty calmly awaits the outcome.

"I am not going to kill you." He raised his eyebrows.

"But, my trusted guard?" Clearly, he was referring to the body on the carpet.

"Well, he is not dead yet. He tried to kill me. Why? I don't know and I don't care. How do I get out of this place without being seen?"

"Why do you need to do that? If what you say is true, then surely you have saved me?" It was becoming a habit for the Flashman family.

"Because somewhere out there is a man who thinks I am here to kill you. And when he discovers that I have done exactly the opposite, then he will kill me. I am his prisoner. Now I do not have time for this. If you value your life, you need to show me a way out. If I were you, I would come with me." It had suddenly occurred to me that the Emperor was an almighty big insurance policy in the right quarters.

Still amazed at the fact we were alone in spite of the noise we must have caused, I started to usher him towards the door, forgetting that Emperor's are not prone to being ushered anywhere.

"I shall not leave the palace. Only a coward would contemplate such a course of action. My enemies," he spat the word out with utter contempt, "would make great play of such shortcomings. No, if I am to die, I shall die here." He seemed to have forgotten the unseemly rush to get off the balcony just before midnight, but I was not going to remind him.

My position now was difficult, impaled firmly on the horns of a dilemma. Did I stay with him and hopefully use him as my passport to freedom, assuming he really did believe I had somehow saved him, or did I just cut and run and draw on the Flashman bank of good fortune?

The decision was taken for me as I stood pondering.

431

"Herr Major. What are you waiting for?"

"Who is this?" demanded the Emperor.

"My name is Dimitrijevic. And this is Kratky, my associate." I was aghast. How the devil had they managed to escape the melee and sneak up on us. "Herr Major Flashman you have already met." I stared from side to side.

"I was about to complete the task," I murmured, hardly daring to breathe.

"I doubt that. I can see from all that has happened already that you were unlikely to do as you were bidden. More likely, you were wondering how His Majesty could help you out of this situation. I see our friend Georges has bitten off more than he can chew."

"Who the hell is Georges?" I spluttered.

"He is a Frenchman. I have long known of his presence here in the palace, as has His Majesty. You should know, Herr Major, before you die, that His Majesty is strongly suspected of sympathy with the cause of the French, and consequently with that of the British. He does not believe in the justice of the German claims for Alsace Lorraine amongst other things. Our French friends therefore were keen for him to become Emperor, as it would strengthen their hand in the political field. Of course, they did not realise initially that my reasons for encouraging the demise of Franz Josef were different to theirs. When they did, Georges here was assigned to the palace to watch over His Majesty. Of course, Georges suspected I was not the loyal servant I pretended to be and presumably had realised that the disturbance this evening was more than an accident. So when you attached yourself to His Majesty, he reasoned that something was up. I was hoping you would manage to do away with friend Georges and by all accounts, that is what has happened. That just leaves His Majesty to deal with. Oh and you of course. It appears I have all the aces." He laughed at this, but he was not amused. It was the sort of laugh that sent a chill down your spine if you had one.[120]

None of us had moved. I was still standing beside the Emperor, Georges was still lying on the floor, quieter now, Dimitrijevic was near Georges looking at us and Kratky was playing sentry just outside the door.

"Put down your gun." This was addressed to me.

I looked at the revolver, realising that if I dropped it, I was halfway to being dead. I knew that he was a better shot than I was and if I didn't drop it quickly, he would probably shoot me anyway and I would not be able to do much about it.

There was silence. Even the groaning had stopped. For a moment, I thought the Frenchman was dead. Without warning, all hell broke loose.

---

[120] Emperor Franz Josef died in November 1916. He was succeeded by his grand nephew, Charles I, whose sympathies were indeed suspect.

Chapter 26

I have been party to more bungled operations, lethal fiascos and monumental disasters than I care to remember. They all have one thing in common. None of the protagonists has the faintest idea what is going on, but afterwards, they will all struggle to present the chaos as a clear outcome to a meticulously planned event. Schonbrunn Palace, New Year's Eve, 1916 was no different. Why has it never been made public? Mostly because the participants are dead, disgraced or simply had nothing to gain from a public display of dirty washing.

The silence was broken by two noises. The first by a fraction of a second was the sound of my gun hitting the floor. The second was Dimitrijevic screaming as a knife was inserted into the back of his leg.

The scene now becomes blurred and it is difficult to assert with certainty what happened next. Dimitrijevic collapsed to the floor letting his gun fall as well. I lunged for my own weapon knowing that fate had delivered me a momentary chance to escape. I collided with the Emperor, who clearly had assumed the same thing and was diving for Georges' gun, and rolled away clutching my head. He snatched up the Luger and all the ammunition fell out as the impact had released the magazine. Kratky, disturbed by the scream no doubt, had put two and two together and came into the room almost on his hands and knees. He obviously remembered the warning about what a dangerous man I was.

How he viewed the mess, I have no idea. All I know is that everybody was on the floor. He gaped around like the idiot he was and without further ado fired two rounds into the Frenchman which settled his hash for him. The firing of shots had me diving for cover behind the furniture and looking for a window.

I peeped out to survey the scene and saw the Emperor raise his gun and fire. His shooting instructor had obviously not played a big part in the royal upbringing as he missed his target, Kratky, by about ten feet and instead blew a large pot with a plant in to pieces. Kratky, disturbed by the fact that he was now a target and that Dimitrijevic was not in a position to guide his actions decided that the time was ripe to decamp. He sprang upright and turned to run.

He was hit by a rather attractive silver horse, which in my panic I had grabbed at and thrown his way. Despite his obvious desire to leave, he definitely did not have any Flashmanovic blood in him, as he stopped briefly to see what had hit him and whether he was injured. This was his undoing. The Emperor had managed to load at least another two rounds and he fired both. The first knocked a large splinter from the door that flew into the corridor and smashed the enormous mirror. The second hit Kratky in the back of the neck and blew the top of his head off. He sprawled forward into the broken glass that was now littering the floor.

I scrambled up from my post and retrieved Dimitrijevic's gun. I was about to send him to join his friend when the Emperor stopped me.

"No, he must be taken alive." I wasn't going to argue.

"I will get help, Your Majesty." I don't know why I called him that as it seems ludicrous now when I consider we were surrounded with corpses and broken furniture. I jumped over the prone Dimitrijevic and peered into the hall. Still no one had appeared so with a swift glance at the mess Kratky had made I retraced my steps. I had not gone far when a pair of soldiers appeared round a corner.

"Was ist los? Ich habe schiessen gehört. Wo ist der Kaiser?"

"Er ist in seinem zimmer. Ich gehe und hole hilfe."

This happened twice in quick succession and I sent them to the Emperor's suite. I rather hoped that when they got there they might put Dimitrijevic out of his misery. But my priority for the moment was leaving the area.

I found my way back to the original party and suddenly realised I was both hungry and thirsty. With a keen disregard for my own safety, which I put down to an unnatural reaction to the scenes I had just witnessed, I stopped to devour some of the delicious pork on the table. I took a large swig at a bottle of wine, another mouthful of pork, stuffed some of it in my pockets as an afterthought and made for the door.

I seemed to be entirely alone. The fireworks had stopped and there was an odd atmosphere. I stepped outside having seen nobody, unusual given the normal crowd of hangers on that swarm around royalty. There were two sentries who were oblivious to the evening's entertainment. But then why should they be anything but? From outside, the gunfire would have been covered by the sound of fireworks. Even if they hadn't, it was unlikely anyone other than those directly involved would have realised anything untoward was taking place. I forced myself to walk as casually as possible to what amounted to the tradesmen's entrance. Neither of the guards was in the least interested. Suddenly I was alone in the street. Where to now?

It was a difficult question. What would happen once the bodies were discovered? What would they do with Dimitrijevic? More to the point, what would they do about me? The Emperor knew who I was and knew I was a prisoner but he apparently had sympathies with the French. However, I was convinced that that was not necessarily a popular view. Plus, the Frenchman who probably could have helped me had tried to kill me believing me to be an assassin, and he was now dead, helped on his way by me. Altogether, I had very few friends in Vienna and probably a larger collection of enemies. I still hadn't answered the question but I had had to leave the immediate area of the palace. It was too cold to stay outside for much longer as I had left my overcoat behind.

The more I thought about it, there was only one answer.

I retraced my steps back to the palace entrance. I had probably forgotten more than these sentries knew about moving unseen and unheard from my time in India and it was simple to slip past them and back into the palace. The hard part was what to do now. Really, I needed to find the Emperor.

I could hear a commotion as I moved through the corridors. I was trying to look both unobtrusive and at home. I could hear a conversation now. I stopped in a doorway and leaning slightly on the door it swung gently open revealing a dark room. I slipped inside to listen.

"Well Sir, what is to be done with him? He cannot stay here."

"Execute him now and have done with it," another voice that I did not recognise added.

"No, no, we must consider. He cannot be working alone."

"Yes but his companion is dead, so let's finish the job." It sounded like a superb idea to me.

"No. He must have other contacts here in the palace. We have to find out who they are and eliminate them. He must be made to talk." Even better. Torture and then a sticky end for friend Dragutin.

"But what about the Englishman? Where is he? He arrived with this animal." I froze. What about him?

"It is perhaps better that he is gone. He went to fetch help he said but that was half an hour ago." Was that all? Still, I didn't think I was going to get a better cue. I slipped out of the room and fortunately still looking suitably dishevelled, hove into view. There were a few gasps of astonishment from the crowd of onlookers and a distinct glare from His Majesty.

"There is another of this gang. I followed him once I had made sure help was on the way, but he caught sight of me and escaped into the streets. I daren't shoot at him for fear of hitting someone else in the dark and I do not know Vienna as well as he does."

I looked around trying to gauge the impact of my words. Blank indifference was the best description. I realised I was going to have an uphill struggle to convince this lot that the best course of action was a fast horse out of here for Flashy.

"You were with this scum. Why should we believe you?"

"Your Majesty, I can only appeal to you as a man of honour." Stretching a point, I know. "Yes I was with this man but as his prisoner. He was trying to force me to harm His Majesty, but how could I, a Flashman, do that to a family we have been honour bound to protect, current differences of opinion notwithstanding? I am an Englishman, not a filthy Serb." It was pretty highhanded but these were Germans and unlikely to have much concern for an irrelevant nation. "I was just waiting for the right opportunity to…."

"To what, Major Flashman? What were you planning to do? Why did you not denounce the traitor earlier? Why did you risk the death of the Emperor?"

Why indeed? I gave my best impression of a trout.

"It wasn't my fault. The Frenchman, he tried to kill me. He knew it all. I was just the innocent victim." It probably wasn't the best line of defence to start whining in front of all these Germans but I was beginning to both regret my return and realise that I was on a hiding to nothing. I stopped talking and stared round my circle of admirers.

"I think we should get rid of him now." This contribution was from some household minion whose opinion clearly should not be taken seriously.

"No. no, not yet. Put him with the traitor."

That was apparently the last word from the Emperor. He nodded to the two guards at the door and they took that to mean I was to be grabbed and dragged away, pleading all the time that I was as innocent as the driven snow. I continued alternately shouting and pleading until they slammed the door of my prison after which I clung to the back of the door. I didn't even try to wrench it open. I just hung on, whimpering at the misfortune that had brought me to this pass.

"So, Herr Major. We meet again."

I nearly had a seizure. The cell was gloomy and I had not seen the other occupant when I was unceremoniously shoved through the door. I turned round slowly and as my eyes adjusted, I could see a body lying on the floor against the far wall. I said nothing.

"You failed me." It was a strange comment to make given that I was standing over him and his leg was swathed in what looked like an old red curtain. I was tempted to kick it.

He was staring up at me with a look of utter contempt. Perhaps at last he realised that all along I had been telling the truth. I was not the hero he imagined me to be and consequently had spoiled his plan to remove the Habsburgs from power. I still found it hard to believe that he thought anything would become of a Serbia free from the clutches of the Austrian empire. Still, it was his fantasy, not mine. I couldn't have cared less about his plans. I was infinitely more concerned with my current plight. My optimistic assessment of my future when I was roaming around outside the palace had been sadly misguided.

"Failed you!" I said. I spat the words out as he had made me angry. He was also defenceless. I was still contemplating kicking him. "How have I possibly failed you? I never asked to be part of your madcap scheme. You never told me about the Frenchman. You knew he was there. I was happy being a prisoner." I was beginning to gabble in my fury.

"You failed me. You failed me in Sarajevo and you have failed me now. For that, I will kill you."

"Well good luck," I sneered. It was easy to sneer at him lying on the floor with his crippled leg. "You can join the queue." I don't know why I said that then. I suppose my thoughts were pretty scrambled and there seemed to be a conspiracy out to finish me off. If it wasn't Richtofen and his gang or the late Madame d'Alprant, it was the Royal Family.

I sat down on the floor, as I was exhausted. We contemplated each other with mutual loathing. If I had been half the man he was, I would have finished him off there and then. I had no illusions that if our situation had been reversed, I would be dancing the Tyburn Jig and be damned to the consequences. He was just that sort of ruthless bastard.

It was a long night. I wasn't convinced that he wasn't exaggerating the extent of his injury to lull me into a false sense of security. I tried to stay awake but I awoke with a start in the morning light. Dimitrijevic was asleep in the same place by the wall. I watched him for some time. When he did wake, he groaned in pain and ignored me. His whole attention was taken up by his leg.

Nobody else seemed interested in us either. A bowl of some despicable gruel was shoved through the door and I ate mine. I considered eating his as well but I couldn't bring myself to do it. It was not through sympathy, only that it was truly inedible. I continued to sit and contemplate my companion and our predicament.

It was a long, long day. Someone brought another meal as it started to get dark. Dimitrijevic was now groaning almost constantly, and his breathing had the hurried sharpness of the deeply unwell.

It was sometime in the late evening that he started to plead with me. He sounded coherent to start with, but when he requested that I return to Sarajevo and explain to some mystery General why the English were about to invade I realised he was off his onion.[121]

Sometime in the night, our captors realised the same thing and removed him. At least that was my first thought when I woke up and he had gone. I must have been in an extremely deep sleep not to hear the accompanying commotion. As I looked around, I realised that it was I that had moved and not he. I felt groggy and sick and wondered why but I could not think any more than that. It required too much effort. At least it was quiet and I could sleep off whatever it was. Not, however, for very long. No sooner had I drifted away again, than the door opened and more gruel appeared. I left it for some time but eventually I had to have some as once the sickness had passed I felt as if I had not eaten in weeks. It tasted different somehow.

Having finished my cold meal, I managed to escape the lethargy and walk across the larger room to a small window. I looked out and recoiled in surprise. Where the view had been the palace, it was now open country. A shiver shot down my spine as my mind selected a number of unlikely, I

---

[121] Colonel Dragutin Dimitrijevic was executed in June 1917. Flashman does not mention his whereabouts after New Year 1916.

hoped, reasons for my having been moved without my knowledge. I realised quickly that someone had laced my food with something nasty. The question once again was where was I, and why was I here?

Recovered completely from my nauseous state, I pondered my position again. Who would bother going to such lengths to move me? Did the Emperor know? Was it good or bad if he did?

The door slammed open and two soldiers came in at a run. I instinctively retreated only to find my back firmly against the wall.

"Don't hit me," I screamed in panic, raising my arms in front of my face. I crouched away from the expected blows and they threw a blanket over my head. One grabbed each arm and between them, they propelled me to the door.

I recovered my voice and yelled for help. I don't know what I expected to happen but all that did was a blow to the stomach that knocked the wind from me. My legs were hardly touching the floor as I stumbled along with the panic rising ever higher. I was hot under the blanket and I wanted to wretch, but I could hardly think as I was bundled down some stairs. I felt the cold as we went outside and I nearly soiled myself. I knew I was going to be shot. I knew that when the blanket was removed I would be looking down the barrels of a dozen rifles. I started praying under my breath and promising to become a reformed character if I was spared, so help me almighty God, Amen.

We all stopped and I started gasping for breath. I wanted to shout but I couldn't as I was still winded from the sudden blow. The soldiers held my arms firmly. In my mind I could almost see the post to which they were about to tie me.

"Gehen sie weg," said a voice close by.

The grip on my arms was released and I stood not knowing what to do, the blanket still obscuring my view. I felt someone pull it and it slipped off onto the floor.

"Herr Major. We have very little time. Do you wish to live?"

I was nearly right. He was holding a revolver but it was not pointing at me. A vision of Madame d'Alprant lying face down swam into view. One of her last questions to me had been along the same lines.

"Yes I do, your Majesty."

"Then you must follow my instructions to the letter."

After all these years, I still cannot decide what it is that gets me into these situations. Fate, bad luck or some all-seeing authority from below that simply delights in seeing my squirming attempts to avoid the latest hellish idea thrust upon me, when all along I know that my only chance is to go along with it. Here I was again.

"I have here a letter. It is to be given to those with the power to carry out its aims, which briefly consist of the withdrawal of German troops from Belgium, the return of Alsace-Lorraine to France and the end of this war."

445

No wonder the French had a man on the inside. Dimitrijevic had said as much in the Emperor's apartments but I had dismissed it as pure fantasy, particularly as Georges himself was not around to explain and up until now, the Emperor had hardly considered me a fit dinner companion.

"Will you take it?"

He had not given me much choice but that did not matter at all. I leapt at the chance. My mind span immediately with the possibilities. I could see it now. A knighthood at least. It never occurred to me that Kaiser Bill might see things differently to the Emperor and refuse his request to withdraw from Belgium and so on. Not that I would have cared if it had. The icing on the cake was my freedom.

"It will not be easy to get you out of Vienna unnoticed." My spirits sank again. "Not everyone here sees this situation as clearly as I do. They may attempt to stop you."

By which he meant kill me. I wanted to shout at him that he was the bloody Emperor and he could do as he pleased couldn't he but I knew it would not have helped. I summoned every statesmanlike nerve and put on my best English front, something that had not been on display much recently. Fortunately, my weakness in trying circumstances seemed conveniently forgotten.

"Your Majesty, I think I can safely assert that the King and his Government will receive this communication from my own hand and I will assure them of the authenticity of the contents. I have no doubt that they will react accordingly."

I knew nothing of the kind. I held out my hand for the letter, which he now seemed reluctant to pass over and for a horrible moment, I thought I had overplayed my part. He contemplated it and me for a few seconds and then virtually threw it at me. He turned on his heel and disappeared. I hoped never to see him again.[122]

The soldiers appeared and hustled me out of what I had noticed was a small courtyard through an arched door to one side. Waiting there was a carriage. I climbed in and found I was not alone. The other occupant simply nodded. I sat down, the door slammed and the driver whipped up the horses. My companion motioned at me to close the curtains. We travelled in silence.

After some hours, punctuated with two brief halts where I assumed the horses were changed, my mute friend produced a hamper from under the seat, which contained some refreshment. I had not realised quite how hungry I was until he opened it. There were cold meats, bread, cheese, some cake and more importantly a bottle of liebfraumilch. I gorged myself until I felt thoroughly sick and bloated.

Our journey continued. It seemed desperately slow and as we dawdled along my fears rose of being intercepted. Simple Simon hardly helped

---

[122] It was rumoured after the war that the last Emperor had sympathies with the French and that he had indeed written a letter expressing these views. Flashman may be providing the proof that this was the case.

with his fascinating conversation and I was left to chew my nails and imagine the worst. Twice I heard hooves approaching and was ready to leap out and run for my life. Both times, they continued past and both times, he never stirred. Either he knew more than he was letting on, or he really was simple.

The dark and cold slowly seeped into every corner of the carriage. I slept occasionally but it was not a restorative rest. I woke with a start once when the carriage stopped and I was alone. The door was open and the cold draught was biting. Surely it could not carry on much longer.

Nothing untoward occurred and the gloom slowly gave way to a half light. We stopped again, and this time Simple Simon ordered me out of the carriage. I stepped out, gazing round looking for signs of trouble but there were none.

"Linz," he announced. Linz was further down my list of unknown places than the Crimea. "Here we catch the train to the border."

"Which border?" I asked. He stared at me as if I was the stupid one.

"Switzerland of course."

"But, how do we get past the war?"

"Austria has a direct border with Switzerland. You do not know this?" he said with the contempt the German has for his ignorant English cousin.

"Why, should I?" I replied matching his with my own contempt for his tin pot empire.

He looked away from me in disgust obviously wondering how I would be of any use to his beloved Emperor.

I thought I heard a whistle in the distance. Then I heard the noise of the train itself and we moved into the station to await its arrival.

"Our seats are here," he said, pointing to the First Class section. I nearly had kittens.

"Surely this is the first place they will look for us," I said. I wasn't sure who they were but I was pretty sure that they would be searching for us and a train seemed a pretty obvious place to start.

"They will be looking for you," he corrected. "But not here. Escaped prisoners do not travel in First Class." He seemed so sure of himself, I almost believed him.

We boarded and found our small but comfortable compartment. There followed the familiar but inexplicable delay of all trains in wartime, even German ones, and two hours later we got under way. They were some of the longest hours I have ever spent, furtively peering out of the window, trying not to look suspicious. The ordeal intensified the further we went as even total war did nothing to reduce the army of officials that swarm everywhere in Germany inserting their noses into everyone else's business. Fortunately, on that score at least, I had chosen the right companion. He gave all of them the rightabout and sent them packing.

The train chugged slowly on and we appeared to climb ever higher. The temperature noticeably dropped and Simple Simon announced that we were entering the Tyrol. I wanted to ask if this made any difference to anything at all but initially at least thought better of it and mumbled something about how attractive the place was. Consequently he expanded at length and I realised quite quickly that be must have been brought up here. I listened politely for a few seconds and then resumed staring out of the window. He got the message as next time I looked at him there was a look of pure fury on his face. It was fortunate he was duty bound to assist me.

We continued in silence for what must have been some hours although I was beginning to lose my sense of time and distance. I woke again and it was dark. Someone was shaking my arm and it was freezing cold.

"We are here."

"Where?"

"Bregenz."

"Where?"

He assumed his exasperated look again. "Bregenz. It is on Lake Constance and it is where we will leave the train." This was apparently all the information I was going to get for the moment. We collected our meagre belongings and made for the door. I then walked into him as he had stopped in the doorway and was looking all around the station, presumably checking for assassins and highwaymen. He didn't do it for long as after I bumped into him, he made an undignified descent on to the platform where he shot upright from his half fall and glared at me with real venom. Luckily, there were no assassins around, as they probably would have noticed this. I descended in a more appropriate fashion and together we left the station. At this point, I realised that we were if not in trouble, then at least not out of it. There was no plan.

"We have to get across the lake," Simple Simon said to no one in particular. He was staring into the distance.

"Presumably you have boats?" I said it in a general fashion, hoping that he did in fact know where to go to find a boat, but with the realisation that he did not even know which way the lake was.

"Of course we have boats," he snapped. He stalked off waving his arms and muttering something and I followed in his wake. Perhaps the strain was telling but given his Germanic nature, he was unable to do anything other than issue orders to me and our imaginary friend the boatman.

After a few minutes evening stroll we found an official of some kind. Simple Simon decided that the best thing to do was demand the way to the lake in the name of the Emperor. The official looked bemused but his natural subservience in the face of natural authority led him to point us in the right direction. We continued on our way but I sneaked a look back to see what he was doing and sure enough, he had doubt written all over him as he stared after us, wondering what on earth we were up to. Being more or less German, he was almost bound to report it to his superior and so on up the chain until it reached someone who could mobilise an Army.

I tried to warn him of this but he was not listening now having regained his confidence and shrugged off my concerns as the ramblings of a filthy foreigner. We reached the lakeside and surveyed the scene. In the dark it was difficult to make out anything but some way along the shore were some lights that at least suggested life. He was virtually running now in his enthusiasm and I was starting to tire.

We reached the lights and to my dismay, he marched straight into the dilapidated building demanding attention.

"House, house," he was shouting, or something very similar. An ancient seadog appeared from somewhere. I retired to the door as his behaviour was bordering on the insane and I had no desire to be cornered. I peered into the darkness but I could see nothing.

A thump on the shoulder nearly had me running for cover.

"It is arranged," he crowed. "This man has a boat and he will take us across the border. I have paid him handsomely. The boat is moored to a jetty a few minutes walk away."

"Where is the border then?"

"In the lake, we cross the German part and then land on the Swiss shoreline."

"German, Jesus Christ, what do you mean German? How come we are so close to Germany?" I spluttered with fear rising fast.

"It is nothing, only a few minutes crossing a remote corner of the Country."

Well he might think it was nothing, but I wasn't so sure that the Germans agreed. They might have realised that it was an ideal place to smuggle anything into Switzerland. I wanted to throttle the idiot who had come up with this. I could see it now, the cream of Vienna looking vaguely at a map and suddenly noticing this place and exclaiming in triumph. If you look at a map, you will see what I mean. Lake Constance is indeed placed suitably in a corner of Austria. The border meets near a place called Altenrhein. The German border is uncomfortably close to the shore and any fool could see that this would be an ideal place to enter Swiss waters, possibly even without encroaching on German territory. My bet would be that the Germans would know this and just might have a little boat or two to inspect anyone attempting the crossing, and who would be able to say afterwards that they had not entered the German part of the lake. The Germans could easily apologise profusely and send you on your way minus any contraband, or absconding prisoners.

My thoughts on the matter were all irrelevant as we were now walking towards the jetty and the boat. We were onboard in pretty short order and the ancient was preparing for sea. I noticed this included a few surreptitious swigs from a convenient bottle.

The engine roared into life with a noise fit to wake the entire town and I was ready to jump ship if pursuit appeared.

"Cast off fore and aft," the ancient shouted, clearly enjoying himself and we obliged. I took the aft position and we drifted away from the wooden pillars. We started moving forwards slowly. Sadly, we stayed moving forwards slowly, but at least we were going in the right direction. The gloom started to envelop us and I started to relax. I took one last look back at the shore and there was nemesis. I knew it was he and he knew it was we in the boat. He had brought a few friends to the party as well. I could only see them for a few seconds before they were swallowed up in the night, but it was enough. We were done for, and there was not a damn thing I could do about it.

I paced up and down the boat. I stared into the darkness every time I reached the stern but I could see nothing. Simple Simon watched me, oblivious to my fears. Captain Hook simply carried on. I could hear him chuckling to himself so presumably the bottle he was carrying was emptying fast.

The time dragged by but slowly, slowly, my fears subsided. There was no sign of pursuit and the further away we got, the more difficult it would be to find us, and of course, they would have no idea where we intended to land.

I stopped my tour of the boat. I considered asking if either of my companions had the faintest idea where we were and whether we had arrived in Swiss waters yet. Not that that would save us if our pursuers really wanted to catch us.

I spun round as I caught a flash of something over the water. I stared hard into the gloom, but I did not see it again. I called out to Simple Simon to come over and have a look. Reluctantly he joined me at the rail and I pointed out where I had seen it. There was nothing.

"Anyway," he said waving his fin airily, "that way must be German territory." He said it because he clearly believed no trouble would come from that direction.

"How do you know? I can't see a thing, and the Captain there has been punishing his liquor so I doubt if he knows where we are either."

He stared at the ancient mariner and decided action was required. He strolled over to what passed for a bridge and I could hear a muttered conversation. We lurched suddenly away from where I had seen the flash and turned through ninety degrees before resuming our stately progress.

"The old fool. It is simple. He must know the lake." He went on in this fashion berating the shortcomings of our driver as if it was entirely his fault that we had happened on him in the middle of the night and demanded a boat ride.

The sky was lightening. Gradually, the shoreline revealed itself and all three of us were now peering at it in the hopes of finding a landing place.

"Is it even Switzerland," I enquired.

"Of course it is Switzerland," he replied. There was a loud crack from behind us, a faint whining noise, a large splash and an explosion. I scrambled out of the scuppers frantically looking for something solid to protect me and gauging the distance to the shore. Simple Simon had run to the stern and was shouting something or other at the boat that was now visible in our wake, all of a few hundred yards away.

We were now in a race. The ancient mariner had not bargained with shellfire and was crouched behind a door.

"Make it go faster," I shouted at him.

"I cannot…"

"Well bugger you then," I added diving for the wheelhouse. There was another bang a little closer and I grabbed every lever I could see and shoved them all as far forward as they would go. The mariner watched in horror and began to complain but was drowned out by another explosion that was close enough to cover the stern in spray. The engine was now running fit to burst but at least as well as producing an appalling screaming noise it appeared to be driving us a little quicker. The shore was coming closer and closer and I could see a slip of beach with a shallow slope running away from it. That was our target and we needed to turn a little to our right, even though that meant giving the Germans a bigger target. I turned the wheel over and we were just settling on our new course when the door suddenly blew off its hinges and all the windows came in. The air was filled with flying glass and I screamed as something seared across the back of my hand. Smoke began to pour out of a hole where the controls used to be. Time to go.

I ran outside again tripping over the wreckage and our whining fool who was struggling to free himself. I glanced backwards and the other ship was still far enough away for my plan. Simple Simon was done for. He was laid out near the stern and his tunic was peppered with small holes and burns. He was conscious but wouldn't be for long. He had a pistol in his hand and it occurred to me that he was better off without that. I snatched it and much to my amazement he hung on like mad for a few seconds before his strength failed him.

"Letter…" he managed to say while I fought him for his gun.

"Overboard," I replied. He gave me a final look of anger and coughed. His breathing was failing and I was moving down the deck to get out of sight of the Germans. I was running, as I knew that the next shot must be imminent. Two more paces and I launched myself at the rail, just as the final shot hit midships and the boat was so much matchwood. I went deep under the water, driven possibly by the blast and I came up spluttering and retching. One deep breath and I struck out for the shore in spite of the pain all over. It was quite close now and a matter of a couple of minutes should see me clear. Something brushed against me and I almost had the conniptions as a man surfaced beside me and grabbed my arm.

"Hilfe, hilfe," it shouted. How he had got ahead of me was a conundrum for another day but a punch to the side of the head released the grip and I was off again. My lungs were heaving with the effort and I could feel cramp fast approaching when my feet struck something solid. I floated over it, three more strokes and there was solid ground. I put my feet down and waded through the chest high water. A few yards to go, faster and faster as the lake shallowed. I was out and stumbling towards the slope. I heard small arms fire behind me, and it gave me the final spur required to stagger over the small ridge and into the first cover I could find. I lay for a few seconds before dragging myself up to the top again to see if they were going to land.

I could have jumped for joy if I had had the strength. The rifles had been aimed at the remains of the boat and whilst I watched, they dragged a limp body out of the water and finally a dead one from the wreckage.

I was free at last. Switzerland, France and home, a place I would never stir from again even if it meant disgrace and ignominy. I admit I was a little light headed from my experience in the water, but I didn't care. My war was over.

Chapter 27

The train from Portsmouth pulled into Waterloo station. It was roughly seven hours late and I was exhausted. The journey from Switzerland took a little longer than the grand tour. It had mostly consisted of fighting officialdom in all its guises. I had to prove who I was. This was almost impossible.

The French authorities were hardly better and I had spent some more time inspecting the walls and ceiling of another cell. But it was all a picnic compared to being on holiday with the Austrians.

I stepped down from the train and hailed a porter. When he ran over, I had to dismiss him instantly as I had forgotten that I had no baggage whatsoever as in between losing my aeroplane, prison and fleeing a sinking ship I possessed nothing whatsoever. It was not the hero's welcome I had envisaged.

I left the station. It was hard to believe there was even a war going on. The muffled people rushed past me going about their business, the traffic was an unceasing stream, there was the odd uniform in the crowd but none of them excited much attention. I stared around me trying to get my bearings. I was about to hail a cab when it occurred to me that I had no money at all.

I walked towards the river, over Waterloo Bridge and up on to the Strand. I strolled down wishing I looked less like the village scarecrow doffing my cap to the ladies until I reached Trafalgar Square. I looked up at Nelson again and crossed towards Whitehall. In the distance, I could just make out St Stephen's tower where the pompous buffoon Lloyd George was no doubt savaging his opponents having forced Asquith to resign in December. I couldn't see what difference it would make myself.

"Flashman?" a voice said from beside a Piccadilly Butcher on a horse. "Is that you?"

"Yes."

"Well I'll be damned. Given you up for dead old man."

The Colonel stared at me for a minute or so before grasping my hand and giving it a hefty shake.

"Well don't just stand there, where can we get a drink? I haven't a penny to my name, I'm just off the boat and clearly a man could die of hunger…"

I said no more. The Colonel whisked me away through the arch and into the building, back through the door I had left by all those weeks ago. Or was it months? Or days? I could not tell. But at least I was not going to leave trussed up like a chicken or blindfolded, or wake up in the company of Dimitrijevic, or the Prince of Wales.

"Feeling better now?" he enquired.

"Much. Anything happened while I have been away?"

"Where can I start?" He looked thoughtful and proceeded to tell me about the minutiae of Government service.

"I really meant with Cumming."

"Ah. Well. Tricky for some time after the Court Martial. Royal favour and so on. Regardless of what one thinks, desperately difficult to maintain any operation like ours without their approval. Cumming is a master of navigating those waters. You are still in our employ. Just don't rock the boat. Well, no more than you have already." He emphasised the last words and I took that to mean I was to carry on as normal, but without ruffling any more royal feathers.

"I was going to resign," I said.

The Colonel stared at me for a long moment. "Resign? You? You can't."

He turned away. I knew there would be no arguing with him.

"So what am I to do with these?" I asked.

"What is.....?"

"The Koh-I-Noor. My Father left it with his documents. Oh and this is a letter to the King. It's from the Austrian Emperor."

THE END

Appendix 1

Sarajevo

The debate over the First World War and its causes will probably never end. It is unlikely that the descent into war will ever be satisfactorily explained. On the face of it, the war was triggered by the assassination of the Archduke Ferdinand in Sarajevo by Gavrilo Princip and his gang, Serbs who wanted independence from the Austro-Hungarian Empire. They claimed to be operating independently although Princip himself had links with members of the Black Hand, a group of Serbian terrorists. Further in the shadows lurked Colonel Dragutin Dimitrijevic, possibly the architect of the plot, possibly working for the Serbian authorities and virtually impossible to verify. Weapons were obtained with the connivance of the Serbian army and Serbian officials helped the group return from Belgrade across the border to Sarajevo, where they carried out their attack. It was so badly mismanaged that it had all but failed when the Archduke's car stopped as the chauffeur had not been informed of the change of plan to visit a hospital. The car stopped directly in front of Princip who took the opportunity to fire into the car, killing the Archduke and his wife.

Following this, the Austro-Hungarian authorities in Vienna decided with German backing that the time was ripe to subdue Serbia. Austrian threats were met with counter threats as the Russians took sides with the Serbs. The dominoes began to fall as the Germans and Russians mobilised followed almost inevitably by the French. Great Britain had guaranteed Belgian neutrality and was drawn in ostensibly when the Germans violated this, although it is unlikely that Britain would have avoided participating in the conflict as there were other more secret commitments, mainly to the French, that would have had to have been honoured if only to maintain the status of the British Empire. The politicians were able to use the Belgian excuse to send an army to Europe, something that would have been very difficult given that public opinion in Britain was set against intervention in mainland Europe.

The war was set against a background of the scramble for Africa, the acquisition of Empires by the major European powers who saw the industrial might and wealth of the British Empire and wanted the same. The numerous small conflicts that this caused were translated to a large-scale war in Europe where the imperial game was fought out with devastating consequences for all concerned.

Appendix 2

Forgotten Victory?

Was the First World War a purely pointless slaughter? Were the British Army lions led by donkeys? If these questions were posed to the average man in the street, the answer would almost certainly be yes. But would he be right?

There is no short answer. To some degree, the Great War, the First World War, the war to end all wars, has been hijacked. Most of the literature concerning the First World War dwells on how terrible it was, but also the waste of life, the lack of anything tangible to show for such sacrifice. It was terrible. It was a cataclysm on an unprecedented scale, but even then only a prelude to the Second World War. The realities of the continuing struggle for power and influence probably caused it to begin, but the continuation for four years was largely due to the inequality between attacker and defender, something that was blatantly obvious. Once the German armies had overreached themselves and retreated to dig in, the mechanisation of the military machine and the ability to throw up impenetrable screens of bullets without any means for the attacking force to avoid them meant there was at the beginning at least, no way to break through a stable defence line. And there lies the nub of the problem. Military technology had developed weapons that could slaughter on an unheard of scale. The machine gun had been used by modern armies for some time, but mostly against poorly armed opponents. When two modern armies came together, it produced stalemate. To break through a defended line required a huge effort of manpower with the associated casualties, but the lack of reliable communications meant local victories were rarely followed up in time to take any advantage. It became a war of attrition and therefore one that Germany had little chance of winning with its far smaller resources, hence the use of tactics such as unrestricted submarine warfare in an attempt to starve the British into submission.

The net result on a human level was thousands of casualties in short periods of time for very little material gain. But was it pointless?

The men who fought it and returned didn't necessarily think so at the time. They were proud of their achievement, they had fought an age-old aggressor to a standstill and won. They had preserved the Empire and the nation, something they considered worthwhile. They were let down by those politicians who failed to make the country they returned to the promised land fit for heroes. The misguided treaty of Versailles set Europe on course for the next confrontation, and the recession of the twenties and thirties with the slavish adherence to the gold standard destroyed notions of a better world. It was in these years that the mood set against the victory of the Great War. Literature began to appear that emphasised the waste of life and spoke of the sordid conditions imposed on soldiers, and worst of all the appalling leadership of the donkeys in charge, both politically and militarily. Magnified by the state of the economy at the time, these ideas took hold and have held sway ever since.

The truth of course is far more complex and impossible to convey satisfactorily briefly, but there has recently been an apparent shift of opinion amongst some scholars and historians who have studied the Great War. I have mentioned some of what I think are important works on the war itself and if nothing else, combined they to my mind convey a balanced view of a terrible period.

The argument will continue until the end of time, in much the same way as we still look back over the years and fight again the Battles of Hastings, or Agincourt, Crecy, Poitiers, Bosworth Field, Edgehill, Naseby, Blenheim, Malplaquet, Trafalgar or Waterloo. Perhaps one way of looking at it is to ask yourself what you would have done in the circumstances. Would you have gone to war to defend the Empire and the nation? Would you have believed that the war would continue as it did for so long?

As for leadership, ask yourself how you might have performed if you were suddenly placed in a position of responsibility leading men into battle with limited training both for you and for them. How would you have made it better?

It wasn't pointless. The men who fought it were not stupid. They believed they were fighting for something regardless of the tragedy of it all. There were plenty of donkeys in charge and some of them caused immense suffering. Politicians made appalling decisions at times, as did Generals, but did we really do it better second time around, and would we be any better if we found ourselves in the same position today?

There were many good men who led from the front and by example, who made sacrifices unheard of in society today to try and preserve their world, whatever its faults and with all its rights and wrongs. They deserve better than a perhaps slightly distorted view.

Despite the time that has passed since the Great War, its imprint on history and the collective memory of the great nations of Europe mean it will take a long time for its ghost to fade. Most families in Great Britain were affected by the war. Many would have lost sons, husbands, fathers and the fact that the huge armies were composed of ordinary citizens as opposed to the convicts and unfortunates of a previous century meant that the image of the soldier was transformed forever from the 'scum of the earth' to the dogged hero fighting for what he believed was right. I believe that the time has indeed come for the 'Forgotten Victory' to be remembered.

Further Reading:

Forgotten Victory by Gary Sheffield
Mud, Blood and Poppycock by Gordon Gorrigan
Tommy by Richard Holmes
The First World War by John Keegan

Sagittarius Rising by Cecil Lewis
The Pity of War by Niall Ferguson
Rules of the Game by Andrew Gordon
The Rise and Fall of the British Empire by Lawrence James
Empire by Niall Ferguson

among many many others!

Appendix 3

The Habsburgs

The Habsburgs were one of the oldest and most prominent of Europe's royal families. They first came to power when Count Rudolf was elected King and Holy Roman Emperor in 1273. By various means, Rudolf acquired Babenburg lands that together with the Tirol became the centre of power for the Habsburgs. In Austria, the Habsburgs ruled without interruption until their complete demise in 1918.

Rudolf's son however was assassinated in 1308 thus denying the Habsburgs the Imperial title, but by judicious marriages and clever diplomacy, they returned when Albert II became Emperor in 1438. The empire remained dominated by the Habsburgs until its abolition in 1806 by Napoleon.

At its height, the empire under Charles V consisted of Spain and its overseas possessions, parts of Italy, the Netherlands as well as the German and Austrian lands. When Charles abdicated in 1556, the empire was divided with Spain, Italy, the Netherlands and the overseas land inherited by his son Philip II while Austria was ruled by his brother, Ferdinand I who also in 1526 had succeeded to the Bohemian and Hungarian thrones.

At the end of the war of the Spanish Succession in 1714, Spain passed to the French Bourbons and with the failure of the male line in

Austria in 1740, succession passed to Maria Theresa. She married the Duke of Lorraine creating the Habsburg-Lorraine house but losing Silesia to Prussia in the war of the Austrian Succession.

Maria Theresa's grandson was the last Holy Roman Emperor. Francis II played a leading role in the opposition to Napoleon and France. In 1804, Francis assumed the title of Emperor of Austria just prior to the dissolution of the empire. His son oversaw further decline until he was compelled to abdicate in favour of Francis Joseph. In his reign, the loss of Italy and Germany meant the empire was reduced to Austria and Hungary.

The final destruction occurred with the end of World War 1, shortly after which the last Emperor Charles I was banished in 1919.

In 1963, the then Archduke Otto was allowed to return to Austria. He became a resident of the Federal Republic of Germany and was elected to the European Parliament.

Appendix 4.

First Day on the Somme.

The first day on the Somme is the greatest tragedy the British Army has ever experienced. 57,000 casualties were inflicted by the Germans, of which just under 20,000 were killed. What made it even more appalling was that it was one of the first real actions for the great citizen army that had been recruited since the beginning of the war. So many of the battalions advancing that day were the 'Pals' battalions consisting of friends who had joined up together from the same factory or workplace, many from the same villages or towns, so many of them killed together which meant that when the news reached England, towns and villages found they had lost a huge percentage of their young men and this concentrated loss was profoundly difficult to bear.

The Somme is another of those great debates of modern times about what the Great War was about and whether it was worth it. But the roots of this particular tragedy lie partly in the training of so many volunteers. With so many men to enlist, arm and train, the system was almost certainly overwhelmed. Regular officers and NCOs found themselves training whole battalions of new men. Of necessity, anyone with promise was promoted and very quickly found themselves leading and training. It was this lack of in depth and lengthy training that led indirectly to the simple tactics on the first day. Combined with the poor intelligence following the artillery barrage, the impossibility of quick and accurate communication and the many other associated difficulties, the troops set off across no-mans-land at a walk in some cases, only to be mown down by the German gunners whose deep dugouts had survived the artillery onslaught.

That anyone reached the German wire at all is a miracle. That any returned is more so.

The Somme tends to be viewed as a one-day experience, but it in fact went on for months with huge casualty figures. But the troops learnt from their mistakes, as did the Commanders. It has been suggested that the Somme was the start of a learning process that led to victory, although this in turn has been compared with the nonsensical notion that the evacuation of Dunkirk was a dress rehearsal for the D Day landings in 1944; it is easy to agree, but I think it is also possible to draw other conclusions. The Somme was important in the first place because it drew in German troops that otherwise would possibly have eventually overwhelmed the French at Verdun. If the French had collapsed, the story of Europe would have been very different. The gain of land was negligible in terms of mileage, but as the battle progressed, the army learnt to combine with the new tanks and with aircraft to forge an all arms fighting machine. It did not bear fruit until 1918 when after the German offensive failed, the

British Army finally advanced out of the trenches leading to the armistice. By this time, the Army was probably as efficient an implement as it would ever be and heralded the all arms blitzkrieg tactics used to such effect twenty years later.

The Somme was a disaster on an unprecedented scale, but it was a disaster that eventually perhaps sowed the seeds of victory.

Appendix 5

Prince Albert Victor

Prince Albert Victor, Duke of Clarence and Avondale is an unresolved conundrum to this day. Born into an extraordinary position as heir to the most powerful empire on earth, his upbringing was probably as far removed from the norm as it is possible to be. Many decisions were taken for him by his powerful and uncompromising Grandmother, Victoria. At the opposite end of the scale, his Father was a renowned womaniser and managed to get himself into numerous minor and a couple of major scandals, despite being eventually a good King. If he was confused, he had plenty of reasons to be so.

He was tutored at home for much of his early life before joining the Navy where he served on Bacchante. He was probably bullied, at least by todays standards, along with his brother. It was a difficult position. How did an heir to the throne have a normal career in the Navy when others either queued up to gain the royal favour or take pleasure in attacking the future King. It is still a valid question as the current heir to the throne apparently had an appalling time at his school, Gordonstoun, where much the same probably occurred.

The mixed messages were accentuated probably by his Cambridge tutor who showed him a far more bohemian lifestyle. It is perhaps from around this time that all started to go awry. The

Cleveland Street scandal blew up in 1889 and the Prince was implicated, despite the fact that he was almost certainly not involved. His name was mentioned in the right ears possibly to deflect some of the mud being slung around. His possible involvement with the Hundred Guineas Club would hardly have helped.

He probably wasn't the brightest star in the sky, but it is unlikely that he was as stupid as he has been made out to be, judging by his writings. If anything, he was probably comparatively immature for his age, hardly surprising in one that had such an odd and sheltered upbringing.

All of this begs the question why? Why has his reputation been so besmirched? Who had anything to gain from it all? Rumours abounded after the Prince's untimely demise that he had been done away with to avoid having a scandal prone possibly homosexual idiot on the throne. The rumours flared up in the 1970s and still persist today, and one only has to look at the conspiracies that surround the again untimely demise of the Princess of Wales to see how quickly and easily rumour can be portrayed as fact. Of course, anything is possible and there have been numerous cases throughout history of this sort of thing going on, but the chances were that Albert would have made a good King.

So the question remains unanswered. Much of the documentation surrounding the Prince is not available to the public and will never be released, or has been destroyed, and without it, it is unlikely that his reputation will ever be recovered. Instead, he will be remembered as a naughty Prince who represented the worst aspects of such a privileged upbringing. For the most recent and balanced view, Andrew Cook's 'Prince Eddy' is a very worthwhile read.

Appendix 6

The Bloodline of Christ

The idea of the Holy Grail being the Cup of Christ as used at the Last Supper has been around for some time. But not as long as most would imagine. In fact, this idea first arose in the twelfth century but did not gain widespread recognition until the publication of Tennyson's Holy Grail in 1859. It is one of the many myths that surround Christianity and Roman Catholicism in particular, and that have been called into question publicly, particularly since the discoveries at Qumran. Having been making their bed for two thousand years, it is hard for the Church to do anything other than lie in it, regardless of any evidence that might dispute some of the widely accepted 'facts' of Christianity. It is unlikely we will ever know the truth about Christianity but some of the alternatives are if anything more fascinating than the official version.

There is some evidence to suggest that the man we all know as Moses was in fact Akhenaten, the Egyptian pharaoh. In time, his heirs led to Saul and David, whose tribes, the Israelites and Hebrews were united by marriage. King Solomon, the son of David, was an advocate of religious toleration and was successful to some degree. But with the decline of the Solomonic regime and the rise of Alexander the Great who defeated the Persian Empire a prophecy was made which foretold of the coming of the messiah. (A messiah was an anointed king or priest.) Alexander's successors, the Romans took some time to conquer and stabilise a Holy land that was in turmoil. In fact, not until Julius Caesar in 63 BC did the troubles abate and the Arab usurper Herod was appointed.

Into these troubled times Jesus was born on 1st March 7 BC. His birth possibly caused something of a stir because he was possibly of royal descent, and as the child of a dynastic marriage, he was supposed to be born in September. Joseph, who probably wasn't a carpenter at all but a master craftsman and himself of the same royal house, had to consult the angels, who were not white with wings but men appointed to the position, to sanction Mary's pregnancy. Once they had done so, Jesus could be declared as the legitimate heir to the house of David. Six years later, and this time without any dispute, his brother James was born. Jesus grew up in a royal and priestly Nazarene society and as he arrived in adulthood, he started to apply his own beliefs. He appointed his twelve delegates to princely service and sought to fulfil the messiah prophecy. It is entirely possible that he married Mary Magdalene. At what is called the Last Supper, which was possibly at Qumran and not in Jerusalem, he was indeed betrayed but it was all about internal power. He was tried by his own priests but handed to the Romans for punishment. Pontius Pilate, the Roman Governor, wasn't in fact very interested and couldn't see why the priests could not just punish Jesus themselves, but eventually, he was sent for crucifixion. It was at this stage that Simon the Zealot masterminded the removal of Jesus from the cross well before he had a chance to die, and in defiance of the priests, effected the resurrection, which was not a miracle at all, but a removal from excommunication. All of which is contrary to the accepted version of events.

Around this time, Paul started to preach about Jesus as divine. In AD37, Jesus' second child and first son Jesus was born. He already had a daughter, Tamar. It was also in these years that the Romans began to see the Nazarenes as a threat. Mary Magdalene went to Gaul where her second son Joseph was born, and the Romans saw fit to sack Jerusalem. The first mention of England is when Joseph of Arimathea, which was also a title and not a single person, arrived in AD36. He returned in AD63 and met Caractacus the Pendragon. The first above ground Christian Church was built at Glastonbury and was dedicated to Saint Mary. This has always been assumed to be Jesus' mother Mary, but it is equally possible that it was dedicated to Mary Magdalene who had just died. St James, otherwise known as Joseph of Arimathea was also buried here. Jesus' second son Josephes had a son, Josue and so began the line of the fisher kings, priest kings by right, not monarchs, at least not until the 5th century when Faramund married Argotta of the Franks.

The next two hundred and fifty years or so saw continual clashes between Rome and the

Christian sects as well as the Pauline falling out with the Nazarenes and his conversion of Jesus into a divine being. As the Roman Empire declined, so Christianity began to flourish until the Emperor Constantine, whose Mother was St Helena, a Briton Princess, in a political masterstroke, realised that converting to Christianity, he could in fact take over the religion, which he did in AD314. He installed his puppet Silvester as Bishop of Rome, and while the true Christians groaned, he turned Christianity into the Imperial Religion, subservient to the Emperor, hierarchical and wealthy. He bastardised it in many ways, not least by moving Jesus' birthday to 25th December as well as introducing Persian and Syrian beliefs and sun worship. At the Council of Nicaea in AD325, Constantine pronounced himself saviour and messiah. What he could not stop though was the continuing decline of Rome and the parallel rise of the Celtic Church and the Merovingian kings who were the male line of the fisher kings, whose beliefs all along were in the traditions of Solomon, military strength, education, agriculture and social progression but not political.

But, in AD496, the Merovingian king Clovis made a mistake. He was fighting the Alamanni near Cologne and in what appeared to be a crucial moment, invoked the name of Jesus and then proceeded to win the battle. His wife, Clotilde, had him baptised and his resultant conversion to Catholicism was followed by many others. Initially Rome paid allegiance to the

Merovingians but at the same time planned their downfall.

Back in England, Anna, the daughter of Joseph of Arimathea had married Bran the Blessed, whose descendants included among others Old King Coel. After the Roman withdrawal in AD410, the bloodline came to the fore and led to a King whose father was King of Scots and whose Mother was possibly descended directly from Jesus and Mary, assuming of course that Jesus did in fact have children. His name was Arthur. He became the Guletic, the military leader, at the age of 16 and was anointed as High King of the Britons. Unfortunately, Arthur became obsessed with the Catholic Church, an obsession that led to a battle where his son Modred fought on the opposite side. Arthur was the first combination of the James and Jesus lines in 350 years, which is possibly why he became such a potent symbol of the grail myths and traditions. The Celtic and Catholic churches continued to develop in parallel until the Synod of Whitby in AD664 where the Catholics scored a significant victory in setting the dates for Easter. Bishop Boniface IV also adopted the title Papa in a blatant attempt to compete with the Celtic Father tradition. Shortly after Whitby, in AD679, the Merovingian King Dagobert was murdered by Pepin the Fat, his mayor, beginning the rise of the Carolingians and the suppression of Dagobert and his family. Dagobert II's son Sigebert was rescued from Pepin and taken to Rennes le Chateau in Languedoc, his mother's home, where in time his descendants included Godefroi de Bouillon, Defender of the Holy Sepulchre. Before this, Charlemagne had expanded the Frankish territories but his incompetent successors allowed the rise of the Capetians when the Imperial title passed to the Saxons. The Hohenstauferns competed with the Papacy for control of the Empire and were defeated in 1268 when the Holy Roman Empire was born, with the Habsburgs in charge. Previous to this, Godefroi had led the first crusade, the only successful crusade, and became King of Jerusalem. He was succeeded by Baldwin I. It was at this time that the Knights Templar first came to prominence when they appeared in Baldwin's Palace. When Baldwin moved to a citadel on the tower of David, the quarters on the site of the Temple of Solomon were left to the Knights. By 1127, the Knights were apparently in possession of the Ark and the hoard of gold hidden there before the Roman conquest in AD70. In 1139, the Pope granted the Knights independence from all but himself, but their knowledge of the true Christianity would eventually lead to conflict, beginning with the massacre of the Cathars in Languedoc by Simon de Montfort in 1208, and the attack on the Templars by Philippe IV on Friday 13th October, 1307. The Templars had had prior warning and evacuated to Scotland, where shortly afterwards they possibly assisted in the defeat of the English at Bannockburn in 1314. The victor of course was Robert the Bruce, a descendant of Kenneth MacAlpin who had united the Picts and Scots and who was himself descended from Aedan, father of Arthur. This line led to the Stewarts whose ancient legacy of kingship was being fulfilled assisted by the Earls of Caithness, guardians of the Kings of the Sangreal, (blood royal, or holy grail) the Sinclair family, descended from Henri de St Clair who fought with Godefroi de Bouillon and whose heirs were at Bannockburn. It is worth noting here that about this time, Edward I removed what he thought was the stone of destiny, but was actually a piece of rubble from a monastery doorway. The real stone, much smaller, of a much darker appearance, was hidden in 1296 by the Abbot of Scone, and has never been revealed.

Having destroyed the power of the Templars the Catholic Inquisition continued with its suppression of supposed heresy. Witchcraft became a target along with the God of Shepherds, Pan, a being with the legs ears and horns of a goat playing a pipe, who was transformed into the devil. Witches were women of course and their oppression continued Peter and Paul's theme of the suppression and submission of women.

The sale of indulgences, ie money for salvation, triggered protests that led to the rise of Martin Luther and his Protestants. This in turn led to the dissolution of the Monasteries in England although Henry VIII had picked the wrong target in purely religious terms, but it fulfilled his selfish aims, also leading to Elizabeth I's excommunication.

Luther was probably successful in part due to his many influential friends who were enemies of the Catholic Church, not the least of which were the still extant Templars and associated societies including the forerunners of what became the Royal Society.

As Europe polarized, the Catholic Inquisition was widened to include Protestants as well as Jews and Muslims. The Spanish Armada was driven by this obsession and it also caused the Huguenot rising of Protestants in France under the sign of the Rosy Cross. The Rosicrucians preached liberty, equality and fraternity.

Against this onslaught, Rome could think of nothing better than to resort to ever more violent means and hunted down heretics, devil worshippers, witches and sorcerers, all as defined by the Church.

The rise of the Rosicrucians awakened the Reformation, but the brotherhood itself in theory dated back to Tuthmosis III and the Egyptian Mystery School whose teachings were furthered by Pythagoras and Plato and in Judaea through the Egyptian Therapeutate at Qumran before Jesus' time. The Therapeutate were allies of the Magi, whose leader Simon the Zealot was a lifelong confederate of Mary Magdalene.

Via such people as Leonardo da Vinci and Francis Bacon, the Rosicrucians became the Royal Society. Wren, Boyle, Newton, Hooke, Halley, Pepys, just some of the names that were associated with it. By the time of Charles I, it was well established. The rise of the Puritans, political allies of the Catholic Church, forced the Society underground, and the Puritan supremacy was sealed with the beheading of Charles I. Oliver Cromwell and his parliamentarians reigned supreme and made Torquemada look somewhat restrained, but after Cromwell's death, the momentum was lost and the eventual restoration allowed the resurgence of the Society with King Charles II of the house of Stuart as its patron.

Previous to this, James I (VI of Scotland) had united the two thrones. There were many objectors in parliament, mostly because James was a Scot and not English. They hatched one of the biggest conspiracies of all time using the Kings debt as a weapon against him and by restricting access to parliament. After Charles I dissolved parliament in 1629, the rise of the Puritans led to the Civil War.

In Scotland, Charles II was crowned at Scone on 1651, some years before the restoration in England. When James II, Charles' brother succeeded, he proposed religious freedom despite being a Catholic himself. He set this down on paper on 4th April 1687. Unfortunately, neither he nor his people were free to do as they pleased, and in 1688, the Whigs, who comprised the wealthy and land owning establishment had James deposed for these proposals.

Parliament had William of Orange crowned along with James' daughter Mary. Still worrying about the Catholics, parliament passed the Act of Settlement in 1701, by one vote. This barred all Catholics from the throne. The Stuarts continued trying to regain the true succession, an effort that led to the Jacobite rebellion and the rise in 1745 of Bonnie Prince Charlie. The throne had by this time passed through Anne to the Hanoverian George I and II.

As history is written by the victor, the Hanoverians managed to pronounce Charlie a drunk and woman hater and generally exclude him and his family. When he died, he left his possessions to his son and daughter, Edward and Charlotte.

His brother Henry had other ideas and claimed to be Henry I of Scots and IX of England intending to disinherit his nephew and niece. However, he later redressed this particular episode and attempted to return the inheritance to Edward via his will. Having then lost everything in the French revolution, he became a pensioner of the British Crown in return for writing a new will that suited the Crown's purpose better. This ambiguous document in theory still left everything to Edward but was phrased 'to Count Stuarton'. When Henry died, no one apparently thought to enquire who Count Stuarton might be, and by suppressing various documents the Hanoverians attempted to pass the inheritance to Charles Emanuel IV, ex King of Sardinia, who had joined an order of Jesuits and was therefore unlikely to have offspring. Charles wrote to Westminster pointing out that the true heir was alive and well and living at his house in Rome. This was ignored by parliament and history effectively shows the inheritance vanishing into thin air.

Refusing to give up, the Stuarts actively encouraged the growth of freemasonry to prolong the true knowledge, but even this was eventually infiltrated by the Whigs who managed to turn it into an allegorical charity where few knew or remembered the true meaning of all they did.

In 1817, a Dr Robert Watson bought some of Cardinal Henry's (Henry I) Stuart documents but the papal police took them and sent them to London. Rightly furious, the Dr pursued his right to the documents only to be found dead in 1838. His cause of death was pronounced as suicide. The documents have never appeared again.

In 1888, Prince Edward's grandson, Charles Benedict James Stuart, 4th Count of Albany, was indeed due to visit London for a grand Stuart exhibition. The show was undermined by Hanoverian agents and Charles was found murdered in Italy. There was no display in 1888. Instead, the following year there was a celebration of the Whig deposal of James. This event, whose patron was the Queen, Victoria, was used to obtain and conceal even more material from the Stuarts.

The Counts of Albany are still extant. Few know much about them, and probably fewer know of their ancestors. But in theory, they are the true royal line, descended, if one wishes to believe it, from King Solomon whose ideas of kingship centred on service to the people.

Unlike parliament, which considers itself to be an irreproachably democratic institution but is in fact nothing of the sort, the current monarchy has, by whatever means, come round to the idea of service to the people. Probably most notably beginning with King George VI and continuing with Elizabeth II and the current Prince of Wales, the monarch has become perhaps something more than a figurehead, perhaps an embodiment of what the people want in a Head of State, someone who can be looked up to as an example but also does not overshadow those who become truly great by their endeavour.

It is interesting to note that since the extreme low point of the death of the Princess of Wales, the monarchy by adapting to the mood of the people saw a new zenith in the year of the Queen's golden jubilee, which oddly began with the death of the Queen Mother, an event that led thousands to file past her lying in state, and then line the route of the procession at her funeral. Parliament stuck its nose in only to find it wasn't wanted, something it finds desperately hard to swallow. More recently of course, the Diamond Jubilee has had a similar effect.

Much of this will sound utterly incredible and downright unbelievable especially if like me one grew up pretty much accepting what one was told with regard to history and religion. But on reading more widely and perhaps more non mainstream work (some of which I have listed below), I find it hard to accept that the established churches and parliaments have got it right. To my mind and whatever one chooses to believe, the origins of Christianity, the bible stories including all that was deemed not suitable for inclusion hundreds of years ago, the legends of the Templar knights and so on did not need embellishment or change to make them interesting in themselves or a suitable basis for a religion. They are perfectly fascinating as they are.

Sources:

Bloodline of the Holy Grail, The Magdalene Legacy, Lost Secrets of the Sacred Ark, by Laurence Gardner.
The Templar Revelation by Lynn Picknett and Clive Prince
The Hiram Key, The Second Messiah by Christopher Knight and Robert Lomas,

Made in the USA
Lexington, KY
19 May 2016